Janice Lynn has a ... University and wo... practice. She lives ... Prince Charming, ... Moxie; and a lot of ... baby bunnies that have moved in since she started her writing career. Readers can visit Janice via her website at: www.janicelynn.net

Susan Carlisle's love affair with books began when she received a bad grade in maths. Not allowed to watch TV until the grade had improved, she filled her time with books. Turning her love of reading into a love for writing romance, she pens hot medicals. She loves castles, travelling, afternoon tea, reads voraciously and hearing from her readers. Join her newsletter at www.SusanCarlisle.com

Married to the man she met at eighteen, **Susanne Hampton** is the mother of two adult daughters, Orianthi and Tina. Her varied career titles have included dental nurse, personal assistant, contract manager and now Medical Romance author. The family also extends to a maltese shih-tzu, a poodle, three ducks and four hens. Susanne has always read romance novels and says, 'I love a *happy ever after* so writing for Mills & Boon is a dream come true.'

The Hot Docs on Call

COLLECTION

July 2019
Hot Docs on Call: New City Nights

October 2019
Hot Docs on Call: Tinseltown Cinderella

August 2019
Hot Docs on Call: Surgeon's Seduction

November 2019
Hot Docs on Call: One Night to Forever?

September 2019
Hot Docs on Call: Hollywood Heartthrobs

December 2019
Hot Docs on Call: Healing His Heart

December 2019
(Christmas Special Edition)
Hot Docs on Call: His Christmas Wish

Hot Docs on Call: His Christmas Wish

JANICE LYNN

SUSAN CARLISLE

SUSANNE HAMPTON

MILLS & BOON

First Published in Great Britain 2019
By Mills & Boon, an imprint of HarperCollins *Publishers*
1 London Bridge Street, London, SE1 9GF

HOT DOCS ON CALL: HIS CHRISTMAS WISH
© 2019 Harlequin Books S.A.

It Started at Christmas... © 2016 Janice Lynn
The Doctor's Sleigh Bell Proposal © 2016 Susan Carlisle
White Christmas for the Single Mum © 2016 Harlequin Books S.A.

Special thanks and acknowledgement are given to Susanne Hampton for her contribution to the *Christmas Miracles in Maternity* series

ISBN: 978-0-263-27994-8

1219

MIX
Paper from
responsible sources
FSC™ C007454

This book is produced from independently certified FSC™ paper to ensure responsible forest management.

For more information visit: www.harpercollins.co.uk/green

Printed and bound in Spain
by CPI, Barcelona

IT STARTED AT
CHRISTMAS...

JANICE LYNN

To Blake Shelton for Retweeting me following his Nashville concert and giving me a total fangirl rush moment. Life is good.

CHAPTER ONE

"Okay, who's the hunk that just winked at you?"

At her best friend's question Dr. McKenzie Sanders rolled her eyes at the emcee stepping out onto the Coopersville Community Theater stage. "That's him."

"That's the infamous Dr. Lance Spencer?" Cecilia sounded incredulous from the chair next to McKenzie's.

No wonder. Her best friend had heard quite a bit about the doctor slash local charity advocate. Was there any local charity he wasn't involved with in some shape, form or fashion? McKenzie doubted it.

Still, when he'd invited her to come and watch the Christmas program, she'd not been expecting the well-choreographed show currently playing out before her eyes. Lance and his crew were good. Then again, knowing Lance, she should have expected greatness. He'd put the event together and everything the man touched was pure perfection.

And these days he wanted to touch her.

Sometimes McKenzie wondered if it was a case of women-chasing-him-toward-the-holy-matrimony-altar burnout that had him focusing on commitment-phobic her. She never planned to marry and Lance knew it. She made no secret of the fact she was a good-time girl and was never going to be tied down by the golden band of death to all future happiness. After his last girlfriend had gone a little psycho when he'd told her flat out he had no intention of ever proposing, Lance apparently wanted a break from tall lanky blonde numbers trying to drag him into wedded "bliss." He'd taken to chasing petite brunettes who got hives at the mere mention of marriage thanks to unhappily divorced parents.

Her.

Despite accepting his invitation and hauling Cecilia with her to watch his show, McKenzie was running as fast as she could and had no intention of letting Lance "catch" her. She didn't want a relationship with him, other than their professional one and the light, fun friendship they already shared. Something else she'd learned from her parents thanks to her dad, who'd chased every female coworker he'd ever had. McKenzie was nothing like either of her parents. Still, she could appreciate fineness when she saw it.

Lance was fine with a capital F.

Especially in his suit that appeared tailor-made.

Lance was no doubt one of those men who crawled out of bed covered in nonstop sexy. He was that kind of guy. The kind who made you want to skip that heavily iced cupcake and do some sit-ups instead just in case he ever saw you naked. The kind McKenzie avoided because she was a free spirit who wasn't going to change herself for any man. Not ever. She'd eat her cupcake and have another if she wanted, with extra icing, thank you very much.

She'd watched women change for a man, seen her own mother do that, time and again. Ultimately, the changes didn't last, the men lost interest, and the women involved ended up with broken hearts and a lot of confusion about who they were. McKenzie never gave any man a chance to get close enough to change her. She dated, had a good time and a good life. When things started getting sticky, she moved on. Next, please.

Really, she and Lance had a lot in common in that regard. Except he usually dated the same woman for several months and McKenzie's relationships never lasted more than a few weeks at best. Anything longer than that just gave guys the wrong idea.

Like that she might be interested in white picket fences, a soccer-mom minivan, two point five kids, and a husband who would quickly get bored with her and have flirtations with his secretary…his therapist…his accountant…his law firm partner's wife…his children's schoolteacher…and who knew who else her father had cheated on her mother with?

Men cheated. It was a fact of life.

Sure, there were probably a few good ones out there still if she wanted to search for that needle in a haystack. McKenzie didn't.

She wouldn't change for a man or allow him to run around on her while she stayed home and scrubbed his bathroom floor and wiped his kids' snotty noses. No way. She'd enjoy life, enjoy the opposite sex, and never make the mistake of being like her mother…or her father, who obviously couldn't be faithful yet seemed to think he needed a wife on hand at all times since he'd just walked down the aisle for the fourth time since his divorce from McKenzie's mother.

Which made her question why she'd said no to Lance when he'd asked her out.

Sure, there was the whole working-together thing that she clung to faithfully due to being scarred for life by her dad's office romantic endeavors. Still, it wasn't as if either she or Lance would be in it for anything more than to have some fun together. She was a fun-loving woman. He was a fun-loving man. They'd have fun together. Of that, she had no doubt. They were friends and occasionally hung out in groups of friends or shared a quick meal at the hospital. He managed to make her smile even on her toughest days. But when it had come to actually dating him she'd scurried away faster than a mouse in the midst of a spinster lady's feline-filled house.

"Emcee got your tongue?" Cecilia asked, making McKenzie realize she hadn't answered her friend, neither had she caught most of what Lance had said as she'd gotten lost in a whirlwind of the past and present.

"Sorry, I'm feeling a little distracted," she shot back under her breath, her eyes on Lance and not the woman watching her intently.

"I just bet you are." Cecilia laughed softly and, although McKenzie still didn't turn to look at her friend, she could imagine the merriment that was no doubt sparkling in her friend's warm brown eyes. "That man is so hot I think I feel a fever coming on. I might need some medical care very soon. What's his specialty?"

"Internal medicine, not that you don't already know that seeing as he works with me," McKenzie pointed out, her gaze eating up Lance as he announced the first act, taking in the fluid movements of his body, the smile on his face, the dimples in his cheeks, the twinkle in his blue eyes. He looked like a movie star. He was a great doctor. What else could he do?

McKenzie gulped back the knot forming in her throat as her imagination took flight on the possibilities.

"Yeah, well, Christmas is all about getting a fabulous package, right? That man, right there, is a fabulous package," Cecilia teased, nudging McKenzie's arm.

Snorting, she rolled her eyes and hoped her friend couldn't see the heat flooding her cheeks. "You have a one-track mind."

"So do you and it's not usually on men. You still competing in that marathon in the morning?"

Running. It's what McKenzie did. She ran. Every morning. It's how she cleared her head. How she brought in each new day. How she stayed one step ahead of any guy who tried to wiggle his way into her heart or bedroom. She ran.

Literally and figuratively.

Not that she was a virgin. She wasn't. Her innocence had run away a long time ago, too. It was just that she was choosy about who she let touch her body.

Which brought her right back to the man onstage wooing the audience with his smile and charm.

He wanted to touch her body. Not that he'd said those exact words out loud. It was in how he looked at her.

He looked at her as if he couldn't bear not to look at her.

As if he'd like to tear her clothes off and show her why she should hang up her running shoes for however long the chemistry held out.

She gulped again and forced more of those possibilities out of her mind.

Loud applause sounded around the dinner theater as the show moved from one song to the next. Before long, Lance introduced a trio of females who sang a song about getting nothing for Christmas. At the end of the trio's set, groups of carolers made their way around the room, singing near the tables rather than on the stage. Lance remained just off to the side of the stage and was directly in her line of vision. His gaze met hers and he grinned. Great, he'd caught her staring at him. Then again, wasn't that why he'd invited her to attend?

Because he wanted her to watch him.

She winced. Doggone her because seeing him outside the clinic made her watch. She didn't want to watch him… only she did want to watch. And to feel. And to…

Cecilia elbowed her, and not with the gentle nudge as before.

"Ouch." She rubbed her arm and frowned. No way could her friend have read her mind and even if she had, she was pretty sure Cecilia would be high-fiving her and not dishing out reprimands.

"Just wanted to make sure you were seeing what I'm seeing, because he can't seem to keep his gaze off you."

"I'm not blind," she countered, still massaging the sore spot on her arm.

"After seeing the infamous Dr. Spencer I've heard you talk about so much and that I know you've said no to, I'm beginning to think perhaps you are. How long has it been since you last saw an optometrist?"

"Ha-ha, you're so funny. There's more to life than good looks." Okay, so Lance was hot and she'd admit her body responded to that hotness. Always had. But even if there wasn't her whole-won't-date-a-coworker rule, she enjoyed her working relationship with Lance. If they dated, she didn't fool herself for one second that they wouldn't end up in bed. Then what? They weren't going to be having a happily ever after. Work would become awkward. Did she really want to deal with all that just for a few weeks of sexy Lance this Christmas season?

Raking her gaze over him, she could almost convince herself it would be worth it...almost.

"Yeah," Cecilia agreed. "There's that voice that I could listen to all night long. Sign me up for a hefty dose of some of that."

"Just because he has this crowd, and you, eating out of the palm of his hand, it doesn't mean I should go out with him."

Cecilia's face lit with amusement. "What about you? Are you included in those he has eating out of the palm of his hand? Because I'm thinking you should. Literally."

She didn't. She wouldn't. She couldn't.

"I was just being a smart aleck," McKenzie countered.

"Yeah, I know." Cecilia ran her gaze over where Lance

caroled, dressed up in old-fashioned garb and top hat. "But I'm serious. He could be the one."

Letting out a long breath, McKenzie shook her head. "You know better than that."

Cecilia had been her best friend since kindergarten. She'd been with McKenzie through all life's ups and downs. Now McKenzie was a family doctor in a small group of physicians and Cecilia was a hairdresser at Bev's Beauty Boutique. They'd both grown up to be what they'd always wanted to be. Except Cecilia was still waiting for her Prince Charming to come along and sweep her off her feet and across the threshold. Silly girl.

McKenzie was a big girl and could walk across that threshold all by herself. No Prince Charming needed or wanted.

Her gaze shifted from her friend and back to Lance. He was watching her. She'd swear he'd smiled at her. Maybe it was just the sparkle in his eyes that made her think that. Maybe.

Or maybe it went back to what she'd been thinking moments before about how the man looked at her. He made her want to let him look. It made her feel uncomfortable. Very uncomfortable.

Which was probably part of why she kept telling him no.

Only she was here tonight.

Why?

"I think you should go for it."

She blinked at Cecilia. "It?"

"Dr. Spencer, aka the guy who has you so distracted."

"I have to work with the man. Going for 'it' would only complicate our work relationship."

"His asking you out hasn't already complicated things?"

"Not really, because I haven't let it." She hadn't. She'd made a point to keep their banter light, not act any differently around him.

If she'd had to make a point, did that mean the dynamics between them had already changed?

"Meaning?"

"Meaning I don't take him seriously."

"He's looking at you as if he's serious."

There was that look. That heavenly making-her-want-to-squirm-in-her-chair look.

"Maybe."

"Definitely."

But then suddenly he wasn't looking at her.

He'd rushed over to one of the dinner tables and wrapped his arms around a rather rosy-faced gentleman who was grabbing at his throat. Everyone at the man's table was on their feet, but looking lost as to what to do.

McKenzie's natural instincts kicked in. She grabbed her purse and phone. Calling 911 as she did so, she rushed over to where Lance gave the man a hearty thrust. Nothing happened. The guy's eyes bulged out, more from fear than whatever was lodged in his throat. The woman next to him was going into hysterics. The carolers had stopped singing and every eye was on what Lance was doing, trying to figure out what was going on, then gasping in shock when they realized someone was choking.

Over the phone, McKenzie requested an ambulance. Not that there was time to wait for the paramedics. There wasn't. They had to get out whatever was in the man's throat.

Lance tried repeatedly and with great force to dislodge whatever was blocking the panicking guy's airway. McKenzie imagined several ribs had already cracked at the intensity of his chest thrusts.

If the man's airway wasn't cleared, and fast, a few broken ribs weren't going to matter. He had already started turning blue and any moment was going to lose consciousness.

"We're going to have to open his airway." Lance said what she'd been thinking. *And pray they were able to establish a patent airway.*

She glanced down at the table, found the sharpest-appearing knife, and frowned at the serrated edges. She'd have made do if that had been her only option, but in her purse, on her key chain, she had a small Swiss army knife that had been a gift many years before from her grandfather. The blade was razor sharp and much more suitable for making a neat cut into someone's neck to create an artificial airway than this steak knife. She dumped the contents of her purse onto the table, grabbed her key chain and a ballpoint pen.

As the man lost consciousness, Lance continued to try to dislodge the stuck food. McKenzie disassembled the pen, removed the ink cartridge, and blew into the now empty plastic tube to clear anything that might be in the casing.

Lance eased the man down onto the floor.

"Does he still have a heartbeat?" she asked, kneeling next to where the man now lay.

"Regardless of whether or not he does, I'm going to see if CPR will dislodge the food before we cut."

Sometimes once a choking victim lost consciousness, their throat muscles relaxed enough that whatever was stuck would loosen and pop out during the force exerted to the chest during CPR. It was worth a try.

Unfortunately, chest compressions didn't work either. Time was of the essence. Typically, there was a small window of about four minutes to get oxygen inside the man's body or there would likely be permanent brain damage. If they could revive him at all.

McKenzie tilted the man's head back. When several seconds of CPR didn't give the reassuring gasp of air to let them know the food had dislodged, she flashed her crude cricothyroidotomy instruments at Lance.

"Let me do it," he suggested.

She didn't waste time responding, just felt for the indentation between the unconscious man's Adam's apple and the cricoid cartilage. She made a horizontal half-inch incision that was about the same depth into the dip. Several horrified cries and all out sobbing were going on around her, but she drowned everything out except what she was doing to attempt to save the man's life.

Once she had her incision, she pinched the flesh, trying to get the tissue to gape open. Unfortunately, the gentleman was a fleshy fellow and she wasn't satisfied with what she saw. She stuck her finger into the cut she'd made to open the area.

Once she had the opening patent, she stuck the ballpoint-pen tube into the cut to maintain the airway and gave two quick breaths.

"Good job," Lance praised when the man's chest rose and fell. "He still has a heartbeat."

That was good news and meant their odds of reviving him were greatly improved now that he was getting oxygen again. She waited five seconds, then gave another breath, then another until their patient slowly began coming to.

"It's okay," Lance reassured him, trying to keep the man calm, while McKenzie gave one last breath before straightening from her patient.

"Dr. Sanders opened your airway," Lance continued. "Paramedics are on their way. You're going to be okay."

Having regained consciousness, the man should resume breathing on his own through the airway she'd created for him. She watched for the reassuring rise and fall of his chest. Relief washed over her at his body's movement.

Looking panicky, he sat up. Lance held on to him to help steady him and grabbed the man's hands when he reached for the pen barrel stuck in his throat.

"I wouldn't do that," Lance warned. "That's what's letting air into your body. Pull it out, and we'll have to put it back in to keep that airway open."

"Is he going to be okay?" a well-dressed, well-made-up woman in her mid-to-late fifties asked, kneeling next to McKenzie a little shakily.

"He should be." She met the scared man's gaze. "But whatever is stuck in your throat is still there. An ambulance is on the way. They'll take you to the hospital where a general surgeon will figure out the best way to remove whatever is trapped there."

The man looked dazed. He touched a steady trickle of blood that was running down his neck.

"Once the surgeon reestablishes your airway, he'll close you up and that will only leave a tiny scar," she assured him.

Seeming to calm somewhat the longer he was conscious, the man's gaze dropped to her bloody finger. Yeah, she should probably wash that off now that the immediate danger had passed.

"Go wash up," Lance ordered, having apparently read her mind. "I'll stay with him until the ambulance arrives."

With one last glance at her patient she nodded, stood, and went in search of a ladies' room so she could wash the blood off her hands and her Swiss army knife.

Carrying McKenzie's purse and the contents she'd apparently gathered up, Cecilia fell into step beside her. "Omigosh. I can't believe that just happened. You were amazing."

McKenzie glanced at her gushing friend. "Not exactly the festive cheer you want spread at a charity Christmas show."

"You and Dr. Spencer were wonderful," Cecilia sighed.

She shrugged. "We just did our job."

"Y'all weren't at work." Cecilia held the bathroom door open for McKenzie.

"Doesn't mean we'd let someone choke to death right in front of us."

"I know that, I just meant…" Cecilia paused as they went into the bathroom. She flipped the water faucet on full blast so McKenzie wouldn't have to touch the knobs with her bloodstained hands.

"It was no big deal. Really." McKenzie scrubbed the blood from her finger and from where it had smeared onto her hands. Over and over with a generous amount of antibacterial soap she scrubbed her skin and then cleaned her knife. She'd rub alcohol on it later that evening, too. Maybe even run it through the autoclave machine at work for good measure.

Cecilia talked a mile a minute, going on and on about how she'd thought she was going to pass out when McKenzie had cut the man's throat. "I could never do your job," she added.

"Yeah, and no one would want me to do yours. They'd look like a two-year-old got hold of them with kitchen shears."

When she finally felt clean, she and Cecilia returned to the dinner theater to see the paramedics talking to the man who'd choked. Although he couldn't verbalize, the man nodded or shook his head in response.

As he was doing well since his oxygenation had returned to normal, they had him climb onto the stretcher and they rolled him out of the large room. Lance followed, giving one of the guys a full report of what had happened. McKenzie fell into step with them.

"Dr. Sanders saved his life," Lance told them.

He would have established an airway just as easily as she had. It wasn't that big a deal.

The paramedic praised her efforts.

She shook off the compliment. It's what she'd trained for.

"You're going to need to go to the hospital, too," Lance reminded her.

Her gaze cut to his, then she frowned. Yeah, she'd

thought of that as she'd been scrubbing the blood from the finger she'd used to open the cut she'd made. Blood exposure was a big deal. A scary big deal.

"I know. I rode here with Cecilia. I'll have her take me, unless I can hitch a ride with you guys." She gave the paramedic a hopeful look.

"I'll take you," Lance piped up, which was exactly what she hadn't wanted to happen. The less she was alone with him the better.

She arched a brow at him. "You got blood on you, too?"

He didn't answer, just turned his attention to the paramedic. "I'll bring her to the hospital and we'll draw necessary labs."

In the heat of the moment she'd have done exactly the same thing and saved the man's life. After the fact was when one started thinking about possible consequences of blood exposure. In an emergency situation one did what one had to do to preserve another's life.

She didn't regret a thing, because she'd done the right thing, but her own life could have just drastically changed forever, pending on the man's health history.

She didn't have any cuts or nicks that she could see on her hands, but even the tiniest little micro-tear could be a site for disease to gain entry into her body.

Whether she wanted to or not, she had to have blood tests.

"Cecilia can take me," she assured Lance. Beyond being alone with him, the last thing she wanted was to have to have him there when she had labs drawn.

McKenzie hated having blood drawn.

Blood didn't bother her, so long as it was someone else's blood. Really, it wasn't her blood that was the problem. It was her irrational fear of needles that bothered her. The thought of a needle coming anywhere near her body did funny things to her mind. Like send her into a full-blown panic attack. How could she be so calm and collected when she was the one wielding the needle and so absolutely terrified when she was going to be the recipient?

She could do without Lance witnessing her belonephobia. He didn't need to know she was afraid of needles. Uh-uh, no way.

McKenzie gave Cecilia a pleading look, begging for her friend to somehow rescue her, but the grinning hairdresser hugged her goodbye and indicated that she was going to say something to someone she knew, then headed out rather than stay for the remainder of the show. Unfortunately, several of the other attendees seemed to be making the same decision to leave.

"I'm going to the hospital anyway, so it wouldn't make sense for someone else to bring you."

"But I…" She realized she was being ridiculous. One of the local doctors going into hysterics over getting a routine phlebotomy check would likely cause a stir of gossip. Lance would end up hearing about her silliness anyway. "Okay, that's fine, but don't you have to finish your show?"

He glanced back toward the dinner theater. "Other than thanking everyone for coming to the show, I've done my part. While you were washing up, I asked one of the singers to take over. The show can go on without me." A worried look settled on his handsome face. "The show must go on. It's for such a great cause and I don't want what happened to give people a bad view of the event. It's one of our biggest fund-raisers."

McKenzie frowned, hating that the incident had happened for many reasons. "It's not the fault of Celebrate Graduation that the man choked. Surely people understand that."

"You'd think so," he agreed, as they exited the building and headed toward the parking lot. "That man was Coopersville's mayor, you know."

"The mayor?" No, she hadn't known. Not that it would have mattered. She'd done what had needed to be done and would have done exactly the same regardless of who the person had been. A life had been on the line.

"Yep, Leo Jones."

"Is he one of your patients?" she asked, despite knowing he shouldn't answer. He knew exactly why she was asking. Did she need to worry about the man's health history? Did Lance know anything that would set her mind at ease?

"You know I wouldn't tell you even if he was."

Yes, she knew.

"But I can honestly say I know nothing about any mayor's health history." He opened the passenger door to his low-slung sports car that any other time McKenzie would have whistled in appreciation of. Right now her brain was distracted by too many possibilities of the consequences of her actions and that soon a needle would be puncturing her skin.

Was it her imagination or had she just broken a sweat despite the mid-December temperatures?

"Thank you," she whispered back, knowing her question had put him in an awkward position and that he'd answered as best he could. "I guess I won't know anything for a few days."

"Probably not." He stood at the car door for a few seconds. A guilty look on his face, he raked his fingers through his hair. "I should have cut the airway, rather than let you do it."

She frowned at him. "Why?"

"Because then you wouldn't be worrying about any of this."

She shrugged. "It was my choice to make."

"I shouldn't have let you."

"You think you could have stopped me from saving his life?"

His grip tightening on the car door, he shook his head. "That's not what I meant."

"I know what you meant and I appreciate the sentiment, but I'm not some froufrou girl who needs pampering. I knew the risks and I took them." She stared straight into his eyes, making sure he didn't misunderstand. "If there are consequences, I'll face them. I did the right thing."

"Agreed, except I should have been the one who took the risks."

"Because you're a guy?"

He seemed to consider her question a moment, then shook his head. "No, because you're you and I don't want anything bad to happen to you."

His answer rang with so much sincerity that, heart pounding, she found herself staring up at him. "You'd rather it happen to you?"

"Absolutely."

CHAPTER TWO

LANCE DROVE TO the hospital in silence. Just as well. Mc-
Kenzie didn't seem to be in the mood to talk.

Was she thinking about what he'd said? Or the events
of the evening? Of the risks she'd taken?

When he'd realized Leo Jones had been choking, he'd
rushed to the man and performed the Heimlich maneuver. Too bad he hadn't been successful. Then McKenzie
wouldn't have any worries about blood exposure.

Why hadn't he insisted on performing the procedure to
open Leo's airway? He should have. He'd offered, but precious time had been wasting that could have meant the difference between life and death, between permanent brain
damage and no complications.

He'd let her do what she'd competently done with quick
and efficient movements. She'd saved the man's life. But
Lance would much rather it was him being the one worrying about what he'd been exposed to.

Why? Was she right? Was it because she was female
and he was male and that automatically made him feel
protective?

Most likely he'd feel he should have been the one to take
the risks regardless of whether McKenzie had been male
or female. But the fact she was female did raise the guilt
factor, with the past coming back to haunt him that he'd

failed to protect another woman once upon a time when he should have.

Plus, he'd been the one to invite McKenzie to the show. If he hadn't done so she wouldn't have been at the community center, wouldn't have been there to perform the cricothyroidotomy, wouldn't have possibly been exposed to something life threatening.

Because of him, she'd taken risks she shouldn't have had to take. Guilt gutted him.

If he could go back in time, he'd undo that particular invitation. If he could go back in time, he'd undo a lot of things.

Truthfully, he hadn't expected McKenzie to accept his invitation to watch his show. She'd shot down all his previous ones with polite but absolute refusals.

He glanced at where she stared out the window from the passenger seat. Why had she semiaccepted tonight?

Perhaps the thought of seeing him onstage had been irresistible. He doubted it. She'd only agreed to go and watch and so had technically not been there as his date.

Regardless, he'd been ecstatic she'd said she'd be there. Why it mattered so much, he wasn't sure. Just that knowing McKenzie had been attending the show had really upped the ante.

Not knowing if she'd let him or not, he reached out, took her hand, and gave a squeeze meant to reassure.

She didn't pull away, just glanced toward him in question.

"It's going to be okay." He hoped he told the truth.

"I know. It's not that."

"Then what?"

She shook her head.

"Seriously, you can tell me. I'll understand. I've had blood exposure before. I know it's scary stuff until you're given the all-clear."

She didn't look at him, just stared back out the window. "I don't want to talk about it."

"What do you want to talk about?"

She glanced toward him again. "With you?"

He made a pretense of looking around the car. "It would seem I'm your only option at the moment."

"I'd rather not talk at all."

"Ouch."

"Sorry." She gave a nervous sigh. "I'm not trying to be rude. I just…"

"You just…?" he prompted at her pause.

"Don't like needles." Her words were so low, so torn from her that he wasn't sure he'd heard her correctly.

Her answer struck him as a little odd considering she was a highly skilled physician who'd just expertly performed a procedure to open a choking man's airway.

When he didn't immediately respond, she jerked her hand free from his, almost as if she'd been unaware until that moment that he even held her hand.

"Don't judge me."

How upset she was seemed out of character with everything he knew about her. She was always calm, cool, collected. Even in the face of an emergency she didn't lose her cool. Yet she wasn't calm, cool or collected at the moment. "Who's judging? I didn't say a word."

"You didn't have to."

"Maybe I'm not the one judging?"

She didn't answer.

"If you took my moment of silence in the wrong way, I'm sorry. I was just processing that you didn't like needles and that it seemed a little odd considering your profession."

"I know."

"Yet you're ultrasensitive about it."

"It's not something I'm proud of."

Ah, he was starting to catch on. McKenzie didn't like

to have a weakness, to be vulnerable in regard to anything.
That he understood all too well and had erected some major
protective barriers years ago to keep himself sane. Then
again, he deserved every moment of guilt he experienced
and then some.

"Lots of people have a fear of needles," he assured her.
They saw it almost daily at the clinic.

"I passed out the last time I had blood drawn." Her voice
was condemning of herself.

"Happens to lots of folks."

"I had to take an antianxiety medication to calm a panic
attack before I could even make myself sit in the phlebotomist's chair and then I still passed out."

"Not unheard of."

"But not good for a doctor to be that way when she goes
around ordering labs for her patients. What kind of example do I set?"

"People have different phobias, McKenzie. You can't
help what you're afraid of. It's not like we get to pick and
choose."

She seemed to consider what he'd said.

"What are your phobias, Lance?"

Her question caught him off guard. He wasn't sure he
had any true phobias. Sure, there were things that scared
him, but none that put him into shutdown mode.

Other than memories of Shelby and his immense sense
of failure where she was concerned.

Could grief and regret be classified as a phobia? Could
guilt?

"Death," he answered, although it wasn't exactly the
full truth.

She turned to face him. "Death?"

His issues came more from having been left behind
when someone he'd loved had died.

When his high school sweetheart had died.

When it should have been him and not her who'd lost their life that horrific night.

When he didn't answer, she turned in her seat. "You are, aren't you? You're afraid of dying."

Better she think that than to know the horrible truth. He shrugged. "Aren't most people, to some degree? Regardless, it isn't anything that keeps me awake at night."

Not every night as it had those first few months, at any rate. He'd had to come to terms with the fact that he couldn't change what had happened, no matter how much he wanted to, no matter how many times people told him it wasn't his fault. Now he lived his life to help others, as Shelby would have had she lived, and prevent others from making the same mistakes two teenagers had on graduation night.

"The thought of needles doesn't keep me awake at night," McKenzie said, drawing him back to the present. "Just freaks me out at the thought of a needle plunging beneath my skin."

Again, her response seemed so incongruent with her day-to-day life. She was a great physician, performed lots of in-office procedures that required breaking through the skin.

"Is there something in your past that prompted your fear?" he asked, to keep his thoughts away from his own issues. Shelby haunted him enough already.

From the corner of his eye as he pulled into the hospital physician parking area he saw her shake her head.

"Not that I recall. I've just always been afraid of needles."

Her voice quivered a little and he wondered if she told the full truth.

"Medical school didn't get you over that fear?"

"Needles only bother me when they are pointed in my direction."

"You can dish them out but not take them, eh?"

"I get my influenza vaccination annually and I'm up to date on all my other immunizations, thank you very much."

He laughed at her defensive tone. "I was only teasing you, McKenzie."

"If you knew how stressful getting my annual influenza vaccination is for me, you wouldn't tease me." She sighed. "This is the one thing I don't take a joke about so well."

"Only this?" he asked as he parked the car and turned off the ignition.

Picking up her strappy purse, she shrugged. "I'm not telling you any more of my secrets, Lance."

"Afraid to let me know your weaknesses?" he taunted.

"What weaknesses?" she countered, causing him to chuckle.

That was one of the things that attracted him to McKenzie. She made him laugh and smile.

They got out of the car and headed into the hospital.

The closer they got to the emergency department, the more her steps slowed. So much so that currently she appeared to be walking through molasses.

"You okay?"

"Fine." Her answer was more gulped than spoken.

Stupid question on his part. He could tell she wasn't. Her face was pale and she looked like she might be ill. She'd made light of her phobia, but it was all too real.

Protectiveness washed over him and he wanted to scoop her up and carry her the rest of the way.

"I'll stay with you while you have your labs drawn."

Not meeting his eyes, she shook her head. "I don't want you to see me like that."

"You think I'm going to think less of you because you're afraid of needles?"

"I fully expect you to tease me mercilessly now that you know this."

Her voice almost broke and he fought his growing urge to wrap her up into his arms. If only he could.

"You're wrong, McKenzie. I don't want to make light of anything that truly bothers you. I want to make it all better, to make this as easy for you as possible. Let me."

"Fine." She gave in but didn't sound happy about it. "Write an order for blood exposure labs. Get the emergency room physician to get consent, then draw blood on our dear mayor. Let's hope he's free from all blood-borne pathogens."

He definitely hoped that. If McKenzie came to any harm due to having done the cricothyroidotomy he'd never forgive himself for not insisting on doing the procedure, for putting her in harm's way. He'd not protected one woman too many already in his lifetime.

McKenzie counted to ten. Then she counted backward. Next she counted in her very limited Spanish retained from two years of required high school classes. She closed her eyes and thought of happy thoughts. She told her shoulders to relax, her heart not to burst free from her chest, her breath not to come in rapid pants, her blood not to jump around all quivery-like in her vessels.

None of her distraction techniques worked.

Her shoulders and neck had tight knots. Her heart pounded so hard she thought it truly might break free from her rib cage. Her breathing was labored. Her blood jumped and quivered.

Any moment she half expected her feet to take on minds of their own and to run from the lab where she waited for the phlebotomist to draw her blood.

Lance sat with her, telling her about Mr. Jones and that the surgeon was currently with him. "Looks like they're taking him into surgery tonight to remove the stuck food and close the airway opening you made."

Only half processing what he said, she nodded. She tried to focus on his words, but her skin felt as if it was on fire and her ears had to strain beyond the burn.

"The surgeon praised the opening you made. He said it would be a cinch to close and would only leave a tiny scar."

Again, she nodded.

"He also said you'd nicked two main arteries and the guy was going to have to be seen by a vascular surgeon. Shame on you."

As what he said registered, her gaze cut to Lance's. "What? I didn't nick a main artery, much less two. What are you talking about?"

The corner of his mouth tugged upward. "Sorry. I could tell your mind was elsewhere. I was just trying to get your attention back onto me."

"I didn't hit two arteries," she denied again.

"No, you didn't. The surgeon really did praise you, but didn't say a thing about any nicked arteries."

"You're bad," she accused.

Not bothering to deny her claim, he just grinned. "Sometimes."

"All the time."

"Surely you don't believe that? I come with good references."

"You get references from the women you've dated?"

"I didn't say the references were from women or from previous dates. Just that I had references."

"From?"

"My mother."

She rolled her eyes and tried not to pay attention to the man who entered the room holding her lab order. He checked over her information, verifying all the pertinent details.

Her heartbeat began to roar in her ears at a deafening level.

"You should meet her sometime," Lance continued as if she weren't on the verge of a major come-apart.

"Nice penguin suit, Dr. Spencer," the phlebotomist teased, his gaze running over Lance's spiffy suit.

"Thanks, George, I'm starting a new trend."

"Pretty sharp-looking, but good luck with that," the phlebotomist said, then introduced himself to McKenzie. "In case you didn't catch it, I'm George."

He then verified her name and information, despite the fact McKenzie had seen him around the hospital in the past. She imagined he had a checklist he had to perform.

So did she. Sit in this chair. Remain calm. Do not pass out. Do not decide to forget the first three items on her checklist and run away as fast as she could.

She clenched and unclenched her sweaty hands.

"She'd like you," Lance continued as if the phlebotomist hadn't interrupted their conversation about his mother and wasn't gathering his supplies.

Oh, she didn't want anyone else to know of her phobia. Why couldn't she just tell herself everything was going to be fine and then believe it? Everything was going to be fine. People did not die from having blood drawn. She knew that logically. But logic had nothing to do with what was happening inside her body.

"McKenzie?"

Her gaze lifted to Lance's.

"You should go to dinner with me sometime."

"No." She might be distracted, but she wasn't that distracted.

"You have other plans?"

"I do."

"I haven't said which day I wanted to take you to dinner. Maybe I wanted to take you out over the holidays."

"Doesn't matter. I don't want to go to dinner with you. Not now or over the holidays."

"Ouch."

"That's my line," she told him, watching George with growing dread.

The phlebotomist swiped an alcohol pad across her left antecubital space. "Relax your arm."

Yeah, right.

Lance moved closer. "McKenzie, you have to relax your arm or he can't stick you."

Exactly. That's why her arm wasn't relaxed.

Lance took her right hand and gave it a squeeze. "Look at me, McKenzie."

She did. She locked her gaze with his and forced her brain to stay focused on him rather than George. That really shouldn't have been a problem except George held the needle he was lowering toward her arm.

She wanted to pull away but she just gripped Lance's hand all the tighter.

She wanted to run, but she kept her butt pasted into her chair. Somehow.

"Keep your eyes on me, McKenzie."

Her eyes were on him, locked into a stare with him. It wasn't helping. All she could think about was George and his blasted needle.

She was going to pass out.

Lance lifted her hand to his lips and pressed a kiss to her clenched fingers.

McKenzie frowned. "What was that for?"

"You've had a rough evening."

"You shouldn't have done that."

"Sure, I should have. You deserve accolades for everything you've done."

"That's ridiculous. I just did my job."

"You're going to feel a stick," George warned, and she did.

Sweat drenched her skin.

Lance took the man's words as permission to do whatever he pleased. Apparently, kissing her hand again pleased him because he pressed another kiss to her flesh. This time his mouth lingered.

"Stop that." She would have pulled away but she was too terrified to move. Plus, her mind was going dark. "I think I'm going to pass out," she warned as the needle connected with its target.

She gritted her teeth, but didn't move. Couldn't move.

"Stay with me, McKenzie."

"No."

He laughed. "You planning to sleep through this?"

"Something like that." Her gaze dropped to where George swapped one vial for another as he drew blood from her arm.

She shouldn't have looked. She shouldn't have.

"Hey."

Lance's rough tone had her gaze darting back to him.

"Stay with me or I might have to do mouth-to-mouth."

"You wouldn't dare."

"Oh, I'd dare." He waggled his brows. "Do you think I have a shot at dating you?"

"Not a chance." She glowered at him. Really? He was going to ask her that now?

"Then I should go ahead with that mouth-to-mouth while you're in a compromised situation."

"I'm not that compromised," she warned, curling her free-from-George fingers into a fist.

"Don't mind me, folks. I'm just doing my job here," George assured them with a chuckle.

"I'm doing my best not to mind you." Actually, she was doing her best not to think about him and that needle.

"You're doing fine," he praised.

Amazingly, she was doing better than she'd have dreamed possible. She glanced toward Lance.

He was why she was doing better than expected. Because he was distracting her. With threats of mouth-to-mouth.

Her heart was pounding from fear, not thoughts of Lance's mouth on hers, not of him taking advantage of her compromised situation.

George removed the needle from her arm. McKenzie glanced down, saw the sharp tip, and another wave of clamminess hit her.

She lifted her gaze to Lance's to tell him she was about to go out.

"McKenzie, don't do it." He snapped his fingers in front of her face, as if that would somehow help. "Stay with me."

But out she went.

CHAPTER THREE

"GIVE IT A REST, McKENZIE. I'm seeing you inside your place." Lance maneuvered his car into the street McKenzie had indicated he should turn at. He'd wanted to punch her address into his GPS, but she'd refused to do more than say she'd tell him where he could go.

Yeah, he had no doubt she'd do exactly that and exactly in what direction she'd point him. He suspected it would be hellish hot there, too.

She crossed her arms. "Just because I passed out, it doesn't give you permission to run roughshod over me."

"Is that what I'm doing?" He glanced toward her. Finally, her color had returned and her cheeks blushed with a rosiness that belied that she'd been as white as a ghost less than an hour before.

Her lips twisted. "Maybe."

"You have had a lot happen tonight, including losing consciousness. Of course I'm concerned and going to make sure you get inside your place, okay?"

"I think you're overreacting."

"I think you're wasting your breath trying to convince me to drop you at the curb and drive away."

"That's not what I said for you to do."

"No, but the thought of inviting me into your place scares you."

"I never said that."

"You didn't have to."

"You're imagining things. I came to your Christmas show."

"You brought a friend." As long as they were bantering she'd stay distracted, wouldn't think about having passed out.

"You were part of the show. It wasn't as if you were going to sit beside me and carry on conversation."

He shot a quick glance toward where she sat in the passenger seat with her arms crossed defensively over her chest.

"Is that what you wanted?" he asked. "For me to be at the dinner table beside you?"

"If I'd been on a date with you, that's exactly what I would have expected. Since I was just there watching your show as a friend and someone who wanted to help support a great cause, it's not a big deal."

"I could take you to a Christmas show in Atlanta, McKenzie. We could go to dinner, or to a dinner show."

"Why would you do that?"

"So I could sit beside you and carry on conversation."

"I don't want you to sit beside me and carry on conversation." She sounded like a petulant child and they both knew it. She was also as cute as all get-out and he couldn't help but smile.

"Isn't that what we're doing right now?"

"Right now you are bringing me home, where you can walk me to my front door, and then you can leave."

"What if I want to come inside?" He couldn't help but push, just to see what she'd say. He had no intention of going inside McKenzie's place, unless it was to be sure she really did make it safely inside.

Her eyes widened. "We've not even been on a date. What makes you think I'd let you stay?"

"You're jumping to conclusions, McKenzie. Just because I said I wanted to come inside, it didn't mean I planned to stay."

"Right," she huffed. She turned to stare out the window.

"Then again, I guess it's a given that I want to stay. I think you and I would have a good time."

She sighed. "Maybe."

"You don't sound enthused about the prospect."

"There is no prospect. You and I are coworkers, nothing more."

"You came to my show tonight."

"Coworkers can support one another outside work without it meaning anything."

"I see how you look at me, McKenzie."

McKenzie blinked at the man driving her home. More like driving her crazy.

How she looked at him?

"What are you talking about? You're the one who looks at me as if you've not seen a woman in years."

"I'm sure I do, but we're not talking about how I look at you. We're talking about how you look at me."

"I don't look at you."

"Yes, you do."

"How do I look at you, Lance?"

"As if you've not seen a man in years."

"That's ridiculous." She motioned for him to make a right turn.

"But nonetheless true. And now that I've had to do mouth-to-mouth to revive you, you know you're dying for another go at these lips." Eyes twinkling, he puckered up and kissed the air.

"You have such an inflated ego," she accused, glad to see him pull into her street. A few more minutes and she'd be able to escape him and this conversation she really didn't want to be having. "Besides, you did not do mouth-to-mouth. I passed out. I didn't go into respiratory arrest."

"Where you are concerned, I didn't want to take any chances, thus the mouth-to-mouth." His tone was teasing. "You were unconscious, so you probably don't recall it. George offered to help out, but I assured him I had things under control."

"Right." She rolled her eyes. She knew 100 percent he'd not taken advantage of her blacking out to perform mouth-to-mouth, even though when she'd come to he'd been leaning over her. She also knew the phlebotomist had offered to do no such thing. "Guess that's something we really do have in common, because I don't want to take any chances either. Not with the likes of you, so you'll understand that there will be no invitations into my house. Not now and not ever."

"Not ever?"

"Probably not."

McKenzie really didn't want Lance walking her to her doorway. Since she'd passed out at the hospital, she supposed she shouldn't argue as it made logical sense that he'd want to see her safely into her home. That was just a common courtesy really and didn't mean a thing if she let him. Yet the last thing she wanted was to have him on her door stoop or, even worse, inside her house.

"You have a nice place," he praised as he drove his car up into her driveway.

"It's dark. You can't really see much," she countered.

"Not so dark that I can't tell you have a well-kept yard and a nice home." As he parked the car and turned off the ignition, he chuckled. "I've never met a more prickly, stubborn woman than you, McKenzie."

She wanted to tell him to not be ridiculous, but the fact of the matter was that he was way too observant.

"I didn't ask you to be here," she reminded him defensively. She was sure she wasn't anything like the yes-women he usually spent time with. "I appreciate your concern, but I didn't ask you to drive me to the hospital or to stay with me while I had my blood drawn or to threaten me with mouth-to-mouth."

He let out an exaggerated sigh. "I'm aware you'd rather have faced George again than for me to have driven you home."

That one had her backtracking a little. "That might be taking things too far."

"Riding home with me is preferable to needles? Good to know."

He was teasing her again, but the thought she was alone with him, sitting in his car parked in her driveway, truly did make her nervous.

He made her nervous.

Memories of his lips on her hand made her nervous.

Because she'd liked the warm pressure of his mouth.

Had registered the tingly pleasure despite the way her blood had pounded from terror over what George had been up to.

At the time, she'd known Lance had kissed her as a distraction from George more than from real desire. She might have been prickly, might still be prickly, but tonight's blood draw had been one of the best she could recall, other than the whole passing-out thing. "Thank you for what you did at the emergency room."

"My pleasure."

"I didn't mean that."

"That?"

"You know."

"Do I?" He looked innocent, but they both knew he was far, far from it.

"Quit teasing me."

"But you're so much fun to tease, McKenzie." Neither of them made a move to get out of the car. "For the record, I was telling the truth."

That kissing her hand had been his pleasure?

Her face heated.

His kissing her hand had been her pleasure. She hadn't been so lost in Terrorville that she'd missed the fact that Lance had kissed her hand and it had felt good.

"I'm sorry tonight didn't go as planned for your Christmas show."

"A friend texted to let me know that they finished the show and although several left following the mayor's incident, tonight's our biggest fund-raiser yet."

"That's great."

"It is. Keeping kids off the roads on graduation night is important."

"Celebrate Graduation is a really good cause." The program was something Lance had helped get started locally after he'd moved to Coopersville four years ago. McKenzie had been away doing her residency, but she'd heard many sing his praises. "Did your school have a similar program? Is that why you're so involved?"

He shook his head. "No. My school didn't. I wish they had."

Something in his voice was off and had McKenzie turning to fully face him. Rather than give her time to ask anything further, he opened his car door and got out.

Which meant it was time for her to get out too.

Which meant she'd be going into her house.

Alone.

It wasn't a good idea to invite Lance inside her place.

She dug her keys out of her purse and unlocked her front door, then turned to him to issue words that caused an internal tug-of-war of common courtesy and survival instincts.

"Do you want to come inside?"

His gaze searched hers then, to her surprise, he shook his head. "I appreciate the offer, but I'm going to head back to the community theater to help clean up."

"Oh."

"If I didn't know better I'd think you were disappointed by my answer."

Was she?

That wasn't disappointment moving through her chest. Probably just indigestion from the stress of having to get blood drawn. Or something like that.

She lifted her chin and looked him square in the eyes. "I'm sorry I kept you from things you needed to be doing."

"I'm sure the crew has things under control, but I usually help straighten things up. Afterward, we celebrate another successful show, which I'm calling tonight despite everything that happened, because you were there and I got to spend time with you."

She glanced at her watch. "You're going out?"

"To an after-show party at Lanette and Roger Anderson's place. Lanette is one of the female singers and who I asked to take over emceeing for me." He mentioned a couple of the songs she'd done that night and a pretty brunette with an amazing set of pipes came to mind.

"She will have their place all decked out with Christmas decorations and will have made lots of food," he continued. "You want to come with me?"

She immediately shook her head. "No, thanks. I ate at the dinner show."

He laughed. "I thought you'd say no."

"You should have said you had somewhere you needed to be."

"And keep you from sweating over whether or not you were going to invite me in? Why would I do that?"

"Because you're a decent human being?"

"I am a decent human being. I have references, remember?"

"Mothers don't count."

"Mothers count the most," he corrected.

When had he moved so close? Why wasn't she backing away from him? Any moment now she expected him to close the distance between their mouths. He was that close. So close that if she stretched up on her tippy-toes her lips would collide with his.

She didn't stretch.

Neither did he close the distance between their mouths. Instead, he cupped her jaw and traced over her chin with his thumb. "You could easily convince me to change my plans."

His breath was warm against her face.

"Why would I want to do that?" But her gaze was on his mouth, so maybe her question was a rhetorical one.

He laughed and again she felt the pull of his body.

"You should give me a chance to make this up to you by taking you to the hospital Christmas party next weekend."

"I can take myself."

"You can, but you shouldn't have to."

"To think I need a man to do things for me would be a mistake. I started wearing my big-girl panties a long time ago."

His eyes twinkled. "Prove it."

"You wish."

"Without a doubt."

Yet he hadn't attempted to kiss her, hadn't taken up her offer to come inside her place where he could have attempted to persuade her into something physical. Instead, he'd said she could convince him to change his plans. He'd given her control, left the power in her hands about what happened next.

"I'll see you bright and early Monday morning, McKenzie."

"Have fun at your party."

"You could go with me and have fun, too."

She shook her head. "I wouldn't want to cramp your style."

His brows made a V. "My style?"

"What if you met someone you wanted to take home with you?"

"I already have met someone I want to take home with me. She keeps telling me no."

"I'm not talking about me."

"I am talking about you."

Exasperation filled her. She wasn't sure if it was from his insistence that he wanted her or the fact that he hadn't kissed her. Maybe both. "Would you please be serious?"

His thumb slid across her cheek in a slow caress. "Make no mistake, McKenzie. I am serious when I say that I'd like to explore the chemistry between us."

Shivers that had nothing to do with the December weather goose-pimpled her body.

"Why should I take you seriously?" she challenged. "We've been standing on my porch for five minutes and you haven't threatened mouth-to-mouth again. Much less actually made a move. I don't know what to think where you're concerned."

That's when he did what she'd thought he would do all along. It had taken her throwing down a gauntlet of challenge to prompt him into action. Lance bent just enough to close the gap between their mouths.

The pressure of his lips was gentle, warm, electric and made time stand still.

Her breath caught and yet he made her pant with want for more. She went to deepen the kiss, to search his lips for answers as to why he made her nervous, why he made her feel so alive, why he made her want to run and stay put at the same time. She closed her eyes and relaxed against the hard length of his body. He felt good. Her hands went to his shoulders, his broad shoulders that her fingers wanted to dig into.

"Good night, McKenzie," he whispered against her lips, making her eyes pop open.

"Unless you text or call saying you want to see me before then, I'll see you bright and early Monday morning. Good luck with your run tomorrow." With that he stepped back, stared into her eyes for a few brief seconds then headed toward his car.

"I wouldn't hold my breath if I were you," she called from where she stood on the porch.

He just laughed. "Thank you for my mouth-to-mouth, McKenzie. I've never felt more alive. Sweet dreams."

"You're not welcome," she muttered under her breath while he got into his car, then had the audacity to wave goodbye before pulling out of her driveway. Blasted man.

McKenzie's dreams weren't sweet.

They were filled with hot, sweaty, passionate kisses.

So much so that when she woke, glanced at her phone and saw that it was only a little after midnight, she wanted to scream in protest. She'd been asleep for less than an hour. Ugh.

She should text him to tell him to get out of her dreams and to stay out. She didn't want him there.

Wouldn't he get a kick out of that?

Instead, she closed her eyes and prayed.

Please go back to sleep.

Please don't dream of Lance.

Please no more visions of Lance kissing me and me begging for so much more instead of watching him drive away.

Please don't let me beg a man for anything. I don't want to be like my mother.

I won't be like my mother.

CHAPTER FOUR

EDITH WINTERS CAME into the clinic at least once a month, always with a new chief complaint. Although she had all the usual aging complaints that were all too real, most of the time McKenzie thought the eighty-year-old was lonely and came in to be around other humans who cared about her.

The woman lived alone, had no local family, and her only relative as far as McKenzie knew was a son who lived in Florida and rarely came home to visit.

"How long have these symptoms been bothering you, Mrs. Winters?"

"Since last week."

Last week. Because when you had severe abdominal pain and no bowel movements for four days it was normal to wait a week to seek care. Not.

"I didn't want to bother anyone."

"Any time a symptom is severe and persistent, you need to be checked further."

"I would have come sooner if I'd gotten worse."

Seriously, she'd seen Edith less than a month ago and it had only been two weeks prior to that she'd been in the clinic for medication refills. Severe abdominal pain and no bowel movement was a lot more than what usually prompted her to come to the clinic. "What made you decide you needed to be seen?"

The woman had called and, although McKenzie's schedule had been full, she'd agreed for the woman to be checked. She'd grown quite fond of the little lady and figured she'd be prescribing a hug and reassurance that everything was fine.

"There was blood when I spit up this morning."

McKenzie's gaze lifted from her laptop. "What do you mean, when you spat up?"

Her nurse had said nothing about spitting up blood.

"It wasn't really a throw-up, but I heaved and there was bright red blood mixed in with the stuff that came up."

Bright red blood. Abdominal pain the woman described as severe.

"Have you ever had an ulcer?"

Edith shook her head. "Not that I know of, but my memory isn't what it used to be."

"I'm going to get some labs on you and will decide from there what our next best step is. I may need to admit you, at least overnight, to see what's up with that bright red blood."

Speaking of labs, she needed to log in and see if her labs from the other night were available online. George had told her they should show up on Monday. She should be notified of the mayor's results today, too.

Although there would still be some risks involved, once she had the mayor's negative ones, she'd breathe much easier. Assuming the mayor's results were negative.

She prayed they would be.

She hadn't allowed herself much downtime to consider the ramifications of her actions. How could she when she'd been so distracted by a certain doctor's kiss? But this morning when she'd run she'd not been able to keep the pending results out of her head. She'd run and run and hadn't wanted to stop when she'd had to turn back or she'd have been late into work.

McKenzie examined the frail little woman in her examination room, then filled out the lab slip. "I'll see you back after your blood is drawn."

She left the room, gave the order to her nurse, then went into the examination room.

An hour later, she was heading toward her office when her cell phone rang. She glanced at the screen and recognized the hospital's number. She stopped walking.

"Dr. Sanders," she answered.

"Hi, Dr. Sanders. This is Melissa from the lab. The ER doc looked over your results and wanted to let you know that all of your labs came back negative, as did those of the subject whose blood you were exposed to. He thought you'd want to know ASAP."

Almost leaning against the clinic hallway wall, she let out a sigh of relief. "He's right and that's great news."

"You know the drill, that you and the person you were exposed to will both need to have routine repeat labs per protocol?"

She knew. She finished the call then clicked off the phone, barely suppressing the urge to jump up and yell, "Yes!"

"Your labs were good?"

She jumped at Lance's voice. She hadn't heard him come up behind her in the hallway.

"Don't do that," she ordered, frowning. Mostly she frowned to keep her face preoccupied because instantly, on looking at him, she had a flashback to the last time she'd seen him.

On her front porch when he'd kissed her and completely rewired her circuitry.

That had to be it because she didn't fantasize about men or kisses or things way beyond kisses, yet that's exactly what she'd done more often than she'd like to admit since Friday night.

"Sorry." He studied her a little too closely for her liking. "I didn't realize I'd startle you or I would have made some noise when walking up."

She stepped into her office and he followed, stomping his feet with each step.

She rolled her eyes.

"So your tests are all negative?"

She nodded without looking at him because looking at him did funny things to her insides.

"Thank goodness." He sounded as relieved as she'd felt. "The mayor's too?"

She nodded again.

"That is great news."

She set her laptop down on her desk then faced him. "Was there something you needed?"

He shook his head. "I was checking to see if you'd heard anything on your labs."

She waved the phone she still held. "Perfect timing."

He waggled his brows. "We should go celebrate."

Not bothering to hide her surprise, she eyed him. "Why?"

"Because you got great news that deserves celebrating."

She needed to look away from those baby blues, needed to not think about his amazing smile that dug dimples into his cheeks, needed to not stare at his magical lips that had put her under some kind of spell.

"My great news doesn't involve you," she reminded him, not doing any of the things she'd just told herself to do.

"Sure it does. I was there, remember?"

How could she ever forget? Which was the problem. So much about that night plagued her mind. Lance acting so protective of her as he'd driven her to the hospital and stayed during her blood draw. Lance taking her home. Lance kissing her.

Lance. Lance. Lance.

Yeah, he had definitely put her under a spell. Under his kiss.

Her cheeks heated at the memory and she hoped he couldn't read her mind. Her gaze met his and, Lord, she'd swear he could, that he knew exactly where her thoughts were.

Don't think of that kiss. Don't think of that kiss. Just don't think at all.

"My news doesn't involve you," she repeated, reminding herself that she worked with him. She wasn't like her father who'd drag any willing member of the opposite sex into his office for who knew what? A relationship with Lance would be nothing short of disastrous in the long run.

Plus, there was how she couldn't get him out of her head. What kind of stupid would she be if she risked getting further involved with someone who made her react so differently from how she did to every other man she'd met? To do so would be like playing Russian roulette with the bullet being to end up like her mother. She was her own person, nothing like her parents.

"You're a stubborn woman, McKenzie." He sounded as if that amused him more than upset him.

"You're a persistent man, Lance," she drily retorted, trying to look busy so he'd take the hint and leave. She wanted out from under those eagle eyes that seemed to see right through her.

Instead, he sat on the desk corner and laughed. "Just imagine what we could accomplish if we were on the same team."

"We aren't enemies." Maybe that was how she should regard him after that treacherous and oh-so-unforgettable kiss.

His gaze held hers and sparked with something so intense McKenzie struggled to keep her breathing even.

"But you aren't willing to be more than my friend."

She wasn't sure if he was making a comment or asking a question. Her gaze fell to her desk and she stared at a durable medical equipment request form she needed to sign for a patient's portable oxygen tanks. Her insides shook and her vision blurred, making reading the form impossible. They did need to just be friends. And coworkers. Not lovers.

"I didn't say that." McKenzie's mouth fell open. What had she just said? She hadn't meant to say anything and certainly not something that implied she'd be willing to share another kiss with him.

She wouldn't, would she?

"You are willing?" He asked what was pounding through her head.

"I didn't say that either." She winced. Poor man. She was probably confusing the heck out of him because she was confusing herself.

Despite her wishy-washiness, he didn't seem upset. Actually, he smiled as if he thought she was the greatest thing since sliced bread. "You want to go get frozen yogurt tonight?"

Totally caught off guard by his specific request, she blinked. "Frozen yogurt? With you?"

Was he nuts? It was December and thirty or so degrees outside. They were having a serious conversation about their relationship and he'd invited her to go get frozen yogurt? Really? That was his idea of celebrating her good news?

Why was she suddenly craving the cold dessert?

"They're donating twenty percent of their take to the Sherriff's Toys for Tots fund tonight. We could sit, eat frozen yogurt. You could tell me about your half marathon on Saturday morning. I heard you won your age division."

Oh.

"You wouldn't say no to helping give kids toys for Christmas, would you?"

No, she wouldn't do that. "You should have gone into sales. Did I mention earlier that you were persistent?"

"Did I mention how stubborn you were?"

A smile played on her lips, then she admitted the truth. "I'll be here until late, Lance. You should go without me, but I can swing by and pick up some frozen yogurt on my way home. That way the kids can get their Christmas toys."

His grin widened, his dimples digging in deep. "You think I won't be here until late?"

"I don't know what you have going on," she admitted. She always made a point to not know what Lance was up to. She hadn't wanted to think about him, hadn't wanted to let his handsome smile and charm get beneath her skin. So much for that. She could barely think of anything else.

"We should correct that."

No, they shouldn't.

"Plus, I plan to go to the hospital to check on a patient." Edith's blood count had come back low enough that McKenzie really was concerned about a gastrointestinal bleed. Hopefully, the gastroenterologist would see her soon. Although she could pull up test results and such remotely from her office, she wanted to put eyes on her patient.

"We could ride to the hospital together, then go get frozen yogurt afterward."

They could, but should they?

"It might cause people to ask questions if we were seen at the hospital together so close on the tails of Saturday night."

"You think my kissing your hand in the lab hasn't caused a few tongues to wag?"

His kissing her hand had caused her tongue to wag when she'd returned his kiss on her front porch.

A sweet kiss that hadn't lasted nearly long enough.

A passionate kiss that had made her want to wind her

arms around him, pull him as close to her as she possibly could and kiss him until she'd had her fill.

"We're already the top story around the hospital. George has told everyone how I saved your life with mouth-to-mouth when you passed out."

Heat flushed her face. "You did not do mouth-to-mouth on me in the lab."

He arched a brow. "You sure? You are still alive."

Very alive. Intensely alive. Feeling more alive by the second beneath his gaze.

"You owe me." His eyes locked with hers. "Say yes."

Needing to break the contact, she rolled her eyes. "I don't owe you."

He let out an exaggerated sigh. "You're right. I'm the one who owes you. Let me make it up to you by taking you out for frozen yogurt."

Her brows made a V. "What do you owe me for?"

"That kiss."

Her cheeks flushed hot and she stared at the durable medical equipment form again, still not able to focus on it. "You don't owe me."

"Sure I do."

"Why?" She refused to glance up at him.

"Because it was an amazing kiss."

It had been an amazing kiss.

"If you said yes to going with me for frozen yogurt, I could repay you."

"With another kiss?"

"Well, I had frozen yogurt in mind, but I like how you think a lot better."

When she didn't immediately answer, he sat down on the edge of her desk and grinned down at her. "But I'm a compromising kind of guy. If you ask nicely, we could do both frozen yogurt and mouth-to-mouth."

McKenzie bit her lower lip. She wanted to say yes.

Way more than she should.

It was only frozen yogurt.

And his lips against hers.

Not giving her breath but stealing hers away.

"You think threatening me with more mouth-to-mouth is going to convince me to say yes?" She made the mistake of looking directly at him.

He stared into her eyes for long moments, that intensity back, then he nodded. "I know it is."

Her eyes widened at his confidence.

"You want me as much as I want you, McKenzie. I'm not sure why you feel you need to say no or not date me, but I'm one hundred percent positive that it's not because you don't want to be with me or that you didn't enjoy that kiss as much as I did."

"That's cocky of you."

"Honesty isn't cockiness."

"Why should I want to be with you?"

He frowned. "We get along well at the clinic and hospital. You make me smile and I make you smile. We have a lot in common, including that neither of us is looking for a long-term relationship," he pointed out. "I'm basically a nice guy."

"Who I work with," she reminded.

"That's really your hang-up? That we work together?"

Sinking her teeth into her lower lip again, McKenzie nodded. It was, wasn't it? It wasn't because he scared her emotionally, that the way she reacted to him emotionally scared her silly, that she was afraid she'd get too attached to him and end up reminding herself of her man-needing mother?

Was fear what was really holding her back?

His gaze bored into her. "If we didn't work together, you'd go out with me? Admit that there was something between us?"

"We do work together so it's a moot point," she said, as much to herself as to him, because she wasn't chicken. She wasn't afraid to become involved with Lance. If she were, that would mean admitting she really was like her mother.

She wasn't.

"But if we didn't work together, you'd go have frozen yogurt with me tonight?"

She closed her eyes then nodded. Lord help her, she would. Probably take some more of that mouth-to-mouth, too. She squeezed her eyes tighter to try to block out the image.

See, she wasn't afraid of Lance. Her reservations were because of their jobs. She heard Lance stir, wondered if he was moving toward her, if he was going to go for more mouth-to-mouth, and, when she opened her eyes, was surprised to see that he was leaving her office.

Seriously, she'd essentially just admitted that she wanted to date him, to share kisses with him, and he was leaving? Not cool.

"Where are you going?" she asked, instantly wishing she could take her question back as she didn't want him to know it bothered her he'd been leaving. *Why had he been leaving?*

"To leave you alone. We're both adults, neither of whom wants a long-term relationship. When we'd both be going in with no long-term expectations and there's no company policy against dating, that you'd use that as your reason doesn't make sense unless the truth is that I've misread the signs that you return my attraction or you're scared. Either way doesn't work for me. Sorry I've bothered you, McKenzie."

CHAPTER FIVE

MCKENZIE BOLTED OUT of her office chair and took off after Lance. She grabbed hold of his white lab coat and pulled him back into her office.

He couldn't just leave like that.

She pushed her office door closed and leaned against it, blocking his access to leave until she was ready to let him go.

"Does that mean we aren't going to be friends anymore?" Did she sound as ridiculous as she felt? He'd asked her out. She'd turned him down. Repeatedly. He'd told her he'd leave her alone. She'd stopped him. What did that say about her?

Dear Lord, she was an emotional mess where this man was concerned. She should have let him go. Why hadn't she?

"You want to just be my friend?" His blue eyes glittered with steeliness. "I'm sorry, McKenzie, but I want more than that. After our kiss, it's going to take time before I can rewire my brain to think of you as just a friend. We can't be 'just friends.' At least, I can't think of you that way."

"Stop this," she ordered, lifting her chin in defiance at him and the plethora of emotions assailing her. "All this because I won't go get frozen yogurt with you? This is ridiculous."

"Not just frozen yogurt, McKenzie, and you know it. I want to date you. As in you and me acknowledging and embracing the attraction between us. As in multiple episodes of mouth-to-mouth and wherever that takes us. I've been honest with you that although I'm not interested in something long term, I'm attracted to you. Isn't it time you're honest with yourself and me? Because to say our working in the same building is why you won't date me is what I find ridiculous."

"But..." She trailed off, not sure what to say. Way beyond her excuse of not wanting to date a coworker, McKenzie was forced to face some truths.

She liked Lance.

She liked seeing glimpses of him every day, seeing his smile, hearing his voice, his laughter, even when it was from a distance and had nothing to do with her. She liked catching sight of him from time to time and seeing his expression brighten when he caught sight of her. She liked the way his eyes ate her up, the way his lips curved upward. She didn't want him to avoid her or not be happy when he saw her. She didn't want to stop grabbing a meal with him at the hospital or hanging out with him at group functions. She enjoyed his quick wit, his easy smile, the way he made her feel inside, even if she'd never admitted that to herself. If he shut her out of his life, she'd miss him. She'd miss everything about him.

"You can date other women," she pointed out, wondering at how her own heart was throbbing at the very idea of seeing him with other women. Not that she hadn't in the past. But in the past she'd never kissed him. Now she had and couldn't stand the thought of his lips touching anyone else's. "You can date some other woman," she continued in spite of her green-flowing blood. "Then we could still be friends."

He shook his head. "You're wrong."

"How am I wrong?"

He bent his head and touched his lips to hers.

McKenzie's heart pounded so hard in her chest she was surprised her teeth weren't rattling. But her thoughts from moments before had her kissing him back with a possessiveness she had no right to feel.

She slid her hands up his chest and twined her arms around his neck, threading her fingers into his dark hair. She kissed him until her knees felt so weak she might sag to the floor in an ooey-gooey puddle. Then she kissed him some more because she wanted him to sag to the floor in an ooey-gooey puddle with her.

The thought that he might cut her out of his life completely gave desperation to how she clung to him.

Desperate. Yep, that was her.

When he pulled slightly away he rested his forehead against hers and stared into her eyes. "That's some mouth-to-mouth, McKenzie."

She shook her head. "Mouth-to-mouth restores one's breath. That totally just stole mine."

Why was she admitting how much he affected her?

He cupped her face in a caress. "I can't pretend that doesn't exist between us. I don't even want to try. I want you, McKenzie. I want to kiss you. Your mouth, your neck, your breasts, all of you. That's not how I think of my 'friends.'"

Fighting back visions of him kissing her all over, she sighed. "You don't play fair."

His fingers stroking across her cheek, he arched his brow. "You think not? I'm being honest. What's unfair about that?"

She let out an exasperated sigh, which had him touching his lips to hers in a soft caress.

Which had her insides doing all kinds of crazy somersaults and happy dances. Okay, so maybe she'd wanted to say yes all along, but that didn't mean everything about him wasn't a very bad idea. Just as long as she kept things simple and neither of them fell under false illusions or expectations, she'd be fine.

When he lifted his head, she looked directly into his gaze.

"I will go to the hospital with you and get frozen yogurt afterward with you, but on one condition."

"Name it."

She should ask for the moon or something just as elaborately impossible. Then again, knowing him, he'd find a way to pluck it right out of the sky and deliver on time.

"No more mouth-to-mouth at work," she told him, because the knowledge that she'd dropped to her father's level with making out at work and to her mother's level of desperation already cut deep.

He whistled softly. "Not that I don't see your point, McKenzie, but that might be easier said than done."

She stepped back, which put her flat against the door. With her chin slightly tilted upward, she crossed her arms. "That's my condition."

"Okay," he agreed, but shook his head as if baffled. "But I'm just not sure how you're going to do it."

Her momentary triumph at his *Okay* dissipated. She blinked. "Me?"

Looking as cool as ever, he nodded. "Now that you know how good I am at mouth-to-mouth, how are you going to keep from pulling me behind closed doors every chance you get for a little resuscitation?"

Yeah, there was that.

"I'll manage to restrain myself." Somehow. He was very, very good at kissing, but there was that whole self-respect thing that she just as desperately clung to. "Now leave so I can work."

And beat herself up over how she'd just proved her parents' blood ran through her veins.

McKenzie looked over Edith's test results while she waited for Lance to come to her office. Her hemoglobin and hematocrit were both decreased but not urgently so. Her abdominal and pelvic computerized tomography scan didn't show any evidence of a perforated bowel or a cancerous mass, although certainly there was evidence of Edith's constipation.

Had the woman really spit up blood? If she had, where had the blood come from? Had she just coughed too hard and had a minor bleed in her bronchus? It wasn't likely, especially as Edith had said it hadn't been like throwing up.

McKenzie had ordered the gastroenterology consult. She suspected Edith would be undergoing an endoscopy to evaluate her esophagus and stomach soon. Then again, it was possible the specialist might deem that, due to her age, she wasn't a good candidate for the procedure.

"You look mind-boggled," Lance said, knocking on her open office door before coming into the room. "Thinking about how much fun you're going to have with me tonight?"

"Not that much fun," she assured him, refusing to pander to his ego any more than she must have done earlier. "I'm trying to figure out what's going on with a patient."

"Want to talk about it?"

"Not really." At his look of disappointment, she relented. "One of my regulars came in today with a history of abdominal pain, constipation, and spitting up blood that she described as not a real throw-up, but spitting up."

"Anemic?"

"Slightly, but not enough to indicate a major bleed. She always runs borderline low, but her numbers have definitely dipped a little. I'm rechecking labs in the morning."

"Have you consulted a gastroenterologist or general surgeon?"

"The first."

"Any other symptoms?"

"If you named it, Edith would say she had it."

"Edith Winters?"

Her gaze met his in surprise. "You know her?"

"Sure. I used to see her quite a bit. She's a sweet lady."

"She has me a bit worried. It's probably nothing. Maybe she drank grape juice with breakfast and that's what she saw when she spat up. I don't know. I just feel as if I'm missing something."

"You want me to have a look at her for a second opinion?"

"Would you mind?"

"I wouldn't have offered if I minded. I'll be at the hospital with you anyway."

"Good point." She got her purse from a desk drawer, then stood. "You ready to go so we can get this over with?"

"'This' as in the hospital or the night in general?"

She met his gaze, lifted one shoulder in a semishrug. "We'll see. Oh, and if you think you're going to get away with just feeding me frozen yogurt, you're wrong. I'm not one of those 'forever dieting and watching her carbs' chicks you normally date who doesn't eat. I expect real food before frozen yogurt."

Lance grinned at the woman sitting next to him in his car. Twice in less than a week she'd been in his car when he'd begun to wonder if she was ever going to admit there was something between them.

He understood her concerns regarding them working together, but it wasn't as if they worked side by side day in and day out. More like in the same office complex and caught glimpses of each other from time to time with occasional prolonged interaction. With other women he might be concerned about a "work romance," but not with Mc-

Kenzie. She was too professional to ever let a relationship interfere with work.

Thinking back over the past few months, really from the time he'd first met her a couple years ago when she'd moved back to Coopersville after finishing her medical training, he'd been fascinated by McKenzie. But other than that he'd catch her watching him with a curious look in her eyes, she hadn't seemed interested in anything more than friendship and was obviously not in a life phase where she wanted a serious relationship.

Not that he wanted that either, but he also didn't want to become last month's flavor within a few weeks. She didn't seem interested in dating anyone longer than a month. It was almost as if she marked a calendar and when thirty days hit, she moved on to the next page of her dating life.

Although he had no plans of marriage ever, he did prefer committed relationships. Just not those where his partner expected him to march her down the aisle.

He owed Shelby that much. More. So much more. But anything beyond keeping his vow to her was beyond his reach.

Since his last breakup he definitely hadn't been interested in dating anyone except McKenzie. If he was being completely honest, he hadn't been interested in dating anyone else for quite some time.

Oddly enough, since she dated regularly and routinely, she'd repeatedly turned him down. Which, since she was obviously as attracted to him as he was her, made no sense. Unless she truly was more a stickler for not dating coworkers than he believed.

"Have you ever dated a coworker in the past?"

At his question, she turned to him. "What do you mean?"

"I was just curious as to why going on a date with me was such a big deal."

"I didn't say going on a date with you was a big deal," she immediately countered.

"My references say that going on a date with me is a very big deal."

"Yeah, well, you might need to update that reference because I'm telling you Mommy Dearest doesn't count."

He grinned at her quick comeback. He liked that about her, that she had an intelligence and wit that stimulated him. "Did you think about our kiss?"

"What?"

He grinned. He knew that one would throw her off balance. "I was just curious. Did you think about our kiss on your porch this weekend?"

"I'm not answering that." She turned and stared out the window.

Lance laughed. "You don't have to. I already know."

"I don't like how you think you know everything about me."

"I wouldn't presume to say I know everything about you by a long shot, but your face and eyes are very expressive so there's some things you don't hide well."

"Such as?"

"Your feelings about me."

"Sorry. Loathing tends to do that to a girl."

There went that quick wit again. He grinned. "Keep telling yourself that and you might convince yourself, but you're not going to convince me. I've kissed you, remember?"

"How could I forget when you keep reminding me?"

He laughed again. "I plan to keep reminding you."

"I have a good memory. No reminders needed."

"I'm sure you do, but I enjoy reminding you."

"Because?"

"You normally don't fluster easily, yet I manage to fluster you."

"You say that as if it's a good thing," she accused from the passenger seat.

Seeing the heightened color in her cheeks, hearing the pitch-change to her voice, watching the way her eyes sparked to life, he smiled. "Yes, I guess I do. You need to be flustered, and flustered good."

"Why am I blushing?"

"Because you have a dirty mind?" he suggested, shooting her a teasing look. "And you liked that I kissed you today in your office and Friday night on your porch."

"Let's change the subject. Let's talk about Edith and her bowel movements."

He burst out laughing. "You have a way with words, McKenzie."

"Let's hope they include *no*, *no* and *no* again."

"Then I just have to be sure to ask the right questions, such as, do you want me to stop kissing you, McKenzie?"

She just rolled her eyes and didn't bother giving a verbal answer.

There really wasn't any need.

They both already knew that she liked him kissing her.

CHAPTER SIX

EDITH DIDN'T LOOK much the worse for wear when Mc-
Kenzie entered her hospital room. The elderly woman lay
in her bed in the standard drab hospital gown beneath a
white blanket and sheet that were pulled up to beneath her
armpits. Her skin was still a pasty pale color that blended
too well with her bed covering and had poor turgor, despite the intravenous fluids. Oxygen was being delivered
via a nasal cannula. Edith's short salt-and-pepper hair was
sticking up every which way about her head as if she'd
been restless. Or maybe she'd just run her fingers through
her hair a lot.

"Hello, Edith, how are you feeling since I last saw you
at the office earlier today?"

Pushing her glasses back on her nose, the woman
shrugged her frail shoulders. "About the same."

Which was a better answer than feeling worse.

"Any more blood?"

Edith shifted, rearranging pillows. "Not that I've seen."

"Are you spitting up anything?"

She shook her head in a slow motion, as if to continue
to answer required too much effort. "I was coughing up
some yellowish stuff, but haven't since I got to the hospital."

"Hmm, I'm going to take a look and listen to you again,

and then one of my colleagues whom you've met before will also be checking you. Dr. Spencer."

"I know him. Handsome fellow. Great smile. Happy eyes."

Lance did have happy eyes. He had a great smile, too. But she didn't want thoughts of that happy-eyed handsome man with his great smile interfering with her work, so she just gave Edith a tight smile. "That would be him."

"He your fellow?"

McKenzie's heart just about stopped.

Grateful she'd just put her stethoscope diaphragm to the woman's chest, McKenzie hesitated in answering. Was Lance her fellow? Was that what she'd agreed to earlier?

Essentially she had agreed to date him, but calling him her fellow seemed a far stretch from their earlier conversation.

She made note of the slight arrhythmia present in the woman's cardiac sounds, nothing new, just a chronic issue that sometimes flared up. Edith had a cardiologist she saw regularly. Perhaps McKenzie would consult him also. First, she'd get an EKG and cardiac enzymes, just to be on the safe side.

"Take a deep breath for me," she encouraged. Edith's lung sounds were not very strong, but really weren't any different from her usual shallow and crackly breaths. "I'm going to have to see why your chest X-ray isn't available. They did do it?"

The woman nodded. "They brought the machine here and did the X-ray with me in bed."

Interesting, as Edith could get up with assistance and had walked out of the clinic of her own free will with a nurse at her side. Plus, she'd had to go to the radiology department for the CT of her abdomen. They would have taken her by wheelchair, so why the bedside X-ray rather than doing it in Radiology?

There might be a perfectly logical reason why they'd done a portable chest X-ray instead of just doing it while she'd been there for her CT scan, McKenzie told herself.

"Is there something wrong?" Edith asked.

"You're in the hospital, so obviously everything's not right," McKenzie began. "It concerns me that you saw blood when you spat up earlier. I need to figure out where that blood came from. Your esophagus? Your stomach? Your lungs? Then there's your pain. How would you rate it currently?"

"My stomach? Maybe a two or three out of ten," Edith answered, making McKenzie question if she should have sent the woman home and just seen her back in clinic in the morning.

Maybe she'd overreacted when Edith had mentioned seeing the blood. No, that was a new complaint for the woman and McKenzie's gut instinct said more was going on here than met the eye. Edith didn't look herself. She was paler, weaker.

"Does anywhere else hurt?"

"Not really."

"Explain," she prompted, knowing how Edith could be vague.

"Nothing that's worth mentioning."

Which could mean anything with the elderly woman.

"Edith, if there's anything hurting or bothering you, I need to know so I can have everything checked out before I release you from the hospital. I want to make sure that we don't miss anything."

McKenzie listened to Edith's abdomen, then palpated it, making sure nothing was grossly abnormal that hadn't shown on Edith's CT scan.

"I'm fine." The woman patted McKenzie's hand and any moment McKenzie expected to be called *dearie*. She finished her examination and was beginning to decide she'd truly jumped the gun on the admission when Lance stepped into the room.

"Hey, beautiful. What's a classy lady like you doing in a joint like this?"

McKenzie shook her head at Lance's entrance. The man was a nut. One who had just put a big smile on Edith's pale face.

"What's a hunky dude like you doing wearing pajamas to work?"

McKenzie blinked. Never had she heard Edith talk in such a manner.

Lance laughed. "They're scrubs, not pajamas, and you and I have had this conversation in the past. Good to note your memory is intact."

"That your fancy way of saying I haven't lost my marbles?"

"Something like that." He turned to McKenzie. "I'm a little confused about why they did a portable chest X-ray rather than do that while she was in Radiology for her CT."

"I wondered that myself. I'll talk to her nurse before we leave the hospital."

"We?" Edith piped up.

Before Lance could say or reveal anything that McKenzie wasn't sure she wanted to share with the elderly woman, McKenzie cleared her throat. "I suspect Dr. Spencer will be going home at some point this evening, and I certainly plan to go home too."

After real food and frozen yogurt.

And mouth-to-mouth.

Her cheeks caught fire and she prayed Edith didn't notice because the woman wouldn't bother filtering her comments and obviously she had no qualms about teasing Lance.

"After looking over everything, I'm thinking you just needed a vacation," Lance suggested.

To McKenzie's surprise, Edith sighed. "You know it's bad when your husband's doctor says you need a vacation."

Edith's husband had been gone for a few years. He'd died about the time McKenzie had returned to Coopersville and started practicing at the clinic. Edith and her husband must have been patients of Lance's prior to his death. Had the woman changed doctors at the clinic because McKenzie hadn't known her husband and therefore she'd make no associations when seeing her?

No wonder he'd been so familiar with Edith.

"What do you think is going on, Edith?" Lance asked, removing his stethoscope from his lab coat pocket.

"I think you and my doctor are up to monkey business."

McKenzie's jaw dropped.

Lance grinned. "Monkey business, eh? Is that what practicing medicine is called these days?"

"Practicing medicine isn't the business I was talking about. You know what I meant," the older woman accused, wagging her finger at him.

"As did you when I asked what you thought was going on," Lance countered, not fazed by her good-natured fussing.

The woman sighed and seemed to lose some of her gusto. "I'm not sure. My stomach has been hurting, but I just figured it was my constipation. Then today I saw that blood when I spit up, so I wasn't sure what was going on and thought I'd better let Dr. Sanders check me."

"I'm glad you did."

"Me, too," the woman admitted, looking every one of her eighty years and then a few. "I definitely feel better now than I did earlier. I think the oxygen is helping."

"Were you having a hard time breathing, Edith?"

"Not really. I just felt like air was having trouble getting into my body."

More symptoms Edith had failed to mention.

"Any weight gain?"

"She was two pounds heavier than at her last office visit a couple of weeks ago," McKenzie answered, knowing where his mind was going. "Her feet and ankles have one plus nonpitting edema and she says her wedding band," which Edith had never stopped wearing after her husband's death, "isn't tighter than normal."

While Lance checked her over from head to toe, McKenzie logged in to the computer system and began charting her notes.

"Chest is noisy." Lance had obviously heard the extra sounds in Edith's lungs, too. They were difficult to miss. "Let's get a CT of her chest and maybe a D-dimer, too."

She'd already planned to order both.

"I've added the chest CT and a BNP to her labs, and recommended proceeding with the D-dimer if her BNP is elevated." McKenzie agreed with his suggestions. "Anything else you can think of?"

He shook his head. "Maybe a sputum culture, just in case, but otherwise I think you've covered everything."

Not everything. With the human body there were so many little intricate things that could go wrong that it was impossible to cover every contingency. Especially in someone Edith's age when things were already not working as efficiently.

They stayed in Edith's room for a few more minutes, talking to her and trying to ascertain more clues about what was going on with her, then spoke with Edith's nurse to check on the reason for doing the portable chest X-ray rather than having it done in the radiology department. Apparently, the machine had been having issues. Edith's nurse was going to check with the radiologist and text McKenzie as soon as results were available.

"Anyone else you need to see before we go?" she asked Lance.

He shook his head. "I went by to check on the mayor prior to going to Edith's room."

"Oh," McKenzie acknowledged, glancing his way as they crossed the hospital parking lot. The wind nipped at her and she wished she'd changed from her lab coat into her jacket. "How is he doing?"

"He's recovering from his surgery nicely. The surgeon plans to release him to go home tomorrow as long as there are no negative changes between now and then."

"That's good."

"You saved his life."

"If I hadn't been there, you would have done so. It's really no big deal."

"He thinks it is a big deal. So does his wife. They are very grateful you were there."

McKenzie wasn't sure what Lance expected her to say. She'd just been at the right place at the right time and had helped do what had needed to be done.

"He wants us to ride on his float in the Christmas parade."

"What?"

"He invited us to ride on his float this Saturday."

"I don't want to be in the Christmas parade." Once upon a time she'd have loved to ride on a Christmas parade float.

"You a Scrooge?"

"No, but I don't want to ride on a Christmas float and wave at people who are staring at me."

Ever since her fighting parents had caused a scene at school and her entire class had stared at McKenzie, as if she had somehow been responsible, McKenzie had hated being the center of attention.

"That's fine," he said, not fazed by her reticence. "I'll do the waving and you stare at me."

"How is that supposed to keep them from staring at me?"

"I'm pretty sure everyone will be staring at the mayor and not us."

"I hope you told him no."

The corner of his mouth lifted in a half grin. "You'd hope wrong."

She stopped walking. "I'm not into being a spectacle."

She'd felt that way enough as a child thanks to her parents' antics. She wouldn't purposely put herself in that position again.

"How is participating in a community Christmas parade being a spectacle?"

She supposed he made a good point, but still…

"Besides, don't people stare at you when you run your races?"

"Long-distance running doesn't exactly draw a fan base." She started toward his car again.

"That a hint for me to come cheer you on at your next run?"

She shook her head. "I don't need anyone to cheer me on."

"What if I want to cheer you on?"

She shook her head again. She didn't want him or anyone else watching her run. She didn't want to expect someone to be there and then them possibly not show up. To run because she loved running was one thing. To run and think someone was there, supporting her, and them not really be, well, she'd felt that disappointment multiple times throughout her childhood and she'd really prefer not to go down that road again.

Some things just weren't worth repeating.

"I tell you what, if you want to come to one of my races, that's fine. But not as a cheerleader. If you want to come," she challenged, stopping at his car's passenger side, "you run."

He opened the car door and grinned. "You're inviting me to be on your team? I like the sound of that."

"There are no teams in the races I run."

"No? Well, maybe you're running in the wrong races."

"I'm not." She climbed into the seat and pulled the door to. She could hear his laughter as he rounded the car.

"You have yourself a deal, McKenzie," he said as he climbed into the driver's seat and buckled his seat belt. "I'll run with you. When's your next race?"

"I just did a half marathon on Saturday morning." She thought over her schedule a moment. "I'm signed up for one on New Year's Day morning. You should be able to still get signed up. It's a local charity run so the guidelines aren't strict."

"Length?"

"It's not a real long one, just a five-kilometer. Think you can do that?" she challenged. He was fit, but being fit didn't mean one could run. She'd learned that with a few friends who'd wanted to go with her. They'd been exercise queens, but not so much into running. McKenzie was the opposite. She was way too uncoordinated to do dancing, or anything that required group coordination, but she was a boss when it came to running.

His lips twitched with obvious amusement at her challenge. "You don't have the exclusive on running, you know."

"I've never seen you out running," she pointed out.

"You've never seen me take a shower either, but I promise you I do so on a regular basis."

Lance. In the shower. Naked. Water sluicing over his body. She gulped. Not an image she wanted in her head. "Probably all cold ones."

Maybe she needed a cold one to douse the images of him in the shower because her imagination was going hot, hot, hot.

He chuckled. "Only lately."

That got her attention. "You're taking cold showers because of me?"

"What do you think?"

"That we shouldn't be having this conversation." She stared at him, unable to help asking again. "I'm really why you need to take cold showers lately?"

He grinned. "I was only teasing, McKenzie. I haven't taken a cold shower in years."

"That I believe."

"But not that I might be rejected and need cold water?"

"I doubt you're rejected often."

"Rarely, but it does happen from time to time."

"Is that why you're here with me?"

"Because you rejected me?" He shook his head. "I'm here with you because you were smart enough to say yes to getting frozen yogurt with me."

"And real food," she reminded him as he put his car into reverse. "Don't forget you have to feed me real food before plying me with dessert."

McKenzie closed her mouth around her spoonful of frozen birthday-cake yogurt and slowly pulled the utensil from her mouth, leaving behind some of the cold, creamy substance.

"Good?"

Her gaze cut to the man sitting across the small round table from her. "What do you think?"

"That watching you eat frozen yogurt should come with a black-label warning."

"Am I dangerous to your health?"

"Just my peace of mind."

McKenzie's lips twitched. "That makes us even."

They'd gone to a local steak house and McKenzie had gotten grilled chicken, broccoli and a side salad. She'd been so full when they'd left the restaurant that if not for Lance's insistence that they do their part to support the Toys for

Tots, she'd have begged off dessert. She'd been happy to discover the old adage about there always being room for ice cream had held true for frozen yogurt. She was enjoying the cold goodness.

She was also enjoying the company.

Lance had kept their conversation light, fun. They'd talked about everything from their favorite sports teams, to which McKenzie had had to admit she didn't actually have favorites, to talking about medical school. They'd argued in fun about a new reality singing television program she'd been surprised to learn he watched. Often she'd sit and have the show on while she was logged in to the clinic's remote computer system and working on her charts. He did the same.

"I'm glad you said yes, McKenzie."

"To frozen yogurt?"

"To me."

Taking another bite, she shook her head. "I didn't say yes to you."

His eyes twinkled. "That isn't what I meant. We can take our time in that regard."

"Really?"

For once he looked completely serious. "As much time as you want and need."

"What if I never want or need 'that'?"

"Then I will be reintroduced to cold showers," he teased, taking a bite of his yogurt and not seeming at all concerned that she might not want or need "that," which contrarily irked her a bit.

"I'm not going to jump into bed with you tonight."

"I don't expect you to." He was still smiling as if they were talking about the weather rather than his sex life, or potential lack thereof.

"But if I said yes, you would jump into my bed?"

"With pleasure."

Shaking her head, she let out a long breath. "This morning, had someone told me I'd go out to dinner with you, go for dessert with you, I'd have told them they were wrong. It's going to take time to get used to the idea that we are an item."

"Does it usually take a while to get used to the idea of dating someone?"

"Not ever," she admitted.

"Why me?"

She shrugged. "I don't know. Maybe because for so long I've told myself I'm not allowed to date you."

"Because of work?"

"Amongst other things."

"Explain."

"I'm not sure I can," she admitted. How could she explain what she didn't fully understand herself? Even if she could explain it to him, she wasn't sure she'd want to. "Enough serious conversation. Tell me how you got started in community theater."

CHAPTER SEVEN

LANCE WALKED MCKENZIE to her front door, and stood on her porch yet again. This time he didn't debate with himself about whether or not he was going to kiss her.

He was going to.

What he wasn't going to do was go inside her place.

Not that he didn't want to.

He did.

Not that he didn't think there was a big part of her that wanted him to.

He did.

But she was so torn about them being together that he'd like her to be 100 percent on board when they made that step.

Why she was so torn, he wasn't sure. Neither of them were virgins. Neither of them had long-term expectations of the relationship. Just that his every gut instinct told him to take his time if that's what it took.

Took for what?

That's what he couldn't figure out.

He just knew McKenzie was different, that for the first time in a long time he really liked a woman.

Maybe for the first time since Shelby.

Guilt slammed him, just as it always did when he thought of her. What right did he have to like another woman? He didn't deserve that right. Not really. He took a deep breath and willed his mind not to go there. Not right now, although maybe he deserved to be reminded of it right now and every other living, breathing moment. Instead, he stared down into the pretty green eyes of the woman looking up at him with a thousand silent questions.

"Well?" she asked. "Are we back to my having to ask for your next move? Seriously, I gave you more credit than this."

He swallowed the lump forming in his throat. "If that were the case, what move would you ask me to make?"

McKenzie let out an exaggerated sigh. "Just kiss me and get it over with."

He tweaked his finger across her pert, upturned nose. "For that, I should just go home."

She crossed her arms. "Fine. Go home."

"See if you care?"

Her brows made a V. "What?"

"I was finishing your rant for you."

"Whatever." She rolled her eyes. "Go home, Lance. Have your shower. Cold. Hot. Lukewarm. Whatever."

Despite his earlier thoughts, he couldn't hold in his laughter at her indignation. "I intend to, but not before I kiss you good-night."

"Okay."

Okay? He smiled at her response, at the fact that she closed her eyes and waited for his mouth to cover hers, though her arms were still defensively crossed.

She was amazingly beautiful with her hat pulled down over her ears and her scarf around her neck. The temperature was only in the upper fifties, so it wasn't that cold. Just cold enough to need an outside layer.

And to cause a shiver to run down Lance's spine.

It had probably been the cold and not the anticipation of kissing McKenzie that had caused his body to quiver.

Maybe.

"Well?" She peeped at him through one eye. "Sun's going to be coming up if you don't get a move on. Time's a-wasting."

She closed her eye again and waited.

Smiling, he leaned down, saw her chin tilt toward him in anticipation, but rather than cover her lips he pressed a kiss to her forehead.

Her eyes popped open and met his, but she didn't say anything.

Her lips parted in invitation, but he still didn't take them. He kissed the corner of each eye, her cheekbones, the exposed section of her neck just above her scarf. He kissed the corners of her mouth.

She moaned, placed her gloved hands on his cheeks and stared up at him. She didn't speak, though, just stood on tiptoe while pulling him toward her, taking what she wanted.

Him.

She covered his mouth with hers and the porch shifted beneath Lance's feet. They threatened to kick up and take off on a happy flight.

Unlike their previous kisses, where he'd initiated the contact, this time it was her mouth taking the lead. Her lips demanding more. Her hands pulling him closer and closer. Her body pressing up against his.

Her wanting more, expressing that want through her body and actions.

Lance moaned. Or growled. Or made some type of strange noise deep in his throat.

Whatever the sound was, McKenzie pulled back and giggled. "What was that?"

"A mating call?"

"That was supposed to make me want to rip off your clothes and mate?"

His lips twitched. "You're telling me it didn't?"

Smiling, she shook her head. "Better go home and practice that one, big boy."

"Guess I'd better." He rubbed his thumb across her cheek. "Thank you for tonight, McKenzie."

"You paid for dinner and dessert. Everything was delicious. I'm the one who should be thanking you, again."

"You were delicious."

She laughed. "Must have been leftover frozen yogurt."

He shook his head. "I don't think so."

She met his gaze and her smile faded a little. "Tell me this isn't a bad idea."

"'This'?"

She gnawed on her lower lip. "I don't do long-term relationships, Lance. You know that. We've talked about that. This isn't going to end with lots of feel-good moments."

"I do know that and am fine with it. I'm not looking for marriage either, McKenzie. Far from it."

"Then we both understand that this isn't going anywhere between us. Not anywhere permanent or long lasting."

"We're clear." Lance wasn't such a fool that he didn't recognize that he'd only kissed her and yet he wanted McKenzie more than he recalled wanting any woman, ever.

Even Shelby.

Then again, he'd been a kid when he and Shelby had been together, barely a man. Old enough to enter into adulthood with her only to lose her before either of them had experienced the real world. Typically, when he dated, Shelby didn't play on his mind so much. Typically, when he dated, he didn't feel as involved as he already felt with McKenzie.

"I'll see you in the morning?" she asked, staring up at him curiously.

"Without a doubt."

Her smile returned. "I'm glad."

With that, she planted one last, quick kiss on his mouth then went into her house, leaving him on her front porch staring at her closed front door and wondering what the hell he was getting himself into and if he should run while he still could.

McKenzie ran as fast as she could, but her feet weren't co-operating. Each time she tried to lift her running shoe–clad foot, it was as if it weighed a ton and she didn't have the strength to do more than lean in the direction she wanted to go. She stared off into the distance. Nothing. There was nothing there. Just gray-black nothingness.

Yet, desperately, she attempted to move her feet in that direction.

Fear pumped her blood through her body.

She had to run.

Had to.

Yet, try as she might, nothing was happening.

Run, McKenzie, run before…

Before what?

She wasn't sure. There was nothing to run to. Was she running from something?

She turned, was shocked to see Lance standing behind her.

Again, she tried to move her feet, but nothing happened. Desperation pumped through her. She had to get away from him. Fast.

She glanced down at her running shoes and frowned. Gone were her running shoes and in their place were con-crete blocks where her shoes and feet should be.

What was going on?

She glanced over her shoulder and saw that Lance was casually strolling toward her. He was taking his time, not in any rush, not even breaking a sweat, but he was steadily closing the gap between them.

Grinning in that carefree way he had, he blew her a kiss and panic filled her.

People were all around, watching them, gawking, pointing and staring.

Run, McKenzie, run.

It's what she did.

What she always did.

But she'd never had concrete blocks for feet before.

Which really didn't make sense. How could her feet be concrete blocks?

Somewhere in the depths of her fuzzy mind she realized she was dreaming.

Unable to run?

People everywhere staring at her?

That wasn't a dream.

That was a nightmare.

Even if it was Lance who was closing in on her and he seemed quite happy with his pursuit and inevitable capture of her.

"The radiologist just called me with the report on Edith's CT and D-dimer." McKenzie stood in Lance's office doorway, taking him in at his desk. His brown hair was ruffled and when his gaze met hers, his eyes were as bright as the bluest sky.

"She has a pulmonary embolism?" Lance asked.

"He called you, too?"

"No, I just figured that was the case after listening to her last night and the things you said."

"That doesn't explain the blood she spat up. She shouldn't have spat up blood with a clot in her lungs. That doesn't make sense."

"You're right. Makes me wonder what else is going on. Did they get the sputum culture sent off?"

"Yes, with her first morning cough-up. Her pulmonologist is supposed to see her this morning. Her cardiologist, too."

"That's good."

Suddenly, McKenzie felt uncomfortable standing in Lance's doorway. What had she been thinking when she'd sought him out to tell him of Edith's test results?

Obviously, she hadn't been thinking.

She could have texted him Edith's results.

She'd just given in to the immediate desire to tell him, to see him, to share her anxiety over the woman's diagnosis. She really liked Edith and had witnessed Lance's affection for her, too.

"Um, well, I thought you'd want to know. I'll let you get back to work," she said, taking a step backward and feeling more and more awkward by the moment.

"Thank you, McKenzie."

Awkward.

"You're welcome." She turned, determined to get out of Dodge as quickly as possible.

"McKenzie?"

Heart pounding in her throat, she slowly turned back toward him. "Yes?"

His gaze met hers and he asked, "Dinner tonight if I don't see you before then?"

Relief washed over her.

"If you do see me before, what then? Do I not get dinner? Just dessert or something?"

He grinned. "You do keep me on my toes."

Since he was sitting down, she didn't comment, just waited on him to elaborate.

"Regardless of when we next see each other, I'd like to take you to dinner tonight, McKenzie. As you well know, I'm also good for dessert."

"Sounds like a plan," she answered, wondering why she felt so relieved that he'd asked, that they had plans to see each other after work hours. He'd been asking her for weeks and she'd been saying no. Now that she was willing to say yes, had she thought he wasn't going to ask?

"Great." His smile was bigger now, his dimples deeper. "We can discuss what we're going to wear for the Christmas parade. I'm thinking you should be a sexy elf."

"A sexy elf, hmm?" she mused, trying to visualize what he was picturing in his mind. He'd make a much sexier Santa's helper than she would. Maybe he should do the sexy-elf thing. "I haven't agreed to be in the Christmas parade," she reminded him.

"It'll be fun. The mayor's float is based on a children's story about a grumpy fellow who hates Christmas until a little girl shows him the true meaning of the holidays. It's a perfect float theme."

"I get to do weird things to my hair and wear ear and nose extensions that make me look elfish for real?" she asked with false brightness.

"You do. Don't forget the bright clothes."

She narrowed her gaze suspiciously. "And you're going to do the same?"

"I'm not sure about doing weird things to my hair." He ran his fingers through his short brown locks. "But I can get into the colorful Christmas spirit if that makes you happy."

This should be good. Seeing him in his float clothes would be worth having to come up with a costume of her own. After all, she had a secret weapon: Cecilia, who rocked makeup and costumes.

"Well, then. Sign me up for some Christmas float happiness."

Cecilia really was like a Christmas float costume secret weapon. A fairy godmother.

She walked around McKenzie, her lips twisted and her brow furrowed in deep thought.

"We can use heavy-duty bendable hair wires to wrap

your hair around to make some fancy loops." Cecelia studied McKenzie's hair. "That and lots of hair spray should do the trick."

"What about for an outfit?"

"*K-I-S-S.*"

"What?"

"Keep It Simple, Stupid. Not that you're stupid," Cecilia quickly added. "Just don't worry about trying to overdo anything. You've got less than a week to put something together. The mayor may not be expecting you to be dressed up."

"Lance says we are expected to dress up."

Cecilia's eyes lit with excitement, as if she'd been patiently waiting for the perfect opportunity to ask but had gotten distracted at the prospect of having her way with McKenzie's hair and costume makeup. "How is the good doctor?"

"Good. Very good."

Cecilia's eyes widened. "Really?"

McKenzie looked heavenward, which in this case was the glittery ceiling of Bev's Beauty Boutique. "I've kissed the man. That's it. But, yes, he was very good at that."

Cecilia let out a disappointed sight. "Just kissing?"

Her lips against Lance's could never be called "just kissing," but she wasn't going to point that out to Cecilia.

"What did you think I meant when I said he was very good?"

"You know exactly what I thought, what I was hoping for. What's holding you back?"

McKenzie shrugged. "We've barely been on three dates, and that's if you count the community Christmas show, which truly shouldn't even count but since he kissed me for the first time that night, I will." Why was she sounding so breathy and letting her sentences run together? "You think I should have already invited him between my sheets?"

"If I had someone that sexy looking at me the way that man looks at you, I'd have invited him between my sheets long ago."

McKenzie shrugged again. "There's no rush."

"No rush?" Shaking her head, Cecilia frowned. "I'm concerned."

"About me? Why?"

"For some reason you are totally throwing up walls between you and this guy. For the life of me I can't figure out why."

McKenzie glanced around the salon. There was a total of five workstations. On the other side of the salon, Bev was rolling a petite blue-haired lady's hair into tight little clips, but the other two stylists had gone to lunch, as had the manicurist. No one was paying the slightest attention to Cecilia and McKenzie's conversation. Thank goodness.

"How many times do I have to say it? I work with him. A relationship between us is complicated."

Cecilia wasn't buying it. "Only as complicated as the two of you make it."

McKenzie sank into her friend's salon chair and spun around to stare at the reflection of herself in the mirror. "I am creating problems where there aren't any, aren't I?"

"Looks that way to me. My question is why. I know you don't fall into bed with every guy you date and certainly not after just a couple of dates, but you've never had chemistry with anyone the way you do with Lance. I could practically feel the electricity zapping between you that night at the Christmas show," she pointed out. "You've never been one to create unnecessary drama. So, as your best friend, that leaves me asking myself, and you, why are you doing it now?"

True. She hadn't. Then again, she never dated anyone very long. Not that three dates classified as dating Lance for a long time. She'd certainly never dated anyone like

Lance. Not even close. He was...different. Not just that he worked with her, but something more that was hard to define and a little nerve-racking to contemplate.

"You really like him, don't you?"

At her best friend's question, McKenzie's gaze met Cecilia's in the mirror. "What's not to like?"

Cecilia grinned. "What? No argument? Uh-oh. This one has you hooked. You may decide you want to keep him around."

"That's what I'm afraid of." Then what? Eventually, he'd be ready to move on and if she were more vested in an actual relationship, she'd be hurt. Being with someone so charismatic and tempting was probably foolish to begin with.

She toyed with a strand of hair still loose from its rubber band. "So, on Saturday morning you're going to make me look like Christmas morning and then transform me into a beautiful goddess for the hospital Christmas party that evening?"

"Sure. Just call me Fairy Godmother." Cecilia's eyes widened again. "Does that mean you're going to go to the hospital Christmas party with Lance?"

McKenzie nodded. She'd just decided that for definite, despite his having mentioned it to her several times. Even if she did insist on them going separately, what would be the point other than that stubbornness he'd mentioned?

Lance stared at the cute brunette sitting on a secured chair on the back of a transfer truck flatbed that had been converted into a magical winter wonderland straight out of a children's storybook.

As was McKenzie with her intricate twisted-up hair with its battery-powered blinking multicolored minilights that were quite attention gathering for someone who'd once said she didn't want anyone staring at her, her elaborate makeup done to include a perky little nose and ear tips, and a red velvet dress fringed with white fur, white stockings and knee-high black boots that had sparkly bows added to them.

She fit in with the others on the float as if she'd been a planned part rather than a last-minute addition by the mayor. Lance liked her costume best, but admitted he was biased. The mayor and his wife stood on a built-up area of the float. They waved at the townspeople as the float made its way along the parade route.

"Tell me this isn't the highlight of your year."

"Okay. This isn't the highlight of my year," she said, but she was smiling and waving and tossing candy to the kids they passed. "Thank you for bringing candy. How did you know?"

"My favorite part of a Christmas parade was scrambling to get candy."

"Oh."

Something in her voice made him curious to know more, to understand the sadness he heard in that softly spoken word.

"Didn't your parents let you pick up candy thrown by strangers?" He kept his voice light, teasing. "On second thought, I should talk to my parents about letting me do that."

"Well, when there are big signs announcing who is on each float, it's not really like taking candy from strangers," she conceded. "But to answer your question, no, my parents didn't. This is my first ever Christmas parade."

"What?"

She'd grown up in Coopersville. The Christmas parade was an annual event and one of the highlights of the community as far as he was concerned. How could she possibly have never gone to one before?

"You heard me, elf boy."

He smiled at her teasing.

"How is it that you haven't ever gone to a Christmas parade before when I know you grew up here and the parade has been around for more decades than you have?"

She shrugged a fur-covered shoulder. "I just haven't. It's not a big deal."

But it was. He heard it in her voice.

"Did your parents not celebrate the holidays?" Not everyone did. With his own mother loving Christmas as much as he did, he could barely imagine someone not celebrating it, but he knew those odd souls were out there.

"They did," McKenzie assured him. "Just in their own unique ways."

Unique ways? His curiosity was piqued, but McKenzie's joy was rapidly fading so he didn't dig.

"Which didn't include parades or candy gathering?"

"Exactly."

"Fair enough."

"You know, I've seen half a dozen people we work with in the crowds," she pointed out. "There's Jenny Westman who works in Accounting, over there with her kids."

She smiled, waved, and tossed a handful of candy in the kids' general direction.

"I see her." He tossed a handful of individually wrapped bubble gums to the kids, too, smiling as they scrambled around to grab up the goodies. "Jenny has cute kids."

"How can you tell with the way she has them all bundled up?" McKenzie teased, still smiling. "I'm not sure I would have recognized them if she wasn't standing next to them."

"You have a point. I think she just recognized us. She's waving with one hand and pointing us out to her husband with the other."

Still holding her smiling, waving pose, McKenzie nodded.

"I imagine everyone is going to be talking about us being together on this float."

"We've had dinner together every night this week. Everyone is already talking about us."

"You're probably right."

"And the ones who aren't will be after tonight's office Christmas party."

"Why? What's happening tonight?"

"You're going as my date. Remember?"

"I remember. I just thought you meant something more."

"More than you going as my date? McKenzie, a date with me is something more."

"Ha-ha, keep telling yourself that," she warned, but she was smiling and not just in her waving-at-the-crowds way of smiling. Her gaze cut to him and her smile dazzled more than any jewel.

"You look great, by the way," he said.

"Thanks. I owe it all to Cecilia. She worked hard putting this together and got to my house at seven this morning to do my hair and makeup. She came up with the lights and promised me that my hair, the real and the fake she brought with her to make it look so poufy and elaborate, wouldn't catch fire. I admit I was a bit worried when she told me she was stringing lights through my hair."

"Like I said, you look amazing and are sure to help the mayor win best float. Cecilia's good."

"Yep. Works at Bev's Beauty Boutique. Just in case you ever need a cut and style or string of Christmas lights dangled above your head on twisted-up fake hair."

"I'll keep that in mind." He reached over and took her gloved hand in his and gave it a squeeze. "I'm glad you agreed to do this."

She didn't look at him, but admitted, "Me, too."

When they reached the final point of the parade, the driver parked the eighteen-wheel truck that had pulled the float. Lance jumped down and held his hand out to assist McKenzie. The mayor and his wife soon joined them. He'd just been discharged from the hospital the day before and probably shouldn't have been out in the parade, but the man had insisted on participating.

"Thank you both for being my honored guests," he praised them in a hoarse, weakened voice. He shook Lance's hand.

"It was our pleasure," Lance assured the man he'd checked on several times throughout his hospital stay despite the fact that he wasn't a patient of their clinic. He genuinely liked the mayor and had voted for him in the last election.

The mayor turned to McKenzie. "Thank you for saving my life, young lady. There'd have been no Christmas cheer this year in my household if not for you."

McKenzie's cheeks brightened to nearly the same color as her plush red dress. "You're welcome, but Dr. Spencer did just as much to save your life as I did. He's the one who did the Heimlich maneuver and your chest compressions."

"You were the one who revived me. Dr. Spencer has told me on more than one occasion that your actions are directly responsible for my still being here."

McKenzie glanced at him in question and Lance winked.

"If there's ever anything we can do." This came from the mayor's wife. "Just let us know. We are forever indebted to you both. You're our Christmas angels."

"We're good, but thank you," Lance and McKenzie both assured them.

"Amazing costume," the mayor's wife praised McKenzie further.

They talked for a few more minutes to those who'd been on the mayor's float, then walked toward the square where the rest of the parade was still passing.

"If it's okay, I'd like to swing by to see Cecelia at the shop."

"No problem," he assured her. "I need to thank her for making you look so irresistibly cute."

McKenzie grimaced. "Cute is not how a woman wants to be described."

"Well, you already had beautiful, sexy, desirable, intelligent, brilliant, gorgeous, breathtaking—"

"You can stop anytime," she interrupted, laughing.

"Amazing, lickable—"

"Did you just say *lickable*?" she interrupted again.

He paused, frowned at her. "Lickable? Surely not."

"Surely so."

"I said *likable*. Not lickable."

"You said lickable."

He did his best to keep a straight face. "You'd think with those elongated ears you'd have better hearing."

She touched one of her pointy ears. "You'd think."

"So maybe I'll just thank her for your costume that's lit up my day so far."

McKenzie reached up and touched her hair. "That would be accurate, at least."

"All the other was, too." Before she could argue, he grabbed her hand and held it as they resumed walking toward Bev's Beauty Boutique.

The wind was a little chilly, but overall the weather was a fairly mild December day in mid-Georgia.

"Oh, goodness, look at you two," Bev gushed in her gravelly voice when McKenzie and Lance walked up to the shop. Lance had met her at a charity function a time or two over the years he'd been in Coopersville. A likable woman even if he did always have to take a step back because of her smoky breath.

Bev and a couple other women were outside the shop, watching the remainder of the parade pass.

"Cecilia, you outdid yourself, girl! McKenzie, you look amazing." Bev, a woman who'd smoked her way to looking older than she was, ran her gaze over Lance's trousers, jacket, and big Christmas bow tie. He'd borrowed some fake ears and a nose tip from the community center costume room from a play they'd put on several years before. "I'm pretty sure you're hotter than Georgia asphalt in mid-July."

McKenzie laughed out loud at the woman's assessment of him. Lance just smiled and thanked her for her hoarse compliment.

"You do look amazing," Cecelia praised her friend. "Even if I do say so myself." She pulled out her cell phone. "I want a picture."

"You took photos this morning," McKenzie reminded as her friend held her cell phone out in front of her.

"Yeah, but that was just you," Cecilia pointed out. "I want pictures of you two together, too. Y'all are the cutest Christmas couple ever."

Reluctantly, McKenzie posed for her friend, then seemed to loosen up a little when she pulled Lance over to where she stood. "Come on, elf boy. You heard her. She wants pictures of us both. If I have to do this, so do you."

Lance wasn't reluctant at all. He wrapped his arm around McKenzie and smiled for the camera while Cecilia took their first photos together.

Their first. Did that mean he thought there would be other occasions for them to be photographed together? Did that imply that he wanted those memories with her captured forever?

"Do something other than smile," Cecilia ordered, looking at them from above her held-out phone.

Lance turned to McKenzie to follow her lead. Her gaze met his, and she shrugged, then broke off a sprig of mistletoe from the salon's door decoration. She held up the greenery, then pulled him to her, did a classic one-leg-kicked-up pose, and planted a kiss right on his cheek with her eyes toward her friend.

No doubt Cecilia's phone camera flash caught his surprise.

He quickly recovered and got into the spirit of things by pointing at the mistletoe McKenzie held and giving an *Oh, yeah* thumbs-up, then posed for several goofy shots and laughed harder than he probably should have at their antics.

All the women and a few spectators laughed and applauded them. A few kids wanted to pose for photos with them, especially McKenzie.

"Is your hair real?" a little girl asked, staring at the twisted-up loops of hair and string of minilights.

"Part of it is real, but I don't normally wear it this way. Just on special days."

"Like on Christmas parade days?" the child asked.

"Exactly."

When they'd finished visiting with her friends, McKenzie hugged Cecilia and thanked her again.

"Don't forget to forward me those pictures," she requested with one last hug.

"I may be calling on you to help with some of our charity events. We're always needing help with costumes and you're good," Lance praised.

Cecilia beamed. "Thank you."

The parade ended and the crowd began to disperse. Customers came to the shop to have their ritual Saturday morning hair appointments and the stylists went back into the salon.

"Now what?" McKenzie asked, turning to face him. Her cheeks glowed with happiness and she looked as if she was having the time of her life.

"Anything you want."

She laughed. "If only I could think of something evil and diabolical."

He took her gloved hand into his. "I'm not worried."

"You should be."

She tried to look evil and diabolical, but only managed to look cute. He lifted her hand to his mouth and pressed a kiss to her fuzzy glove.

"You wouldn't hurt a fly."

"I definitely would," she contradicted. "I don't like flies."

"Okay, Miss Evil and Diabolical Fly-Killer, let's go grab some hot chocolate and see what the Christmas booths have for sale that we can snag."

"Sounds wonderful."

CHAPTER EIGHT

"YOU LOOKED AMAZING TODAY," Cecilia told her as she ran a makeup pencil over McKenzie's brow with the precision of an artist working on a masterpiece.

"Thanks to you and the fabulous work you did getting me ready for the mayor's float," McKenzie agreed, trying to hold perfectly still so she didn't mess up what her friend was doing to her face.

"I have to admit, I had fun. Then again, I had a lot to work with."

"Yeah, right," McKenzie snorted. "Let's just hope you can pull off another miracle for tonight, too."

"For your work Christmas party?"

"Yes." She cut her eyes to her friend. "What did you think I meant?"

"You've never asked me to help doll you up in the past for a mere work party."

"This one is different."

"Because of Lance?"

Because of Lance. Yes, it seemed that most everything this week had been because of Lance. Lots of smiles. Lots of hot kisses. Lots of anticipation and wondering if tonight was the night they'd do more than "mouth-to-mouth."

"I suppose so. Can't a girl just want to look her best?"

"Depends on what she's wanting to look her best for."

"For my party."

"And afterward?"

"Well, I'm hoping not to turn into a pumpkin at midnight, if that's what you're asking."

"No pumpkins," Cecilia promised. "Wrong holiday. But what about that mistletoe this morning?"

"What about it?"

"You've gone to dinner every night this week, ridden on a Christmas float with him, and you are going as his date to the Christmas party. That's big, McKenzie. For you, that's huge. What changed?"

"Nothing."

"Something has to have changed. You were saying no to the guy left and right only a week ago."

"You were the one who said I was crazy for not going out with him."

"You *were* crazy for not going out with him. He seems like a great guy. Lots of fun, hot, and crazy about my bestie. I like him."

"You've only been around him twice," McKenzie reminded.

"During which times he helped save a man's life and made you laugh and smile more than I've seen you do in years."

There was that.

"I was in character."

"Yeah right." Cecilia threw McKenzie's words back at her. "If I'd been you, I'd have used that mistletoe for more than a kiss on the cheek."

"I'm sure you would have."

"But you didn't need to, did you?"

"I'm not the kind of girl to kiss and tell." Which was hilarious because Cecilia had been her best friend since before her first kiss and she'd told her about pretty much all her major life events. Plus, she had already told Cecilia that she and Lance had kissed.

Cecilia leaned back, studied McKenzie's face, then went back to stroking a brush across her cheeks. "Even if you hadn't already told me that you kissed Lance on the night of the Christmas show, I'd know you had."

"How would you know that?"

"I can tell. The same as I can tell that, despite our conversation the other day, what you still haven't done is have sex with him."

Could Cecilia see inside her head or did her friend just know her that well?

"And how is it you know that?"

Cecilia's penciled on brow arches. "Am I wrong?"

"No," she admitted. "I've not had sex with him."

Not that he'd made any real plays to get into her bed. He hadn't. Which surprised her.

"The tension between you two is unreal."

"Tension? We weren't fighting today."

"Sexual tension, McKenzie. It's so thick between you two that you could cut it with a knife."

There was that. Which made his lack of pushing beyond their nightly kisses even more difficult to understand.

"I see you're not denying it."

"Would there be any point?"

"None." Cecilia leaned back again and smiled at what she saw. She held a hand mirror up for McKenzie to see what she'd done. "Perfect."

McKenzie stared at her reflection. Cecilia had done wonders with her face. McKenzie rarely wore more than just mascara and a shiny lip gloss that she liked the scent of. Cecilia had plucked, brushed, drawn and done her face up to the point where McKenzie barely recognized the glamorous woman staring back at her. "Wow."

"How much do you want to bet that when Lance sees

you he'll want to forget the party and just stay here and party with you?"

"Not gonna happen." Not on her part and, based on the past week, not on his part either. But anticipation filled her at the thought of Lance seeing her at her best. "Help me into my dress?"

"Definitely. I want to see what underwear you're wearing."

McKenzie's face caught on fire. Busted. "What?"

"You heard me," Cecilia brooked no argument. "I'll know your intentions by your underwear."

McKenzie sighed and slipped off her robe.

Grinning, Cecilia rubbed her hands together. "Now that's what I'm talking about."

"This doesn't mean a thing, you know."

"Of course it doesn't. That's why you aren't wearing granny panties."

McKenzie stuck her tongue out at her friend. "I never wear granny panties."

"Yeah, well, you don't usually wear sexy thongs either, but you are tonight."

"Works better with the material of my dress. No unsightly panty lines that way."

Cecilia had the audacity to laugh. "Keep telling yourself that."

"Fine. I will. Think what you like."

Cecilia laughed again. "Here, let's get you into your dress, let me do any necessary last-minute hair fixes, and then I'm out of here before Dr. Wonderful shows up."

"He's not that wonderful," McKenzie countered.

"Sure he's not. That's why you're a nervous wreck and wearing barely-there panties and a matching bra."

Cecilia laughed and slid McKenzie's sparkly green dress over her head and tugged it downward.

"A real best friend wouldn't point out such things," Mc-

Kenzie pointed out to the woman who'd been a constant in her life since kindergarten. "You know, it's not too late to trade you in for a less annoying model."

Cecilia's loud laughter said she was real worried.

"Have I told you how beautiful you look?"

"Only about a dozen times." McKenzie ran her gaze over Lance. He had gone all out and was wearing a black suit that fit so well she wondered if it was tailor-made. He'd washed away all traces of his Christmas parade costume. His hair had a hint of curl, his eyes a twinkle, and his lips a constant smile. "Have I mentioned how handsome you look in your suit?"

"A time or two." He grinned. "I'm the envy of every man in the building."

"Hardly."

"It's true. You look absolutely stunning."

"Cecilia gets all the credit. She's the miracle worker. I sure can't pull off this…" she gestured to her face and hair "…without her waving her magic wand."

"Your fairy godmother, huh?"

"That's what I've called her this week."

"She's definitely talented," he agreed. "Then again, she had a lot to work with because on your worst day, you're beautiful, McKenzie."

"That does it. No more spiked Christmas punch for you." She made a play for his glass, but he kept it out of her reach.

"Is the punch really spiked?"

"It must be," she assured him, "for you to be spouting so many compliments."

He waggled his brows and took another drink. "I don't think so."

The Christmas party was being held in a local hotel's conference room. There were about two hundred employees in total who worked for the clinic. With those employees and their significant others, the party was going full swing and was full of loud commotion from all directions.

Several of their coworkers had commented on how great they looked tonight, how great they'd looked in the Christmas parade, how excited they were that they were a couple.

Those comments made McKenzie want to squirm in her three-inch heels. All their coworkers now knew without a doubt that they were seeing each other as more than friends.

She'd known this would happen. She'd allowed this to happen.

Several of her female coworkers stared at her with outright envy that she was with Lance. She couldn't blame them. He was gorgeous, fun, intelligent and charming. He didn't seem to notice any of their attention, just stayed close to McKenzie's side and tended to her every need.

Well, almost every need.

Because more and more she'd been thinking of Cecilia's teasing. Yeah, her green dress fit her like a glove right down to where it flared into a floaty skirt that twirled around her thighs when she moved just right. But she hadn't had to wear teeny-tiny underwear because of the dress. She'd worn them because…

"That's the first time I've not seen a smile on your face all evening," Lance whispered close to her ear.

"Sorry," she apologized, immediately smiling. "I was just thinking."

Which, of course, led to him asking what she'd been thinking about.

She just smiled a little brighter, grabbed his hand, and tugged him toward the dance floor. "Dance with me?"

"I thought you'd never ask," he teased, leading her out onto the crowded dance floor. "I've been itching to have you in my arms all evening."

"All you had to do was ask."

"Well, part of me was concerned about the consequences of holding you close."

"Consequences?" She stared into his eyes, saw the truth there, then widened her eyes. "Oh."

"Yeah, oh."

"I guess it's a good thing girls don't have to worry about such things."

His eyes remained locked with hers, half teasing, half serious. "Would that be a problem for you, McKenzie?"

A problem?

Her chin lifted. "I'm not frigid, if that's what you're asking."

"It wasn't, but it's good to know." He pulled her close and they swayed back and forth to the beat of the music.

"You smell good," she told him, trying not to completely bury her face in his neck just to fill her senses totally with the scent of him.

"I was just thinking the same thing about you. What perfume are you wearing?"

"Cecilia sprayed me with some stuff earlier. I honestly don't know what it's called, just that she said it was guaranteed to drive you crazy. Of course, she didn't tell me that until after she'd hit me with a spray."

He nuzzled against her hair. "She was right."

"Feeling a little crazy?"

"With your body rubbed up against mine? Oh, yeah."

She laughed. "I'll let her know the stuff works."

"Pretty sure if you had nothing on at all I'd be feeling just as crazy. Actually, if you had nothing on at all, my current level of crazy would be kid's stuff in comparison."

She wiggled closer against him. "Well, that makes sense. We're both just kids at heart."

"True, that." His hands rubbed against her low back. "Were you thinking about our coworkers just a few minutes ago?"

She knew when he meant and at that time it hadn't been thoughts of their coworkers that had robbed her of her smile. No, it had been thoughts of what she was anticipating happening later in the evening. Not that she was sure that's what would happen, but she'd questioned it enough that she'd shaved, lotioned, powdered, perfumed and dressed in her sexiest underwear.

Because all week Lance had kissed her good-night, deep, thorough passionate kisses that had left her longing for more. She hadn't invited him in and he hadn't pushed. Just hot good-night kisses night after night that left her confused and aching.

Mostly, she just didn't understand why he hadn't attempted to talk his way into her bed. Or at least into her house. He'd still not made it off the front porch.

He might not push for more tonight either. She was okay with it if he didn't. It was just that something had felt different between them today on the Christmas float, and afterward when they'd weaved their way from one booth to another. All week she'd felt as if she was building up to something great. From the moment he'd picked her up at her house this evening and had been so obviously pleased with the way she looked and how she'd greeted him—with lots of smiles—the feeling had taken root inside her that tonight held magical possibilities that she wasn't sure she really wanted in the long run, but in the short term, oh, yeah, she wanted Lance something fierce, thus the itsy-bitsy, barely-there thong.

"Should I be concerned about how quiet you are?" he asked.

"Nope. I'm just enjoying the dance."

"Any regrets?"

His question caught her off guard and she pulled back enough to where she could see his face. "About?"

"Coming to the party with me."

"Not yet."

He chuckled. "You expecting that to change?"

"Depends on your behavior between now and the time we leave."

"Then I guess I better be on my best, eh?"

"Something like that."

Not that she could imagine Lance not being on his best behavior at all times. He was always smiling, doing something to help others. Never had she met a man who volunteered more. It was as if his life's mission was to do as much good as he possibly could in the world. Or at least within their small community.

The music changed to an upbeat number and they danced to a few more songs. The emcee for the evening stopped the music and made several announcements, gave away a few raffle items.

"Now, folks." The emcee garnered their attention. "I'd like to call Dr. Lance Spencer to the stage."

Lance glanced at her. "Do you know anything about this?"

McKenzie shook her head. She didn't have a clue.

Pulling McKenzie along with him, he headed up toward the makeshift stage. She managed to free her hand just before he stepped up onto the stage. No way was he taking her up there with him. Who knew what was about to happen? Maybe he had won a raffle or special door prize or something.

"Dr. Spencer," the emcee continued, "I'm told you make a mean emcee."

"I wouldn't say 'mean,'" Lance corrected, laughing.

"Well, a little birdie tells me you've been known to rock a karaoke machine and requested you sing to kick off our karaoke for the evening."

Lance glanced at McKenzie, but she shook her head. That little birdie wasn't her.

Always in the spirit of things, Lance shrugged, and told the emcee the name of a song. As the music started, microphone in hand, he stepped off the stage and took McKenzie's hand again.

"I need a singing partner."

Her heart in her nonsinging throat, McKenzie shook her head. He wasn't doing this. She didn't want to make a spectacle of them by pulling her hand free of his, but her feet were about to take off at any moment, which meant he was either coming with her, hands clasped and all, or she'd be doing exactly that.

"Come on," he encouraged. "Don't be shy. Sing with me, McKenzie. It'll be fun."

By this time, the crowd was also really into the spirit of things and urging her onto the stage. She heard a female doctor whose office was right next to hers call out for her to go for it.

McKenzie's heart sank. She wasn't going to be able to run away. Not this time. She was surrounded by her coworkers. Her hand was held by Lance.

She was going to have to go onstage and sing. With Lance. Nothing like a little contrast to keep things interesting.

A singer she was not.

She closed her eyes.

What had been a great night had just gone sour. Very, *very* sour.

She blamed Lance.

Lance realized he'd made a mistake the moment he'd put McKenzie on the spot. Unfortunately, his request wasn't something she could easily refuse with their coworkers now cheering for her to join him. She could either sing or be seen as a total party pooper—which she wasn't and he knew she'd resent being labeled as one.

McKenzie's eyes flashed with fear and he wasn't sure what all else.

He'd messed up big time.

Faking a smile, she stepped up onto the stage with him. He still held her hand. Her palm was sweaty and her fingers threatened to slip free. He gave her a reassuring squeeze. She didn't even look at him.

Lance sang and McKenzie came through from time to time, filling the backup role rather than taking a lead with him, as he'd initially hoped. Mostly, she mumbled, except during the chorus. With almost everyone in the crowd singing along, too, maybe no one noticed.

McKenzie noticed, though. The moment the song was over, she gave him the evil eye. "For the record, I don't sing and if you ever do that to me again, it'll be the last time."

"That's funny," he teased, planning to keep their conversation light, to beg her forgiveness if he needed to. "I just heard you do exactly that."

"Only a tone-deaf lunatic would call what I just did singing."

"I thought you sounded good."

"You don't count."

"Ouch." He put his hand over his heart as if she'd delivered a fatal blow. "My references say I count."

She flashed an annoyed look his way. "You're really going to have to get over those references."

"Or use them as a shield against the walloping you seem determined to deliver to me."

"Not everyone enjoys being the center of attention."

"Tell me the truth. You didn't have fun onstage just then? Not even a little?" he coaxed.

McKenzie stared at him as if he was crazy. He *was* crazy.

"I detested being onstage in front of my coworkers." She frowned as they moved onto the dance floor. Her body remained rigid, rather than relaxing against his like it had during their earlier dances. "For the record, I really don't like people staring at me. Put it down to bad childhood memories of when my parents thrust me into situations where I got a lot of unwanted attention."

When he'd gone after her to sing with him, he'd never considered that she might not enjoy being onstage. He'd just selfishly wanted her with him.

"I'm sorry, McKenzie. If I'd known how you felt, I wouldn't have put you in the spotlight that way. I definitely would never intentionally upset you. It was all in fun, to kick off the night's karaoke. That's all."

"I know you didn't intentionally pull me up there to upset me," she admitted. "I just prefer you not to put me in situations where all eyes are on me. I have enough bad childhood flashbacks as it is."

"What kind of childhood flashbacks?"

"Just situations where my parents would yell and scream at each other regardless of where we were and no matter who was around. Way too often all eyes would be on me while they had a knock-down, drag-out. When people stare at me, it gives me that same feeling of humiliation and mortification."

"I'm sorry your parents did that to you and that I made those negative feelings come to surface. But, for the record, maybe you're finally getting past those old hang-ups because you were smiling." She had been smiling. Mumbling and smiling.

"I was faking it."

"Ouch." His hand went to his chest and he pretended

to receive another mortal blow. "Not good when a man's woman has to fake it."

"Exactly. So you should be careful what situations you put me into where I might have to fake other things," she warned with a half smile. "I don't sing. I barely dance. Take note of it."

He pulled her to him, his hand low on her back, holding her close. "You dance quite nicely when you aren't in rigor mortis. However, I'll make a note. No more singing and barely dancing. Got it."

"Good."

"Also, for the record, when I put you in a certain situation, there will be no need for faking it."

Her chin tilted up and she arched a brow in challenge. "How can you be so sure?"

"Because I'll use every ounce of skill, every ounce of sheer will, every ounce of energy I have to make sure I blow your mind," he whispered close for her ears only. "My pleasure will be seeing your pleasure. Feeling your pleasure."

"That sounds...fun. Maybe you should have tried your hand at that instead of pulling me onstage with you."

He swallowed. Was she saying...?

"I want you, McKenzie. I haven't pushed because I know you still have a lot of mixed emotions about being with me, but when you're ready I want to make love to you. I've made no pretense about that."

"Sex. You want to have sex with me," she corrected, resting her forehead against his chin. "I'll let you know when I'm ready."

Lance's heart beat like a drum against his rib cage. "I'll be waiting."

"Don't hold your breath."

"I'd rather hold yours."

That had her looking up.

"Kiss me, McKenzie."

"Here? Now? On the dance floor? Around our cowork-ers? Are you crazy?"

He glanced around the dim room. The dance floor was crowded with couples, some of them stealing kisses. There were some single women who were dancing in a circle off to one side of the dance floor. One of the admin girls cur-rently had the microphone and was belting out a tune. No one was paying them any attention.

McKenzie's gaze followed his, no doubt drawing the same conclusions, but she shook her head anyway. "No. I'm not one of those girls who is into public displays of affection."

"You kissed me in front of Bev's Beauty Boutique."

"That was different."

"How was that different? Other than it being in broad daylight and in the middle of the square with half the town in the near vicinity?"

"I can't explain how that was different, but it was." Her lower lip disappeared between her teeth. "Don't push me on this, please."

He sighed. "It would probably have been a bad idea for you to kiss me here, anyway."

"Why is that?"

Did she really not know how much she affected him? How much he was having to fight sweeping her up into his arms and carrying her out of the ballroom and straight to the first private place he could find where he could run his fingers beneath her sparkly green dress?

"I think I've already mentioned how much I want you and the effect you have on me."

"But… Oh." Her eyes widened as she moved against him.

"Yeah. Oh."

To his surprise, her body relaxed and he'd swear the

noise that came out of her mouth was a giggle. Not that McKenzie seemed the giggling type, but that's what the sound had most resembled.

Regardless, her arms relaxed around his neck and just to prove how ornery she was and to his total surprise her lips met his in a soft kiss that only lasted a few seconds but took his breath and made his knees weak.

"There," she taunted. "I kissed you in public."

"Not sure what made you change your mind, but thank you." He studied her expression and he'd swear there was a mischievous glint in her eyes. "I think. Because if I didn't know better I'd think you were trying to set me up for embarrassment."

There was the sound again. Definitely a giggle. "Would I do that after our conversation, with you pointing out the obvious differences in the way our bodies react?"

A grin tugged at his lips. "Yeah, you would."

Her eyes sparkled. "Did it work?"

He pulled her close and let her feel for herself that his body was indeed reacting to her, making him uncomfortable in the process. Then again, he'd left her front porch this way every night the past week.

She tilted her face toward him. "I think it did."

"You think?" He shook his head, then stroked his finger across her cheek.

He held her close until the slow dance ended then they moved to a couple of fast songs. Despite what she'd said, McKenzie could dance. She could definitely sing too if she wouldn't let her own self-doubt get in the way.

Laughing, McKenzie fell into his arms. "Hey, Lance?"

"Hmm?" he asked, kissing the top of her head just because he could, because it felt right and wonderful.

"I'm ready."

"Already?" He'd figured they'd be one of the last to

leave, not one of the first. Still, if she was done partying, he'd take her home. Then he met her gaze and what she meant glittered brightly in her emerald eyes. "Really?"

She nodded. "Let's get our coats, please."

"Yes, ma'am."

"Such good manners," she praised.

Lance grinned. "Just wait until I show you what else I'm good at."

CHAPTER NINE

YES, IT HAD been a while since she'd had sex, but McKenzie wasn't a virgin. She enjoyed sex, was athletic enough to have good stamina and a good healthy drive so she felt she was decent in the sack. So why was she suddenly so nervous?

Because she'd essentially agreed to have sex with Lance.

With Lance!

Wasn't that what the dress, the hair and makeup, *the sexy undies* had all been about? Leading up to his taking them off her, kissing her body, running his fingers though her hair, making her sweat from the intensity of their coming together?

Sex with Lance.

Lance, who did everything perfectly.

He looked perfect.

Danced perfectly.

Doctored perfectly.

Made love perfectly?

That was the question.

She gulped and had to fight to keep her eyes on the road and off the man driving his car toward her house. He hadn't looked at her and seemed to have no desire to make small talk, which she appreciated. He was as lost in his thoughts as she was.

What was he thinking?

About sex? With her?

Sometimes she wondered why he even bothered. He'd been asking her out for weeks before she'd agreed to go to the Christmas show at the community center. Why hadn't he just moved on to someone else who was more agreeable?

Ha. She was agreeable tonight. She was practically throwing herself at him.

When he'd realized what she'd meant, he'd taken her hand and, with a determined gleam in his eyes, had made a beeline for their coats, not stopping to chat with any of their coworkers and friends as they'd left.

She took a deep breath.

Lance asked, "Second thoughts?"

She glanced toward him. "No, but I feel like a teenager sneaking off from a high school dance to mess around."

He wasn't looking at her, but she'd swear Lance's face paled, that his grip on the steering wheel tightened to the point his skin stretched white over his knuckles.

When he didn't comment, she asked, "You?"

"No regrets, but we don't have to do this if you're not sure."

"I'm sure." He still looked way tenser than she felt a man on his way to getting what he'd been supposedly wanting for weeks should look. Which made her uneasy. Maybe they were talking too much and not having enough action.

Maybe she was boring him with all her conversation.

They were still another ten minutes from her house. What were they supposed to do during the drive?

Then again, she wasn't the one driving so the possibilities were only limited by her imagination.

She'd always had a good imagination. A vivid imagination.

She wiggled in the seat, enjoying the car's seat warmers. "Nice seaters you've got here."

His gaze flicked her way. "Seaters?"

"Seat heaters. Yours are awesome." Seat belt still in place, she twisted as best she could toward him and wiggled her hips. "I'm feeling all toasty warm."

He kept his eyes on the road, but his throat worked and his fingers flexed along the steering wheel. "Things getting hot down there?"

Yes, this was much better than their terse silence. This was fun. As fun as she wanted to make it.

As fun as she could imagine it.

With Lance her imagination was working overtime.

Odd because even though the thought of sex with him made her nervous, she felt no hesitation in unbuttoning her coat and slipping her arms free, and running her palms down her waist, hips, thighs, letting her fingers tease her skirt hem.

"Maybe. Give me your hand and I'll let you check for yourself."

"McKenzie." Her name came out as half plea, half groan. "I need to concentrate on the road. I don't want to wreck."

"You won't. I only need one hand. You keep your eyes on the road and your other hand on the steering wheel. No worries. I'll take good care of you."

"You think I can touch your body and not look?" His voice sounded strained.

She liked it that his voice sounded strained, that what she was doing was having a profound effect on him. "Can't you?"

"I'm not sure." He sounded as if he really wasn't.

Which made McKenzie giddy inside. He wanted her. Really wanted her. She knew this, but seeing the reality of his desire was something more, was the cherry on top.

"Let's find out." She reached for him and he let her pull his right hand to her thigh. "See, I have faith in your ability to let your fingers have some fun. You've got this."

"Fun? Is that what you call between your legs?"

Excited from how much she could see he wanted her, she reached her free hand out and ran her fingers over his fly. "It had better be what I'm calling between your legs by morning."

"McKenzie." This time her name was a tortured croak.

She smiled, liking the hard fullness she brushed her fingertips over. That was going to be hers before the sun came up. Oh, yeah. He really was perfect.

"You're testing my willpower," he ground out through gritted teeth when her fingers lingered, exploring what she'd found and become fascinated by.

That made two of them. Her willpower was in a shambles. How she'd gone from teasing to totally turned on she wasn't sure, but she had. So much so that she wiggled against the seat again, causing his hand to shift on her thigh and make goose bumps on her skin.

"I have no doubt that you've never failed a test." She placed her free hand over his and guided him beneath the hem of her dress.

"There's always a first."

"Not this time," she told him, gliding his hand between her thighs to where she blazed hotly, and not from the car's seat warmers.

"You sure about that?"

"Positive," she assured him, "because if you lose your willpower we have to stop, and where's the fun in that?"

"Fun being where my fingers are?"

"Exactly." She shifted, bringing him into full contact with those itty-bitty panties she'd put on earlier.

"If I get pulled over for speeding to get us home quicker?"

She squeezed her buttocks together in a Kegel, pressing against his fingers. "Not sure how you'd explain to the officer why you were going so fast."

"I'd tell him to look in my passenger seat and he'd understand just fine."

For all his talk, the speedometer stayed at the speed limit, which she kind of liked. Safety mattered. Even when your passenger was seducing you. That he wasn't gunning the engine of the sports car surprised her, though. She'd have bet money he'd be a speed demon behind the wheel, but she couldn't think of a time she'd been in his car when he'd been going too fast or pulling any careless stunts.

His thumb brushed lightly over her pubic bone and she moaned, forgetting all about safety.

She gripped his thigh and squeezed. "That feels good."

"I couldn't tell."

He didn't have to look at her for her to know he was smiling, pleased with her body's reaction to his touch. She heard his pleasure in his voice, felt it in the way his fingers toyed over the barely-there satin material.

"Might be time to turn that seater off since you're already steamy down there."

She tilted her hips toward his touch. "Might be, but I'm sure I could get hotter."

"You think?"

"I'm hoping."

He slowed the car and turned into her street. "Thank God we're almost there."

"Not even close," she teased. "But if you move those fingers just so, maybe."

"McKenzie." Her name was torn from deep within him. "You're killing me."

His fingers said otherwise. His fingers were little adventurers, exploring uncharted territory, staking claims in the wake of his touch.

She closed her eyes, holding on to his thigh, spreading her legs to give him better access. Gentle back-and-forth movements created cataclysmic earthquakes throughout her body.

Yearnings to rip off her clothes hit her. To rip off *his* clothes, right then, in the car, to give him free access to touch with no material in the way.

Why couldn't she?

Why couldn't she take her panties off?

That wasn't something she'd ever done before, but she was an adult, a responsible one usually. If she wanted to suddenly go commando, she could do that, right?

She hiked her dress up around her thighs, looped her fingers through the tiny straps of her thong and wiggled them down her legs. She probably looked ridiculous raised up off the seat to remove them, but who cared?

His eyes were on the road and now there was nothing to keep him from touching her. Not her panties, but her, as in skin to skin. She needed that. His skin against hers. His touch on her aching flesh.

"If I were a stronger man, I'd make you wait until we're at least in your driveway before I touched you for real," he warned.

"Good thing you're not a stronger man," she replied as his fingers slid home. "Very good thing."

His touch was light, just gentle strokes teasing her.

"This isn't fair," he complained.

"Life isn't fair. Get over it."

He laughed. "No sympathy from you."

"Hey, you've been trying to get in my pants for weeks now. Why would I feel sympathetic toward you when you're getting what you want?"

"I want more than to get into your pants, McKenzie. I want a relationship with you."

"Here's a news flash for you—if you're in my pants, you're in a relationship with me."

"For thirty days or less?" he asked.

"I'm not putting a time limit on our relationship. Move your fingers faster."

"Not until you promise you'll give me two months."

Two months? Why two months?

"This isn't as business negotiation."

"True," he agreed. "But if you want my fingers to do more than skim the surface, you'll give me your word. I want two months. Not a day less. Not a day more."

She moved against him, trying to get the friction she craved. "Two months?"

"Two months."

Ugh. He was pushing for more than she usually gave. It figured. Then again, what was two months in the grand scheme of life?

"I don't have to agree to this to get what I want. It's not as if you're going to turn down what I'm offering."

He chuckled. "Confident, aren't you?"

"Of that? Yes, you're a man."

"I won't be used for sex, McKenzie."

"Isn't that usually the woman's line?"

"These are modern times and you're a modern woman."

She arched further against his hand. "Not that modern."

"Two months?" He teased her most sensitive area with the slightest flick of his finger.

"Fine," she sighed, moving against his fingers. "You can have two months, but I won't promise a day more."

He turned into her driveway, amazing since she hadn't even realized they were that close to her house. Hadn't even recalled that they were in her street or even on the planet, for that matter. All that existed was the two of them inside his car.

He killed the engine, turned toward her, and moved her thighs apart, touching where she ached.

"I knew you could find it if you tried hard enough," she teased breathlessly.

"Oh, I'm definitely hard enough."

She reached out and touched him again. He was right. He definitely was.

Lance leaned toward her, taking her mouth as his fingers worked magic. Sparkles and rainbows and shooting-stars magic.

Her inner thighs clenched. Her eyes squeezed tight then opened wide.

Her body melted in all the right places in a powerful orgasmic wave that turned her body inside out. Or it felt like it at any rate.

Sucking in much-needed oxygen, she met his smug gaze.

Two months might not be nearly enough time if that was a preview of the main event.

Bodies tangled, Lance and McKenzie tossed a half dozen pillows off her bed and onto the floor with their free hands. A trail of clothes marked their path from the front door to her bed. His. Hers.

"I want you, McKenzie," he breathed, his hand at the base of her neck as his mouth took hers again. Long and hard, he kissed her.

McKenzie was positive she'd never been kissed so possessively, never been kissed so completely.

Even when his mouth lifted from hers, she didn't answer him verbally. She wasn't sure her vocal cords would even work if she tried.

Her hands worked, though. As did her lips. She touched Lance and kissed him, exploring the strong lines of his neck, his shoulders, his chest.

"So beautiful."

Had she said that or had he? She wasn't sure.

His hands were on her breasts, cupping her bottom, everywhere, and yet not nearly all the places she wanted to be touched.

"More," she cried, desperation filling her when it was him she wanted, him she needed. "Please. Now, Lance. I want you now."

Maybe her desperation was evident in her tone or maybe he was just as desperate because he pushed her back onto the bed, put on the condom he'd tossed onto the nightstand when they'd first entered the room, then crawled above her.

With his knee he spread her legs, positioned himself above her. "You're sure?"

What was he waiting for?

She arched her hips, taking him inside, then moaned at the sweet stretching pleasure.

That was what she had been wanting for a very long time.

Breathing hard, Lance fell back against the bed.

She'd been amazing.

Beautiful, fun, witty, sexy, actively participating in their mating, urging him on, telling him what she wanted, what she needed. Showing him.

The chemistry between them was unparalleled. Never had he experienced anything like what they'd just shared.

"That. Was. Amazing."

He grinned at her punctuated words. "My thoughts exactly."

He turned onto his side and stared at her. "You are amazing."

"Ha. Wasn't me."

"I think it was."

"Right. I assure you that I've been there every time I've had sex in the past and it's never been like that so it must be you who is amazing."

His insides warmed at her admission. "For the record, it's never been like that for me either."

Her expression pinched and she scooted up on a pillow.

Shaking her head, she went for the sheet that was bunched up at the foot of the bed. When she'd covered her beautiful body, she turned to him.

"I don't really think I need to say this, not with a man like you, but I'm going to, just in case. I don't want there to be any confusion."

He knew from her words, her tone what she was going to say. He was glad. He felt the same, but hearing the reminder was good and perhaps needed.

"Despite your amazing orgasm-giving ability, I'm not looking for a long-term relationship."

"Me, either," he assured her, trying not to let his ego get too big at her praise.

"I guess that's crude of me, to talk about the end when we're still in bed and I feel wonderful. But we work together so we need to be clear about the boundaries of our relationship so work doesn't become messy."

The thought of ending things with her, not being able to touch her, kiss her, make love to her and experience what they'd just shared, because it might make things messy, wasn't a pleasant thought, but it should be.

He didn't want marriage or kids, didn't want that responsibility, that weight on his heart, that replacing of Shelby. He'd made a vow to his first love. He owed Shelby his heart and more. McKenzie was right to remind them both of the guidelines they'd agreed to. Setting an end date and clear boundaries was a smart move.

Two months for them to enjoy each other's bodies, then move on with their lives. Him with his main focus being his career and charity work in memory of Shelby. McKenzie with her career and her running and whatever else filled her life with joy.

Two months and they'd call it quits. That sounded just right to him.

* * *

Staring at the oh-so-hot naked man in her bed, McKenzie hugged the sheet tighter to her.

Please agree with me, she silently pleaded.

She'd just had the best sex of her life and couldn't fathom the idea of not repeating the magic she'd just experienced.

But she would do just that if he didn't agree.

Already she was risking too much. That's why she usually ended her relationships after a month, because she didn't want pesky emotional attachments that might lead her down the paths her parents had taken. She didn't want a future that held multiple marriages and multiple divorces like her father. Neither did she want the whiny, miserable, man-needing life her mother led.

Bachelorettehood was the life for her, all the way.

Hearing Lance agree that they'd end things in two months was important, necessary for them to carry on. She simply wouldn't risk anything longer. Already she was giving him double the time she usually spent with a man.

He deserved double time.

Triple time.

Forever.

No, not forever. She didn't do forever. Two months, then adios, even if he was an orgasm-giving god.

"Promise me," she urged, desperately needing the words.

"Two months sounds perfect."

Relief flooded her, because she hadn't wanted to tell him to leave. For two months she didn't have to.

CHAPTER TEN

"YOU CAN'T BE working the entire Christmas holiday," Lance insisted, following McKenzie to the hospital cafeteria table where she put down her food tray.

She'd gotten a chicken salad croissant and a side salad. He'd gone for a more hearty meal, but had ended up grabbing a croissant as well.

Sitting down at the table, she glanced at him. "I'm not, but I am working at the clinic half a day on Christmas Eve and then working half a day in the emergency room on Christmas morning." She'd done so the past few years so the regular emergency room doctor could have the morning off with his kids and she liked filling in from time to time so she kept her emergency care skills sharp.

"When will you celebrate with your parents?"

Bile rose up in her throat at the thought of introducing Lance to her parents. Her mother would probably hit on him and her dad would probably ask him what he thought about wife number five's plastic surgeon–constructed chest. No, she wouldn't be taking Lance home for the holidays.

Actually, when she'd talked to her mother a few days ago, Violet had said she was going to her sister's for a few days and spending the holidays with her family. She hadn't mentioned Beau, the latest live-in boyfriend, so McKenzie wasn't sure if Beau was going, staying or if he was history. Her father had planned a ski trip in Vermont with his bride and a group of their friends.

"We don't celebrate the holidays like other folks."

"How's that?"

"We'll meet up at some point in January and have dinner or something. We just don't make a big deal of the day. It's way too commercialized anyway, you know."

"This coming from the winner of the best costume in the Christmas parade."

She couldn't quite keep her smile hidden. The call from the mayor telling her she'd won the award had surprised her, as had the Christmas ornament he'd dropped by the clinic to commemorate her honor.

"Cecilia is the one who should get all the kudos for that. She put my costume together."

"But you wore it so well," he assured her, giving her a once-over. "You wear that lab coat nicely, too, Dr. Sanders."

She arched a brow at him and gave a mock-condescending shake of her head. "You hitting on me, Dr. Spencer?"

"With a baseball bat."

She rolled her eyes. "Men, always talking about size."

He laughed.

"Speaking of size, you should see the tree my mother put up in her family room. I swear she searches for the biggest one on the lot every year and that's her sole criterion for buying."

"She puts up a live tree?"

"She puts up a slew of trees. All are artificial except the one in the family room. There, she goes all out and insists on a real tree. There's a row of evergreens behind my parents' house, marking Christmases past."

McKenzie couldn't even recall the last Christmas tree her mother had put up. Maybe a skimpy tinsel one that had seen better days when McKenzie had still been young enough to ask about Santa and Christmas. Violet had never been much of a holiday person, especially not after Mc-Kenzie's father had left.

"She wants to meet you."

McKenzie's brow arched. "Why would she want to do that? For that matter, how does she even know about me?"

"She asked if I was seeing anyone and I told her about you."

Talking to his mother about her just seemed wrong.

"She shouldn't meet me."

"Why not?"

"Mothers should only meet significant others who have the potential for being around for a while."

"Look, telling her I was dating someone was easier than showing up and there being some single female there eager to meet me and plan our future together. It's really not as big a deal as you're making it for you to come to my parents' at Christmas."

Maybe not to him, but the thought of meeting his family was a very big deal to her. She didn't meet families. That implied things that just weren't true.

"Obviously you haven't been paying attention," she pointed out. "I'll be here on Christmas, working."

"The shifts are abbreviated on the holidays. What time will you get off?"

"Oh, no. You're not trapping me that way."

He gave her an innocent look. "What way?"

"The way that whatever time I say you're going to say, 'Oh, that's perfect. Just come on over when you're finished.'"

"Hey, McKenzie?"

She frowned at him, knowing what he was about to say.

"The time you get off from the emergency room is perfect. Just come to my parents' house when you're finished."

"Meeting parents implies a commitment you and I don't have," she reiterated.

"There'll be lots of people there. Aunts. Uncles. Cousins. People even I've never met. It's a party. You'll have fun and it's really not a big deal, except it saves me from my mother trying to set me up with every single nonrelated female she knows."

How in the world had he talked her into this? McKenzie asked herself crossly as she pushed the Spencers' doorbell.

She didn't do this.

Only, apparently, this year she did.

Even to the point she'd made a dessert to bring with her to Lance's parents. How corny was that?

She shouldn't be here. She didn't do "meet the parents." She just didn't.

Panic set in. She turned, determined to escape before anyone knew she was there.

At that moment the front door opened.

"You're here."

"Not really," she countered. "Forget you saw me. I'm out of here."

Shaking his head, he grinned. "Get in here."

"I think I made a mistake."

His brows rose. "McKenzie, you just drove almost an hour to get here and not so you could get here and leave without Christmas dinner."

"I've done crazier things." Like agree to come to Christmas dinner with Lance's family in the first place.

"Did you make something?" He gestured to the dish she held.

"A dessert, but—"

"No buts, McKenzie. Get in here."

She took a deep breath. He was right. She was being ridiculous. She had gotten off work, gone home, showered, grabbed the dessert she'd made the night before and typed his parents' address into her GPS.

And driven almost an hour to get here.

"Fine, but you owe me."

He leaned forward, kissed the tip of her nose. "Anything you want."

"Promises. Promises."

He grinned, took the dish from her, and motioned her inside. "I'm glad you're here. I was afraid you'd change your mind."

"I did," she reminded him as she stepped into his parents' foyer. "Only I waited a bit too late because you caught me before I could escape."

"Then I'm glad I noticed your headlights as your car pulled into the driveway, because I missed you last night."

He'd driven to his parents' home the afternoon before when he'd finished seeing his patients. It had been the first evening since their frozen yogurt date that they'd not seen each other.

She'd missed him too.

Which didn't jibe well, but she didn't have time to think too much on it, because a pretty woman who appeared to be much younger than McKenzie knew she had to be stepped into the foyer. She had sparkly blue eyes, dark brown hair that she had clipped up, black slacks and the prettiest Christmas sweater McKenzie had ever seen. Her smile lit up her entire face.

Lance looked a lot like his mother.

"We are so glad you're here!" she exclaimed, her Southern drawl so pronounced it was almost like something off a television show. "Lance has been useless for the past hour, waiting on you to get here."

"Thanks, Mom. You just called me useless to my girl." Lance's tone was teasing, his look toward his mother full of adoration.

McKenzie wanted to go on record that she wasn't Lance's girl, but technically she supposed she was. At least for the time being.

"Nonsense. She knows what I meant," his mother dismissed his claim and pulled McKenzie into a tight hug. She smelled of cinnamon and cookies.

Christmas, McKenzie thought. His mother smelled of Christmas. Not McKenzie's past Christmases, but the way Christmas was supposed to smell. Warm, inviting, full of goodness and happiness.

"It's nice to meet you," McKenzie said, not quite sure what to make of her hug. Lance's mother's hug had been real, warm, welcoming. She couldn't recall the last time her own mother or father had given her such a hug. Had they ever?

"Not nearly as nice as it is to finally meet one of Lance's girlfriends."

Did he not usually bring his girlfriends home? He'd said her being there was no big deal. If he didn't usually bring anyone home, then her presence was a big deal. She wanted to ask, but decided it wasn't her place because really what did it matter? She was here now. Whatever he'd done with his past girlfriends didn't apply to her, just as what he did with her wouldn't apply to his future girlfriends.

Future girlfriends. Ugh. She didn't like the thought of him with anyone but her. His smile, his touch, his kisses, they belonged to her. At least for now, she reminded herself.

"I'm glad you're here." Lance leaned in, kissed her briefly on the mouth, then took her hand. "I hope you came hungry."

Her gaze cut to Lance's and she wondered if he'd read her thoughts again?

"Take a deep breath. It's time to meet the rest of the crew," he warned.

"Be nice, Lance. You'll scare her off. They aren't that bad and you know it," his mother scolded.

Lance just winked at her.

Two hours later, McKenzie had to agree with Lance's mother. His family wasn't that bad. She'd met his grandparents, who were so hard of hearing they had everyone talking loudly so they could keep up with the conversation, his aunts and uncles, his cousins, and a handful of children who belonged to his cousins.

It was quite a bunch: loud, talking over one another, laughing, eating and truly enjoying each other's company.

The kids seemed to adore Lance. They called him Uncle Lance, although technically he was their second cousin.

"You're quiet," Lance observed, leaning in close so that his words were just for her ears.

"Just taking it all in," she admitted.

"We're something else, for sure. Is this similar to your family get-togethers?"

McKenzie laughed. "Not even close."

"How so?"

"I won't bore you with my childhood woes."

"Nothing about you would bore me, McKenzie. I want to know more about you."

She started to ask what would be the point, but somehow that comment felt wrong in this loving, warm environment, so she picked up her glass of tea, took a sip, then whispered, "I'll tell you some other time."

That seemed to appease him. They finished eating. Everyone, men and women, helped clear the table. The kids had eaten at a couple of card tables set up in the kitchen and they too cleared their spots without prompting. McKenzie was amazed at how they all seemed to work together so cohesively.

The men then retired to the large family room while

the women put away leftovers and loaded the dishwasher. All except Lance. He seemed reluctant to leave McKenzie.

"I'll be fine. I'm sure they won't bite."

He still looked hesitant.

"Seriously, what's the worst that could happen?"

What indeed? Lance wondered. He had rarely brought women home and never to a Christmas function. His entire family had been teasing him that this must be the one for him to bring her home to Christmas with the family. He'd tried to explain that he and McKenzie had been co-workers and friends for years, but the more he'd talked, the more he reminded them that he'd already met and lost "the one," the more they'd smiled. By the time McKenzie arrived, he'd been half-afraid his family would have them walking down the aisle before morning.

He didn't think she'd appreciate any implication that they were more than just a casual couple.

They weren't. Just a hot and heavy two-month relationship destined to go nowhere because McKenzie didn't do long-term commitment and his seventeen-year-old self had vowed to always love Shelby, for his heart to always be loyal to her memory.

What was the worst that could happen? He hesitated.

"Seriously, Lance. I'm a big girl. They aren't going to scare me off."

"I just…" He knew he was being ridiculous. "I don't mind helping clean up."

"Lance Donovan Spencer, go visit with your grandparents. You've not seen them since Thanksgiving," his mother ordered. "That will give me and your girl time to get to know each other without you looming over us."

"Looming?" he protested indignantly.

"Go." His mother pointed toward the door.

Lance laughed. "I can tell my presence and help is not

appreciated or wanted around here, so I will go visit with my grandmother who loves me very much."

"Hmm, maybe she's who you should list on your references," McKenzie teased him, her eyes twinkling.

"Maybe. Mom's been bumped right off."

"I heard that," his mom called out over her shoulder.

He leaned in and kissed McKenzie's cheek. "I'm right in the next room if their interrogation gets to be too much."

"Noted." McKenzie was smiling, like she wouldn't mind his mother's, aunts' and cousins' questions. Lord, he hoped not. They didn't have boundaries and McKenzie had boundaries that made the Great Wall of China look like a playpen.

"Lance tells me you two have only been dating for a few weeks," his mother said moments after Lance left the kitchen.

"You know he's never brought a woman home for Christmas before, right?" This came from one of Lance's cousins' wives, Sara Beth.

"He seems to be head over heels about you," another said. "Told us you two work together and recently became an item."

"We want the full scoop," one of his dad's sisters added.

"Um, well, sounds like you already know the full scoop," McKenzie began slowly. She didn't want to give Lance's family the wrong idea. "We have been friends since I returned to Coopersville after finishing my residency."

"So you're from Coopersville originally? Your family is still there?"

"My mother is. My dad lives here in Lewisburg."

His mother's eyes lit up with excitement. "We might know him. What's his name?"

She hoped they didn't know him. Okay, so he was a highly successful lawyer, but personally? Her father was a mess. A horrible, womanizing, cheating mess. If Lance's mother knew him, it probably meant he'd hit on her. No the impression McKenzie wanted Lance's mother to have of her.

Avoiding the question, she said instead, "I don't have any brothers or sisters but, like Lance, I do have a few cousins." Nice enough people but they rarely all got together. Really, the only time McKenzie saw them was when one of them was sick and was seen at the clinic. "My parents divorced when I was four and I never quite got past that."

She only added the last part so Lance's family would hopefully move on past the subject of her parents. Definitely not because she wanted to talk about her parents' divorce. She never talked about that. At least, not the nitty-gritty details that had led up to her world falling apart.

"Poor thing," Lance's mother sympathized. "Divorce is hard at any age."

"Amen," another of Lance's aunts said. "Lance's Uncle Gerry is my second husband. The first and I were like gasoline and fire, always explosive."

The conversation continued while they cleaned up the remainder of the dishes and food, jumping from one subject to another but never back to McKenzie's parents. She liked Lance's noisy, warm family.

"Well, we're just so happy you're here, McKenzie. It's about time that boy found someone to pull him out of the past."

McKenzie glanced toward the aunt who'd spoken up. Her confusion must have shown because the women looked back and forth at each other as if trying to decide how much more to say.

Sara Beth gave McKenzie an empathetic look. "I guess he never told you about Shelby?"

Who was Shelby and what had she meant to Lance?

"No."

The woman winced as if she wished she could erase

having mentioned the woman's name. "Shelby was Lance's first love."

Was. An ominous foreboding took hold of McKenzie.

"What happened?"

"She died." This came from Sara Beth. Every pair of eyes in the room was trained on McKenzie to gauge her reaction, triggering the usual reaction to being stared at that she always had.

Lance's first love had died and he'd never breathed a word.

"Enough talk about the past and anything but how wonderful it is to have McKenzie with us," Lance's mother dried her hands on a towel and pulled McKenzie over to the counter for another of her tight, all-encompassing hugs. "Truly, we are grateful that you are in my son's life. He is a special man with a big heart and you are a fortunate young woman."

"Yes," McKenzie agreed, stunned at the thought someone Lance had loved had died. Was he still in love with Shelby? How had the woman died? How long ago? "Yes, he is a special man."

CHAPTER ELEVEN

"YOU SURE ABOUT THIS?" McKenzie asked the man stretching out beside her. He wore dark running pants that emphasized his calf and thigh muscles and a bright-colored long-sleeved running shirt that outlined a chest McKenzie had taken great pleasure in exploring the night before as they'd lain in bed and "rung in" the New Year.

Lance glanced at her and grinned. "I'll be waiting for you at the finish line."

She hoped so. She hoped Lance hadn't been teasing about being a runner. He was in great shape, had phenomenal endurance, but she'd still never known him to run. But the truth was he hadn't stayed the whole night at her place ever, so he could do the same as her and run in the early morning before work. They had sex, often lay in bed talking and touching lightly afterward, then he went home. Just as he had the night before. She hadn't asked him to stay. He hadn't asked to. Just, each night, whenever he got ready to go, he kissed her good-night and left.

Truth was, she'd have let him stay Christmas night after they'd got back from his parents'. He'd insisted on following her back to her place. Despite the late hour, he'd come in, held her close, then left. She hadn't wanted him to go. She'd have let him stay every night since. He just hadn't wanted to. Or, if he had wanted to, he'd chosen to go home anyway.

Why was that? Did it have to do with Shelby? Should she tell him that she knew about his first love? That his family had told her about his loss? They just hadn't told her any of the details surrounding the mysterious woman Lance had loved.

Maybe the details didn't matter. They shouldn't matter.

Only McKenzie admitted they did. Perhaps it was just curiosity. Perhaps it was jealousy. Perhaps it was something more she couldn't put her finger on.

She'd almost asked him about Shelby a dozen times, but always changed her mind. If he wanted her to know, he'd tell her.

Today was the first day of a new year. A new beginning.

Who knew, maybe tonight he'd stay.

If not, she was okay with that, too. He might be right in going, in not adding sleeping together to their relationship, because she didn't count the light dozing they sometimes did after their still phenomenal comings together as sleep. Sleeping together until morning would be another whole level of intimacy.

"You don't have to try to run next to me," she advised, thinking they were intimate enough already. Too intimate because imagining life without him was already becoming difficult. Maybe they could stay close friends after their two months were up. Maybe. "Just keep your own steady pace and I'll keep mine. We'll meet up at the end."

Grinning, he nodded. "Yes, ma'am. I'll keep that in mind."

They continued to stretch their muscles as the announcer talked, telling them about the cause they were running for, about the rules, etc. Soon they were off.

McKenzie never tried to take the lead early on. In some races she never took the lead. Not that she didn't always do her best, but sometimes there were just faster runners for that particular distance. Today she expected to do well, but perhaps not win as she was much more of an endurance runner than a speed one.

Lance ran beside her and to her pleased surprise he didn't try to talk. In the past when she'd convinced friends to run with her, they'd wanted to have a gab session. That was until they became so breathless they stopped to walk, and then they often expected her to stop and walk with them.

McKenzie ran.

Lance easily kept pace with her. Halfway in she began to wonder if she was slowing him down rather than the other way around. She picked up her pace, pushing herself, suddenly wanting distance between them. Without any huffing or puffing he ran along beside her as if she hadn't just upped their pace. That annoyed her.

"You've been holding out on me," she accused a little breathily, thinking it was bad when she was the one reverting to talking. Next thing you knew she'd be stopping to walk.

"Me?" His gaze cut to her. "I told you that I ran."

"I've never seen you at any of the local runs and yet clearly you do run."

"I don't do organized runs or competitions."

Didn't do organized runs or competitions? McKenzie frowned. What kind of an answer was that when he clearly enjoyed running as much as she did? Well, maybe almost as much.

"That's hard to believe with the way you're into every charity in the region," she said. "Why wouldn't you participate in these fund-raisers when they're an easy way to raise money for great causes? For that matter, why aren't you organizing races to raise money for all your special causes?"

McKenzie was a little too smart for her own good. Lance was involved with a large number of charities and helped support many others, but never those that had to do with running.

He did run several times a week, but always alone, always to clear his head, always with someone else at his side, mentally if not physically.

High school cross-country had been where he'd first met Shelby. She'd been a year older than him and had had a different set of friends, so although he'd seen the pretty brunette around school he hadn't known her. She'd have been better off if he never had.

"No one can do everything," he answered McKenzie.

"I'm beginning to think you do."

"Not even close. You and I just happen to have a lot in common. We enjoy the same things."

She shook her head. "Nope. I don't enjoy singing."

"I think you would if you'd relax."

"Standing onstage, with people looking at me?" She cut her gaze to him. "Never going to happen."

Keeping his pace matched to hers, he glanced at her. "You don't like things that make people look at you, do you, McKenzie?"

"Nope."

"Because of your parents?"

"I may not have mentioned this before, but I don't like talking while I run. I'm a silent runner."

He chuckled. "That a hint for me to be quiet?"

"You catch on quick."

They kept up the more intense pace until they crossed the finish line. The last few minutes of the race Lance debated on whether or not to let McKenzie cross the finish line first. Ultimately, he decided she wasn't the kind of woman who'd appreciate a man letting her win.

In the last stretch he increased his speed. So did McKenzie. If he hadn't been a bit winded, he'd have laughed at her competitive spirit. Instead, he ran.

So did she.

They crossed the finish line together. The judge declared Lance the winner by a fraction of a second, but Lance would have just as easily have believed that McKenzie had crossed first.

She was doubled over, gasping for air. His own lungs couldn't suck in enough air either. He walked around, slowly catching his breath. When he turned back, she was glaring.

"You were holding out on me," she accused breathlessly, her eyes narrowed.

"Huh?"

"You were considering letting me win." Her words came out a little choppy between gasps for air.

"In case you didn't notice..." he sucked in a deep gulp of air "... I was trying to cross that finish line first."

"You were sandbagging."

He laughed. "Sandbagging?"

"How long have you been running?"

"Since high school." Not that he wanted to talk about it. He didn't. Talking about this particular subject might lead to questions he didn't want to answer.

"You competed?"

He nodded.

"Me, too." She straightened, fully expanding her lungs with air. "I did my undergraduate studies on a track scholarship."

Despite the memories assailing him, the corners of Lance's mouth tugged upward. "Something else we have in common."

McKenzie just looked at him, then rolled her eyes. "We don't have that much in common."

"More than you seem to want to acknowledge."

"Maybe," she conceded. "Let's go congratulate the guy who beat us both. He lives about thirty minutes from here.

His time is usually about twenty to thirty seconds better than mine. He usually only competes in the five-kilometer races, though. Nothing shorter, nothing longer."

They congratulated the winner, hung out around the tent, rehydrating, got their second and third place medals, then headed toward McKenzie's house.

They showered together then, a long time later, got ready to go and eat.

The first day of the New Year turned into the first week, then the first month.

McKenzie began to feel panicky, knowing her time with Lance was coming to an end as the one-month mark came and went. Each day following passed like sand swiftly falling through an hourglass.

Then she realized that the day before Valentine's Day marked the end of the two months she'd promised him. Seriously, the day before Valentine's?

Why did that even matter? She'd never cared if she had a significant other on that hyped-up holiday in the past. Most years she'd been in a casual relationship and she'd gotten a box of chocolates and flowers and had given a funny card to her date for the evening. Why should this year feel different? Why did the idea of chocolates and flowers from Lance seem as if it would be different from gifts she'd received in the past? Why did the idea of giving him a card seem to fall short?

She'd be ending things with Lance the day before every other couple would be celebrating their love.

She and Lance weren't in love. She wasn't sure love even truly existed.

A vision of Lance's grandparents, married for sixty years, his parents, married for forty years, ran through her mind and she had to reconsider. Maybe love did exist, but not for anyone with her genetic makeup. Already her dad was complaining about his new wife and had flirted outrageously with their waitress when they'd had their usual belated Christmas dinner a few weeks back. Hearing that his new marriage would be ending soon wouldn't surprise McKenzie in the slightest. Her mother, well, her mother had taken up the vegan life because Beau was history and her new "'love" was all about living green. Her mother was even planning to plant out her own garden this spring and wanted to know if McKenzie had any requests.

McKenzie had no issue with her mother trying to live more healthily. She was glad of it, even. But the woman enjoyed nothing more than a big juicy steak, which was what she ordered on the rare occasions she met McKenzie for a meal—usually in between boyfriends or at Christmas or birthdays.

McKenzie had managed both meals with her parents this year without Lance joining them. Fortunately, his volunteer work oftentimes had him busy immediately following work and she had scheduled both meals with her parents on evenings he had Celebration Graduation meetings.

"You've been staring at your screen for the past ten minutes," Lance pointed out, gesturing to her idle laptop. "Problem patient?"

He'd come over, brought their dinner with him, and they'd been sitting on her sofa, remotely logged in to their work laptops and charting their day's patients while watching a reality television program.

McKenzie hit a button, saving her work, then turned to him. "My mind just isn't on this tonight."

"I noticed." He saved his own work, set his laptop down on her coffee table and turned to her. "What's up?"

"I was just thinking about Valentine's Day."

His smile spread across his face and lit up his eyes. "Making plans for how you're going to surprise me with a lacy red number and high heels?" He waggled his brows suggestively.

Despite knowing he was mostly teasing, she shook her head. "We won't be together on Valentine's Day. Our two months is up the day before. The end is near."

His smile faded and his forehead wrinkled. "There's no reason we shouldn't be able to spend Valentine's Day together. I have the Celebration Graduation Valentine's Day dance at the high school that I'll be helping to chaperone. It ends at ten and it'll take me another twenty to thirty minutes to help clean up. But we can still do something, then we'll call it quits after that."

She shook her head. "You already had plans for that evening. That's good."

She, however, did not and would be acutely aware of his absence from her life, and not just because of the holiday.

"I hadn't really thought about it being the end of our two months. You could volunteer at the dance with me."

She shook her head again. "Not a good idea."

"Think you'd be a bad influence on those high schoolers?" Even though his tone was teasing, his eyes searched hers.

"I probably would," she agreed, just to avoid a discussion of the truth. They would be finished the night before. There would be no more charting together, dining together, going to dances or parties together, no more running together, as they'd started doing every morning at four. Lance would be gone, would meet someone else, would date them, and, despite what he claimed, he would very likely eventually find whatever he was looking for in a woman and marry her.

Was he looking for someone like Shelby?

What was Shelby like?

Why had he still not mentioned the woman to her?

Then again, why would he mention her? He and McKenzie were temporary. He owed her nothing, no explanation of his past relationships, no explanation of his future plans.

Yet there were things about him she wanted to know. Suddenly needed to know.

"Do you want kids?" Why she asked the question she wasn't sure. It wasn't as if the answer mattered to her or was even applicable. She and Lance had no future together.

To her surprise, he shook his head. "I have no plans to ever have children."

Recalling how great he was with his cousins' kids, that shocked her. Then again, had she asked him the question because she'd expected a different answer? That she'd expected him to say he planned to have an entire houseful, and that way she could have used that information as one more thing to put between them because, with her genetics, no way could she ever have children.

"You'd make a fantastic dad."

His brow lifted and he regarded her for a few long moments before asking, "You pregnant, McKenzie?"

Her mouth fell open and she squished up her nose. "Absolutely not."

"You sure? You've not had a menstrual cycle since we've been together. I hadn't really thought about it until just now, but I should have."

Her face heated at his comment. They were doctors, so it was ridiculous that she was blushing. But at this moment she was a woman and he was a man. Medicine had nothing to do with their conversation. This was personal. Too personal.

"I rarely have my cycle. My gynecologist says it's because I run so much and don't retain enough body fat for proper estrogen storage. It's highly unlikely that I'd get pregnant. But even if that weren't an issue," she reminded him, "you've used a condom every single time we've had sex. I can't be pregnant."

Not once had she even considered that as a possibility. Truth was, she questioned if her body would even allow her to get pregnant if she wanted to, which she didn't. No way would she want to bring a baby in to the world the way her parents had.

"Stranger things have happened."

"Than my getting pregnant?" She shook her head in denial. "That would be the strangest ever. I'm not meant to have children."

His curiosity was obviously piqued as he studied her. "Why not?"

"Bad genetics."

"Your parents are ill?"

How was she supposed to answer that one? With the truth, probably. She took a deep breath.

"Physically, they are as healthy as can be. Mentally and emotionally, they are messed up."

"Depression?"

"My mother suffers from depression. Maybe my dad, too, really. They both have made horrible life choices that they are now stuck living with."

"Your dad is a lawyer?"

She nodded.

"What does your mom do?"

"Whatever the man currently in her life tells her to do."

Lance seemed to let that sink in for a few moments. "She's remarried?"

McKenzie shook her head. "She's never remarried. I think she purposely stays single because my father has to pay her alimony until she remarries or dies."

"Your father is remarried, though?"

"At the moment, but ask me again in a month and who knows what the answer will be."

"How many times has he remarried?"

She didn't want to answer, shouldn't have let this conversation even start. She should have finished her charts, not opened up an emotional can of worms that led to conversations about her menstrual cycle, pregnancy and her parents. What had she been thinking?

"McKenzie?"

"He's on his fifth marriage."

Lance winced. "Hard to find the one, eh?"

"Oh, he finds them all right. In all the wrong places. He's not known for his faithfulness. My guess is that he's to blame for all his failed marriages. Definitely he was with his and my mother's."

"There's always two sides to every story."

"My mother and I walked in on him in his office with his secretary."

"As in…"

Feeling sick at her stomach, McKenzie nodded. She'd never said those words out loud. Not ever. Cecilia knew, but not because McKenzie had told her the details, just that she'd figured it out from overheard arguments between McKenzie's parents.

"How old were you?"

"Four."

CHAPTER TWELVE

LANCE TRIED TO imagine how a four-year-old would react to walking in on her father in a compromising situation with a woman who wasn't her mother. He couldn't imagine it. His own family took commitment seriously. When they gave their word, their heart to another they meant it.

His own heart squeezed. Hadn't he given his word to Shelby? Hadn't he promised to love her forever? To not ever forget the young girl who'd taught him what it meant to care for another, who'd brought him from boyhood to manhood?

He had. He did. He would. Forever.

He owed her so much.

"That must have been traumatic," he mused, not knowing exactly what to say but wanting to comfort McKenzie all the same. Wanting not to think of Shelby right now. Lately he'd not wanted to think of her a lot, and had resented how much he thought of her, of how guilty he felt that he didn't want to think of her anymore.

How could he not want to think of her when it was his fault she was no longer living the life she had been meant to live? When if it wasn't for him she'd be a doctor? Be making a difference in so many people's lives?

"It wasn't the first time he'd cheated."

Lance stared at McKenzie's pale face. "How do you know?"

"My mother launched herself at them, screaming and yelling and clawing and...well, you get the idea. She said some pretty choice things that my father didn't deny."

"You were only four," he reminded her, trying to envision the scene from a four-year-old's perspective and shuttering on the inside at the horror. "Maybe you misunderstood."

She shook her head. "He doesn't deserve you or anyone else defending him. He doesn't even bother defending himself anymore. Just says it's genetic and he can't help himself."

"Bull."

That had McKenzie's head shooting up. "What?"

"Bull. If he really loved someone else more than he loved himself then being faithful wouldn't be an issue. It would be easy, what came naturally from that love."

McKenzie took a deep breath. "Then maybe that's the problem. No one has ever been able to compete with his own self-love. Not my mother, not his other wives or girlfriends and certainly not me."

There was a depth of pain in her voice that made Lance's heart ache for her. "Did he have more children?"

McKenzie shook her head. "He had a vasectomy so that mistake would never happen again."

"Implying that you were a mistake?"

McKenzie shrugged.

"He's a fool, McKenzie. A stupid, selfish fool."

"Agreed." She brushed her hands over her thighs then stood. "I'm going to get a drink of water. You need anything?"

"Just you."

She paused. "Sorry, but the discussion about my parents has killed any possibility of that for some time."

"Not what I meant."

She stared down at him. "Then what did you mean?"

Good question. What had he meant?

That he needed her?

Physically? They were powerful in bed together. But it was more than sex. Mentally, she challenged him with her quick intelligence and wit. Emotionally...emotionally she had him a tangled-up mess. A tangled-up mess he had no right to be feeling.

He'd asked her to give him two months. That's all she planned to give him, that's all he'd thought he'd wanted from McKenzie.

Usually he had long-lasting relationships even though he knew they were never going anywhere. He'd always been up-front with whomever he'd been dating on that point. When things came to an end, he'd always been okay with it, his heart not really involved.

With McKenzie he'd wanted that time limit as much as she had, because everything had felt different right from the start.

She made him question everything.

The past. The present. The future. What had always seemed so clear was now a blurred unknown.

That they had planned a definite ending was a good thing, the best thing. He had a vow to keep. Guilt mingled in with whatever else was going on. Horrible, horrible guilt that would lie heavily on his shoulders for the rest of his life.

"I'll take that glass of water after all," he said in way of an answer to her question. Not that it was an answer, but it was all he knew to say.

"Yeah, this conversation has left a bad taste in both our mouths."

Something like that.

"Edith came in to see me this morning."

Lance glanced up from his desk. "How is she doing?"

McKenzie sank down in the chair across from his desk.

"Quite well, really. She had a long list of complaints, of course. But overall she looked good and the latest imaging of her chest shows that her pulmonary embolism has resolved."

"That's fantastic. She's a feisty thing."

"That she is."

He studied her a moment then set down the pen he held, walked around his desk, shut his office door, then wrapped his arms around her.

"What are you doing?"

"Shh…" he told her. "Don't say anything."

Not that his arms didn't feel amazing, but she frowned up at him. "Don't tell me what to do."

He chuckled. "You're such a stubborn woman."

"You're just now figuring that out, Mr. Persistence?"

"No, I knew that going in."

"And?"

"I can appreciate that fact about you even if it drives me crazy at times."

"Such as now?"

He shook his head. "Not really because for all your protesting, you are still letting me hold you."

"Why are you holding me? I thought we agreed we wouldn't do this at work? You promised me we wouldn't."

"This is a hug between friends. A means of offering comfort and support. I never promised not to give you those things when you obviously need a hug."

"Oh." Because really what could she say to that? He was right. She obviously had needed a hug. His hug.

Only being in his arms, her body pressed close to his, her nostrils filled with his spicy clean scent, made her aware of all the other things she needed him for, too.

Things she didn't need to be distracted by at work.

She pulled from his arms and he let her go.

"Sorry I bothered you. I just wanted to let you know about Edith and that I'd be at the hospital during lunch."

"I'll see you there."

"But—"

"I'll see you there," he repeated.

"You're a persistent man, Lance."

"You're a stubborn woman, McKenzie."

A smile tugged at her lips. "Fine, I'll see you at the hospital at lunch."

Lance had a Celebration Graduation meeting for last-minute Valentine's Day dance planning that he'd tried to convince McKenzie to attend with him. She didn't want to get too involved in his pet projects because their days together as a couple were dwindling. The more entangled their lives were the more difficult saying goodbye was going to be.

McKenzie's phone rang and she almost didn't answer when she saw that it was her mother. When she heard what her mother had to say she wished she hadn't.

"I'm getting married."

Three little words that had McKenzie dropping everything and agreeing to meet her mother at her house.

Violet's house was the same house where McKenzie had grown up. McKenzie's father had paid for the house where they'd lived when he'd first been starting his law career. He'd also provided a monthly check that had apparently abdicated him of all other obligations to his daughter.

"Whatever is going through your head?" McKenzie asked the moment she walked into her mother's living room. She came to a halt when she saw the man sitting on her mother's sofa. The one who was much younger than her mother. "How old are you?"

"What does it matter how old he is?" her mother interrupted. "Age is only a number."

"Mom, if I'm older than him, I'm walking out of this house right now."

Her mother glanced at the man and giggled. *Giggled.* "He's eight years older than you, McKenzie."

"Which means he's ten years younger than you," McKenzie reminded her. She wasn't a prude, didn't think relationships should be bound by age, except for when it came to her mother. Her mother dating a man so much younger just didn't sit well.

"Yes, I am a lucky woman that Yves has fallen for me in my old, decrepit state," her mother remarked wryly. "Thank goodness I'll have him around to help me with my walker and picking out a nursing home."

"Mom…" McKenzie began, then glanced back and forth between her mother and the man she was apparently engaged to. She sank down onto her mother's sofa. "So, maybe you should tell me more about this whole getting-married bit since I know for a fact you were single at the beginning of the year."

She was used to her father marrying on a whim, but her mother had been single since the day she'd divorced McKenzie's father almost three decades ago. Violet dated and chased men, but she didn't marry.

"I met Yves at a New Year's Eve party."

"You met him just over a month ago. Don't you think it's a little quick to be getting engaged?"

"Getting married," her mother corrected, holding out her hand to show McKenzie the ring on her finger. "We're already engaged."

The stone wasn't a diamond, but was a pretty emerald that matched the color of her mother's eyes perfectly.

"When is the wedding supposed to take place?"

"Valentine's Day."

Valentine's Day. The first day McKenzie would be without Lance and her mother was walking down the aisle.

She regarded her mother. "You're sure about this?"

"Positive."

"Why now? After all this time, why would you choose to marry again?"

"The only reason I've not remarried all these years is because I hadn't met the right person, McKenzie. I have had other proposals over the years, I just haven't wanted to say yes until Yves."

Other proposals? McKenzie hadn't known. Still, her mother. Married.

"Does Dad know?"

"What does it matter if your father knows that I'm going to remarry? He has nothing to do with my life."

"Mom, if you remarry Dad will quit sending you a check every month. How are you going to get by?"

"I'll take care of her," Yves popped up, moving to stand protectively by Violet.

"And how are you going to do that?"

"I run a health-food store on the square."

McKenzie had read about a new store opening on the square, had been planning to swing by to check out what they had.

"He more than runs it," Violet bragged. "He owns the store. Plus, he has two others that are already successful in towns nearby."

So maybe the guy wasn't after her mother for a free ride.

"You know I don't need your permission to get married, McKenzie."

"I know that, Mother."

"But I had hoped you'd be happy for me."

McKenzie cringed on the inside. How was she supposed to be happy for her mother when she worried that her mother was just going to be hurt yet again? She'd seen her devastation all those years ago, had watched the depression take hold and not let go for years. Why would she want her mother to risk that again? Especially with a man so much younger than she was?

She must have asked the last question out loud because her mother beamed at Yves, placed her hand in his and answered, "Because for the first time in a long time, maybe ever, I know what it feels like to be loved. It's a wonderful feeling, McKenzie. I hope that someday you know exactly what I mean."

Lance hit McKenzie's number for what had to be the dozenth time. Why wasn't she answering her phone?

He'd driven out to her place, but she wasn't home. Where would she be? Cecilia's perhaps? He'd drive out there, too, but that made him feel a little too desperate.

Unfortunately, he was the bearer of bad news regarding a patient she'd sent to the emergency room earlier. The man had been in the midst of a heart attack and had been airlifted to Atlanta. When the hospital hadn't been able to reach McKenzie they'd called him, thinking he might be with her.

He would like to be with her. He should be with her. Instead, he'd sat through the last meeting before the Valentine's Day dance. They had everything under control and the event should be a great fund-raiser.

But where was McKenzie?

He was just getting ready to pull out of her driveway when her car came down the street and turned in.

"What are you doing here?" she asked, getting out of her car. "It's almost ten."

Yeah, he should have gone home. He didn't have to tell her tonight. Nothing would have been lost by her not finding out about the man until the next morning.

"I was worried about you."

"I'm fine."

"I'll go, then. I was just concerned when you didn't answer your phone."

"Sorry. I had my ringer turned off. I was at my mother's."

Her mother that he'd not met yet.

"She's getting married."

"Married?"

"Seems after all this time she's met the man of her dreams."

"You don't sound very happy about it."

She shrugged. "He's growing on me."

"Someone I know?"

"Unlikely. He just opened up the new health-food store on the square."

"Yves St. Claire?"

Her brows veed. "That's him. You know him?"

"I met him a few days after he opened the store. Great place he has there. Seems like a nice enough fellow."

"And?"

"And what?"

"Doesn't he seem too young for my mother?"

"I've never met your mother so I wouldn't know, but age is just a number."

"That's what she said."

"If I were younger than you, would it matter, McKenzie?"

"For our intents and purposes, I suppose that depends on how much younger. I don't mess with jailbait."

He laughed, leaned back against his car. "Glad I have a few years on you, then."

"Do you want to come inside?"

Relief washed over him. "I thought you'd never ask."

February the thirteenth fell on a Friday and McKenzie was convinced that the day truly was a bad-luck day.

Today was it. The end of her two months with Lance.

She'd promised herself there would be no fuss, no muss, just a quick and painless goodbye. He had his dance to-morrow night and no doubt by next week he'd have a new love interest.

But she couldn't quite convince herself of that.

Something in the way Lance looked at her made her think he wouldn't quickly replace her but might instead take some time to get over her.

Unfortunately, she might require that time, too.

Lots and lots of recovery time, though perhaps not the three decades' worth her mother had taken to blossom into a woman in love.

Her mother was in love. And loved.

Over the past several days McKenzie had been fitted for a maid-of-honor dress and had met Yves's best friend for his tux fitting. Her mother was getting married at a local church in a small, simple ceremony the following day.

"You're not planning to see me at all tonight?" Lance asked.

She shook her head. "My mother's wedding-rehearsal dinner is tonight."

"I could go with you."

"That would be a bad idea."

"Why?"

"Our last night together and we go to a wedding re-hearsal? Think about it. That's just all kinds of wrong. Plus, I don't want you there, Lance."

He winced and she almost retracted her words. Part of her did want him there. Another part knew the sooner they parted the sooner she could get back to the regularly sched-uled program of her life. Her time with Lance had been a nice interlude from reality.

"I should tell you that Yves invited me to the wedding."

"I don't want you there," she said.

"I'll keep that in mind." Without another word, he left her office.

McKenzie's heart shuddered at the soft closing of her office door as if the noise had echoed throughout the building.

She went to her mother's rehearsal dinner, smiled and performed her role as maid of honor. Truth was, watching her mother and Yves left her heart aching.

Feeling a little bereft at the thought she was soon to be single again.

Which was ridiculous.

She liked being single.

She thrived on being single.

She didn't want to be like her parents.

Only watching her mother glow, hearing her happy laughter, maybe she wouldn't mind being a little like her mother.

McKenzie got home a little after eleven. She'd not heard from Lance all evening. She'd half expected him to be waiting in her driveway.

No, more than half. She had expected him to be there.

That he wasn't left her feeling deflated.

Their last night together and they weren't together.

Would never be together again.

Sleep didn't come easily but unfortunately her tears did.

This was exactly why she should never have agreed to more than a month with him. Anything more was just too messy.

Lance sat in the fourth pew back on the groom's side. There were only about fifty or so people in the church when the music started and the groom and his best man joined the preacher at the front of the building. The music changed and a smiling McKenzie came down the aisle. Her gaze remained locked on the altar, as if she was afraid to look around. Maybe she was.

Maybe she had been serious in that she really hadn't wanted him to attend. Certainly, she hadn't contacted him last night. He'd checked his phone several times, thinking she might. She hadn't. He'd told himself that was a good thing, that McKenzie sticking to their original agreement made it easier for him to do so too.

Their two months was over.

The music changed and everyone stood, turned to watch the bride walk down the aisle to her groom.

Lance had never met McKenzie's mother, but he would have recognized the older version of McKenzie anywhere. Same green eyes. Same fine bone structure.

Seeing McKenzie made his insides ache.

Part of him wanted to ask her for more time, for another day, another week, another month.

But he couldn't.

Wouldn't.

He'd vowed to Shelby that he'd remain committed to her memory.

To spend more time with McKenzie would be wrong.

He wasn't free to be with her and never would be.

"You invited Dad?" McKenzie whispered, thinking her knees might buckle as she took her mother's bouquet from her.

Her mother's smile was full of merriment, but she didn't answer, just turned back to her groom to exchange her vows.

The exchange of wedding vows was brief and beautiful. McKenzie cried as her mother read the vows she'd written for a man she'd known for less than two months.

Less than the time McKenzie had been dating Lance.

McKenzie outright wept when Yves said his vows back

to her mother. Okay, so if the man loved her mother all his days the way he loved her today, he and McKenzie would get along just fine and her mother was a lucky woman.

The preacher announced the happy couple as Mr. and Mrs. Yves St. Clair and presented them to their guests.

A few photos were taken, then the reception began. McKenzie spotted Lance talking to a tall blonde someone had told her earlier was Yves's cousin. A deep green pain stabbed her, but she refused to acknowledge it or him. She headed toward her father, who was downing a glass of something alcoholic.

"I can't believe you are here."

He frowned into his empty glass. "She invited me."

"You didn't have to come."

His gaze met hers. "Sure I did. Today is a big day for me, too."

"Freedom from alimony?" she said drily.

For the first time in a long time her father's smile was real and reached his eyes. "Exactly."

"She seems really happy."

That had her father pausing and glancing toward her mother. "Yeah, she does. Good for her."

"What about you? Where is your wife?"

He shrugged. "At home, I imagine."

He excused himself and went and joined the conversation with Lance and the blonde. No doubt he'd have the blonde cornered in just a few minutes.

He must have because Lance walked up shortly afterward to where McKenzie stood.

"You look very beautiful," he said quietly.

Okay, so a smart girl wouldn't let him see how his words warmed her insides. A smart girl would play it cool. McKenzie tried. "Cecilia works wonders."

"She is indeed talented."

Their conversation was stilted, awkward. The conversation of former lovers who didn't know what to say to each other.

"I see you met my father," she said to fill the silence.

Shock registered on Lance's face. "That was your father?"

McKenzie laughed at his surprise. "Yes. Sorry he moved in on Yves's cousin while you were talking her up."

"I wasn't talking her up," he replied. "And, for the record, had I been interested in her no one would have moved in, including your father." He glanced around until his gaze lit on where her father still chatted with the blonde, who laughed a little too flirtatiously. "Isn't he married?"

She nodded. "Fidelity isn't his thing. I've mentioned that before."

Lance's expression wasn't pleasant. "Seems odd for him to be here, at your mother's wedding."

"I thought the same thing, but my mother invited him and he came. They are a bit weird that way. Something else I've mentioned."

Lance's gaze met McKenzie's and locked for a few long seconds before he glanced at his watch as if pressed for time. "Sorry to rush off, but I've got to head out to help with the Valentine's Day dance tonight."

"Oh. I forgot." Had her disappointment that he wasn't going to stay for a while shown? Of course it had.

He reached out, touched her cheek. "McKenzie, there's so much I could say to you."

"But?"

"But you already know everything I'd say."

"Not everything."

His brow rose and she shook her head. Now wasn't the time to ask him about Shelby. That time had come and gone.

Apparently he agreed because he said, "It's been fun."

She nodded, hoping the tears she felt prickling her eyes didn't burst free.

"Your car door was unlocked and I left something for you in the front seat of your car."

Her gaze lifted to his. "What? Why would you do that?"

"Just a little something for Valentine's Day."

He'd gotten her a gift for Valentine's Day? But they'd ended things the day before. She had not bought him the standard card. "I didn't get you anything."

"You didn't need to. Our two months is finished, just as we are." He glanced at his watch again. "Goodbye, McKenzie." Then, right there in the reception hall in front of her mother, her father and her brand-new stepfather, Lance kissed her.

Not a quick peck but a real kiss. Not a dragged-out one but one jam-packed with emotion all the same. One that demanded the same emotion back from her.

McKenzie blinked up at him. He looked as if he was about to say something but instead shook his head and left.

"Who was that man, McKenzie?" her mother asked, immediately joining her as Lance exited the building.

"That's what I want to know," her father practically bellowed. "Why was he kissing you?"

"Why is he leaving?" Her mother asked the more pressing question.

"He's just someone I work with," she mumbled, not wanting to discuss Lance.

"She gets that from you," her mother told her father. "The idea she's supposed to kiss people she works with."

"Violet," her father began, crossing his arms and giving her a sour look.

But her mother seemed to shake off her thoughts and smiled. "Come, let me introduce you to your much younger, more virile and loyal replacement."

"Sure took you long enough," her father gibed.

"Some of us are more choosy than others."

McKenzie watched her parents walk away together, bickering back and forth. It wasn't even six in the evening and exhaustion hit her.

Much, much later, after she'd waved sparklers at her mother and Yves's exit, McKenzie gathered up her belongings from the church classroom where the bridal party had gotten ready.

When she got into her car, her gaze immediately went to the passenger floorboard where she saw a vase full of red roses. On the passenger seat was a gift box. Chocolates?

She doubted it due to the odd box size. She ripped open the package, and gave a trembling smile at what was inside.

A new pair of running shoes.

CHAPTER THIRTEEN

"YOU'RE NOT RIGHT, you know."

McKenzie didn't argue with her best friend. Cecilia was correct and they both knew it. Then again, one didn't argue with a person streaking hair color through one's hair.

"I think you should talk to him."

"Who said this was about him?" Okay, so maybe she was feeling more argumentative than she should be.

Cecilia's gaze met McKenzie's in the large salon mirror in front of her styling chair. "You're still upset about your mother getting hitched? I thought you were over that."

"I am over that." How could she not be when her mother was happier than McKenzie recalled her ever being? When she'd morphed into an energetic, productive person who suddenly seemed to have her act together?

Yves had taken her to South America to a bird-watching resort for their honeymoon. Since they'd returned her mother seemed as happy as a lark, working at the health-food store with her new husband.

This from a woman who'd never really held a job.

"Then it has to be Lance."

"Why does it have to be Lance?"

"The reason you're lost in your thoughts and moping around like a lovesick puppy? Who else would it be?"

"I'm not," she denied with way too much gusto.

"Sure you are."

"I meant I'm not a lovesick puppy," she countered, because at least that much was true.

Cecilia laughed. "Keep telling yourself that, girlfriend, and maybe you'll convince one of us."

McKenzie didn't say anything, just sat in the chair while Cecilia dabbed more highlight color onto her hair, then wrapped the strand in aluminum foil.

"Have you tossed out the roses yet?"

What did it matter if she still had the roses Lance had given her on Valentine's Day? They still had a little color to them.

"I'm not answering that."

"It's been a month. They're dead. Let them go."

"I thought I might try my hand at making potpourri."

"Sure you did." Cecilia had the audacity to laugh as she tucked another wet strand of hair into a tinfoil packet. "What about the shoes?"

"What about them?"

"Don't play dumb with me. I've known you too long. Have you worn them yet?"

That was the problem with best friends. They had known you too long and too well.

"I've put them on," she admitted, not clarifying that she'd put them on a dozen times, staring at them, wondering what he'd meant by giving her running shoes. "They're a perfect fit."

"I wouldn't have expected otherwise. He pays attention to details."

Lance did pay attention to details. Like the fact she ran away when things got sticky. Then again, he hadn't tried to convince her not to. Not once had he mentioned anything beyond their seeing each other on Valentine's Day. If she'd agreed, would he have asked for more? No matter how many times she asked herself that question, she couldn't convince herself that he would have. She wasn't the only one who ran.

Maybe she should have gotten him a pair of running shoes, too.

She bit the inside of her lower lip. "You think I messed up letting him go, don't you?"

Cecilia's look was full of amusement. "If you were any quicker on the uptake I'd have to call you Einstein."

"It wasn't just my choice, you know. He walked away that night at my mother's rehearsal."

"He gave you roses and running shoes."

Yeah, he had.

"Running shoes? What kind of a gift is that anyway?"

"The kind that says he knows you better than you think he does. You're a runner—physically, mentally, emotionally. He also gave you red roses. What does that say?"

"Not what you're implying. He never told me that he loved me."

"Did you want him to?"

"I don't know."

"Sure you do." Cecilia pulled another strand of hair loose, coated it in dye, then wrapped it.

"He was in love with a woman who died. I can't compete with a ghost."

"She's gone. She's no longer any competition."

"Cecilia!"

"I don't mean to be crude, McKenzie, but if he's in love with a woman who is no longer around, well, she's not a real threat. Not unless you let her be."

"He never even mentioned her to me."

"There are lots of things you still haven't told him. That's what the rest of your lives are for."

"He and I agreed to a short-term relationship."

"You didn't have a signed contract. Terms can change."

"Ouch!" McKenzie yelped when Cecilia pulled a piece of hair too tightly.

"Sorry." But the gleam in her eyes warned that she might have done it on purpose. "You could have kept seeing him. You should have kept seeing him."

"He didn't want to go beyond our two months any more than I did."

"Sure you didn't. That's why you're miserable now that you're not with him anymore."

"I'm not miserable," McKenzie lied. "Besides, I see him at work."

"How's that?"

"Awkward. Strange. As bad as I was afraid it would be. I knew I shouldn't become involved with a coworker."

"So why did you?"

"Because…because I couldn't not."

Cecilia's face lit with excitement that McKenzie had finally caught on. "Exactly. That should tell you everything you need to know about how you feel about the man. Why you are so intent on denying that you miss him makes no sense to me."

"I miss him," she admitted. "There, does that make you happy? I miss Lance. I miss the way he looks, the way he smiles, the way he smells, the way he tastes. I miss everything about him."

Cecilia spun the chair to face her straight on, her eyes full of sympathy. "Girl, how can you not see what is so obvious?"

McKenzie's rib cage contracted tightly around everything in her chest. "You think I'm in love with him."

"Aren't you?"

McKenzie winced. She wasn't. Couldn't be. She shouldn't be.

She was.

"What am I going to do?"

"Well, you are your mother's daughter. Maybe you should grab the happiness you want instead of being afraid it's always going to be just outside your grasp."

All these years she'd not wanted to be like her mother, but her mother had been happy, had been choosing to be single, but not out of fear of love. If her mother, who'd borne the brunt of so much hurt, could love, could trust, why couldn't McKenzie?

If her mother could put her heart out there, be in a committed relationship, find happiness, why couldn't McKenzie?

Maybe she wasn't like her father. Maybe she wasn't like her mother either.

Maybe she was tiny pieces of both, could learn from their mistakes, learn from their successes and be a better person.

Right now, she wasn't a better person. Right now, she didn't even feel like a whole person. She felt like only half a person, with the other half of her missing.

Lance.

"I want him back," she admitted, causing Cecilia's eyes to widen with satisfaction.

"Good. Now, how are you going to make it happen?"

"He didn't want more than our two months, Cecilia. He was as insistent on our ending point as I was," she mused. "I wasn't the only one who let us end at two months. He didn't fight to hang on to me." He hadn't. He'd walked away without a backward glance. "His heart belongs to another woman."

"Another woman who can't have him," Cecilia reminded her. "If you want Lance back, then you don't worry about whether or not he's fighting for you. You fight for him. You show him you want him in your life. Show him how much he means to you."

She did want Lance back and, Lord help her, she wanted

to fight for him, to show him she missed him and wanted him in her life.

"How am I supposed to do that?"

Cecilia's gaze shifted to the back of a flyer posted on the salon's front door. A flyer someone from Celebration Graduation had dropped by a week or so ago, advertising a St. Patrick's Day show at the Senior Citizen Center.

"I have the perfect idea."

McKenzie could see her friend mentally rubbing her hands together in glee. "Why do I get the feeling I'm not going to like this?"

Lance shoved the giant four-leaf clover to the middle of the stage, trying to decide if the light was going to reflect off the glittery surface correctly or if he should reposition the stage prop.

"That looks great there," one of the other volunteers called out, answering his silent question.

He finished arranging props on the stage, then went to the room they were using as a dressing room to get ready for the actual show. He was emceeing.

The event hadn't been a planned Celebration Graduation fund-raiser, but the Senior Citizen Center had approached him with the idea and the earnest desire to help with the project. How could he say no?

Besides, he'd needed something to focus on besides the gaping hole in his chest.

He should be used to having a gaping hole in his chest.

Hadn't he had one since he'd been a seventeen-year-old kid and the love of his life had been killed in a car accident?

Only had Shelby really been the love of his life? Or had she just been his first love and their relationship had never been able to run its natural course to its inevitable conclusion?

Which was his fault.

He winced at his thoughts. Why was he allowing such negativity into his head?

It had been his fault Shelby was no longer alive. He'd promised her that her death wouldn't be in vain, that her life wouldn't be forgotten. He'd vowed to keep her alive in his heart and mind. Wasn't that why he did the volunteer work?

Wasn't that why he headed up Celebration Graduation?

So that no other teen had to go through what he and Shelby had gone through?

So that there were other options in teens' lives besides making bad choices on graduation night?

If only their school had offered a Celebration Graduation program. If only he and Shelby had gone to the event rather than the party they'd been at. If only he hadn't given in to peer pressure and drunk. If only he'd not let her drink, not let her get into that car for him to drive them home that night.

If only.

If only.

If only.

Hadn't he spent a lifetime playing out if-onlys in his head? What good had they ever done? He couldn't go back to that night, couldn't bring Shelby back. All he could do was carry on and make a difference in other teens' lives.

He did make a difference in other teens' lives. Both at his job where he counseled and encouraged teens to make good decisions and with Celebration Graduation.

Shelby would be proud of the man he'd become.

At least, he thought she would.

That's what kept him going, knowing that he was living his life to make a difference for others.

He couldn't let anything, anyone get in the way of that.

"There's a full house out there already," one of the other cast members told him, taking one last look in the mirror before moving to the doorway. "This was a great idea, Dr. Spencer."

"I can't take the credit. The Senior Citizen Center approached me," he admitted.

"Well, I'd say they've sold out the show," Lanette said, peeping through a curtain to look at the crowd. "There's only a few seats left and it's still a good fifteen minutes before showtime."

Lance had called the cast members from the Christmas show and gotten them on board to do a St. Patrick's Day show. They'd kept it simple, doing numbers that they all already knew, but that would be fun for the audience. Lance had even convinced a magician to come in and do a few tricks between sets. If the guy worked out, Lance hoped to have him perform on graduation night at the kids' lock-in to help pass their time in a fun way.

Seven arrived and Lance went out onto their makeshift stage. He welcomed the crowd, apologized to the ones standing in the back of the room, but applauded them on participating in something that was for such a worthy cause.

He moved to the side of the stage. Four of the female performers came out onstage, holding sparkly four-leaf clovers the size of dinner plates. The performers changed and a male singer crooned out a love ballad that had Lance's throat clogging up a little.

He didn't want to think about Shelby. He didn't want to think about McKenzie.

He couldn't stop thinking about either.

The crowd cheered each performance.

They finished the first half of the show, went to the back to grab a drink and change costumes while the magician did his show. Lance found himself laughing at some of the tricks and trying to figure out how a few others were done. The crowd loved the show. Soon the singers were back onstage and sang a few more songs. Lanette had the lead in the next number and took the stage with a bright smile.

"Okay, folks, this is a little different from what's on your program, but sometimes the best performances are the unexpected, impromptu ones," Lanette began, causing Lance to frown.

He was unaware of any changes to their schedule and certainly there weren't any planned impromptu performances that he knew of.

That's when he saw her.

McKenzie, wearing her sparkly green dress that she must have had hidden beneath a jacket for him to have not noticed her before because she glimmered with every step she took toward the stage.

What was she doing?

But even before Lanette handed her the microphone, he knew.

McKenzie was going to sing.

The question was why.

And why was his heart beating so crazily in his chest with excitement over what she was about to do when he had no right to feel that excitement?

To feel that joy that McKenzie was there?

Any moment McKenzie expected her heels to give way and she would fall flat on her face. Definitely she was more comfortable in her running shoes than the three-inch heels she'd chosen to wear because Cecilia had told her they made her legs look phenomenal.

Who cared how good her legs looked if she was flat on her butt from her feet going out from under her?

Or maybe it was because her knees were shaking that she feared falling.

Her knees were shaking, knocking together like clackers. Why was she doing this? Wouldn't a simple phone call or text message have sufficed? No, she'd had to go along with Cecilia's idea that she had to do something big, something totally out of character to convince Lance she was playing for keeps.

Cecilia had arranged a voice coach who'd worked with McKenzie every night that week. Cecilia had called a client who happened to be one of the female singers in the show and arranged for McKenzie's surprise performance. Lanette had been thrilled to help because she'd seen McKenzie and Lance save the mayor's life and had thought them a perfect couple even back then.

Now it was all up to McKenzie.

She hated people looking at her and the entire room's eyes were all trained on her, waiting to see what she was going to do. To see if she was going to cry or scream out like her parents.

No, that's not why they were here. That's not why they were looking at her. They were here for entertainment. Entertainment she was about to add to, and perhaps not in a good way.

She couldn't sing.

A week with a voice coach wasn't going to fix that. A year with a voice coach couldn't.

But she'd learned what her voice's strengths were and what her weaknesses were. Her performance wasn't going to have any agents lining up to sign her, but hopefully her putting herself out there for him would impress a certain man enough for him to rethink two months, for him to open up his heart and let her inside, to at least give her, give them, a chance.

The music started up as she made her way up the steps to the stage. One step. Two steps. Three steps. On the stage without falling. Yes, now, if she could just stay upright during her song, she totally had this.

She made her way over to Lance, smiled at him suggestively as she ran her finger along his shirt collar. His body heat lured her in, making her want to touch him for real, but common sense said she was on a stage, everyone was watching, the show must go on and this wasn't that kind of show.

Taking a deep breath first that she hoped the microphone didn't pick up, she broke into a song about going after what she wanted and making it hers.

If he walked away from her, she'd look a fool.

She'd feel a fool.

But, even more, he might not forgive her for interfering in his show.

Still, she agreed with Cecilia. She had to make a grand gesture to show Lance that she was serious about wanting him in her life, that she was willing to take risks where he was concerned, that she'd fight for him.

That she'd sing for him.

So she sang.

His eyes searched hers and she couldn't quite read his expression.

Fine. She was going to do this, was going to put her heart into it, and whatever happened happened.

She played her eyes at him, did her best to be sultry and seductive without being trashy, and felt a huge weight lift off her when Lance grinned.

Thank God. At least he wasn't going to have her look a fool on the stage.

To those in the audience he looked believable. To McKenzie he looked more beautiful than anything she'd ever seen.

She finished the song.

Shaking his head, he wrapped her into his arms, spun her around, and kissed her forehead.

"Ladies and gentlemen, give it up for Dr. McKenzie Sanders."

The room filled with applause.

"Bow," Lance whispered, squeezing her hand.

Feeling a bit silly, she did so.

He led her off the stage and round to the back as Lanette took to the stage again to perform another song.

"What are you doing here?" he asked the second they were out of sight of the audience.

Ouch. Not exactly what she'd hoped to hear him say. Then again, what had she expected? For him to immediately know what her song had meant? He was a man. Sometimes men had to be hit over the head with the obvious for them to recognize the truth, or so her best friend had told her repeatedly.

"I'm here to sing for you."

His brow lifted. "I thought you didn't like singing?"

"I don't."

"Then why?"

"Because I want to be a part of the things you enjoy. Two months wasn't enough time. I want more. I need more."

He considered her a moment, glanced at the other crew members who were backstage, then pulled her toward the back. "Obviously we need to talk, but this isn't the time or the place."

"Obviously," she agreed, knowing the other cast members were watching them curiously.

"I have to be there for the last song. All the cast members will be onstage for it. I give my thanks to the cast and the Senior Citizen Center, and then we'll take our bows."

"I can wait."

The others lined up to take the stage as soon as Lanette's number ended. Lance glanced toward her and looked torn.

"Go. I'll be here when you're finished."

"You're sure?"

"In case you haven't figured it out just by my being here, I'm planning to stick around, Lance. Two months wasn't enough time. At least, not for me. Unless... You're not see-ing anyone else, are you?"

She'd not even considered that he might already be see-ing someone else. She couldn't imagine it. Not with the way he looked at her. But sometimes people did stupid things.

"There's no one else, McKenzie. Just you."

Although his face went a ghostly white at his own words, they put such joy into her heart that she threw her arms around him and kissed him, letting every bit of feeling in-side her show in her kiss.

One of the other singers cleared his throat, reminding them that Lanette's number was coming to an end.

"Sorry," McKenzie apologized, then took it back. "No, I'm not sorry. Not that I kissed you anyway. Just that I haven't kissed you every night for the past month. I've missed you."

Lance pulled away from McKenzie without saying any-thing.

He'd already said enough.

He'd said there was no one else.

Just her.

How could he have said that?

His insides shook.

A crushing weight settled onto his chest.

One that made breathing difficult, much less saying any-thing as he took to the stage.

He went through the motions, had the cast bowing at the appropriate times, the crowd applauding, and the cast ap-plauding the Senior Citizen Center. But he couldn't keep his mind on what he was doing, no matter how much he tried.

Just her. Just McKenzie.

Not Shelby.

How could he have said *Just McKenzie*?

How could he feel that?

He owed Shelby his dedication, his life, because he'd taken hers.

Then it was time for Lance to thank everyone for attending and for their donations to Celebration Graduation.

Only when he went to thank them did more words spill out than he'd meant to say. Words he'd never spoken out loud. Not ever.

"I've had people ask me in the past why I'm so passionate about Celebration Graduation," he began, staring out into the audience without really seeing anyone. "Most of the time I come up with an answer about how I believe in the cause and want to do my part. The truth goes much deeper than that. The truth is that I'm the reason programs such as Celebration Graduation need to exist. At the end of my junior year my girlfriend, who'd just graduated from high school, was killed in a car crash because I made the bad decision to drive while under the influence of alcohol. I lost control of the car and hit a tree. We were both airlifted to a trauma hospital. She died later that night."

McKenzie covered her mouth with her hand.

Oh, God. She should have known, should have figured out the truth behind Shelby's death. Only how could she have?

"So the truth is that my passion about Celebration Graduation, which gives teenagers an alternative to how they spend their graduation night, comes from my own past mistakes. I lived through what I hope to prevent from ever happening again." Lance's voice broke and for a moment McKenzie didn't think he was going to be able to say more, but then he continued.

"Through Celebration Graduation I hope to keep Shelby's memory alive, to make her life, her death matter, for her to make a difference in others' lives because she was a very special person and would have done great things in the world had she gotten the chance."

Tears ran down McKenzie's face. Dear Lord, she was devastated by the pain inside him. By the guilt inside him. She could hear it wrenched from him. He had loved Shelby.

He did love Shelby.

Lance's heart belonged to another. Irrevocably.

"Thank you for being here today, for helping me keep Shelby alive in my heart, and for making a difference in our youth's lives through this wonderful program."

At first there was a moment of silence, as if the audience wasn't sure whether to applaud or just sit there, then a single person clapped, then the room burst into applause.

McKenzie watched Lance say something to Lanette. She nodded, and he disappeared off the opposite side of the stage.

McKenzie waited at the side of the stage, but Lance didn't reappear. After they'd mingled with the crowd, the other performers returned.

"He told me to tell you he was sorry but that he had to leave," Lanette told her in a low voice so the others couldn't hear.

"He left?" McKenzie's heart pounded. He'd left. How could he do that, knowing she was backstage? Knowing she'd come to fight for him?

But she knew.

She recognized exactly what he'd done, because it was something she excelled at.

He'd run.

CHAPTER FOURTEEN

LANCE KNELT BESIDE the grave, thinking himself crazy for being at a cemetery at this time of night. The show hadn't ended until after nine, and by the time he'd realized where he'd been headed it had been almost eleven.

He hadn't consciously decided to go to Shelby's grave, but it's where his car had taken him. Maybe it was where he needed to go to put things into proper perspective.

Because for a few minutes he'd allowed himself to look into McKenzie's eyes while she'd sung to him and he'd acknowledged the truth.

He was in love with her.

Right or wrong, he loved her.

And she loved him. Perhaps he'd always known she felt that way, had seen the truth in her eyes when she'd looked at him, had felt the truth in her touch, in her kiss.

She looked at him the way her mother looked at Yves. The way his mother looked at his father. The way his grandmother looked at his grandfather.

Tonight, while she'd sung to him, McKenzie had looked at him with her heart shining through every word.

In the past she'd fought that feeling, had been determined not to allow herself to be hurt by making the mistakes her parents had made. Tonight she'd put everything on the line and he'd felt exhilarated to realize she was there for him, that she loved him and wanted him.

Then reality had set in.

He wasn't free to accept her love, to return her love. He'd vowed his love to another he owed everything to.

And he'd resented his vow. He'd resented Shelby.

The guilt of that resentment sickened him.

"Forgive me, Shelby. Forgive me for that night. Forgive me for not keeping you safe," he pleaded over the grave, much as he had many times in the past.

"Forgive me for still being here when you're not."

Wasn't that the crux of the matter?

He'd lived and Shelby hadn't.

How many times had he wished he could give his life for hers?

Standing at this very graveside, he'd vowed that his heart would always belong to her, that he'd never love another, never marry another. Even at seventeen he hadn't been so naive as to think he'd spend his life alone, so he had dated over the years, had been in relationships, but not once had he ever been tempted to sway from his promise to Shelby.

Until tonight.

Until McKenzie.

With McKenzie everything had changed.

With McKenzie he wanted everything.

Because he really did want McKenzie.

"Forgive me, Shelby. Forgive me for the way I feel about McKenzie. You'd like her, you know. She's a lot like what you might have been at her age. She loves to run, just as you did. And she's a doctor, just as you always planned to be. And I love her, just as I planned to always love you."

Guilt ripped through him.

He swiped at moisture on his face.

This was crazy. Why was he here? Then again, he felt crazy. He'd told everyone at the Senior Citizen Center his most guarded secret. He'd told them he'd essentially murdered Shelby.

The authorities hadn't seen it that way. Neither had Shelby's parents or his own family. She'd been eighteen to his seventeen. She'd been caught drinking in the past, he'd been a stupid kid trying to fit in with her older friends, but he knew that he shouldn't have been drinking or driving.

Memories of that night assailed him. For years he'd blocked them from his mind, not wanting to remember.

Shelby dancing. Shelby smiling and laughing. Shelby so full of life. And liquor. She'd been full of that, too.

She'd wanted more, had been going to take his car to get more, and he'd argued with her.

Even with being under the influence himself, he'd known she'd been in no shape to drive. Unfortunately, neither had he been and he'd known it, refusing to give her his keys.

She'd taken off running into the darkness, calling out over her shoulder that if he wouldn't take her, she'd just run there.

He should have let her. She'd have run herself sober.

Instead, to the teasing of her friends that he couldn't control his girlfriend, he'd climbed into his car and driven down the road to pick her up.

But he hadn't been taking her to the liquor store when he'd wrecked the car.

He'd been taking her home.

They'd been arguing, her saying she should have known he was a baby, rather than a man.

He'd been mad, had denied her taunts, reminded her of just how manly she'd said he was earlier that evening, and in the blink of the eye she'd grabbed at the steering wheel and he'd lost control of his car and hit the tree.

The rest had come in bits and pieces.

Waking up, not realizing he'd wrecked the car. The smells of oil, gas and blood.

That was the first time he'd realized blood had such a

strong odor. His car had been full of it. His blood. Shelby's blood.

He'd become aware of people outside the car, working to free them from the crumpled metal, but then he'd lost consciousness again until they'd been pulling him from the car.

Shelby had still been inside.

"I can't leave her," he'd told them.

"We've got her, son," a rescue worker had said. "We're taking you both to the hospital."

"Tell her I love her," he'd said. "That I will always love her."

"We will, son. They're putting her in the helicopter right now, but I'll see to it she gets the message."

"Tell her now. Please. Tell her now." He'd tried to get free, to go to her, but his body hadn't worked, and he'd never got to tell her. He had no idea if the rescue worker had carried through with his promise or not.

But as soon as Lance had been released from the hospital, he'd told Shelby himself.

Kneeling exactly where he currently knelt.

He'd been guilt-ridden then. He was just as guilt-ridden now.

"I'm so sorry, Shelby. I love her. In ways I didn't know I could love, I love McKenzie."

He continued to talk, saying all the things that were in his heart.

For the first time peace came over Lance. Peace and self-forgiveness. Oh, there was a part of him that would never completely let go of the guilt he felt that he'd made such bad choices that night, but whether it was the late hour or his own imagination he felt Shelby's presence, felt her forgiveness, her desire for him to let go and move on with his life.

Was he being self-delusional? Believing what he wanted to believe because he wanted McKenzie?

"I need a sign, Shelby. Give me a sign that you really do forgive me," he pleaded into the darkness.

That was when he looked up and saw a ghost.

McKenzie couldn't stay in the shadows any longer. For the past half hour she had leaned against a large headstone, crying, not knowing whether to make her presence known or not. She hadn't purposely tried to keep her presence from him initially. He just had been so lost in his thoughts, in his confessions that he hadn't noticed her.

Lance had run away from her.

Only he loved her. She'd known he loved her even before she'd heard his heart-wrenching words, and she hadn't been willing to give him up without a fight. Especially not to someone who'd been gone for over fifteen years.

She'd listened to him, cried with him and for him from afar, and had prayed for him to find forgiveness, to be able to let his guilt go.

When he'd asked for a sign she'd swear she'd felt a hard shove on her back, making her stumble forward, almost falling in the process.

"Shelby?"

Her heart broke at the anguish in his voice. "It's McKenzie, Lance."

Wiping at his eyes, he stood. "McKenzie? What are you doing here?"

"I followed you."

"You followed me from the Senior Citizen Center?"

"It wasn't difficult as slowly as you drive." Which she now finally understood. He liked his fast sports car, but never got it up over the speed limit.

"I didn't see you."

"I didn't think you had. I sat in my car for a few minutes after you first got here. I realized where you were going and was going to give you privacy, but it's after midnight and we're at a cemetery and I'll admit I got a little freaked out, sitting in my car by myself."

"You shouldn't be here, McKenzie."

Yeah, he might think that.

"You're wrong. This is exactly where I should be. Right beside you."

"I don't understand."

"You love me," she told him. "And I love you. And maybe you love her, too, but she isn't here anymore." At least, McKenzie didn't think she was. That had been her imagination playing tricks on her when she'd felt that shove. "I am here, Lance. I used to be terrified that I'd make all the same mistakes my parents made, but I'm not anymore. I'm not like my father, although I may be more like my mother than I realized. You told me that my father did those things because he loved himself more than my mother or me."

"I shouldn't have said that, McKenzie."

"Sure you should have. You were right. But guess what, Lance Donovan Spencer? I love you that much. I love you enough to know that you are who I want, that you are the man I admire above all others, that you are the person I love enough to know that being faithful won't be a problem because I don't want anyone but you."

"Don't admire me, McKenzie. I'm not worthy. You heard what I admitted to back at the Senior Citizen Center."

"I heard and I love you all the more for it."

In the moonlight, she saw the confusion on his face. "How can you love me for something I detest myself for?"

"Because in the face of adversity you learned from the lessons life threw at you and you became a wonderful man who is constantly doing things for others, who is constantly trying to save others from the agony he suffers every day, from Shelby's fate."

"You make me sound like a hero. I'm not."

"To me, you are a hero. You are my hero, Lance. You're

the man who made me know what love is, both to feel and to receive it."

He closed his eyes.

"Don't try to tell me you don't love me, because I heard you say it," she warned. "But I already knew, deep down, I knew. That's why I sang to you, why I followed you. Because of love and my trust in that love."

"I don't deserve you."

"I'm stubborn and prideful and prone to run when things get sticky, but take a look at these." She raised one foot up off the ground. While she'd been sitting in her car, waiting for him to come back to his, she'd changed out of her heels and into the pair of running shoes he'd given her. "See these? My man gave them to me for Valentine's Day so I could run to him. He doesn't know it yet, but I have a pair for him in my car so, that way, the next time he runs, he can run to me, too."

"You knew I was going to run away tonight?"

"My singing is pretty bad. I wasn't expecting you to swoon with the sudden realization that everything was going to be perfect."

"Your singing was beautiful."

"I've heard of being blinded by love, but I'm pretty sure you must be tone-deaf from love."

"I do love you, McKenzie."

"I know."

"I made Shelby a promise."

"One you've kept all these years. It's time to let go. You asked Shelby to give you a sign, Lance. I'm that sign. The way we feel about each other." She wrapped her arms around him and leaned her forehead against his chin. "I don't need you to forget Shelby. She's part of what's made you into the man you are, the man I love, but you have to let the guilt go. You can't change the past, only the future. I want to be your future."

"What are you saying, McKenzie?"

"That I want a lot more than two months to see what the future holds for us."

Lance held the woman in his arms tightly to him. He couldn't believe she was here, that they were standing by Shelby's grave at midnight.

He couldn't believe McKenzie was laying her heart on the line, telling him how much she cared.

"If we do this," he warned, his heart pounding in his chest, "I'm never going to let you go, you do realize that?"

She snuggled closer to him and held on tight. "Maybe you weren't paying attention, but that's the idea."

EPILOGUE

"THE EMCEE JUST winked at you."

McKenzie nodded at her mother. "Yep, he did."

"He has a disgusting habit of doing that," Cecilia accused with a shake of her head.

"You're just jealous," McKenzie teased her friend.

"Ha. I don't think so. My hunky boyfriend is Santa, baby," Cecilia countered, making McKenzie laugh.

"Yeah, yeah. Quit pulling rank just because Santa has the hots for you."

"I could dress as Santa if you're into that kind of thing," Yves offered Violet.

"Eww. Don't need to hear this." McKenzie put her fingers over her ears. "La-la-la. I'm finding my happy place, where I *didn't* just hear my stepdad offer to dress up as Santa to give my mom her kicks."

Yves waggled his brows and gave Violet a wink of her own. McKenzie's mother giggled in response. McKenzie just kept her hands over her ears, but she couldn't keep the smile from her face at how happy her mother was or how much in love the two newlyweds were.

"Ahem." Cecilia nudged her arm. "The emcee is trying to get your attention."

"He has my attention." And her heart. The past nine months had been amazing, full of life and happiness and embracing her feelings for Lance, with him embracing his feelings for her. Sure, there were moments when her old insecurities slipped through, but they were farther and farther apart. Just as Lance's moments of guilt were farther and farther apart.

He'd even been asked to speak at the local high school the week before graduation to talk to the kids about what had happened with Shelby. McKenzie had been so proud of him, of the way he'd opened up and shared with the kids his tragedy, how he'd lived his life trying to make amends, but one never really could. The Celebration Graduation committee had surprised Lance by setting up the Shelby Hanover Scholarship in her honor and had made the award to its first recipient following Lance's talk at the high school.

"Yeah, well, he's motioning for you to join him onstage," Cecilia pointed out. "He gonna have you croon for him again?"

"I hope not." McKenzie still didn't enjoy singing or having everyone's eyes on her, but the emcee aka the most wonderful man in the world truly was motioning her to come up onto the stage.

She got onto the stage. "Please tell me I'm not about to embarrass myself by singing some Christmas ditty."

Grinning, he shook his head. "You're not about to embarrass yourself by singing."

"Phew," she said. "That's a relief to everyone in the audience."

One of the performers brought over a chair and set it down behind where McKenzie stood next to Lance. She glanced around at the chair, then looked at Lance in question.

"Have a seat, McKenzie."

She eyed him curiously. "What's going on?"

The look in his eyes had her concerned. His grin had faded and he actually looked nervous.

"Lance?"

"Sit, please."

McKenzie sat, which must have cued the music because it started up the moment her bottom hit the seat.

When she caught the tune, she smiled.

All the performers came out onto the stage and began singing. Lance stood in front of her, his eyes full of love. When the song ended, she got to her feet and kissed him.

The crowd cheered.

"You have me, you know," she whispered, for his ears only.

"I sure hope so or I'm about to look like the world's biggest fool."

She arched a brow at him. "Lance?"

"Have a seat, McKenzie."

Her gaze met his and her mouth fell open as she sat back down.

A big smile on his face, Lance dropped to one knee, right there on the Coopersville Community Center's stage, with half the town watching.

"McKenzie, at this show last year you saved the mayor's life," Lance began. "But without knowing it, you saved mine, too."

McKenzie's eyes watered.

He wasn't doing this.

He *was* doing this.

"This past year has been the best of my life because I've spent it with you, but more than that you've helped me to be the person I was meant to be, to let go of things that needed to be let go of, and to embrace the aspects of life that needed to be embraced."

"Lance," she whispered, her hand shaking as he took it in his.

"I can't imagine my life without you in it every single day."

"You'll never have to," she promised.

"I'd like to make that official, get it in writing," he teased, drawing a laugh from their audience. "McKenzie, will you do me the honor of becoming my wife?"

McKenzie stared into the eyes of the man who'd taught her what it meant to love and be loved and felt her heart expand even further, so much so that she felt her chest bursting with love.

"Oh, yes." She nodded, watching as he slipped a diamond ring onto the third finger of her left hand.

He lifted her hand, kissed her fingers. "I love you, McKenzie."

"I love you, too, Lance."

Lance lifted her to her feet, kissed her.

The curtain fell, closing them off from the applauding audience.

"Merry Christmas, McKenzie."

"The merriest."

* * * * *

THE DOCTOR'S SLEIGH BELL PROPOSAL

SUSAN CARLISLE

To Carol, I love you for being my sister—if not
by birth, of my heart.

CHAPTER ONE

SCREECHING VEHICLE BRAKES caught Dr. Chance Freeman's attention. That would be his three new staff members arriving. They should have been here last night but bad weather had delayed them. He'd needed them desperately. His other team had left that morning and today's clinic had been shorthanded and almost impossible to manage.

Chance glanced up from the baby Honduran boy he was examining and out the entrance of the canvas tent located in a clearing near a village. Beyond the long line of waiting patients, he saw a tall, twentyish woman jump down from the rear of the army surplus truck. She wore a tight green T-shirt, a bright yellow bandana round her neck and tan cargo pants that clung to her curves.

Great. High jungle fashion. He'd seen that before.

Shoulders hunched, he drew his lips into a tight line, stopping a long-suffering sound from escaping. Years ago he'd helped Alissa out of a Jeep. She'd believed in being well dressed in any environment as well. They had been newlyweds at the time. That had only lasted months.

Everything about this new staff member's regal bearing screamed she didn't belong in the stifling heat of a rain forest in Central America. He bet she wouldn't last long. In his years of doing medical aid work he'd learned to recognize those who would stick out the tough conditions and long hours. His guess was that she wasn't one of them. Everything about her screamed upper crust, big city. Pampered.

When had he become so cynical? He hadn't even met her yet and he was already putting her in a slot. It wasn't fair not to give her a chance just because she reminded him of his ex-wife. Still, he didn't have the time, energy or inclination to coddle anyone, even if he desperately needed the help.

From under her wide-brimmed hat she scanned the area, her gaze coming around to lock with his. She tilted her head, shielding her eyes with a hand against the noon-day sun. One of her two companions said something and she turned away.

Shaking off the spell, Chance returned to the child. He'd hardly looked down when there was a commotion outside. People were screaming and running. *What was going on?*

He didn't have to wait long to find out. Two men carried another man into the tent. He was bleeding profusely around the face and neck area and down one arm. Quickly handing the baby to his mother, Chance cleared the exam table with his arm.

"Put him here. What happened?"

The men lifted the injured man onto the table. Despite Chance's excellent Spanish, they were talking so fast he was having to work to understand them. Apparently, the man had been attacked by a jaguar while trying to save one of his goats.

A feminine voice asked from the end of the table, "What can I do to help?"

A fragrant scent floated in the air. He was tempted to lean forward and inhale. There was a marked difference between the feminine whiff and the odor of the sweaty bodies around him. Unfortunately, he would need to warn her not to wear perfume in this part of the world because it attracted unwanted insects.

Chance looked up into clear blue eyes that made him think of the pool of water at the bottom of his favorite waterfall. The woman he'd just seen climbing off the truck waited. She'd removed her hat and now he could clearly see a long blonde braid falling over a shoulder. With her fair coloring she would burn in no time in the hot Honduran sun.

"Start with cutting away the clothing."

She stepped to the table. The paper on the table was soaked with blood. He glanced up to see her face blanch as she viewed the man who would be disfigured for life from the deep lacerations.

"Don't faint on me," Chance said through clenched teeth. "Michael, get over here." He nodded toward the other table. "Go help there. Michael and I'll handle this."

She moved off to see about the case Michael was working on. Chance didn't have time to ponder why someone in the medical profession couldn't handle this type of injury.

He and Michael worked to piece the Honduran man back together. It may have been the largest number of stitches he'd ever put into a person. There would be a long recovery time.

"We need some help here," Michael called as he finished suturing an area.

The woman stepped to the table again.

Chance glared at her. "I thought I told you—"

She gave him a determined and unwavering look. "I've got this." She turned to Michael. "What do you need?"

"Bandage this hand," he said.

"I'll take care of it." The words were full of confidence as fingers tipped in hot pink picked up the saline and four-by-fours sitting on the table and began cleaning around the area.

Chance had to stop himself from rolling his eyes. That manicure wouldn't last long here and there wouldn't be another forthcoming either. He moved on to the next laceration. As he looked at the man's arm Chance kept a watchful eye on the new staff member. With the efficiency of few he'd seen, she'd wrapped and secured the dressing and moved on the next spot.

At least she seemed to have recovered from whatever her earlier issue had been. He was used to temporary help, but he still wanted quality.

Many who came to help with the Traveling Clinic were filled with good intentions and the idealism of saving the world but didn't have the skills or common sense required to work in such primitive settings. The clinic served the medical issues in the small villages outside of La Ceiba. Making it even more difficult was that the locals were often hesitant about asking for help.

A jaguar attack wasn't the clinic's normal kind of injury but they did see a number of severe wounds from accidents. He needed staff that could handle the unexpected and often gruesome. If Chance wasn't such a sceptic he'd have given the new woman points for her recovery but he'd been doing this type of work for far too long. Had seen staff come and go.

He was familiar with people who left. His mother had done it when he'd been a child. He'd been seven when she'd just not been there. His father was a world-renowned surgeon and had been gone much of the time. With his mother's absence Chance had starting acting out in an effort to keep his father's attention, even to the point of stealing. That had got him sent to boarding school. Even in that restrictive environment Chance had pushed back.

In a stern voice the headmaster had said, "It's time for

you to decide if you're going to amount to anything in your life. Right now I'd be surprised if you do."

He was the one man in Chance's life who had taken a real interest in a scared and angry boy. The grizzled and gruff headmaster had believed in him, had taken time to listen. Unlike his father. Chance had wanted to make the headmaster proud and had made a change after that conversation. He'd focused on his studies. Dedicated his life to helping others. But in the area of personal relationships he had failed miserably over and over to the point he had long ago given up. Those, apparently, he wasn't capable of having.

Why were dark memories invading now? Maybe because the new woman reminded him so much of his ex-wife, Alissa, whose defection always made him think of his mother. Two females who had rejected him. He'd moved past all that long ago. His worry now was how to keep the clinic open. Pondering old history did nothing to help with the present problem.

He watched the new woman as he changed gloves. Her movements were confident now. Marco, a local man who served as clerk, translator, and gofer for the clinic, entered the tent with a distressed look on his face. He hurried to her and said in his heavily accented voice, "I know not where you are. Please not leave again without telling. Much danger here. Not get lost."

She looked at him. "I'm sorry. I saw the emergency and thought I should come help."

"It's okay, Marco. I'll explain. See to the other two," Chance said to the short, sturdy man.

"*Sí*, Dr. Chance." Marco nodded and hurried out of the clinic.

Chance gave her a pointed look. "Please don't leave the clinic area until we've talked."

Her chin went down and she nodded. "I understand.

By the way, my name is Cox. Dr. Ellen Cox. Like Bond. James Bond." She flashed him a grin.

She was a cheeky little thing. He wasn't certain he appreciated that.

He finished up with the injured man and sent him off in a truck to the hospital in La Ceiba. He would check in on him when they got back to town. Chance cleaned up and moved on to his next patient, who was an older woman with an infected bug bite. It would be necessary to drain it.

Before starting the procedure, he stepped to the table next to his, where a five-year-old girl sat. Digging into his pants pocket, he pulled out a peppermint and handed the piece of candy to her. She removed the clear plastic cover and plopped it into her mouth, giving Chance a wide, toothy grin. He'd given a child a second of happiness. He just wished he could make more of a difference. What he did wasn't enough.

As Chance returned to his patient, Ellen joined him.

Since she was so enthusiastic he'd let her see to the woman as he watched. "We're going to need a suture kit, a box of four-by-fours and bandages. Supplies are in the van." He gestured toward the beat-up vehicle that had been parked partially under the tent so that the back end was protected from the daily afternoon rain and could function as a portable storage room. Chance waited as she hurried after the supplies.

Returning to his side, she placed the kit on the bed and a bottle of saline water as well. "I'll get a pan." She was gone again.

Chance spoke to his patient in Spanish, reassuring her that she would be fine and that what he was going to do wouldn't take too long. A few moments later Ellen was back with the pan and plastic gloves for herself.

He helped the older woman lay back on the table.

Ellen gave the patient a reassuring pat on the shoulder and then turned her attention to opening the suture kit, placing it where he could easily reach the contents. Taking the plastic gloves off the top, he pulled them on. She did the same with hers. Removing the blue sterile paper sheets, she placed them on her patient's leg around and under the inflamed area.

Chance handed her the scalpel. She took it without question.

Michael called, "Chance, you got a second to look at this?"

"Go ahead. I can handle this," Ellen said.

Chance hesitated then nodded. He liked to oversee the new staff for a week or so just to make sure they understood the locals and the type of work they were doing but she should be able to handle a simple case.

The patient's eyes had grown wide when he'd left. Ellen moved to his side of the table and began speaking to her in a mix that was more English than Spanish. As she distracted the woman by having her pay attention to what she was saying instead of what she was doing, the woman calmed down to the point of smiling a few times.

Chance glanced Ellen's way now and then to see how she was doing. By the time he returned the patient was bandaged and ready to leave. Ellen had done a good job.

Chance moved on to the next person waiting. She assisted him. They were just finishing when Marco returned with the two other new staff members. He introduced the man as Pete Ortiz and the woman as Karen Johnson, both nurses. Ellen moved off across the short aisle of tables to help Chance's colleague, Michael Lange. Because Pete spoke fluent Spanish, Chance sent him to do triage and Karen stayed to help him.

Working in Honduras on and off for eight years had

only made Chance see the needs here grow. There had been a time he'd thought he might really make a difference but the people needed real clinics, brick-and-mortar buildings with dedicated doctors, not just a few coming in and out every few weeks.

He loved this country—the weather, which he much preferred to the cold of the north, the coast. Scuba diving was one of his greatest day-off hobbies. Walking through a rain forest and being surprised by a waterfall was amazing. But most of all he liked the open, generous smiles of the people. In Honduras he had found home.

The Traveling Clinic had been his idea years ago and he'd worked long and hard to gain funding for the idea. The clinic was a successful concept but money was forever a problem. Again tomorrow the clinic would be stopping at a different village and the locals would line up. Some would wait all day for care. The day would start just as this one had. Never enough, and more left to do.

A couple of times during the afternoon hours the sound of laughter reached his ears. Michael and the new doctor seemed to enjoy working together. That was what he'd thought when his wife had spent so much time helping his clinic colleague, Jim. They had gotten along so well she'd returned to the States with him.

The sun was only touching the tops of the trees by the time Chance saw his last patient. Michael was finishing up with his as well. Now all that was left was to break down the clinic, load the trucks, and head for a hot shower. He leaned up against the nearest exam table, finishing a note on his patient's chart.

"Doctor, if you'll excuse me, I need to fold this exam table." Ellen gave him a pointed look as she flipped her hair back, implying he needed to move.

She reminded him of a teenager, looked no older than a fresh-out-of-high-school girl, even though she must be at least twenty-eight to his tired forty-one-year-old eyes. Breaking down the clinic was the job of Marco and the local men he'd hired to help him. As much as Chance was amazed by her zeal, she needed to understand a few things about the culture and dangers here. "Marco and his men will take care of that."

"I can get—"

He lowered his voice. "I'm sure you can but they take their jobs and positions seriously. I don't want them to feel insulted."

"Oh. I didn't realize." She stopped what she was doing.

"Now you do. You need to tread more carefully, Dr. Cox. There are cultural and safety issues you should be aware of before you go off willy-nilly. Don't be reckless. This isn't Los Angeles, New York or wherever you are from."

A flash of something in her eyes he couldn't put a name to came and went before she said, "New York."

He looked at her a second. "There're not only animals in the jungle that could hurt you, as you saw today, but there's a major issue with drug traders. Neither play around or allow second chances. You should never go out alone. Even in the villages or clinic compound, always have someone with you."

"Are you trying to scare me?"

Did she think this was some exotic vacation spot? "No, I'm trying to keep you out of harm's way." He looked straight at her. "If you don't follow the rules, you don't stay around here long."

Her lips tightened as she glanced toward the men working to break down the clinic. "I'm sorry I upset Marco. I saw the number of people waiting and thought I should get to work."

"You would be no good to them if you get hurt."

"Your point is taken."

"Chance," Michael called.

"Just remember what I said." He walked away to join Michael beside the supply van.

Half an hour later the tent was down and everything stowed in the vehicles. Now their party was bumping along the narrow dirt road toward the coast. Chance rode in the supply van, with one of the locals driving, while Michael was a passenger in the truck. The others rode in the rear of it. The hour-long trip to the resort might be the toughest part of the day. As the bird flew, the distance wasn't far; however, the roads were so rough and winding it seemed to take forever to make the return drive. Chance usually tried to sleep.

For some reason his thoughts went to the young doctor traveling in the truck behind him. She'd worked hard, doing her share and some more. There was no way she was napping while sitting on that hard metal bench. If she complained, he would point out that the ride was just part of doing this type of medical work. Anyone who stayed with it learned to accept the hardship.

Ellen's head bumped against one of the support frames running around the bed of the truck. Taking a nap was almost impossible. She pulled a jacket out of her duffel bag and folded it up then stuffed it between her head and the unforgiving metal.

Looking out through the slats, she watched the fascinating countryside go by. The vegetation grew rich and huge. Some of the leaves were the size of an umbrella. And so green. It looked impossible to walk through. She'd never seen anything like it. The flowers were such vivid colors. A pink hibiscus always caught her attention.

As the plane had been coming in that morning she'd looked down on the coastline of the county. The pristine white sand against the blue-green of the water had made her want to experience it for herself. It was a beautiful country. She already loved it.

Completely different from New York, the city of buildings and lights. She'd worked at an inner-city clinic that saw pregnant teenagers and babies with colds. It was nothing compared to the type of patients and conditions she'd experienced today. It had been exhilarating. Except for that one moment when she'd looked at that man and all the memories of her mother caught in the car had come flooding back.

The Traveling Clinic cared for people who truly needed it. These people had no other way of getting medical care. They hadn't made poor life choices like the drug addicts and drunks in the city. Here they had nothing, and the clinic offered them something they desperately needed. And they still had a bright smile to share.

The type of work she'd done today was why she'd become a doctor. As a child, a car accident had killed her mother and had left Ellen in the hospital for weeks. There she'd learned the importance of good medical care. The staff had loved and given special attention to the little girl who had lost so much. Ellen had determined then that she wanted to work in the medical field, do for people what had been done for her.

The only sticking point had been her father. As a Manhattan socialite and the only child of an overprotective father, she'd worked at being taken seriously when she'd announced she was going to medical school. Ellen desired to do more than chair committees and plan fancy fund-raisers. She'd wanted to personally make a difference, get to know the people she was helping.

When Ellen had started practicing at the inner-city clinic her father had pitched a fit, saying it was too risky and he didn't want her to work there.

"You're acting like your mother. She went in head first

and then thought," he'd said more than once to her as she'd been growing up.

Ellen had told him he had no choice. A number of times she'd noticed a man hanging around when she'd come and gone from the clinic. Some days later she'd found out he had been hired by her father to watch over her because he'd been concerned about her safety.

A few weeks later she'd heard Dr. Freeman speak with such passion about his work in Honduras that she had been hooked. She wanted to make that kind of difference, offer that kind of care. The next day she'd applied to join his staff. It had taken her six months but she was finally here.

After her decision to come to Honduras, she'd thought of not telling her father but she loved him too much to just disappear. Instead, she'd told him she was going to Honduras but not specifically where she would be, fearing he'd send someone to watch over her. Again he'd accused her of not thinking it through. She'd assured him she had. For once she wanted to do something on her own, free from her father's influence.

Her head bounced again. The picture of Dr. Freeman's displeased look when she'd frozen came to mind. Her lips formed a wry smile. Later she had seen a small measure of respect in his eyes.

The wheels squealed to a painful halt. Ellen looked out the end of the truck to see a gorgeously groomed area. Where were they? The others filed off the vehicle and she brought up the rear. With her feet on the ground, she looked around. It appeared as if they were in the back parking lot of a resort.

A couple of Honduran helpers pulled her bag, along with Pete's and Karen's, down from the truck. She hadn't met her fellow staff members until the time had come to board the flight to Honduras. Pete was a nice guy who was looking for a change after a bad marriage and Karen was a middle-aged woman who thought working with the clinic would be a nice way to see a new country. Ellen had liked them both immediately.

Their group was joined by the two doctors. She'd enjoyed working with Michael Lange. He seemed fun and laid back. The same couldn't be said about Dr. Freeman. From what she could tell, he was an excellent doctor. Everything she'd heard about him had been glowing. But on the Mr. Congeniality scale he was pretty low. He could work on his warm welcomes. He hadn't even taken the time to offer his name.

After hearing him speak Ellen had expected him to have less of a crusty personality. He acted as if he'd seen too much and couldn't leave it behind. He was as strikingly handsome as she remembered. With thick, dark, wavy hair with a touch of white at the temples that gave him an air of authority, he was someone who held her attention. Even when she hadn't been working directly with him she had been conscious of where he'd been in the tent. She generally didn't have this type of reaction to a man.

"I'll show Ellen to her hut," Michael said.

"No, she's next to me," Chance said. "You see to, uh, Pete and…" He looked at the other nurse. "It's Karen, isn't it?"

"That's correct." Karen picked up her bag.

"Okay. Dinner is at seven in the private dining room behind the main one." Dr. Freeman headed toward a dirt path between two low palmetto plants. There was a small wooden sign there giving arrowed directions to different areas of the resort. "Coming, Dr. Cox? I've got a call to make to the States before it gets too late."

He'd not offered to carry her luggage. If he thought she couldn't or wouldn't carry her own bag, he had another thought coming. Grabbing her duffel, she pulled the strap over her shoulder and hurried after him. The man really was egotistical.

She followed him along a curving path through groomed vegetation beneath trees filled with blue and yellow chattering macaws. She lagged behind when she became caught up in her surroundings. The place was jaw-dropping beautiful. Completely different from any place she'd ever seen.

"Dr. Cox." The exasperation in the doctor's voice reminded her of a father talking to a distracted child. She didn't like it.

"It's Ellen."

"Come along, *Ellen*. I still have work to do tonight." He took long strides forward.

From what she could tell, he had more than put in a day's worth of work. What could he possibly need to do tonight? "Coming, sir."

He stopped and glared down his nose at her. "The *sir* isn't necessary."

"I just thought that since you were acting like a general I should speak to you as such."

"Ellen, you'll find I'm not known for my sense of humor." He continued on down the path as if he didn't care if she followed him or not.

"I'm sure you're not," she murmured. Hefting her bag strap more securely over her shoulder, she focused on catching up. They moved farther into the landscape until they came out in a small grassy opening where two huts stood with only a huge banyan tree separating them. Each had a thatched roof and a dark-stained wooden porch with what looked like comfortable chairs with bright floral pillows.

The space was perfect as a romantic getaway. "This is amazing. I expected to live in a tent and have to use a bathhouse."

"You have a top-of-the-line bath. We work hard and the board believes the least it can do is provide a nice place to stay. The resort gives us a deal." Dr. Freeman pointed to the structure on the left. "That hut is yours. Follow the signs around to the dining room. If you need something, call zero on the phone." With that he headed toward the other hut.

Well, she wouldn't be counting on him to be the perfect neighbor.

Ellen climbed the three steps to the main door. There was a hammock hanging from one post to another. The living arrangements weren't what she'd expected but she wasn't going to complain.

She swung the door open and entered. Her eyes widened. She sucked in a breath of pleasure. Talk about going from one extreme to another. As rough as the working conditions were, the living quarters were luxurious. She'd lived well in New York but even by those standards this was a nice living space.

The floor plan consisted of an open room with a sitting area on one side and the bed on the other. The ceiling was high with a slow-moving fan that encouraged a breeze through the slated windows. A gleaming wood floor stretched the length of the room. The only area of it that was covered was in the sitting area, where two chairs and a settee created a cozy group. A large bright rug of red, greens and yellows punctuated the space.

But it was the bedroom side that made the biggest impression. A large square canopy bed made of mahogany with identical twists carved into each of the four posts sat there. If she was going to spend a honeymoon somewhere, this would be her choice.

She'd come close to a wedding a couple of times but it seemed like her father stepped in and changed her mind just as she was getting serious. It was as if he couldn't trust her to know who and what she wanted. That was one of the reasons she'd come to Honduras. At least here she could make her own decisions.

The open-air shower, shielded from any onlookers by plank walls, was a new experience. At first she found it intimidating but as the warm water hit her shoulders Ellen eased into the enjoyment of the birds in the trees chirping at her. She was officially enchanted.

Half an hour later, Ellen headed down the plant-lined walk in the direction of what she hoped was the dining area. She turned a curve and a crystal-blue swimming pool that resembled a fern-encircled grotto came into view. The resort was truly amazing.

Beside it Dr. Freeman sat on a lounger, talking on the phone. He wore a T-shirt, cargo shorts and leather thong shoes. His legs were crossed at the ankles. He appeared relaxed but the tone of his voice said that was far from the case. She wasn't surprised. Her impression had been that he didn't unwind often.

"Look, we need those supplies. We have to raise the money." He paused. "I can't be in two places at once. You'll have to handle it. And about the staff you're sending me, I've got to have people who'll stay longer than six weeks. No more short term. The people of rural Honduras need a standing clinic." He glanced in her direction.

Ellen continued toward a tall open-air building, hoping it was where she should go. Footfalls followed her.

"Eavesdropping, Dr. Cox?"

She looked back at him. "I wasn't. I was just on my way to dinner. And I told you I prefer Ellen. When you say Dr. Cox it sounds so condescending."

"I'm sorry. *Ellen.*"

She now wished she hadn't insisted he call her by her first name. His slight accent gave it an exotic note that sent a shiver up her spine. Not wanting to give that reaction any more analysis, she said, "I'm hungry."

"The dining room is this way." He started up the steps to the building and she joined him.

They entered a large open space with a thatched roof supported by huge poles. A wooden desk with a local man standing behind it was located off to one side. He waved in their direction as they crossed the gleaming wooden floor. Ellen followed him around one of three groupings of wicker furniture toward a shuttered doorway that stood open. Inside were tables with white cloths over them and low lighting. Dr. Freeman kept moving then stopped at a single door and opened it.

"Close the door behind you," he instructed.

Ellen did as he asked. They were now in a small room where a long table was set in the middle and a buffet area along one wall. The other members of their group were already there, talking among themselves. They grew quiet as she and Dr. Freeman joined them.

"I thought you guys would already be eating."

"Not without you, boss," Michael said with a grin.

"You know better than that. Well, if no one else is going to start, I am." Dr. Freeman picked up a plate off the stack on the buffet table. Everyone else followed his lead and lined up. Unsure of the protocol or the seating arrangement, Ellen moved to the back of the line. A minute or two later, with her plate full of chicken and tropical fruit, she considered which chair to take.

"Come and sit beside me," Michael offered.

With a smile Ellen took the open seat. She glanced at Chance. His eyes narrowed as he looked in their direction.

She and Michael discussed where she was from and what she thought of her hut then he asked, "So, Ellen, what brings you to our little slice of the world?"

She shrugged. "I wanted to work where I could make a difference."

"You weren't doing that where you were?" Dr. Freeman asked.

She hadn't realized he'd been listening to their conversation.

"Yes, but these people really need someone here. I was seeing young mothers and babies. I found my job necessary and rewarding but there was a tug to do something more. Others were there to help those girls but not enough here to help these. I wanted to come here."

"How did you find out about us?" Michael asked.

"I heard Dr. Freeman speak. I knew this was where I wanted to be."

"Well, Chance, you made a convert."

Dr. Freeman shrugged and went back to eating.

"So, what did you think about the work today?" Michael asked.

"It was different, I have to give you that. But I loved it." She glanced toward the end of the table where Dr. Freeman was sitting.

"You might feel differently after a few days of hot, unending work," Dr. Freeman drawled.

"Aw, come on, Chance, don't scare her." Michael smiled at her. "Don't worry about him. The great Chance Freeman has seen so many people come and go here he's a little cynical about all the new ones. Many don't stay the full six weeks. Some have only lasted days. It's made him a little jaded."

"That's enough, Michael."

The doctor's snap didn't seem to faze Michael. He just grinned. Ellen looked at Dr. Freeman. "I don't plan to be leaving anytime soon, Dr. Freeman."

"Dr. Freeman?" Michael chuckled. "We're a casual

bunch around here. First names work just fine. Especially after hours. Isn't that right, Chance?"

He leaned back in his chair. "Sure."

After that Michael turned his attention to Pete and Karen, asking them about themselves.

Ellen concentrated on her dinner and was glad to have Dr. Freeman…uh, Chance's attention off her. When everyone had finished laughing at a story Michael told, Chance tapped on the table with the back of his fork to gain their attention.

"Okay, we need to talk about tomorrow. We'll be in the Tooca area. Near the river. This is our first time there so let's be on our toes. We'll need to be at the trucks at four a.m., ready to roll. Get some sleep and be ready for a really long day."

Ellen shuffled out of the dining room with the rest of the group. It turned out that Karen was housed not far from her so they walked back toward their huts together. After leaving Karen, Ellen continued along the path lit only by lights in the vegetation. Thankfully the porch lights were on at her and Chance's huts. One of the staff at the resort must have come by while she'd been at dinner.

Ellen had just crawled under the covers when the light flicked on inside Chance's hut. His silhouette crossed in front of the window. His passion for what he did was a major factor in why she'd come to Honduras. It was obvious he needed nurses and doctors to help him. So what was his problem with welcoming her?

CHAPTER TWO

THE SUN WAS SLOWLY topping the nearest palm tree when the caravan of three vehicles pulled into a clearing near the River Sico. Chance climbed out of the Jeep that had been leading the caravan and walked over to speak to the local village leader, who was there to greet him. Returning to his staff, who were already beginning to set up the tent, he searched for Ellen. To his surprise she was all smiles and asking what she could do to help. The early hour didn't seem to bother her. Did nothing faze the woman?

She'd traveled for over ten hours the day before, put in five hours of work, and had had to wake up at four a.m. and ride in the back of an uncomfortable truck, and she was still chipper. He was afraid her fall would be hard. No one could keep up that positive attitude for long.

Still, he was having a hard time not liking her. And she was certainly nice to look at. Too much so.

Marco and his crew had the tent erected in no time and were working on setting up tables as Chance directed the van driver into place.

Ellen came to stand beside him. "Good morning. Michael said I should see you about my duties."

"Did you sleep well?"

Her brows drew together as if she was unsure of his motive for asking. "Actually, I did. Thanks for asking."

"You're going to need that rest because we have a long, full day ahead of us. We all kind of do what's needed when needed. The lines are blurred between the doctors and nurses here. So you'll know what supplies we have and where they are stored. Why don't you supply each station with bandages, suture kits, saline bottles and antiseptic? Any basic working supplies you are familiar with."

"Will do."

"Under no circumstances do you open the locked box behind the seat of the van without permission. There's a prevalent drug problem here and we have to be careful drugs are not stolen. There's only one key and I have it. If you need something you must see me."

"I understand."

"When you're finished putting out supplies you'll be needed to work triage. People are already lining up."

A steady stream of patients entered the tent over the next four hours. Karen worked with him and she seemed comfortable with all he'd asked her to do. He'd had little time to check on Ellen. When he had, she'd been either leaning over, intently listening to a patient, or in a squatting position, speaking to the mother of a child.

At noon the patients dwindled to nothing. Chance stepped outside the tent, hoping for a breeze. Ellen walked toward him.

"Are we done here?"

Chance let out a dry chuckle and waved his hand to discourage a fly. "Not by a long shot. Everyone stops for lunch. We'll start over with twice the number in an hour. Marco should have our food ready. Get something to eat and drink then take a moment to rest."

With the back of her hand Ellen pushed away the strand

of hair sticking to her forehead. Some of it remained and Chance was tempted to reach out and help her. He resisted the urge. Getting involved on a personal level even with something as benign as moving her hair wasn't going to happen.

"You can wash up behind the tent. Remember what I said about not straying from the area." He turned and walked off toward Michael, who had just exited the clinic. Watching out of the corner of his eye, he saw Ellen headed round the tent.

"The new crew is really working out," Michael said when Chance reached him.

"Yeah."

"Ellen seems especially capable."

"She won't last long."

"Why? Because she's blonde and beautiful?" Michael said drily.

"That has nothing to do with it."

"Sure it does. They aren't all Alissa. I have a feeling this one might surprise you."

Chance huffed. "It won't matter. She'll do her six weeks and we'll have to train someone else. Just see to it you don't get too attached."

Michael grinned and raised his brows. "Me? Get attached? But there's nothing wrong with a little fun."

"Just don't let it affect the clinic work." Michael was a good guy but Chance didn't need any personal relationship getting in the way of work. He knew first-hand how emotional upheaval could make the working situation difficult. It had been his own issue with his wife and the affair that she had been having with his colleague that had done it last time. He'd lost all the staff and had almost had to give up the clinic altogether. The only way he had survived had been to push forward and devote all his off time to finding new funding for the clinic.

"Have I ever?" Michael said, his grin growing to a smile.

They both knew it had. Michael was known for showing the young female members a good time while they were in Honduras. For some reason Chance didn't like the idea of him doing so with Ellen. "Let's get some lunch before patients start lining up again. I noticed they are coming in by the canoe load now. In the future we need to think about setting up near rivers so that more people will have access."

Michael's look sobered. "We need to think about where we're going to get some major support so that we can build a permanent building to work out of."

"I know. I'm going to have to go to the States soon and start doing some fund-raising." Chance didn't like the dog and pony show he seemed to have to put on for all the wealthy potential donors to get money but understood the necessity. Give them a good time and they would give was the motto. Still, it was so little in the face of so much need.

Sympathy filled Michael's voice. "But you hate the idea."

"I'm more about the work and less about begging for money."

"Maybe it's time to find someone who'll handle fundraising full time."

Chance had tried before but nothing had worked out. "I need to check on a couple of things and I'll get lunch." Michael headed round the tent and Chance entered the clinic to find Ellen replenishing supplies. "What're you doing? I thought I told you to get some lunch and rest."

"Marco didn't have everything set out yet so I came to check on the supplies and get things ready for this afternoon."

"I appreciate what you're doing but I've seen people burn out pretty quickly here."

She looked at him. "Doctor, I can assure you that I am nowhere near being burned out."

"It sneaks up on you."

For a moment she gave him a speculative look. "Is that what has happened to you?"

The statement seared him. "What do you mean?"

"You seem to care about these people but at the same time don't welcome the people who come to help you. You've been trying to run me off from the minute I got here."

Anger rose in him. Was he letting the past boil over that much? "I have not. There's not enough help as it is. Why would I discourage anyone?"

"I'm wondering the same thing."

"I want you to know the facts. And you don't seem the type cut out for this kind of work."

"And you have decided this by..." she cocked her head "...the clothes I wear, the color of my eyes, my shoes?"

"Your age. Your looks. You attitude. In my experience someone like you only comes to a place like this as a lark, running from something, looking for adventure or to prove something." She flinched. So he had touched a nerve. What had brought her here?

"Why, Dr. Freeman, I do believe you're a bigot. And it must be nice to be all-knowing. It doesn't matter what you think. The real question is have you had any problems with the work I have done so far?"

She had a way of cutting to the point. He hadn't. In fact, he'd been surprised at her knowledge and efficiency. He said nothing.

"That's what I thought. Now, if you don't mind, I'll get that lunch you think I need so badly." She stalked out of the tent.

Wow, there might be more to the blonde bombshell than he'd given her credit for. Had he really been that tough on her? Unfair? She had certainly stood up to him. Been a capable doctor. Maybe he should cut her some slack.

By the time Chance had made it to the lunch table Ellen was finished with her meal and headed toward the front of the clinic. "Remember not to go out of sight of the clinic or one of us."

"I'll heed your warning, Doctor," she said in a sarcastic tone as she kept moving, not giving him time to respond.

Despite what she said, it didn't ease his concern. He felt responsible for all his staff but for some reason Ellen seemed so naive that she required more attention. A couple of times the new people hadn't taken his warnings seriously and had almost gotten in trouble. He couldn't let that happen to her.

He returned to the front and took a seat on a stool just inside the tent door. Ellen was sitting on a blanket she'd apparently taken from the supply van. Chance tried not to appear as if he was watching but she claimed his attention. As she sat, a few of the village girls approached. Ellen spoke to them in a soft voice, halting a couple of times as if searching for the correct word. One of the girls tentatively picked up Ellen's hand and touched her fingernail.

"You like my polish?" Ellen smiled and held her fingers out wide.

The child nodded and the other girls stepped closer, each stroking a nail in wonder.

"Stay here and I'll be right back." Gracefully she rose and headed for the transport truck as if on a mission. She climbed onto the back bumper and reached in to pull out a backpack. Looking through a side pocket, she removed a small bottle. After dropping the bag back into the truck, she returned to the girls. Ellen sat and the children gathered around her again. She patted the blanket and invited them to join her, then opened the bottle. Taking one of the girls' hands, Ellen placed it on her bent knee and applied polish to a nail. There was a unified sound of awe.

What the hell? The woman had brought fingernail polish into the jungle.

Bright smiles formed on dark faces. Small bodies shifted closer in an effort to have a turn. Ellen had their complete attention. Her blonde head contrasted against those around her. The girls giggled and admired their nails, showing them off to their friends before jumping up and running to display them for someone else. As one left another joined Ellen.

Her mirth mingled with the children's. The sound was unusual in the rain forest yet seemed to belong. Like the sweet song of birds in the trees.

Chance walked toward her. It was time to get started again or patients would go unseen and he couldn't let that happen. He stood over the little group. "You seem to have created a stir."

Ellen looked at him with a grin on her face and moved to stand. "Every female likes to do a little something special for herself."

She wobbled and Chance reached for her elbow, helping her to stand. A shot of awareness he'd not felt in years went through him. It was both exciting and disturbing. To cover his reaction he said, "Even if they can't have it all the time."

Ellen glared at him. "Especially then. A moment of pleasure is better than none."

What would it be like to share pleasure with her? Whoa, had the noon sun gone to his head? That wasn't something he should be thinking about in regard to any of his staff and certainly not about this too young, too idealistic newcomer. Life had taught him that picking women wasn't his strong suit.

Chance released her arm as if it had turned into a hot

coal. "I'll see you in the clinic. You'll be working with Michael this afternoon until I think you know the ropes well enough to handle cases on your own."

Ellen didn't know what had gotten into Chance but she was relieved that she didn't have to assist him. Working with Michael was easy and fun so why did it seem anticlimactic next to helping Chance? There was an intriguing intensity about him that tugged at her.

He had seemed so much larger than life when she'd heard him speak. The passion and compassion he felt for the people of Honduras had vibrated through her with each of his words. She'd been drawn to this place. But she'd fought too long and too hard to make her own decisions and Chance was too bossy for her taste. She didn't need another man overseeing her life.

One of the girls who'd had her nails done was Chance's patient at the next table. Despite having her back to them, Ellen overheard him say, "Your nails are so pretty."

She smiled. Mr. Gruff and Groan might have a heart after all.

During the rest of the afternoon and into the dimming light of evening came the continuing blur of people with open wounds, bug bites, sores, to serious birth defects. Thunder rolled in the distance and the wind whipped the tent as the last of the patients were being seen.

"Get started on putting things away. We need to get on the road before this hits," Chance called to everyone as he finished cleaning a wound on the calf of his last patient, a middle-aged man.

Ellen began storing the supplies in the van. As she passed by Chance he said, "Ellen, would you get an antibiotic out of the med cabinet for me?" He held up a key attached to a ring.

"Sure." Her hand brushed his larger one as she took it. A tingle went through her. Why this reaction to him of all people? She wasn't looking for that. Hadn't come here expecting it. She hurried toward the van.

Entering the vehicle, she made her way down the small isle to where the med box was located. Constructed of metal and bolted to the floor for security, it was situated behind the bench seat. She went down on her knees in front of it. The light was so poor she fumbled with the key in the lock. Slipping her hand into the side leg pocket of her cargo pants, she pulled out her penlight. She balanced it on a nearby shelf, directing the beam toward the lock.

The screech of the driver's door opening drew her attention. She glanced over her shoulder. A thin young man held a knife in her direction. Fear made her heart pound. Her hand holding the lock shook. She opened her mouth to scream.

The man leaned over the seat bring the knife to her neck. *"Tranquillo."*

Ellen remained quiet as he'd asked. She glanced out the end of the van. What was she going to do? She couldn't give him the meds and she had to protect the others.

The tip of the knife was pushed against her skin. The man hovered over her. He smelled of sweat and wet clothes.

"What do you want?" she asked.

"The drugs," the man bit out. "Open the box."

The urgent demand in his voice told her he meant business. When she didn't immediately move he pressed the knife against her and growled, "Now."

Panic welled in her. She couldn't give him the drugs but the blade at her neck reminded her that she couldn't put him off long either.

With relief and renewed alarm she heard Chance call, "Ellen?"

"Say no word," the man whispered, slipping down behind the seat but still holding the knife to her neck.

She had to warn Chance.

Why hadn't Ellen returned? Chance headed toward the van.

He had finished applying the bandage around the man's leg. All he needed to do now was give him the antibiotics and they could get on the road. A commotion outside caught his attention. A young man who looked like he was in his twenties was being helped into the tent by another Honduran about the same age. There was a rag soaked in blood on his arm. Michael and Karen were aiding them. Marco and one of his men had started setting up the exam table they had just folded. They could handle the situation. He wanted to know what Ellen was doing.

He instructed his patient to remain where he was. The rear of the van had been driven under the back of the tent. The area was shadowy because the portable lamps were being used around the exam tables. With the dimming light of the day, compounded by the storm, it was hard to see.

As Chance neared the open doors he saw the small glow of what must be Ellen's penlight. "Hey, what's taking you so long?"

She was on her knees on the floor, facing the medicine box. Her head turned slowly toward him. Even in the disappearing light Chance could see the fear in her eyes. She looked as if she was imploring him to leave. There was a slight movement behind her. Ellen shook her head almost imperceptibly.

Chance kept eye contact and nodded. "Hurry up, I need those meds."

"Yes, sir."

Sir? She knew he didn't like being called sir. Something was definitely wrong.

He backed away from the van. The others were still busy with the injured patient. Rushing past them and outside, he started round the tent when he met Marco. In a low voice he told him that Ellen was in trouble and to give him to the count of ten then run inside the clinic, hollering for help. Marco nodded and Chance circled the outside of the tent until he could see the driver's side van door. It stood open. He could make out the outline of a man in the seat with his back to the door and one leg on the running board. Dread seized him. The man must have a weapon on Ellen.

Giving thanks for the storm brewing, which would cover any noise he made, Chance moved out to the edge of the clearing and followed it around until he was facing the front of the van. When the thunder rolled again Chance ran as fast as he could and slammed his body into the door. The man let out a startled yelp and twisted in the seat, reaching for his leg. Chance grabbed the door and swung it hard again. This time it hit the man in the head and he dropped to the ground, along with a knife.

"Ellen!" Chance barked. "Ellen, are you okay?"

"I'm fine." She sounded shaken.

Marco joined him. Chance left him to tie the vandal up while he climbed into the van. Looking over the seat, he saw Ellen still sitting on the floor, with her head in her hands. "Are you hurt?"

She said nothing.

He reached out and placed a hand on her shoulder. "Ellen, are you hurt? Did he cut you?"

Slowly she looked up. "No." She held up his keys. "And I didn't let him get any drugs. Do I get atta-girl points?"

"Hell, woman, I'd rather he'd had all the drugs than hurt you."

A stiff smile came to her lips. "Aw, you do care." She looked away and a loud sniff filled the air.

"What's going on?" Michael called from the end of the van.

"A guy was trying to steal drugs. Had Ellen at knife-point," Chance answered.

Michael climbed in, went to Ellen and gathered her into his arms. She buried her face in his chest. For some reason Chance wished he was the one she had turned to. He left the van and spoke to Marco, who'd already tied the man up, but his thoughts were still with Ellen. The trespasser admitted that he was with the injured man Michael had been caring for. The injury had been a small self-inflicted wound and used as a diversion.

The rest of the staff had to know what had happened in detail before they returned to packing up. Chance gave the short version on what he'd done before Ellen told her side. He was all too aware of Michael's arm around her shoulders the entire time. Why shouldn't she seek reassurance and comfort from him?

Marco would see to it that the Honduran authorities picked up the man they had captured and looked for the other two. Little would be done to them because Honduras had larger drug problems than these petty thieves.

Half an hour later it was dark and the trucks were loaded and ready to leave.

"Ellen, come on up here," Michael called from the cab of the truck. "I think you're still a little shaken up."

"I'm okay back here." She climbed in the rear with Karen and Peter.

She was tough. Chance admired her for that. After those few minutes of emotion with Michael she'd joined in and helped store the supplies, acting as if nothing had happened.

* * *

That evening at dinner Chance watched as Michael stood and tapped his fork against a glass.

"We have a few awards to give out tonight. First, to the great Dr. Freeman, for his heroic use of a van door to apprehend a drug dealer." Michael grinned. "Well done, Chance." He placed a second plate of dessert near him.

Chance smiled and nodded. Why did Michael have to make a big deal of what happen?

"And last but not least, to Dr. Ellen Cox, who held herself together under pressure and didn't give up the key to the drug cabinet." Michael held up his drink glass. The others joined him. A soft clinking of glass touching glass sounded around the room. "For you a flower." He bowed as he presented her with a large orange Bird of Paradise.

Ellen smiled but it didn't quiet reach her eyes. Had she been and was she still more scared than she let on?

"Chance deserves all the accolades. I did nothing." Ellen looked directly at him with sincerity in her eyes. "Thanks for saving me."

Examining the terror coursing through him when he'd realized Ellen was being threatened was something he didn't want to look at too closely. The emotion had been too strong, raw. Still he couldn't deny the relief that had replaced the terror when he'd known she was okay.

Satisfaction he'd not felt in a long time filled him. His look held hers as he nodded. Why did he suddenly feel like standing and thumping his chest?

Ellen rolled to the left and minutes later to the right. She'd been trying to sleep for hours. The sound of rain with the steady dripping off the hut roof would normally lull her to sleep but not tonight. At least the adrenalin rush she'd experienced today should have had her in a deep sleep but it didn't seem to come.

She rubbed the back of her neck. The feel of the man's breath on her skin and the prick of the tip of the knife remained. Even after a hot shower and neck massage the ache between her shoulders blades remained. Would it ever go away? Could she forget that feeling of helplessness? Fear for the others?

It had been that same feeling she'd had when she'd been trapped in the car with her mother. They had been making a simple trip to buy Ellen a dress. It had been a pretty day but the traffic had been heavy. Her mother had sped up to go through a traffic light that had turned yellow. The next thing Ellen had known they'd been upside down and her mother's blood had been everywhere.

Her mother had said, "Your father always says I take too many chances." Then the life had left her.

Slinging the covers away, Ellen slid out and grabbed the thin blanket off the end of the bed, wrapping it around her shoulders. She headed out the front door. Maybe if she watched the rain for a few minutes she could sleep.

She walked to the porch rail. The shower had eased and a full moon was making an appearance every now and then behind the clouds. When it did the soft glow made the raindrops on the ferns surrounding the hut glisten. She stood there, absorbing the peace.

"Can't sleep?"

She yelped and spun toward Chance's hut. He climbed out of the hammock wearing nothing but tan cargo shorts that rode low on his hips. She couldn't help but stare. "Have you been there since I came out?"

"Yep."

"Why didn't you say something?" she snapped.

"I thought you needed a few moments to yourself. What happened today can be hard to process."

He wiped all the times he'd been less than warm away

with one compassionate comment. "Yeah, it got to me more than I wanted to admit at dinner."

He came down the steps and started toward her hut. "You wouldn't be human if it hadn't affected you. And you are very human."

She looked down at him. Her heart fluttered as she watched his half-naked body coming toward her. "What's that supposed to mean?"

He started up her steps. "That you're one of the most empathetic and naturally caring doctors I've ever worked with. You feel things more strongly than most. There's no way you wouldn't be upset about being held at knife-point."

"Wouldn't anyone be?" How did he know so much about her when they'd only known each other such a short time?

He came to stand an arm's length. "Sure they would, but I have a feeling you were not only worried about yourself but the rest of us. Or what would happen to the local boy if you gave up the drugs. Your heart is too tender for this type of work."

"I thought caring was what it took to work here." She continued to watch a small stream of water flow over a large leaf and to the ground.

"Yeah, but it also makes for a great victim."

Ellen turned to face him, propping a hip against the rail. She was no victim. When her mother had died she'd proved that. "You know, there was a moment there that I thought you might be trying to cheer me up. I should have known better."

"Look, you did good today. Held it together. I don't know if anyone could have done better. How was that?"

The corner of her mouth lifted. "Better. But it lacked a ring of sincerity. By the way, I really do appreciate you saving me."

"That's what I do, save people."

Was he embarrassed by the praise? "You make it sound like it's no big deal but to them it is. And to me it was."

He bowed. "Then you're welcome. Let's just hope I don't have to do it again."

This time she had the idea that his words were to cover up his awkwardness at being thought a hero. "It would suit me just fine for it not to happen again as well."

Chance moved toward the steps. "We have another early morning so you best get to bed."

"I'm sorry if I woke you."

He looked up at her from the walk. "Not a problem. The view was well worth it."

"Uh…"

"A woman in the moonlight dressed in a sexy see-through gown is always worth being woken up for. Get some sleep. You'll need it tomorrow."

Yeah, as if she was going to sleep after that statement.

Two days later Ellen scanned the clinic area. Since the incident with the vandals, she looked over her shoulder any time she was alone. Being held at knifepoint had rattled her more than she wanted to show. She had been paralyzed by fear. No way was she going to let on how much what had happened in the van stayed with her. If she showed weakness around Chance, he would see to it that she was sent home. She was determined to stay and continue her work. Ellen was surprised to find that she'd drifted off to sleep after their conversation on her porch. He'd managed to make her think of something else besides what had happened. She wouldn't have thought that was possible. Had his last remark been to get the incident off her mind or had he meant what he'd said?

She glanced at him working at the next exam table. He was great with the patients and got along with the others in the group. Was even known to laugh on occasion. It was a wonderful full sound. He didn't treat her differently in an obvious way but she sensed something...perhaps that he was weary of her for some reason. Her assignments were almost always with Michael. That suited her. At least she didn't have to deal with Chance's moods or with her uncontrollable thirst to understand him better.

Chance never sat beside her if there was a choice of another open chair at dinner. They were never alone even if they were going to their huts at the same time. Apparently for him to approach her porch had been completely out of character. It was as if she had the plague and he was highly susceptible. Sometimes she thought about just forcing the issue and asking him what his problem was, but why should it matter? She had come to Honduras to work, not to get caught up in the great Dr. Chance Freeman's life.

And she was working. Hard. It was invigorating. The days were long but satisfying. It was as if she had been liberated from a cage. She belonged here. Her father may not like it but she wouldn't be returning to New York to work ever again.

Minutes later Karen was called to assist Michael with a patient while Ellen was still doing a wound cleaning. When she finished Karen and Michael were still involved with the patient so she was left with no choice but to help Chance.

"Ellen, would you mind calling the next patient?"

She did as he asked. A highly deformed man entered the tent with the help of a woman who Ellen guessed was his mother. The man had elephantiasis. His arms and legs were enlarged, as were areas of his head and neck. She couldn't prevent her intake of breath. The only case she'd ever seen had been in a medical textbook.

"We mustn't make him feel unwelcome," Chance said

from close enough behind her that she felt the warmth of his body.

He spoke to the man in Spanish and he returned a lop-sided smile that appeared sincere.

"Ricardo is one of my regular patients."

"Hello, Ricardo," Ellen said, giving him her most genuine smile. "Nice to meet you."

Ricardo gave her the same smile he'd given Chance.

"We're going to need to get some blood work today, Ricardo." Chance said, pulling on gloves.

The man nodded and spoke but it came out as gibberish.

Ellen went to get a blood sample kit. She returned and Chance said, "Ricardo, do you mind if Ellen draws your blood?"

Ricardo nodded his head in agreement. As she pressed to find a good vein Ricardo said, "Pretty."

"Yes, she is," Chance answered as he continued to examine Ricardo.

She smiled at Ricardo. "Thank you. You are very sweet."

Even with his distorted face she could see his discomfort. This man was a gentle giant who'd been given a bad deal in life by contracting elephantiasis.

Chance finished his examination and gave Ricardo a supply of antibiotics before he left. With him gone Chance asked, "You've never seen someone with a major case of elephantiasis, have you?"

"No. I had no idea. I'm sorry I reacted poorly."

"Don't worry about it. It's hard not to."

There was that compassion she rarely saw but which pulled her to him. "What can you really do for him?"

"For right now he's getting the antibiotic diethylcarbamazine but that only really deals with the symptoms. He has lymphatic filariasis. It's from worms introduced by mosquitoes. It's common in the tropics. Ricardo is just one of many. If you stay around long enough you will see more. Ricardo's case is getting bad enough he'll need surgery to keep walking."

"Where will he go to have that?"

"I had hoped we would have a standing hospital built by now but we're still working on the funding. Right now he'll have to go to the city or hope a visiting group of orthopedists is able to come here."

"That's sad." Her heart hurt for Ricardo and the others like him. These people needed more help.

Their next patient entered and ended their conversation but the needs in the small tropical country remained on Ellen's mind. Chance was working hard to do what he could but it wasn't enough. What would happen if he didn't get the funding required and the clinic closed?

The rest of the afternoon was one more patient after another. Once again a storm built and seemed primed to dump water over them. As much as Ellen enjoyed rain, every day was a little much. Thirty minutes after the last patient was seen the clinic was dismantled and she, Karen and Peter were running for the truck as the first fat drops of water fell.

"You guys will be drenched. We're going to have to double up in the cabs," Michael yelled over the sound of thunder and wind. "Ellen, you go in the van. Karen and Peter, we'll just have to make do in the truck cab."

The rain started coming down in sheets. Ellen didn't hesitate before running to climb into the van. Marco was already in the driver's spot. Her bottom had hardly hit the seat before she was being pushed across it by Chance. His body leaned heavily against hers as he slammed the door. He moved off her but she was still sandwiched between him and Marco. The gearshift on the floor forced her legs into Chance's space. She shifted to an upright position but remained in too close contact with him.

"Maybe I should just ride in the back of the truck," she murmured.

Chance looked out the window shield. "Not in this storm. Scoot over."

"To where? I'm practically sitting in Marco's lap now." She shifted away from him but it made little difference. Her right side was sealed to his left from shoulder to knee.

Marco put the truck into gear and it launched forward. They hadn't gone far when the truck hit a bump that almost brought her down in Chance's lap. She squirmed away from him. Gritting her teeth, she did her best not to touch him any more than necessary. Her mind as well as her body were hyperaware of even his breathing. She'd be sore in the morning from her muscles being tense in her effort to put space between them.

The storm continued to rage around them as they traveled over the muddy roads. Finally, they reached the poorly maintained paved road. She was exhausted and the cab was warm and steamy. With the steady swish-swish of the wipers the only sound in the cab, Ellen's chin soon bobbed toward her chest. Sometime during the ride her head came to rest against a firm cushion.

A hand on her arm shook her. "We're home."

Ellen jerked straight. She'd been leaning against Chance's shoulder. "I'm sorry. I didn't mean to fall asleep on you."

He ignored her, reached for the door handle and said a little stiffly, "Since it's so late we won't be eating in the dining room tonight. A supper tray will be brought to your hut."

A light rain fell as she climbed down from the van. "I'm glad. I don't think I have the energy to walk up to the main building."

Karen joined them and handed Ellen her backpack. "I'm headed for a hot shower and bed."

"Me too," Ellen agreed. "I'll walk with you. Good night," she said to the group in general.

"We have another early morning tomorrow. Be here ready to go at six a.m.," Chance called after them.

Karen mumbled, "Slave driver."

Ellen giggled. "And a few other things."

Foliage dripped around them and the moon shone above as they walked along the path toward their huts.

"Chance is something else, isn't he?" Karen said with admiration in her voice.

"He's something all right," Ellen mumbled.

"Very good looking, and super smart. I can see why the women that come down here are known to get crushes on him."

Ellen huffed. "Where did you get that bit of info?"

"Michael told me."

"Well, I won't be developing one, that's for sure." Ellen pushed a strand of escaped hair out of her face. Wasn't she already headed that way? She stood in front of Karen's hut.

She'd stopped at the top of her steps and looked at Ellen. "What is it with the two of you anyway?"

"He doesn't like me for some reason."

Karen gave her a searching look. "Aren't you over-reacting?"

"I don't think so. I'm too tired to worry about what Dr. Freeman thinks of me tonight. See you in the morning." Ellen continued along the path.

"Well, you're blind if you don't see how attractive he is," Karen called after her.

Ellen was well aware of how handsome Chance was but it wasn't enough to overlook his controlling and some-times overprotective attitude where she was concerned.

The shower water couldn't get hot enough for her. Ellen stood in it until it started to cool. She loved this shower. It was almost like she was skinny dipping. With a towel wrapped around her, she entered the back door of the hut just as a light came on in Chance's. She watched as he pulled his safari shirt off over his head and let it drop to the floor. From her vantage point she was a voyeur but she couldn't stop herself from looking.

Chance was older than any other men she had been attracted to but he still had a nice body. He flipped his belt out of the clasp then looked up. It was as if they were standing inches apart and he was reading her every thought. Heat flashed over her. She released the blind but it hadn't fallen between them before she saw a sexy grin cross his lips.

CHAPTER THREE

CHANCE LAY BACK in the lounger located in a recess surrounded by plants near the pool. Only a person who looked carefully or passed him could see him, while he had an open view of most of the water. He needed some down time, just like the others. Thank goodness Friday was the transition day for guests so this afternoon there were few around. The resort would be full for the week by the next evening.

He'd worked his staff hard over the last week. They had moved to five different areas in five days, with each day starting at four a.m. The team not only needed a break but deserved one. Michael had volunteered to show the others around Trujillo. Karen and Peter had taken him up on the suggestion but for some reason Ellen had declined to join them. Chance had paperwork to see to and a conference call to make so he'd remained behind as well. He'd not seen Ellen since that morning and assumed she was resting in her hut.

In the short time since the three new staff members had arrived, their clinic team had turned into a cohesive group that worked well together. Ellen had assisted him some but mostly he'd stationed her with Michael or given her triage duty. She and Michael had become regular buddies. When there weren't patients to see, they had lunch together, laughing over something that had happened. It reminded him too much of Alissa and his ex-colleague Jim.

Even Marco and his crew gave Ellen special attention. She shared her sunshine with everyone but him. It wasn't that she wasn't civil, it was just that he didn't receive the same warmth. The times she had worked with him they had said little outside the need-to-know arena. He shouldn't have cared but he felt left out. When she'd first arrived he'd wanted it that way but now he wasn't so sure. The more he was around her the more he admired her. She wasn't the pampered princess he'd wanted to believe she was.

Ellen was an excellent doctor. When she was working triage she recorded what was wrong and had everyone in order of need so that no time was wasted between patients. Maybe it was time to let her start handling patients on her own. They could see three times more patients if he did.

After the excruciating return ride to the resort, when she'd fallen asleep against him, and later, when he'd caught her watching him undress, he'd renewed his vow to stay clear of her as much as possible. He'd be lying if he said he hadn't enjoyed the feel of a soft body against him. But wouldn't he have reacted the same to any female contact?

There wasn't much opportunity for a sex life around here but when he'd found companionship he'd been discreet about it. After his wife had left he'd been the favorite subject of discussion and he hadn't enjoyed it. He preferred his private life to remain just that—private. A few times in Honduras he'd met a woman of interest and when he'd return to the States he had a few ladies he regularly stayed in contact with, so he had hardly been celibate. Still, there was something about Ellen that made his hormones stand up and take notice whenever she was near, as if he had been a monk and left the order.

If the ride home hadn't been painful enough, the fact that she'd been watching him undress while wearing nothing but a towel had made him even more sexually aware. Every time they were alone it was like she was teasing him, daring him to come closer. He was confident this was something she did unconsciously yet it was still there, pulling him to her. As his body heated with need he imagined stepping across the short space between their huts and taking her in his arms. That would have shown her not to be poking the bear. Instead, she'd let the blind down, shutting him out.

He understood that feeling. In this case, he was glad she had. Even a short moment of pleasure would turn into a bad idea in the long run. Despite how she might act about work here, she wasn't the type to stay with him. No woman was. His life was in Honduras. She would never be satisfied with him or living here for the long run. He wasn't her prince charming.

Chance opened one eye to a slit at the soft pad of feet along the bricks around the pool. Ellen stood there in a blue bikini, preparing to dive. He shifted uncomfortably in the chair as his body reacted to all the beautiful skin on display. Her hair was down around her shoulders. The woman was going to be his undoing. He'd been played for a fool before and if he wasn't careful he would give Ellen the opportunity to do the same again.

With a perfect arch, she dove into the pool and surfaced. As she swam to one end and back, he was fascinated by each smooth movement she made. What he wouldn't do to be the water flowing around her. He had to get some control but that wasn't going to happen right now. On her next pass he stood. Hopefully his baggy swim trunks would disguise most of his body's reaction to her.

A yelp of surprise came from her when he stepped into her view.

"Hey." He watched as all that long blonde hair swirled around her on the surface of the water.

"Hi. I didn't see you sitting there."

He stepped closer. "I thought you would've gone to town with the others."

"I thought about it. But I hate to admit that after the pace we've kept this week I needed a little extra rest. I can be a tourist on our next day off."

"Do you like being a tourist?"

"I do. I love to see new places. See how others live." She held on to the edge of the pool.

Her position gave him a tantalizing view of her breasts scantly covered in triangles of dark blue that reminded him of a sky just before a storm. "So what do you think of Honduras?"

"I like it. The people are wonderful. Every day is exciting."

"Some days, too much so." Like the day she had almost been stabbed. It still sent fear though him when he thought about it.

Ellen pushed away and floated toward the other side of the pool. Chance took a seat on the edge, letting his feet dangle in the water.

"So why aren't you off doing something exciting on your day off? Surely you get away from work sometimes," she asked.

"Not as much as I would like." He enjoyed watching her tread water. She had managed to put as much space as possible between them. For that he was grateful. He was far to attracted to her. "When I get a couple of days I like to spend them scuba diving. Hiking in the jungle."

She moved closer. "I would love to learn to scuba dive. My father said no when I was a kid. Never took the time to learn after I started college. And hiking? After all the lectures you've given me about safety, you hike in the jungle?"

"I stay on the touristy trails. More than one person has gotten into trouble, venturing off too far."

"Michael offered to take me to see a waterfall one day." With a kick, she swam away from him again.

"I wouldn't get too attached to Michael if I were you." Chance didn't like how that sounded. Like a jealous middle-schooler. "Hey, I shouldn't have said that. It's none of my business what you two do after hours."

She headed for deeper water. "I'm pretty sure Michael flirts with every woman in his age group who comes down here. I don't take anything he says seriously."

That's what his wife had said when he'd questioned her about her relationship with Jim. Still, coming from Ellen he wanted to believe her.

"Anyway, I'm down here to work, not play around." She started toward the shallow end.

"But it's always nice to have a friend."

Could they be friends? He wasn't so sure. This attraction would also be vibrating between them.

"Well, I think I'll get a nap in before dinner. See you later." Ellen took the steps out of the pool, giving him a tantalizing view of her backside that included a sexy swing of her hips.

Chance slipped into the water and began making strong, sure laps until he was exhausted.

Ellen paused in the doorway of the restaurant. Maybe she'd just eat in the main dining area tonight. She'd given thought to having her meal brought to her hut but she wasn't going stay in such a beautiful place and hole up in her room.

She'd made it halfway to the private dining room when her name was called. She recognized that voice.

Chance sat at a table overlooking a bubbling water fixture among ferns. A candle flickered in the lantern on the table. "We have to eat out here tonight. Not enough of us to prepare the extra room for. You're welcome to join me but I'm almost done."

She looked around the area at all the empty tables. Hating to cause any of the staff more work, she still wasn't sure she wanted to eat a meal with Chance in such a romantic setting. Maybe she should order her food then make an excuse to carry it back to her hut. "Okay."

Chance half stood as she took her seat cross from him.

After feeling vulnerable at the pool in nothing but her swimsuit, she wasn't sure she could handle more time between the two of them. Every nerve in her body had been aware of Chance watching her leave the pool. It had been exciting and terrifying at the same time.

Apparently she was worrying for no reason. Chance ate and shuffled papers he had spread out on the table without paying any notice to her. She finally asked, "So what are all these?"

"Med invoice forms. I'm expecting a shipment any day." He didn't look at her.

"You do work all the time."

He glanced up. "Someone has to do the paperwork."

"Can't someone else do that?"

He made an exaggerated scan of the room. "You see someone else volunteering?"

"I'll be glad to. It wouldn't hurt you to accept help sometimes."

He put down the paper he had been reviewing. "Do you always say what you're thinking?"

"Not always." She certainly didn't where her father was concerned and kept some of her thoughts about him to herself.

A waiter showed up with her meal. They fell into silence as they both ate. For some reason she didn't even think to ask to take her meal to the room. "You know, I could help with those. I'm a pretty good organizer. Maybe I can set up a system that'll make it easier for you."

"Don't you get enough work during the day not to want more?"

She shrugged. "I want to help. That's what I'm here for."

He looked at her. "And why is that? Here in Honduras?"

"Because of you." She wanted that passion and conviction she'd heard in his voice in her life.

"That's right, you said. Where was the fund-raiser?"

"In New York about six months ago." She'd spent the next few months trying to convince her father that her life's calling was in Honduras. He'd spent the time fighting the idea.

"That long ago."

"Yeah, it took me awhile but I made it."

Chance looked at her instead of the papers. "Why not sooner?"

"Well, mostly because of my father."

Chance lifted his chin in question. The man had a way of getting people to talk to him. He was practicing that bedside manner she'd seen him use on his patients. It was powerful when turned on someone. She was that person now. The feeling that if he turned up the charm she couldn't resist him anything filled her. Caution was what she needed to use.

"I'm an only child with an overprotective father. Make that way overprotective."

"I guess if I had a beautiful daughter and she wanted to come down here to work I'd be concerned also."

He'd said she was beautiful. Other men had but for some reason she especially liked hearing it from Chance.

"I love my father but after my mother died he just couldn't stand the thought of losing me too. He seemed to think that making all the decisions in my life was the answer to keeping me safe."

"He wouldn't be pleased to know what happened the other day, would he?"

"No, he wouldn't, and I don't plan to tell him. It would only worry him. He already thinks I take too many risks."

"Risks?"

"Yeah, like going into medicine, working in an inner-city clinic, or like coming down here."

"Then I'd better see that you get home safe."

Anger shot though her. "That's not your job. I can take care of myself. I don't need someone else watching over me."

"Whoa." He held up a hand. "I stepped on a tender spot. Sorry." He went back to looking at his papers.

Taking a deep breath, she focused on her meal again. She watched the candle flicker and listened to the tinkle of water in the fountain then glanced at Chance. He was a handsome man. One of those who drew a woman's attention naturally. There was an aura about him that just made her want to know him better. But what she didn't need was someone caging her after she'd finally found her freedom.

Done with her meal, she asked, "Of all the places in the world, why did you decide to start a clinic in Honduras?"

Chance looked up. "I came here to do summer work with one of my professors while in med school."

"That was it. You decided to start the Traveling Clinic?"

"Yeah, something like that. I saw the hardship and wanted to work here."

Something about his tone made her think there was more to it than that. "So you decided to make it your life's work."

"It sort of evolved into it." He took a bite of the fruit they'd been served for dessert.

"How's that?"

Chance put his fork down. "You're full of questions."

"No more than you were."

"Okay, so I had high hopes that I could make life better for the Hondurans. Make a real difference. But that, like everything else, costs money. Each year that has been harder to come by."

"So when you made fun of me for trying to save the world you weren't any different your first time in Honduras."

A sheepish look came over his face. "Yeah, I know that stars-in-the-eyes look. I've had it and seen it hundreds of times. I've also seen people go home defeated by the amount of need here."

"Is that why you're so tough on me, because you don't want me to be discouraged?"

He crossed his arms on the table. "I just want you to understand what you're getting into. This isn't a fairy-tale world."

"What makes you think I need that?"

"Look at you. Your polished nails. You don't belong here. This isn't a place for you."

She leaned toward him. "Who gave you such a narrow view of women and their abilities?"

"That would be my ex-wife, who came down here and stayed a few months before she left me for my colleague."

By the tone of his voice he was still terribly bitter. She

couldn't keep the amazement in her voice from showing. "You were married?"

"Don't sound so surprised. Even I can make a mistake."

"Mistake? That's a sad view of marriage."

"But honest. Enough on that subject." Chance returned to the papers at his fingertips.

He had been hurt, deeply. Did he judge all women by his ex-wife's behavior? Even her? Maybe that's why he treated her so unfairly. A few minutes later, she pushed back from the table. "Thank you for the stimulating company but I think I'll call it an evening."

To her disbelief Chance gathered his work, stood and stuffed the forms in his back pocket. "I'll walk back with you."

She didn't question his motives; instead, she said thank you to the waiter and headed for the door. Chance caught up with her and they walked out of the main building.

She needed to apologize for spying on him but she couldn't bring herself to say anything. They continued walking.

At her hut Ellen said, "Uh, about the other night, the window and all. I'm sorry."

"Don't be. I was flattered."

She shifted from one foot to the other, not meeting his eyes. "Still, I shouldn't have been invading your privacy. It won't happen again."

"That's a shame. I found it flattering."

"Why am I not surprised?" Where she had been embarrassed now she was indigent. He was enjoying her discomfort.

"What man doesn't appreciate a lovely woman admiring him?"

"My, you have an ego."

He grinned. "I'm just teasing you."

"Since when do you tease?"

"Maybe I'm finding a new side to my life."

"Could another one be you getting over your issues with me?"

Suddenly the current of awareness between them went up three notches. The air almost sparked. He stepped into her personal space. "Sweetheart—" the word was more growl than endearment "—I don't think so. I have too many where you are concerned. The main one is wanting you."

Her heart quickened. She'd not anticipated that declaration. In fact, by the way he'd treated her she hadn't been sure he even liked her. Chance stepped closer. She refused to back away. His head lowered and an arm went around her waist. He drew her against him. His mouth found hers and she forgot to think. She hung on for dear life. It wasn't a simple meeting of lips. Too many emotions roiled in her and flowed between them. The kiss was a mixture of shock, amazement, taking, giving, and abrupt release.

Without a word Chance left her staring after him as he stalked off past his hut and up the path.

On weak legs Ellen slowly climbed the steps to her porch. What had brought that on?

For days he'd treated her as if she was an interloper in his world. Out of nowhere he'd kissed her like there was no tomorrow.

Then he'd abruptly let her go. Why? What had suddenly turned him against her? There had been something real between them and just as quickly he'd broken the connection as if it was something he wanted no part of. Her arms went around her waist and she squeezed. Being pushed away hurt.

She knew what she had been thinking. No one had kissed her like that in her life. The electric ripple had rolled through her, making her ultra-aware of her body and his. She'd come close to marrying other men who had never had that effect on her. What if she had never known those brief moments of passion with Chance?

How far would she have allowed Chance to go? By her reaction to his kiss, too far. She bit her lower lip. Even now her lips still tingled.

But could she afford to act on her feelings again? Coming to Honduras had been her way of finding her place in the world. A space she chose and to make hers. Not one that her father oversaw or controlled. Did she want to get involved in something that might hurt her chances of staying here?

It really wasn't an issue. Chance had walked way.

Chance hesitated at the bottom step to Ellen's hut. He had no choice but to knock on her door. Never having been an indecisive person, he couldn't understand why this time it was so difficult to do something so simple. Maybe because he was afraid she'd chew him out for the abrupt way he'd grabbed her, kissed her and walked off. He deserved her disdain even if he had done the right thing. Now he had a larger issue. A shipment of drugs was coming in and he needed to meet the plane. She'd offered to help with the paperwork and this was one of the times he needed her.

Needed her. Unfortunately, that seemed to be happening on a number of levels.

He prided himself on facing problems head on but the thought of approaching Ellen so soon after their kiss had him feeling uneasy. The kiss they'd shared had rattled his nerves and his convictions. He wanted more than a kiss and that shook him to the core. She shouldn't interest him, shouldn't affect him in any way, but she did, far too much. He'd spent the night vacillating between berating himself and wanting to crawl into Ellen's bed. The latter he wasn't going to do under any circumstances. He had to stop whatever was happening before it got out of hand.

He wouldn't kiss her again.

For him, controlling his emotions had been a lifetime thing. He done it when his mother had left, when his father had sent him to boarding school, separating him and his sister, and yet again when the headmaster had stated frankly he would never amount to anything. He would do so again where Ellen was concerned. It was necessary if he didn't want to lose his sanity, or, worse, hurt her.

She was a good doctor and he was as well. They were in Honduras to help people and that was what they would do. Their relationship would remain professional. He wasn't some teen whose body ruled his brain or some lovestruck young man who went after the first beautiful woman he'd seen in a while. As a mature man he could handle any fascination he might feel for her, especially a woman he wasn't sure he liked.

Chance gave the door a sharp, solid tap. There was no response. His knuckles rapped against the wood once more.

"Coming." The word had a groggy sound.

Ellen opened the slatted door and stood on the other side of the screen door.

"Did I oversleep?" Panic filled her voice.

Her mass of hair fell in disarray around her face. The temptation to open the door, take her in his arms and walk her backwards to the bed almost got the better of his control. How much was a man supposed to take? Chance sucked in a breath.

"No. Were you serious about helping with the paperwork?" He sounded gruff and formal even to his own ears.

She blinked twice. "Yes."

"Then I need you to come with me. We have a shipment.

I want to show you how to handle it and what's involved."
He was already making his way down the steps again.

"Okay. Give me ten minutes."

"I'll get us something to eat and meet you at the truck."
He didn't wait for her to answer before heading along
the path.

As good as her word, which he was coming to learn
was ingrained in Ellen's makeup, she showed up at the
Jeep dressed and ready to go right on time. He'd never
known a woman as attractive as she who could be dressed
on such short notice. His ex-wife would have certainly
balked at his request, expecting at least an hour to prepare herself to go out in public, even in the wee hours of
the morning.

Ellen climbed into the seat beside him and he handed
her a cup of juice and a banana. "Breakfast of champions."

"Or the crazy," she mumbled.

Chance grinned. He found she had that effect on him
more often than most. There was never a dull moment
around Ellen. He was learning to like it. Putting the Jeep
in gear, he headed toward the road that would take them
to the nearby airstrip.

Ellen yawned. "Why so early? It's three a.m."

"This is when a plane was available to bring supplies
in. We use volunteers and have to work around their
schedule. This plane was making another delivery and
just added us as an extra stop."

"Oh. You couldn't have told me about this last night?
I would have been ready."

"I didn't know for sure and I had other things on my
mind." Like kissing you, holding you, taking you to bed.

A soft sound of realization came from her side of the
cabin.

"Uh, Ellen, about that kiss. Look, I'm sorry, I shouldn't
have done that. You didn't come down here to have an af-

fair and I certainly don't make it a habit of taking advantage of young women. It won't happen again." Out of the corner of his eye he saw her shift towards him in the seat.

"For starters, I'm old enough to take care of myself and I make my own choices about who I kiss, not you."

"But I took advantage of the situation…"

He felt her glare. "Chance, just shut up and drive."

Half an hour later they had reached the airfield. Marco and a couple of the others were helping set out lanterns along a dirt runway.

"This looks a little illegal to me," Ellen said as they waited on the plane circling the field.

"It would be by American standards but by Honduran ones it's the only way to get the drugs safely into our hands." Chance pointed toward a car sitting near the tree line. "That's one of the officials. We'll give him the papers, a little cash and he'll sign off on them."

"So it is illegal?"

"No, we just have to get our shipments in a less orthodox method so that we don't draw the drug traffickers' attention. This way we're not robbed on the road. Marco, Ricardo and Perez will ride as an armed escort back to the resort just to be sure."

"Is this how it's handled every time?" Ellen sounded excited by the whole idea.

"Pretty much, but we change up meeting points and times. Nothing's the same twice."

"Interesting. I kind of like this cloak-and-dagger stuff."

Chance grinned. He could see her as a femme fatale. "Rest assured, it's necessary and not something to take lightly."

The plane's wheels touched the runway, throwing up dust.

"Do you ever see the humor in something or do you always take everything seriously?"

"When it comes to my work it's serious."

And unfortunately where you are concerned it is serious as well.

Chance stepped on the gas and raced after the plane. They needed to have it unload and gone before anyone took notice. He pulled to a stop beside the plane. Thrusting some papers into Ellen's hand, he said, "As I call out the meds, you mark them off the list."

"Got it."

By the time he had the first box in his hands and was placing it in the trunk, Ellen was standing at the hood with a penlight in her mouth and the papers spread across it.

"Do you have a pen?"

"No."

She dug through her bag a second. "Never mind. I've got something."

"Amoxicillin."

"Okay," she called.

"Penicillin."

There was a pause. "Got it."

The government representative stood beside her as Chance named the medicine labeled on each of the boxes. The man didn't ask to see inside any of them. When it came time for him to sign the government form, Chance slipped him some bills and he went away smiling. The price of doing business. The process went on for another fifteen minutes.

Chance looked at Marco and his crew. "Okay, guys, are you ready to go?"

"*Sí.* We behind you."

Chance climbed into the Jeep. Ellen was already there, holding a paper by the corner as she flapped it. "What're you doing?"

"Making sure it's dry."

The paper must have sucked up moisture from the

night air. Chance breathed a sigh of relief that they were loaded and headed back to the resort. He was always on edge when waiting in the open. Drug traffickers were everywhere and as far as he and they were concerned his cargo was gold. The antibiotics were not the most valuable of drugs for resale but they certainly were important to the work of the clinic.

He glanced at Ellen. She'd gathered the forms firmly in her hands. He started the Jeep and they were soon turning into the resort entrance and driving round to the staff parking lot. Chance pulled into a slot next to the van. He waved at Marco as he turned in behind them then back out again on his way home.

"Marco isn't staying?"

"No, we're safe here. Now we need to get these counted and stored." Chance opened the back end of the van.

"How can I help?"

How like Ellen not to complain and join in. "As I bring you the boxes, open them, count the contents and store them in the lockbox."

"Will do."

Over the next half hour they worked together, getting the medicine into place. Ellen did everything he asked. With all the boxes in the van, he joined her inside it as well. Being in the tight area with her made him even more aware of his desire. Working shoulder to shoulder, with hands brushing on occasion, he questioned his judgment at having Ellen help him over asking Karen.

He'd chosen Ellen because she had offered and seemed good at this type of work. The other part of his reasoning had been to see how she reacted to the clandestine operation that was sometimes necessary. He was pleased, she'd come through like a champ.

With the medicine stored, Chance climbed out of the van and offered his hand to Ellen. She hesitated a second before she placed hers in his then jumped the short distance to the ground.

To his disappointment she let go of his hand. "Bedtime."

She yawned. "Past it."

"Tomorrow's clinic is in a village not far away. You and I will sleep in. The others will go ahead and we'll catch up with them before midmorning."

She pulled her bag out of the Jeep. "I can go earlier if I'm needed."

"No, you need your rest."

"But—"

What was the problem? The idea that she'd have to ride out with him? Or she wanted to spend time with Michael? "No buts. Be here at nine ready to go."

"Okay, but before I go I need to ask you a question." It had been worrying her all night. Ellen had to get some kind of answer for his behavior in front of her hut.

He stopped and turned. She moved toward him. Looking him straight in the eyes, she asked, "Why did you kiss me?"

A stillness came over Chance then he wiped his hand over his face. "Let's not get into it again. I've already apologized. It won't happen again."

"You didn't answer my question." Ellen refused to back down until he gave a reason. She said softly, "Why?"

"What do you want me to say? Because I wanted to more than anything in the world."

Did he mean that? Joy swelled in her chest. She stepped closer. "If that's the truth, why not?"

"Come on, Ellen, this isn't a good idea."

"Probably not. But I still want to know." She continued to study his face in the dim light.

"Look, you deserve more than I can or am willing to give."

"I don't remember asking for anything. And if I was, you don't get to decide that for me. My father has done that all my life and I don't need you taking his place. I choose what I want." Since when did he think she wasn't capable of making her own decisions?

"The most that can be between us is an affair. You don't want that. Go to bed, Ellen. Forget about what happened."

"Just for the record, I asked about a kiss, you are the one that brought up an affair. Good night, Chance."

That would give him something to think about. She took the path leading to their huts.

After a few hours of sleep, which were not refreshing by any standard, Ellen was sitting in the truck, waiting for Chance. She'd decided after their discussion that she would do her job, be as much help as she could be to the clinic, and stay out of Chance's way. He'd made it clear where he stood regarding her and she would respect that. That was just as well for her, she didn't need to get involved with someone who thought they knew all the answers where her life was concerned.

Chance walked up looking as if he hadn't fared any better since they'd parted than she had. His hat was crammed on his head and his aviator sunglasses were in place.

"Good morning," she offered.

Chance climbed into the driver's seat. "Mornin'."

"It came around pretty quickly."

A grin covered his lips. The one she didn't see often. "Nights like last night remind me I'm not as young as I used to be."

"I can understand that," Ellen mumbled as he started the Jeep and pulled out of the lot.

She looked at Chance's large, capable hands on the steering wheel and then moved her eyes up to his face to settle on his mouth. She like his full lips that remained far too serious far too often. As he slowed, her attention went to his strong thigh muscles flexing and contracting as he pressed the gas pedal after shifting gears.

He intrigued her, made her want to know more about him, figure out what made him react to her as he did. It wasn't just his kisses, his air of authority but his devotion to the people he was trying to help that fascinated her. Yet the hurt from the night before wasn't easy to let go of. There was still an ache behind her heart. No one liked being rejected, especially when they were told it was for their own good.

Ellen peeled an orange that she had taken from the bowl in her hut. Breakfast had been delivered without her request. It was her guess that Chance had seen to it. "Want some?"

"No, thank you."

"You sure?" She offered a couple of slices, holding them out. "I bet you didn't eat much for breakfast."

After shifting gear again, he reached out and took the slices from her.

A shiver of warmth went through her. All it took was one innocent touch and her heart rate jumped. If she was going to keep her promise to herself, she would have to get a handle on her reaction to Chance.

Ellen pulled a slice off the orange and popped it into her mouth, making an effort not to let it show how rattled she was. What she needed to do was focus on something else. "Tell me what you need done to get the paperwork in order."

"I have to see that everything is turned in on time and

in order to the foundation as well as to the government representative. I need help doing what we did last night and an inventory of supplies done regularly. I also need shipments set up. Have papers in order for customs."

For the next few minutes Chance continued to list different areas where he needed assistance.

"Where's the paperwork right now?" Ellen threw the orange peel out of the window.

"Most of it is on a table in my hut."

He was a control freak? Did he think he could do everything? "Have you been seeing to it since the clinic opened?"

"Pretty much, but lately it has been more difficult. The foundation is now required to submit items it didn't have to in the past. I have to admit I hate doing it as well."

"But you didn't plan to ask for help, did you?"

He glanced at her. "I let you help last night, didn't I?"

Chance had, but she had a feeling that was a rarity. She suspected she should feel honored.

By the time she and Chance arrived at the clinic area there was a line of people waiting.

"I should have come on with the others," Ellen said as she hopped out of the car. "So many waiting."

"It doesn't do them any good if you're so tired that you don't know what you're doing. They'll be seen. We won't leave until we do." Chance grabbed his to-go bag off the backseat.

He sounded like he knew from experience what bone tired meant. As if he'd been there before.

"I just hate the never-ending need here."

A weary look came over Chance's face. "I know what you mean. I often wonder if we'll ever make headway."

The statement was like a thump to her chest. She would've never thought she'd hear that discouraged tone from Chance. The great man who had stood at the podium and proudly shared the work being done in Honduras on behalf of the people. The work the clinic was doing. His voice made him seem demoralized. As if he could give up the effort. Didn't he see that just being here, his caring was making a real difference in these people's lives? Marco and his crew were better off just by the pay.

She walked beside him. "But it's worth it. We do make a difference. I see it in every place we go."

"Yeah, but it doesn't appear any different when we return. These people need local permanent clinics."

Was he just tired? She'd never heard him talk like this. "Then why do you keep on doing it?"

"Because no one else is. Where would these people go for help if the clinic wasn't here? Where would I go?"

A cloud of sadness settled around her. Why did he think he had no other place to go? What had happened to him? Where was his family?

Ellen followed Chance into the tent where the clinic was already in full swing. He took his spot at a table where Karen was prepping a patient for an exam. Peter was doing triage. Ellen joined Michael and went to work.

In the middle of the afternoon a mother brought in a baby who had a cleft palate. He was thin but had bright eyes. Not only his looks suffered from his mouth deformity but his ability to eat had as well. Ellen's heart went out to the child like it had to no other. The mother also had a three-year-old with her.

Michael lifted the older child onto the table. As he did the mother watched intently. Michael examined the boy and then said to the mother, "You'll need to clean this area."

The baby in her arms began to squirm.

"May I hold him?" Ellen asked.

The mother looked unsure but she handed the boy to Ellen.

She looked into the baby's face. With the right funding and the right people, how many children with cleft palates could be given a better life? Maybe she could get some support from her father and his contacts. Her fear was that in return his demand would be that she return to New York.

Michael said to her, "Chance will see the baby. He handles all the cleft palates."

Chance looked up when Michael called his name.

"Can you see this little boy now or do you want them to wait?" Michael asked.

"I'll be ready for him in a second."

He looked at Ellen, who was speaking baby talk to the child. She was absorbed in the child's happy but distorted sounds. Motherhood would suit her. She would make a good wife to someone. The idea left a sour taste in his mouth.

His voice was gruff when he said, "Ellen, bring him here and let me have a look."

She did as he asked.

"Hold him while I check him out." Chance pulled his stethoscope from around his neck and put the earpieces in place. He leaned close, placing the disk on the child's chest. The soft smell filled his nostrils. *Ellen.* Would her scent always remind him of flowers? She'd stopped wearing perfume after he'd explained it wasn't a good idea but still he would know her aroma anywhere.

Chance glanced up to find her watching him. They were so close he could see the black flecks in her blue eyes. He had to count the baby's heartbeats twice. Returning his attention to the child's chest didn't help matters. One of Ellen's breasts, covered in a tight T-shirt, was only inches from his hand. He dreamed of touching. Just once…

He closed his eyes and opened them again. Only by focusing on a tree outside the tent door was he able to record the child's respirations accurately the first time. The fascination with Ellen had to stop. Someone was going to notice. Worse, he was going to act on his desires.

The boy baby looked well cared for but thin. He would need surgery to continue to grow, for his teeth to form correctly and for him not to develop ear problems. Chance had just finished his examination when the mother, along with the older child, joined him and Ellen.

"Please continue to hold the boy," he said to Ellen. She smiled and nodded, appearing glad to do so. "I need to take some pictures." He then spoke to the mother, telling her he could help the child but that he would need surgery. That he wanted to take some pictures of the boy's mouth for the doctors.

The mother gave her agreement but she continued to look concerned.

"Ellen, I need you to hold him in front of you so I can get some pictures from different angles. Just stand where you are and try to keep him happy."

"That's not a problem. He's precious."

Chance hurried to the van and brought back the high-resolution camera then began taking pictures. The boy remained happily in Ellen's arms.

He wasn't surprised people were content around her. If it wasn't for the fact he was fighting his attraction to her all the time, he'd feel the same way around her.

Minutes later Chance had all the pictures he needed. "Ellen, get Marco to help you get all the information you can about names and where she lives so that we can contact her when the team comes down here. Marco knows what to do."

"Okay." She placed a kiss on the child's cheek and handed the boy back to his mother.

Despite the pretty picture, Chance was aware of the price of becoming too emotionally involved. Ellen would get hurt if she rushed in and opened her heart too freely.

He made sure that didn't happen to him.

Fifteen minutes later Ellen returned. He was between patients. "We got all the information you requested," she said.

"Good. The plastic surgery team should be here the week after next. We'll put the boy on the list. They'll have a full week of surgery."

"He's a cute little thing." She looked out the clinic door wistfully. "It's a shame he has to go through surgery."

"I could tell you liked him."

"How can you not?"

"Be careful, Ellen. Your bleeding heart is showing. Don't get too attached. You'll get hurt."

"You keep telling me that." She gave him a direct look. "Yeah, maybe. But if you never get attached you might miss out on something wonderful."

Pete asked her for some help and she left him. Chance had the idea that her remark had more to do with what was happening between them than dealing with their patients. He had closed himself off. Had meant to. How many times could he get kicked in the teeth and still survive? It had already happened twice. If he became involved with Ellen it would occur again. He was confident her kick would be the hardest of them all. He wouldn't give her up easily, but give her up he would.

CHAPTER FOUR

THE STAFF ATE supper together that night. Afterwards Ellen and Karen took a walk around the resort before heading for their huts. When Karen had said good-night and left, Ellen glanced at Chance's place. A light was on inside. She shrugged. Tonight would be as good a time as any to tackle those reports he was concerned about. Maybe he had time now to show her what needed doing.

A roll of thunder from the west arrived just as a soft rain began to fall. Ellen climbed the steps of Chance's hut. The main door was open. She knocked, at the same time looking through the screen.

"You looking for me?" The low rumble came from the hammock hanging near the edge of the porch.

Startled, she turned. "Are you spying on me again?"

"Hey, you're the one on my porch, looking into my hut."

The hammock swung slowly as he spoke. She stepped toward him, close enough to look down at him. Chance was stretched out with his hands behind his head and his legs crossed, wearing a T-shirt and cargo shorts. He appeared more relaxed than she'd ever seen him. Chance carried a heavy burden with all he did to make the clinic function. He deserved his down time.

"I came over to see if you wanted me to look at that

paperwork but I can see you're taking some time for yourself. We can do it tomorrow."

A streak of lightning flashed in the darkening sky seconds before thunder hit. Ellen yelped, jumped, and grabbed the rope supporting the end of the hammock where Chance's head lay. It swung. She tipped forward and down on top of him.

Strong arms circled her waist. "There's nothing to be afraid of."

With her palms she pushed against his chest. "I'm sorry. I didn't mean to fall on you."

Lightning flashed again. She shuddered.

"Don't worry, I have you."

There was security in those words. She looked into his eyes and found compassion there.

"It'll pass soon."

She relaxed into him. Found sanctuary. "Thanks. I've not been too fond of lightning since I was a child."

Chance continued to hold her but his body remained tense as if he was trying not to get too close, even though they were touching from shoulder to toes.

The lightning eased. She looked at him. "I think I'm good now. If you'll give me a little push, I can get off you."

Instead of doing as she requested, his lips found hers and her world exploded with pleasure. The hammock drifted to the side as he brought her up alongside him. She entwined her legs with his. He wore shorts and her bare legs brushed against his rougher ones. She stifled a moan.

Chance's hand slid down to cup her butt then squeezed it, lifting her against him. The knit tank top sundress she wore rode up her legs. He ran a hand along the back of a thigh, setting her skin tingling. She flexed into him. The evidence of his desire stood long and ridged between them.

Ellen didn't question why Chance was kissing her after he'd made it clear earlier he didn't want her. She didn't care. He wanted her now. That was what mattered.

Chance's tongue demanded entrance and she gladly offered it. Her center throbbed. She was crazy for this man, had been since she'd heard him speak so passionately about the people he cared about. Even then she'd been half in love with him.

Vaguely aware of the rain falling around them as if curtaining them from the outside world, her hands shook as they pushed upward over his T-shirt and circled his neck, letting her fingers curl into his hair. His scalp was warm.

Chance's mouth left hers to nuzzle behind her ear. His fingers found her leg and the edge of her panties. Tracing the elastic, he teased her. His other hand splayed across her back, holding her close.

Ellen rolled her head to the side, giving Chance better access to her neck. He whispered, "Sweet, sweet El."

She slipped a hand under the hem of his shirt and found warm skin waiting there. His muscles rippled as her fingers brushed over them on her way around his waist to his back. It was heaven to touch Chance, to have him near.

His lips traveled over the line of her jaw and back to her mouth. He placed small hungry kisses on her mouth before he captured her lips completely in a hot kiss, full of need and question.

Ellen squeezed his neck and gripped his back, squirming against him.

"Woman, you're killing me."

"Good." Her lips found his and took command.

Abruptly Chance rolled forward, causing her to slide behind him, her face buried between his shoulder blades. The thump of steps on the boards of the porch stopped her complaint.

"Chance, I need to see you about your plans for the surgery team." At Michael's words Ellen went stone still.

"I'll meet you up by the reception area," Chance said.

"It'll just take a minute." Michael said.

Ellen grinned against Chance's back and brushed a fingertip over his waist. His hand captured hers and squeezed, holding it in place. Her body shook with a giggle.

Chance said tightly, "I'll see you up front."

There was silence for a second, then an "Oh…" from Michael. He added, with humor wrapping the word, "Gotcha."

As the sound of his footsteps disappeared, Ellen kissed the back of Chance's neck and ran her hands around his waist beneath his shirt. She snickered. "We almost got caught."

Chance's swung his feet to the floor and stood. He turned and offered her a hand. "I think you should go."

Really! She could kick Michael for showing up. Finally Chance was letting her in, showing his true feelings, and Michael barged in. Maybe she had been stepping over an edge that would end up hurting her but it would have been a wonderful trip down. Chance's touch sent her body into awareness overdrive.

As soon as Michael had left, Chance had turned cold. What was he afraid of? She wouldn't let him walk away as if nothing had happened. This time she wasn't going to stand for it.

Putting her hand in his, she let Chance pull her to a standing position. As soon as she had, he let her go and stepped back. She glared at him as she straightened her dress, then stepped close enough that her chest came into contact with his. His eyes widened but he didn't move. How much humiliation could she take?

"Dr. Freeman, I don't know what you're playing at but I'm tired of it. We're both adults. I'm old enough to know what I want and to be responsible for my decisions. I've made it clear I want you. I know you want me too. You made that obvious minutes ago. So give it a rest. It's not me you are protecting, it's yourself."

He said nothing but his jaw muscle jumped. She'd made her point. Shaking all over, she said, "I'll be going now."

Had he been gut punched? Chance stood there looking at the spot where Ellen had stood. He hadn't planned on what had happened. The second she'd fallen into his arms he'd been unable to let her go. If Michael hadn't walked up Chance had no doubt where it would have ended. His bed. Every fiber in his being wished it had.

Ellen was angry. She should be. He deserved every word she'd said. She felt used. What had he been thinking? That's just it, he didn't think around her. He'd wanted her to stay away. After tonight it looked like she would without him saying it again. Why didn't that make him feel better?

She been right about him protecting himself. He was afraid of her. Ellen had the capability of taking his heart and crushing it.

Inhaling a few deep breaths, he headed to the lobby area to meet Michael.

He was sprawled in a chair, flipping through a magazine as if he wasn't really interested in the material. When Chance approached, he sprang out of the chair with a wide grin on his face. "Sorry, man, I didn't mean to break something up. I had no idea."

Chance didn't want to talk about what had happened

between him and Ellen. His nerves were too raw. The need still too intense. "What do you need to know?"

"Oh, yeah, yeah. You're in a hurry to get back to Ellen."

Michael had seen her. Chance had tried his best to protect her. What was or wasn't between them, he wanted it to remain theirs alone.

Michael was saying, "I think it's great and about time. Ellen's crazy about you. I've tried to get something going but she'll have none of it. But you, she can't seem to keep her eyes off. Even when we're working she knows where you are all the time."

She did? Chance hadn't been aware. Maybe he hadn't wanted to. Regardless, he didn't want to discuss Ellen with Michael. "What did you need from me?"

Michael looked at him a second then said, "I need the list of patients and their diagnoses to fax to the surgery team ASAP."

"I need to double-check the info. Can I get them to you first thing in the morning?"

Michael grinned. "I'm sure that'll be soon enough."

"Good. See you then." Chance started back toward his hut.

A few minutes later he shuffled through the papers on his desk, the same ones that Ellen had come over to work on before he had distracted her. He looked at the drug list from a few nights before. Beside each drug there was a pink dot. What the hell?

That damn fingernail polish. The same that had covered her nails as she'd raked them over his skin just a few minutes earlier. And the ones he wished were still pulling him close.

He had to figure out a way around this obsession with Ellen. All he need to do was endure a few more weeks and she would be gone. The bigger question would be how would he survive after that?

* * *

Despite Ellen's anger with Chance, she was still basking in the glow of his kisses days later. She didn't like it but couldn't seem to do anything about it.

What would have happened if Michael hadn't interrupted them? Would Chance have forgotten all the opposition he'd put up against her and taken her to bed? Would she have let him? Could she have resisted?

Even now she wished she could be alone with him again. But she had no intention of allowing that. She wanted someone who trusted her to make her own decisions.

She looked at him sitting at the head of the table as if he were the patriarch of a family. Forking another piece of the succulent fruit off her dinner plate, she scanned the table. The staff was sitting down together for the first time in over a week. She relished it when they ate in their dining area, almost like they were a family. It had been just her father and her for so long that she enjoyed a meal with the large, boisterous group.

Chance tapped his fork against his glass. "Okay, listen up. Here's the plan for the next couple of days."

Everyone quieted.

"We'll be going to two outlying villages that are farther away from here than we normally go. Because of this, we'll have more armed guards than usual. Security will be extra-tight. We'll be in drug-trafficker country. They shouldn't bother us unless we give them a reason. And we'll be making every effort not to do that."

Ellen's newfound freedom shook a little. They were going to spend the night in the jungle? This was more than she'd expected when she'd decided to come to Honduras. She looked at Chance again. Everything was more than she'd expected.

"Is there a problem, Ellen?"

"No, sir."

His eyes narrowed at the use of *sir*. "You're welcome to stay here if you're not comfortable." His blue gaze bored into her. Daring her.

Was he trying get her to stay here? "No. I'm good. I wouldn't miss it."

His look moved to Peter and then Karen. They both nodded.

"Good. There has been some trouble with the local traders and we need to be very careful about every move we make. Don't ask any questions of the patients that aren't medical." He looked at her. "Don't leave the clinic area unescorted for any reason. My priority is everyone's safety. Take no chances. Pack for a two-night stay. Enjoy the comforts of home tonight because we'll be sleeping in the trucks or on the ground for the next couple of nights. Any questions?"

Ellen listened as the others talked and made comments about the plans. She couldn't decide if she was excited or terrified. Either way, this was the type of work she'd come to Honduras to do and she would do it without complaint.

"Pack light but be sure to have your long pants and long-sleeved shirts, hat and boots. Don't forget the bug spray and sunscreen." He looked at her. "This won't be a picnic. So be prepared."

He acted as if she had been complaining. Not once, to her knowledge, had she not risen to expectations. If she hadn't been sure she could do it she hadn't let on and had forged ahead. She was tired of trying to prove herself to him.

The next day consisted of a long drive into the interior of the country. Ellen had been told by Michael that the people they would be seeing had only seen a doctor a few times. She was looking forward to helping them.

She'd kept her distance from Chance whenever she

could. Disgusted with him for not facing the fact that he cared for her, she was also furious at herself for letting it matter. She was slowly accepting he was right. If they had a relationship and it went bad, she didn't think she could continue to work here. She would have to look elsewhere for a clinic. But would she like the country and the people as much as she loved this one? It would be better if they just remained professionals. But could she face Chance every day without her feelings showing?

They arrived at the village where they were to work by midafternoon. Before they had finished setting up people were waiting. Again, Ellen worked primarily with Michael, only occasionally swapping to help Chance. At those times they were almost too formal in their interactions. A couple of times the others gave them strange looks or knowing smiles. Would it be worse if they were together?

As the day ended, Marco and his men set up a food table. There were double the number of helpers, with two of them stationed on the perimeter of the area with rifles. Folding chairs were placed at the table so that everyone could sit in comfort to eat.

Growing up in New York City, Ellen hadn't had a chance to do any real camping. She'd attended summer camp but there had been beds with mattresses and running water. This was going to be rough camping and she was rather looking forward to the new adventure after the initial shock. The most interesting aspect so far was the tent structure with covered sides that had been set up as a bathroom area.

While they were eating Chance announced, "Ladies, you may have first turn in the bathroom. You'll find your sleeping bags in the back of the truck. Don't forget to pull the mosquito netting over you when you go to sleep.

Marco's men will be keeping watch tonight. Don't get up and wander around. Get some sleep. We'll start early tomorrow."

Ellen and Karen headed straight to the bathing area after dinner. They were allowed nothing more than a sponge bath but that was better than nothing. They changed into clean work clothes, which they would sleep in. Ellen left her bra off for ease of sleeping and planned to slip it on before anyone noticed in the morning. When she and Karen stepped out of the tent the men were already lined up, waiting to get in. Ellen pulled her towel up against her chest to cover the fact she was braless.

Chance was at the end of the line but she didn't met his gaze as she passed him.

There was a lantern burning in the truck and her and Karen's sleeping bags were already rolled out on the benches across from each other, their nets hanging from the side rails of the truck.

"I've always loved camping out," Karen said as she slipped into her bag.

"This is a first for me."

"Really? And no complaints. I like that about you. Always a good sport."

"Thanks. I wish others thought that." Ellen helped Karen adjust her net around her.

Karen lay back. "You really have a thing for Chance."

"I've sure tried not to." Ellen opened her bag.

"I've worked with many doctors but I've never seen one more dedicated than Chance. Sometimes people can't see past their job."

"I think most of it has to do with him thinking he needs to protect me."

Karen harrumphed then murmured, "It's more like the fact he has the hots for you that's bothering him."

He might but Chance had made it clear he wasn't going to act on them.

Ellen settled into her bag, turned the lantern down and pulled the net around her. Lying back, she looked up at the stars. This was an amazing country. Even with the poverty, need and sometimes danger she'd be happy to live here forever.

Sometime during the night Ellen woke, needing to go to the restroom. After debating having to get out of the sleeping bag, climb down out of the truck and walk across the camping area to the bathroom tent, she decided she had no choice. Using her penlight and moving as quietly as possible, she made her way there.

She was returning to the truck when a figure loomed near her. A hand touched her arm. She jerked away.

"Shush. You'll wake the whole camp." Chance stood close enough that she could feel his breath against her cheek. "What're you doing out here, wandering around? I've told you it isn't safe."

Ellen clenched her teeth. "I had to go to the restroom. Why should it matter to you anyway? You've made it clear you don't care about me."

Chance's fingers wrapped around her forearm and he pulled her behind the clinic tent, putting it between them and where the rest of the group slept. His arms crushed her against him and he growled, "You make me crazy. And the problem isn't that I don't want you but that I do." His mouth found hers.

Despite everything her brain told her about him hurting her again, her body told her to take what she could. She dropped her light and her hands clutched his waist. His tongue caressed the interior of her mouth and she join in the sweet battle. One of Chance's hands slipped under her shirt and slid over her ribs to cup her breast.

He groaned.

A flash of awareness went through her. Her flesh tingled. Reveled in Chance's touch. He took her nipple between two fingers and gently tugged.

Her womb contracted.

"Sweetheart," he murmured against her lips. He pushed the shirt higher. The moist night air touched her skin seconds before Chance leaned her over his arm. She held on as his wet, warm mouth covered her nipple and sucked. His tongue circled and teased her. Blood flowed hot and heavy to her center, feeding the throbbing there.

She moaned. Chance stood her up and his mouth covered hers. His hands went to her hips and brought them against his. With a hand behind his neck, she held his lips to hers.

"Mr. Chance, I heard a noise." Marco stood nearby.

Chance continued to hold her close as he said over his shoulder, "Everything is fine. Miss Ellen got lost. I'll see her back."

"Sí." By the tone of Marco's answer he saw through that lie.

With Marco gone, Chance tugged Ellen's shirt back into place. "Let's get you back to bed. We'll talk about this later."

Ellen's heart flew. At least this time he wasn't walking away mad, apologizing or denying that there was something between them.

He picked up her penlight then took her elbow, guiding her around the tent toward the truck. There he gave her a quick kiss and brushed her already sensitive breast with the knuckle of his index finger before he handed her the light and walked off into the darkness.

On shaky legs, Ellen climbed into the truck and into her sleeping bag. Her heart thumped as if she had been running and her center burned as she relived every second of the last few minutes before she finally drifted into a dream of Chance doing it all again.

Had he lost his mind? Chance walked the few paces to his tent. Ellen was driving him beyond reason. He'd always been a sensible adult, one who thought before he acted, yet when he was around Ellen he came unglued. She brushed against him and all he could think of was kissing her, having her. It had become worse when he'd discovered her bare breast. Heaven help him. He'd almost taken her behind the clinic tent. Worse, he still wanted to.

He had to get Ellen out of his system.

Chance slapped at his pants leg in frustration. They were both adults. She had more than proved that with her warm welcome when he'd kissed her. So why couldn't they have a short and satisfying affair while she was here? He would make it clear there would be no ties when the time came for her to leave.

Maybe it was time to stop protecting her. If he didn't do something soon, he wouldn't be able to concentrate on his work. One thing he did know was that he would not be able to push her away any longer. No matter the reason, he wanted her beyond sanity. He would have her.

Come morning, he assigned Ellen to work with Michael as usual. If he'd assigned her to assist him after all this time the others would notice, especially Michael. He wasn't ready to answer questions about his feelings for Ellen.

Throughout the day he would meet Ellen's gaze and she would smile. Once they grabbed for a bandage at the same time. Their hands touched. By his body's reaction he was reverting back to his youth. When they stopped for lunch he sat under a banana tree to eat and watched as Ellen and Karen walked to the truck that doubled as their bedroom. Even Ellen's walk had him turned on.

Michael squatted on his heels beside him. He looked off toward the two women as well. With humor hanging on each word, he said, "I never thought I would have seen it. The untouchable Chance Freeman has fallen hard."

Chance cut his eyes to him. "What does that mean?"

"You have it bad for Ellen."

"You're crazy." Chance picked up a tiny stick and threw it.

"So it's okay if I go after her?"

"You already said she wasn't interested."

"I haven't given her the full court press," Michael said with a smile.

"Leave it alone, Michael," Chance growled.

"Then I suggest you do something about it." Michael looked at the women again.

"You know, it's none of your damn business." Chance didn't need pushing toward something he had every intention of taking care of himself.

Michael chuckled. "No, I guess it isn't but it's nice to see the cool, calm and collected Dr. Freeman squirm." His grin grew larger. "I'll see that the clinic is ready for this afternoon around two."

Michael had been a friend for a number of years and had often listened into the early morning hours to Chance's sad story of his poor choices where women were concerned. More than once they had handled issues having to do with the clinic together. If Michael wasn't such a friend, he would've never gotten away with those remarks about Ellen.

The afternoon work went every bit as well as the morning had. It was dusk when a couple of gunshots rang out in the distance.

"What's that?" Karen asked in alarm.

Michael, appearing unconcerned, continued to store

equipment. "Drug dealers most likely. We've been lucky we haven't heard more shots."

Fifteen minutes later Chance stepped out of the clinic to see a boy of about twelve run into the clearing and stop. He gave the area a wide-eyed look as if searching for something. Ellen slowly approached him from the direction of the truck. She spoke to him.

Chance hurried toward them. As usual she wasn't considering the danger. The boy could be luring her into the jungle. Kidnappings happened often for ransom in this area. She didn't have to step beyond the clearing but a few paces before she wouldn't be seen. Not wanting to spook the boy, Chance slowed as he joined them.

As he came closer the boy said something about his father being shot and asking for her to come help. Chance's heart rate jumped. That had to have been the shots they'd heard. The boy's father must be working with the drug traffickers or had crossed their path.

"Must come," the boy cried. He stepped forward with his hand out as if he were going to take Ellen's.

Chance stepped closer to Ellen and told the child, "You'll need to bring him here."

"Can't. He no walk," the boy said as he looked back toward the opening in the foliage he'd just come out of. "Hurry. Lots blood."

"Then have someone carry him here." Chance made it a firm statement.

The boy looked around as if expecting someone to pop out of the jungle. "No one help. Afraid."

Chance shook his head. "Then I'm sorry."

Ellen gave him a pleading look. "Chance, we have to help."

"My first concern is the staff of this clinic, their safety. Leaving this area would not be safe. The drug traffickers have free rein. We don't even know the boy is telling the truth."

"He die. Please." The boy looked from Ellen to Chance and back again, tears forming in his eyes. "It not far. Promise."

"We have to help him," Ellen begged.

Chance was torn. If it was true he wanted to give the help. But what if it was a trap?

Ellen grabbed his arm and squeezed as she looked at him.

"How far?" Chance asked the boy.

He said a village name Chance wasn't familiar with.

By this time Marco had joined them. Chance looked at him, "How far?"

"Ten-minute walk," Marco said.

"Okay, I'll get supplies and you get my to-go bag." Ellen left before he could say more.

"Should be safe. I send Ricco with you." Marco waved Ricco over.

"Tell me what happened to your father and what part of his body has been hurt," Chance said in rapid Spanish to the boy. Heaven help them if they ran into trouble. He'd let his better judgment be overshadowed by Ellen's beautiful eyes. That unrestricted, forge-forward determination might get them all into trouble. Yet he felt the pull to go as well. There was a patient who needed his help regardless of the danger.

Ellen hurried into the clinic tent and snatched up Chance's bag then headed for the supply van. At first she'd been angry with him for hesitating to help the boy's father. As far as she was concerned, if a person was hurt you had to do whatever was needed to take care of them. Chance's hardline stance didn't impress her. As he spoke more to the boy she saw the sympathy in his eyes. It wasn't that

Chance didn't want to go, it was more that he was responsible for everyone and couldn't make snap decisions. The fact they were going showed that Chance really did care.

Grabbing suture kits, she stuffed them in his bag. She took a couple of bottles of saline out of a storage basket. Finding a spare backpack by the shelf, Ellen dropped the bottles in. She added additional supplies that from her experience might be needed.

Chance entered the van. "I need to get some antibiotics. The boy says his father was shot in the leg."

Ellen stood, letting Chance come behind her. Their bodies bumped in the close quarters. Minutes later, they had what they thought they might need. She left the van first, with him right behind.

"Hand me that backpack," he ordered.

"I can carry it." Ellen offered him his to-go bag instead.

Chance glared at her. "You're not going. Ricco and I will handle this."

"Ricco has medical experience now? How's he supposed to handle a gun at the same time he's helping you? I'm going." Ellen watched his mouth form a tight line. He wasn't going to agree.

"Peter or Karen—"

Ellen huffed. "Karen couldn't keep up the pace and Peter is needed here. We can stand around and argue about this while a man is dying or we can get going." She turned to leave the tent.

He grabbed her under the arm, jerking her round to face him. "You can go *only if* you agree to follow my orders to the letter. No arguments. No going rogue. Either you agree or you stay here. This is still my clinic and my call."

She glared at him and said through her teeth, "I promise to do as you say."

Chance searched her face. "Okay, let's go take care of this patient."

Ellen had no doubt that he didn't like the idea of her going but he recognized he clearly needed her help. She adjusted the pack on her back as he slung the strap of his bag across his chest. At a lope he crossed the clearing and Ellen followed close behind.

"You ready?" Chance asked Ricco, who nodded. "Ellen, I want you between Ricco and me."

She moved into position.

To the boy Chance said, "Take us to your father."

The boy dipped his head under a large leaf and moved into the jungle. Chance followed with Ellen and seconds behind her Ricco. The path was little more than a foot wide. She wouldn't have even said there was one if she hadn't been behind Chance. As they walked he held leaves and vines back. She accepted them and did the same for Ricco.

"Stay close and don't speak unless necessary," Chance hissed over his shoulder.

Underfoot was dark packed dirt crisscrossed with roots. Her boots were so new they didn't make the best hiking wear. A couple of times she caught a toe on a root but righted herself before she tripped. Once Ricco caught her arm before she fell.

Another time Chance stopped and she bumped into his back. He cautiously looked around. The boy was standing a few feet in front of him, looking down the path. They waited then moved forward at a slower pace. Finally, they broke out of the jungle into an open space next to a creek with five small huts. The roofs were pieces of tin or plastic tarps peaked just enough for rain to roll off. The walls were little more than uneven boards wired together to form a square. The boy led them through knee-high grass to one of the stacks closest to the water.

He stepped through an opening into a hut that had no door. Chance and she followed. Ricco stayed on guard outside. The sun was almost over the horizon, making it dark inside. The boy told a woman there that he had brought the doctors.

Ellen could make out someone lying on an old mattress on the dirt floor across the room. Chance was already stepping that way and Ellen joined him.

"We have to have some light here." He sounded exasperated as he went down on his knees to speak to the barely conscious man.

Ellen pulled off the backpack, opened it and removed a flashlight. Clicking it on, she held it over Chance's head.

He glanced up. "Well done, Ellen. I should have known you'd consider the details."

She couldn't help but be pleased with his praise.

"Can you point the light toward the left some?"

Ellen did as he requested. From her vantage point she could see the dark-skinned man was maybe thirty, dressed in a torn shirt with baggy shorts. One leg of the pants was pulled high on his leg. Below that on his thigh were two dirty rags covered in blood. Even if they could help him, fighting infection would be the larger battle.

"Look at this," Chance said with revulsion in his words.

She understood his feelings. "Two shots. He really needs to be in a hospital."

"Agreed, but that would be in a perfect world and this isn't one. Nearest hospital is too far away and he would never make it, even if he would allow us to take him."

Ellen leaned closer for a better look. "He's lost a lot of blood. He needs a transfusion."

"I'm O. Have you ever done a transfusion outside a hospital?"

"No."

"Then I'll set that up and you can take care of the wounds while I'm giving blood. Ever removed a bullet?"

She gave him a wry smile. "I saw it done during emergency rotation."

"Can you handle it?"

"Sure I can. So if I understand this right, you're going to lie around while I do all the work?"

"Funny lady." Chance reached for his pack.

She came down on her knees beside him.

Chance called to the boy to come and hold the flashlight and asked the woman to get them some hot water. He then prepared a syringe of antibiotic and injected it into the man's arm. "It'll be too little, too late, but it's better than nothing."

Ellen could identify with his frustration. She pulled the saline bottles out of the backpack as Chance removed supplies from his bag. Slipping on gloves, she lifted the bandage off the upper hole in the man's leg. It was still oozing. She opened up some four-by-fours and placed them over it, then gave the same attention to the other one. As Ellen worked Chance was busy setting up an IV line. With efficiency and precision that she admired, he'd already inserted the needle into the man's arm.

Chance spoke to the boy again and he dashed out the door. The woman arrived with the water. Ellen continued to clean around the first wound. The boy returned with a wooden chair that had seen better days and a lantern. Chance placed the chair close to the mattress. Ellen took the lantern, situating it so she could get the most out of its light.

"I'm ready for you to finish this IV," Chance said.

"Let me change gloves." Ellen stripped off the ones she'd been wearing and pulled on clean ones. She moved close to Chance. Taking his arm under hers, she held his steady and began pressing on the bend in his elbow for a good vein. She was close enough to catch the natural scent of him.

"You know, you really are beautiful."

She glanced up then down again. "You're not already light-headed, are you?" With a firm, steady push she inserted the large IV needle into his arm. "Hand me one of those tape strips."

"No, just speaking the truth." He handed her a strip from the ones he'd placed on the backpack. "This isn't your first stick. Nicely done."

"Thank you. Yes, I've done a few in my time." She looked him straight in the eyes. "But I'm always open to a first time in other areas." His eyes widened slightly before he started pumping his fist and blood flowed to their patient.

"You'd better get busy on those holes or you'll be wasting my blood."

"I'm on it." She removed her gloves and replaced them with clean ones again. "I'll have them taken care of and get back to you in a minute."

Ellen carefully cleaned around the surface of the first wound. She was going to have to remove the bullet and not damage the nearby artery while doing it. Even in the best of situations that would still have a degree of difficulty. Under these conditions that was upped a hundred times. Ellen counted on her skill to save this man, if not her experience.

Locating large tweezers, she cleaned the blood away and went after the bullet. She pursed her lips tightly as she continued to search. Finding the bullet, she grabbed it and pulled it out. The wound bled anew. She dropped the bullet to the floor and snatched some four-by-fours and placed them over the hole.

"Nice job, Doctor."

"Thanks, but I have to stop this bleeding. Could you apply pressure while I get the sutures ready?"

"Sure. Now I'm assisting you."

She glanced at him. "Problem with that?"

"Not at all." After she'd helped him pull on a glove, he put two fingers in the center of the pads.

Minutes later Ellen had the wound sutured closed. She checked on Chance as she worked. She didn't need him passing out. He seemed comfortable. The entire time she worked she was conscious of him watching her.

As she applied the final piece of tape to the bandage Chance said, "You handled yourself well, Dr. Cox."

"Thank you. How're you doing?" She took the patient's vital signs. He was stable, but barely.

"I think I'm about at the end of my giving. Head's a little light."

"Well, let me try to stand and I'll see about you." She pushed up but her knees were stiff and didn't want to move.

"Give me your hand and I'll pull."

She took his hand. It was a struggle but she finally made it to her feet.

"Walk around a minute and get some feeling back into your legs."

Ellen took his suggestion and made a couple of circles around the shack.

Returning to Chance, she removed the needle and applied a pressure bandage. "Now, sit there for a while. I don't need two patients. I'll have to admit this is out of my usual wheelhouse. Even in a clinic in the middle of New York City, what we have done here is over the top."

"If it makes you feel any better, this is a little extreme for me as well."

"Thanks for that. I thought you might remind me again that I shouldn't be here."

"I only acted that way because I was afraid that you had bitten off more than you could chew. These conditions are harsh."

What he didn't say was that today was an example of that. She had a patient waiting and couldn't worry about that now. Going down on her knees again, she started caring for the last bullet wound. With the lower one, the bullet had gone clean through. Working as efficiently as possible with the few supplies as she had left, she closed the wounds Done, she started cleaning up.

In all the medical work she had ever done she'd never felt better or more confident about herself than she did at this moment. This work was what she had been born for.

She looked at him. "We're not all the hothouse flowers you think we are."

"I know that now. You've more than proved it." Chance looked around the shack. "It seems we're here for the night. We need to keep an eye on him." He nodded toward the injured man.

Ellen placed a hand on their patient's head. "Infection is our enemy now. And you don't need to do any activity for a while either."

Chance looked in the direction of the woman and boy, who waited in the corner in what was nothing more than a makeshift kitchen. There was a small table and a bench with a shelf above it. A bucket sat on the bench. Chance spoke to the boy, "Can you find us something to sleep on? A blanket for your father? Something to eat?"

"Sí." The boy left and the woman went out the door behind him.

Chance stood and walked to the doorway. Ellen joined him. Chance spoke to Ricco. He nodded and move to the corner of the building, his gun at the ready. She and Chance continued to stand there. The night sounds were almost overwhelming as animals as well as bugs communicated.

"This is an amazing country," Ellen said. "I know why you keep coming back."

"It is."

She looked at him. "You love it here, don't you?"

"If I said I didn't, you would call me a liar."

Ellen smiled. "That I would."

The boy returned carrying a rolled-up tarp. They followed him inside. He placed it on the floor. "Sleep." He pointed to it.

Chance chuckled. "All the comforts of home."

"Better than the dirt." Ellen sat on it with her legs crossed.

"Do you ever see the negative in anything?" Chance asked, taking the chair again.

"Sometimes but it's better to see the positive because the negative is usually far too obvious."

The woman came in holding two banana leaves. She handed one to her and the other to Chance. Ellen had never seen anything like it.

"Pulled pork and vegetables. It's cooked in the ground. You'll like it." Chance picked up a bite between his thumb and forefinger and put it in his mouth.

Ellen wasn't so eager. She looked at it more closely in the dim light then moved it around with a tip of a finger.

"This is the first time I've seen you squeamish about something. You need to eat."

"I'm just not sure about this. I usually have my food on a plate."

Chance chuckled. "Just pretend that you're at a baseball game and you're having a hotdog."

"My father has box seats for the Mets and a cook comes in."

Chance's fingers stopped halfway to his mouth. "Just who is your father?"

"Robert Cox." Even in the low light she could see Chance's eyes widen.

"As in Cox Media."

"Yes. That's my father's company."

"So why in the hell are you down here? You don't need the money or even to work."

She glowered at him. "I'm a doctor because I want to help people. And today shows that I'm needed. Even by you." In a show of defiance, she picked up a finger full of food and plopped it into her mouth. "That's good."

The boy came in again, this time with two bottled drinks. He gave them each one.

Chance said, "No matter how far out of civilization you get, soda companies are there. Thank goodness. We don't need to drink the water."

Ellen finished off her meal and stood. "Let me have those." Chance handed her his leaf and bottle. "I'll put this away and then check the patient. You need to sleep. Work on building new blood cells."

"Yes, ma'am."

"No argument?" Ellen looked at him.

"Nope."

"We really have gone into a different world." She placed the stuff she held on the bench then stepped over to her patient. He seemed comfortable enough. There was a low fever but that was expected. "We'll need to get him out of here and to a hospital tomorrow."

"Agreed," Chance said as he lay out on the tarp. "Come on, you need some rest as much as I do."

Ellen stretched out beside him, leaving as much space as possible between them. She put her arm under her head, trying to get comfortable.

"Come over here," Chance said. "You can use my shoulder for a pillow."

The tarp made a crinkling sound as she shifted closer. She laid her head on his broad shoulder. He moved his arm around her and his hand settled on her waist.

In a sleepy voice he said, "I've dreamed of sleeping with you but never in a shack in the middle of the jungle."

Ellen rolled toward him and her arm went across his waist. She didn't care where it was, just that she was near him.

CHAPTER FIVE

CHANCE ROSE A couple of times during the night to check on their patient. Each time Ellen curled into the warm spot he had left. When he returned she moaned her appreciation as he took her into his arms again. That kind of treatment he could get used to.

He looked out the doorway at the full moon. It was well after midnight. Their patient had spiked a fever. After giving him another dose of antibiotics, Chance used a four-by-four to bathe his head. Under these conditions there wasn't much more he could do. He joined Ellen again.

"How's he doing?" she murmured.

"Fever's down. Go back to sleep."

"Next time I'll get up."

He pulled her close again. "Deal."

The sky was still more dark than light when Chance was shaken awake. "Must go," the boy said in a low urgent whisper. "Now."

Chance was instantly alert.

The boy was already picking up Chance's to-go bag and putting things in it. "Bad men come. Must hide."

Chance stood and helped Ellen to her feet.

"They find you, they kill you." The boy didn't slow down.

His statement propelled Chance into action. "Ellen,

make sure we have everything picked up that might indicate who we are. Leave nothing behind." He grabbed her backpack and finished putting their things, even the paper covers, into the pack. Done, he zippered it up.

"What's going on?" Ellen looked around as if unsure what to do first.

"Drug traffickers. They're looking for our patient over there. If they find us they'll kill me and ransom you. If you're lucky."

"What about our patient?" She started toward the man.

"We've done all we can for him. Now we have to take care of ourselves." He thrust the backpack at her. "Put it on. Do exactly as I say. No more questions." He took his pack from the boy and pulled the strap over his shoulder. "Let's go."

"Ricco?" she asked.

The boy went to the door and stopped. "He leave when the men come close. Hide. Then warn doctors." The boy waved them on. Instead of heading across the grassy field, the boy led them to the edge of the jungle. There he went into a squat. Chance followed suit and pulled Ellen down beside him. The boy searched the area.

There was a stillness in the air as if nature was waiting for something to happen. No birds chattered in the trees or monkeys swung from limb to limb. Seconds later voices broke the silence. The boy put his finger across his mouth. They waited, waited. The sounds came no closer.

The boy, followed by Ellen and then Chance ran stooped over around the edge of the field for a time until they ducked into the foliage near a large banyan tree. At almost a run they headed down a path that was harder to follow than the one they had been on the day before.

They had been moving at a fast pace for about ten minutes when Ellen tripped and went down on her hands. Chance grabbed her by the waist and pulled her to her feet.

"Are you all right?" he whispered close to her ear.

She nodded.

Chance looked at the boy, who had paused. He waved them forward.

"We have to move." Chance took Ellen's hand and started after the boy.

As they ran Chance tried to push the leaves back so they wouldn't slap Ellen in the face but wasn't always successful. She kept up despite the difference in their size and the fact she was wearing chunky boots. A few minutes later the boy pulled to a stop and squatted on his heels.

Ellen took a seat on a large root. Strands of hair hung around her face. Her cheeks were bright red. Her deep breathing filled the air along with his and the boy's.

Standing, the boy said quietly, "I must go to my father. You follow path to river, then go down river to Saba." The boy headed up the path the way they had come.

"He's leaving us?" Ellen whispered in disbelief.

"Yes. He'll be missed and we'll be in more danger."

"Won't they know we have been there when they see his father?"

"Maybe they won't look that closely or hopefully they don't even check the shack." Chance offered her his hand and she took it. "We need to put as much distance between us and them as we can."

He hurried down the path but not at a run and Ellen kept pace with him. As they went the birds started to call at each other and the animals scurried off. At least the jungle was accepting them. If the traffickers were close and they heard no noise they would know where he and Ellen were.

They had been walking for about an hour when Chance stopped and led Ellen off the path. Stepping through the vegetation about ten feet, he found a large fig tree that would give them plenty of cover.

"Why're we stopping?"

"You need to rest." He looked around. "Hell, I need to rest. Take a seat."

Ellen pulled off her pack and dropped it to the ground. Satisfied that they were out of sight of the path, Chance joined her on the ground.

"Any way you have some food in that bag?"

He grinned. "As a matter of fact I do. Two or three breakfast bars."

"That's what I love, a man who's prepared for a quick run through the jungle."

Chance chuckled and started searching though his bag. No one was prepared for this situation but he didn't want to scare her by saying that. He pulled out a bar. Tearing it open, he handed her half of it. "It's more like a man who has had to go a day without a meal."

"Do you know where we are?"

This was a conversation he wasn't looking forward to having. It would go one of two ways: she would panic or she would take it in her stride. So far Ellen had been a good sport but this was more than they both had bargained for when he'd agreed to go help the boy's father. "Three days is my best guess if we don't run into trouble."

"Three days!" Her voice rose. Birds squawked and flew away.

"Shush, we don't know who else is nearby."

Ellen's brows grew together and she looked around with concern. "Sorry."

"Just be careful from now on. We have to walk and it won't be an easy one. Even following the river, we have to circle any villages we come to. We don't know who we can trust."

"We really are in a mess. I'm sorry I insisted that we

help the father." She took a bite of the bar. "Now I've put us in danger."

"It didn't take much for me to agree. Let's not worry about it. We need to make plans. First, we have to conserve what food we have. Which consists of two and a half bars. We'll need water." He was now talking more to himself than her.

"We have the two saline bottles. We can fill them up at the river."

"No, we mustn't drink the water unless we have no other choice. The chance of getting a parasite is too great. We'll collect rain water. We'll just have to make do until it rains." Thankfully it did that almost daily.

By the deflated look on Ellen's face he suspected she was thirsty now but she didn't say anything.

"Do you have any idea where we are?"

"Some but we're far deeper in-country and north than I've ever been." Maybe he shouldn't be quite so truthful with her but he couldn't bring himself to lie either. He finished his half of the bar and put the paper in his bag. "We'd better get going."

They both stood. He gave her a hand signal to stay and stepped out to check the path then waved her to join him. Chance offered his hand. Ellen took it. She trusted him to get them out of this. He just hoped he'd earned her faith.

Ellen realized she was in over her head this time. She'd done what her had father worried would happen. Taken a risk. It was starting to take a great deal of effort to contain her fear. The pace Chance set had her feet aching and her body sweating. By the time the rush of the river could be heard the sun was high in the sky.

Her mouth was desert dry and her clothes stuck to her skin. She couldn't remember being more miserable but she refused to say anything or ask to slow down. There was no way she would be responsible for putting them in more danger. She'd already placed them in enough.

Chance stopped. "Stay here. I'll be right back."

She nodded but didn't like the idea of being left. By the sound of the water the river was around the next bend. Surely Chance wouldn't be gone long. When he was no longer in sight panic pushed its way into her chest. She looked up the path from the direction they had come. Then back to where Chance had gone. What if something happened to him and she was left out here alone? What if he got hurt and needed her? What if those men found him? Why didn't he hurry?

With a flow of relief that had to equal the river in size, she saw Chance coming back.

When he joined her again he gave her a searching look. "You okay? Hear something?"

She gave him a weak smile. "I'm fine. Everything is fine."

"That might be stretching the truth. River's right ahead. There's a path running beside it. We'll use it but we'll have to be careful not to run into anyone."

"You lead, I follow."

"When we get down a way we'll stop and cool off for a while."

"Gives me something to look forward to."

Chance started down the path. "I'll give you this, Ellen Cox, you're a trouper."

The path widened and she walked beside him. "You might want to save that praise until you see how I do over the next few of days."

He took her hand and squeezed it. "We'll make it."

Ellen couldn't contain the "Aw" that came out at the sight of the river. It was breathtaking. The water flowing over the white rounded boulders whooshed and boiled as it made its way to the coast. The contrast of the vivid vegetation framing it and the blue of the sky above made for a perfect picture. If it hadn't been for the situation they were in she would have sworn she was in paradise.

Chance let go of her hand and stood beside her. "It's just one of the many things I love about this country, the beauty."

They started moving again. "Still, you've had a hard time dealing with all the needs you see and keeping the hospital going."

"I have to admit that the struggle to retain staff, find funding and most of all making a real difference here has started to eat away at me."

It was the first time she'd heard him really share his feelings about anything personal. "So your plan was to discourage help when it shows up?"

As they walked along the path beside the river he pointed down, "Watch the rocks. We don't need a twisted ankle to deal with."

A couple of minutes went by as they maneuvered over a narrow, difficult area. Back on a wider section, Ellen said, "You didn't answer my question."

"I don't discourage people from coming. In fact, I encourage them. We need the help down here."

"I didn't get that kind of welcome."

"Only because you reminded me of my ex-wife at first, then because you didn't. I wasn't sure you could handle this type of work. I was concerned for your safety. Still am." He took her hand and helped her down over a slippery area.

It was nice to have someone care but she was a survivor. She'd learned that when her mother had died and during those days in the hospital. "But there's more to it."

It took him a second to answer. "I was attracted to you and I didn't want to be."

"Why's that such a bad thing?"

"Because I have nothing real to offer you."

Before she could get him to clarify that statement he said, "Here's a good place to rest." The river slowed and created a pool. "I'll keep watch while you clean up. Just be sure not to swallow any water despite how temping it might be."

Ellen crouched beside the river. She must look a fright. Cupping her hands, she splashed water onto her face. She did it again, rubbing her hands down her cheeks, and was amazed at the dirt that came off. The water felt wonderful. Cool and refreshing. Cupping another handful of liquid, she ran her hand along the back of her neck. Now, if she could just have a drink.

She sat on a rock and started working with her boot-lace. "I'm going to take my boots off and cool off my feet for a second."

"No. Don't." Chance's tone was sharp. "You won't be able to get them back on because your feet will be so swollen. Hopefully, we'll be somewhere tonight where you can remove them."

Ellen started re-lacing her boot. So much for the pleasure of having water run over her throbbing feet. Done, she stood. "Your turn."

Chance stepped to the river and began cleaning himself. As she expected, he poured and splashed the water into his hair. He slung his head back. His hair curled and dripped around the collar of his safari shirt. In an odd way he belonged to the wild uncertain world around them.

While he was doing that she checked up and down the path. Pulling her band from her hair, she let it fall then gathered it again, working to get all the loose strands back under control.

The shrill call of a bird had her jerking around to search the area behind them. She looked back at Chance. He was on guard as well.

Stepping away from the river, he picked up his bag and came to her. "Come on, we're both tired and jumpy. We need to rest. Get out of the heat. We'll start again in an hour or so." He pushed leaves of rhododendron the size of a man and vines out of the away, putting distance between them and the path. They soon came to a banyan tree.

"This should do. We have cover here." He bent over and weaved his way between the roots that grew almost head high in abundance around the tree.

Ellen followed.

Chance put his satchel on the ground, lay down and used the bag as a pillow. Ellen took the space beside him, doing the same with her backpack. After they were settled and still, the birds started talking again. She looked up into the tree, catching glimpses of sky through the thick canopy.

"Chance," she whispered.

"Mmm?"

"Tell me about your ex."

He rolled his head toward her and opened one eye. "Why do you want to know about her?"

There was a hint of pain in his voice. She must have destroyed him.

"Because I think she is part of the reason why you've been trying to stop anything from happening between us."

Chance looked away. She wasn't sure if his eyes were closed or if he was staring off into the distance.

He took a deep breath and let it out slowly. "I met her at a fund-raiser. She was all about looks, which worked because she had them. In spades. Blonde, blue-eyed, leggy."

Ellen's lips tightened. *Like her.*

"I fell for her right away. She liked the good things in life and she was more than glad to hitch a ride with me. What she didn't bargain on was living in Honduras. She came from a middle-class background where they camped on vacation and didn't have the comforts of high living so I thought she would do fine down here, especially staying at the resort. It didn't take her long to start complaining about the heat, the bugs, the rain and most of all having to spend the day by herself. She wanted nothing to do with the clinic. There wasn't enough to do and she was lonely."

Ellen could hear the disgust and disappointment in his voice.

"One of my buddies from med school came down to work for six weeks. She had been so unhappy that when she started spending time with Jim and smiling again I was glad. Suddenly she wanted to come out with us and help at the clinic. I thought it was a good idea. The more she saw maybe the more she'd want to help. Yeah, right. It turned out they were having an affair. He was from an old Boston family with the name and money to please her. When he left, she went with him." The last he all but spit out.

"I'm sorry that happened to you."

"It was a long time ago. I've moved on."

Ellen had never known a person more in denial. "You do know I'm nothing like her?"

"Yeah, I figured that out pretty quickly." There was a contrite note in his voice. "I was tough on you there at first."

"You think?"

He smiled slightly.

"So those question and comments about Michael and me was you being jealous?"

"I wouldn't say that."

She leaned over him and looked into his eyes. "I would."

Their gazes held for a long time before he said, "Lie back, Dr. Cox, and get some rest. You're going to need it."

Ellen did as he asked with a grin on her face. He cared

far more than he let on. Could she have a relationship with Chance and still maintain the freedom she'd fought so hard to gain? From what she'd learned about him, he had a strong need to protect. Could she handle that?

The sounds of the birds as they took flight from the top of the trees woke her. Chance rolled over her and put a finger to her lips. His body remained rigid and still. Seconds later the voices of males speaking in Spanish reached her ears. They were on the path. She only caught a few words because the dialect was so different. Words like "find" and "American" she understood.

They were looking for them!

Chance saw the fear in Ellen's eyes. Her body trembled beneath him. She'd heard the men. They were in more danger than he'd believed. The drug traffickers were determined to find them. Ellen's eyes were wide with terror. She squirmed as if wanting to run.

He brushed his lips over hers as he shook his head. Bringing his hand to her cheek, he held her so that he could deepen the kiss. Ellen opened. Her tongue mated with his. Fingers weaved into the hair at the nape of his neck and her body softened. She kissed him with the passion of a person hanging on to life. An arm came down to his waist then pushed under his shirt and grasped his back.

Heaven help him, Chance wanted her. Here. In the jungle. On the ground. Beneath this tree. But he couldn't. He must keep her safe.

His lips remained on hers as he listened for the men. They had moved on but they were going the same way as them. They would have to wait here and let them get further down river then cross over. Find somewhere to hole up for the night. It would mean more time in the jungle but getting Ellen back in one piece would be worth it.

She quit kissing him. He opened his eyes. Hers were fixed on him. He put his finger to her lips. She kissed it. Thankfully the panic had cleared from her eyes. Passion and questions filled them now.

"Shh."

She nodded. He rolled off her and sat up. She did the same. They waited there, just listening, for what seemed like an eternity. The birds settled again. All he could make out was the usual jungle sounds.

Standing, he extended his hand and helped her to her feet. He put his finger to his lips again then gently pushed the undergrowth back as they made progress toward the river. Ellen was glued to his back as if they were one. He paused and carefully searched the area before they stepped out onto the path.

Using a low voice, he said, "We have to cross the river and find somewhere to stay the night. Maybe they'll give up by tomorrow."

She nodded.

"We need to do it here. I'm afraid to go downstream any farther. We'll cross at those rocks." He pointed down the river just below the pool. "Guess what? You get to take those boots off after all. We don't want to get them wet or they'll be even harder to walk in. Tie the laces together and put them around your neck."

Ellen did as he instructed without question. Minutes later they were ready to go. Chance led her across some rocks and down into the water and up again. There was a section where the water was moving fast between two large rocks close to the bank. It was moving rapidly enough that Ellen wouldn't be strong enough to walk through it without assistance.

"I'll step over then help you though." Chance didn't wait for a response. They had to get out of the open. There was no way of knowing if the men would come back this way. He held on to the rock and put a foot into the gushing water. Secure, he took a long step, making it across the flow. He offered his arm to Ellen. She grasped his forearm and he hers. He swung her more than helped her over the divide. She now stood a little in front of him.

In his peripheral vision he saw a flash of color. He pushed Ellen into the deeper water surrounding a large rock. When he did so he slipped. He was headed down the river and right into the sight of the men looking for them.

His bag strap held him back. Seconds later he felt a tug across his chest.

"Help," Ellen whispered close to his ear.

Using a foot, Chance pushed against a rock beneath the water and back toward her. He did it once more. Now at least half of his body was behind the rock, lying over Ellen's. She held tightly to the strap, pulling him against her chest. The water tugged at him as it flowed over his legs but Ellen held steady. They stayed in that position without daring to look to see where the men were for a long time. The shadows were long on their side of the river before Chance had the nerve to lean forward. Scanning the area, he saw no sign of human life.

He worked to find adequate footing then managed to get turned around and to the bank. Ellen took his hand and he brought her over to join him. They climbed out of the water and moved into the vegetation. Sitting, he said, "Thanks for saving my butt back there."

"Think nothing of it." She sounded exhausted.

"When did you see—?"

"About the same time you did. I couldn't think of anything to do but hold on."

"You did well." What he didn't want to tell her was that they had bigger problems now. Like it was getting dark and they had no safe place to stay for the night. "Let's get our boots on. We need to get moving. The good news is that they were headed upstream so the chances of us meeting them again is slim."

"So there'll be no more distraction kisses?"

"I hope not."

"Shame, I rather enjoyed it."

He grinned. "I did too. Get your shoes on. We need to get going."

"I'm afraid they're wet." Ellen dumped water out of one of hers.

"We'll have to wear them anyway."

They both had their boots on and were ready to go in a few minutes. Once again Chance led, pushing plants out of the way. It was rough walking but they made headway. He almost kissed the ground when they came to a path. Keeping the sound of the river to his right, he could be sure they were still headed toward the coast.

Now to find a place for them to stay for the night. They were both soaking wet. He was starting to chap and Ellen must be also. But still no complaint. He shook his head. The woman with hot pink fingernails had just saved his life. Who would have thought?

Where did she find that fortitude? In his experience with women they would have broken down long ago. As the daughter of Robert Cox she'd grown up in a privileged home. He couldn't imagined her having done anything that would prepare her for this type of undertaking. It was nice to have someone he wasn't having to reassure all the time. A partner in the effort.

They walked about an hour without seeing any obvious good place for shelter. Under the tree canopy it was almost dark. He had to find something soon. As if in answer to his prayer, a giant kapok tree came into view. It was so large that its trunk and roots created a cave of sorts. They had just made it to the tree when rain started to fall. Ellen stood with her mouth open, letting the drops off a leaf fall into her mouth. He wished he could let her continue but they had to see to their needs first.

"Get the bottles and put them where they'll collect water. I'll make sure we don't have any company inside this tree. Then we need to get out of these clothes and shoes. We can't take a chance on a fire but we do need to give our bodies relief from the damp."

Chance left her to see about the drinking water while he checked out the tree. There was just enough room for them to both lie down. At least it was dry. He returned outside and found a banana tree and started stripping leaves from it. He would use them to clean out any ants or spiders that might want to share their room. They couldn't afford to be bitten.

He'd just finished and had their bags inside when Ellen joined him, soaking wet. She had one full bottle of water in her hand.

"I poured what I had in one. I'll go out after the other in a few minutes. Have some." She handed it to him like she was giving a Christmas present. "It's wonderful."

Chance gladly took a swallow. And another, before handing it back to her. "Drink all you can so we can fill it up again."

She did as he said and passed it to him once more.

"I think we're safe here so we need to get out of these clothes. There's a root we can hang them on. They won't dry completely but it's better than nothing." Chance started unbuttoning his shirt. He couldn't help but watch Ellen pull her T-shirt over her head. Why couldn't there be more light? Beneath she wore a sports bra.

"Please, don't look at me like that. I'm not used to undressing in front of a man."

Chance unbuckled his belt, bent over and removed his boots then dropped his pants. "You certainly have nothing to be ashamed of. You're amazing."

"From what I can see of you, you're not so bad yourself. So you're a briefs guy. And I would have said boxers."

She'd given thought to what type of underwear he wore? He rather liked that idea.

Ellen sat on a banana leaf and removed her boots then stood. The sound of a zipper drew Chance's attention away from hanging clothes. In the dim light he could see a strip of white bikini panties. Once again he had to remind himself to focus on keeping them alive instead of his baser desires.

"Hand me those," he said in a gruff voice.

She gave him her pants.

"We need to go through our packs and see what we have that we can use to gather food and attend to our feet. I don't know about you but mine feel like shriveled-up prunes." The job needed to be done but it would also keep his mind off the half-naked woman sharing a tree bedroom in the middle of nowhere with him. It should have been the stuff that dreams were made of. Instead they were in a nightmare.

He'd worked hard all day to sound upbeat and not to show his fear and concern. Gut-wrenching anxiety filled him any time he let himself think about their situation. People with guns were after them, they were dehydrated, had no real food, their feet were blistered, they were insect bitten, and exhausted. He just couldn't let on to Ellen how dire their situation was.

She sat on a banana leaf again and opened her backpack. She started laying things out. When she found the flashlight she start to turn it on.

"Wait until we have everything out so we don't waste the batteries."

"It's so wet it might not work."

"It's the kind sealed for water. It should be fine."

She went back to digging in the pack. "What's this?" She held a rag with its ends tied. She opened it carefully. It was food like the boy had bought them last night.

"The boy must have put it in there when he was packing things up."

"I don't care how it got here, I'm just grateful to have it. I'm starving." She handed one to him.

They stopped what they were doing and took a moment to eat. Neither said anything about saving some but they only ate a little. Chance gave his back to her and she put them both back into the rag and tied it.

"Okay, what else do we have?" she asked.

Most of what they had was medical supplies, which did them little good for food or drink.

"Let me see that light. I want to look at your feet."

"Why, Doctor, that's a kinky idea." Ellen brought her feet around in his direction.

"Funny. You keep that up and I might tickle them." Chance shined the light on her feet. He wanted to cry. They had blisters and were bleeding in some places. "I have some antibiotic ointment I'm going to put on these. Why didn't you say something?"

"We couldn't stop, could we?"

"No."

"Then what was the point? I'm sure yours are just as bad. Finish up with mine and then I'll see to yours."

He gently applied the ointment to her feet but it wouldn't really help much. The air and time out of her boots were the best healer. "Before you do mine, let me go out and see to the water." Chance picked up the bottle and headed outside. He soon returned to find her repacking their bags.

"It's your turn." Chance wiped as much dirt off his feet as possible and sat down to let her examine them.

Her hands were gentle as she checked each angry spot and applied the cream. She was an above-average doctor.

"We're both in sad shape but we'll survive. My father will never believe this. I'll be lucky if he lets me out of town again."

Chance placed banana leaves so that they had a bed of sorts. He put his bag and her pack on it and lay back. Patting the area beside him, he said, "Join me."

Ellen did but didn't touch him.

He clicked off the flashlight. "Would you mind keeping me warm?"

She placed her head on his shoulder and wrapped an arm around his waist. Shifting, she got comfortable and he became uncomfortable. He could so easily roll over and make love to her but he was bone weary and she could only be just as tired. They needed their rest more than release.

"These banana leaves make you think a dirty tarp isn't so bad."

Chance chuckled and kissed her temple. "You never cease to amaze me."

The soft sound of her even breathing brought the only feeling of peace he'd found all day.

CHAPTER SIX

THEY HAD BEEN walking since sunrise and Ellen's feet were already screaming. Even with the attention Chance had given them they'd still had to go back into damp leather boots. It hadn't been a pleasant experience. To have a thick, dry pair of socks would have been wonderful. But that was only a fantasy.

Ellen had wanted to work in a developing country but this was more than she had planned on. Sleeping in a tree in only her underwear hadn't been a scenario she would have imagined. She had slept, though. Exhausted from hiking, swimming and raw fear, she'd been fast asleep as soon as her head had snuggled into Chance's shoulder. Despite her lack of clothing, she'd been warm the entire night nestled against Chance.

Sometime she had been jerked awake by the sound of a wild animal growling.

"Shush, sweetheart. He's a long way off. Go back to sleep." Chance's hand had caressed her hip and waist.

For once she'd appreciated his protection. She hadn't questioned further and had soon been asleep again. How did Chance do that? Make her feel secure by just being there? She'd been consumed by fear the day before. She'd run down a path in the jungle without question because

Chance had said that was what they needed to do, and had been confident he would take care of her.

He'd distracted her by kissing her when she'd been so sure the bad men just feet away would find them. The kiss had started out as something to help her keep quiet but had turned into a passionate meeting of lips, as all of her and Chance's kisses had. Her distress had disappeared with only a touch from him.

The pinnacle of her terror had been those seconds before she'd wrapped her hands around his bag strap and pulled him back against her. It had taken all her strength but she'd managed by sheer determination. Her heart had been in her throat and there had been a roaring sound in her ears. Losing him hadn't been something she would even consider. If he had been washed away and the drug traffickers had seen him they would have shot at him. She couldn't let that happen. After they'd climbed out of the river the look on Chance's face had aid he was proud of her. She'd wanted to dance a gig in happiness that they'd been alive but she'd been afraid they'd be seen or heard.

Ellen watched Chance walking ahead of her a few paces. He was confident and watchful at the same time. He had to move a leaf or push away a vine more often than she because he was taller. His clothes clung to his body in the tropical dampness. Occasionally he pushed his hair back with a hand when he glanced over his shoulder to check on her.

She and Chance had become a true partnership through this ordeal. He was no longer pushing her away. Last night he'd trusted her to see to something as important as the water. He saw her as a competent person, something that her father would never open his eyes to. Someone who could take care of herself. For that alone she adored Chance. She looked at his broad shoulders and the back of his handsome head. Her heart was full.

Sometime later Chance called for a rest stop. They shared a bottle of water. There was little better than the feel of the liquid going down her parched throat.

"I'd like half a bar, if that's okay?" Ellen said.

"Sure. I'll join you." Chance pulled a food bar out of a side pocket of his bag. Opening and breaking it, he gave her a piece.

Ellen found a seat on a nearby root. "So how long should it take us to get to Saba?"

"Maybe tomorrow evening if we're lucky. If we can keep the same pace as we have been. How are your feet?"

"Much like yours, I imagine."

His chuckle was a dry one. "My boots are more broken in than yours. I'm sure your feet are dying to get out and dry out."

"It may be a long time before I can wear open-toed shoes again. I'm pretty sure I'm going to lose some skin."

Chance sat beside her and took one of her hands in his. He stroked a fingertip much like the Honduran girls had. Her nails were no longer neatly polished. A number of them were broken and chipped. Dirt circled the cuticles. Under any other circumstances she wouldn't have let him look at them. Now she was just too tired to argue.

"I'm sorry." He sounded sad.

"For what?"

"Your nails."

"I thought you hated them. Thought they were…frivolous."

"No. They're one of the nicest things about you."

"Really? You could have fooled me. You acted like I had committed a crime when I brought out my polish."

He kissed a knuckle. "Yeah, but you made those girls' day." He kissed another. "I couldn't fault you for that." He touched his lips to a different knuckle. "When we get out of this I'll see that you get a day of pampering at the resort. Including a manicure and pedicure."

"What about you? You'll deserve something."

"I'll get to enjoy you." He gave her a quick kiss.

Warmth seeped through her that had nothing to do with the steamy weather or the sun beaming down on them. They still hadn't had that talk he had promised but she was going to see to it that they did.

"Come on, it's time for some more walking." Chance stood and helped her up.

It was around noon when the sound of the river grew louder.

"We're getting closer to the river," Ellen said.

"Yes. I think this path leads to a ford. It's time we crossed back over," Chance said. "Wait here and I'll check it out."

Her chest tightened. "I'm going with you. I don't like it when you leave."

He regarded her a moment. "You know, that's the first complaint you've made since we started this trek."

"Complaining does no good. I learned that a long time ago." That lesson had been clear when she'd been trapped in a car with her mother and later in the hospital. Even with her father she'd found out that she didn't make headway by complaining. It hadn't been until she'd forced the issue by coming here that she'd made a step away from him.

Chance took one of her hands in his. "Why now?"

"Because I'm afraid that something will happen and you won't come back." Was that how her father felt? This was the fear he knew when he thought of losing her?

"I won't be out of your sight two minutes. Promise."

She tapped her wristwatch. "I'm going to time you."

"I expected nothing less. While I'm gone think about

what you want to do when we get back to the resort. I want to hear every detail." He hurried off.

She was so busy making plans for their return, she forgot to check her watch. As good as his word, Chance was soon back.

"Did you miss me?" he asked with a grin.

"Always." But at least this time she hadn't been a big bundle of nerves thanks to him giving her something else to ponder. Maybe that's what her father needed—something else to focus on besides her. He'd not dated since they had lost her mother. It was time for him to move on. Past time.

Maybe it was time for her to embrace life more as well. She'd taken a major step by coming to Honduras but not in her personal life. Working so hard to earn her independence, she'd put her love life on hold. Was it time for her to open up? Let someone in? Should that person be Chance? If she did, would he accept her?

"This is a good place to cross. The river is wide but not running fast."

Ellen picked up her pack. "At least I don't have to worry about saving your butt."

"Did I say thank you for that?"

She smiled. "I think you did but feel free to do so again."

"Thanks. Let's get moving."

She hurried to catch up with him. There was the old Chance. Focused.

The river was much wider than it had been where they had crossed before. The rocks were not nearly as large and were spaced so that one large step or jump could get her from one to another. There was a real possibility they could cross without getting wet.

"I want to lead this time." Ellen wasn't sure what had gotten into her when she said that.

Chance looked surprised. "Okay."

Ellen chose her path carefully, managing to get out into the middle of the river without any mishaps. There the water was moving faster and the gap between the rocks was wider. She hitched up her pack, preparing to jump. Pushing off hard, she jumped over the water and landed on her hands and knees on top of the next rock. Chance stepped up beside her. He took her forearm and helped her up.

"You're the most determined woman I know."

"Thanks." Ellen moved on across the river. When she reached the other side she waited for Chance to join her, which he soon did. "Come on. We need to get going." She headed down the path.

"So are you usurping my authority now?"

"I just thought I'd like to lead for a while. You know the saying: if you aren't the lead dog, the view never changes."

He released a bark of laughter. The birds reacted by screaming and flying away.

"Shush," she said.

Chance looked contrite then searched the area. His gaze came back to her. "No more smart remarks from you."

"You can't blame me for that. You were the one being loud."

They didn't walk long before the sound of civilization could be heard over the flow of water. Chance took the lead again, making his way into the greenery under a large tree. From their location they could see women doing laundry at the riverbank. There was an open field of high grass between the women and a group of huts sitting back against the jungle.

Chance put his mouth close to her ear. "We'll have to stay here until they leave. We might as well rest."

They slowly and as quietly as possible removed their packs. He leaned his back against the tree and she scooted up next to him. The women's chatter lulled her to sleep.

"Ow!" Ellen woke, slapping at her pants leg. She'd been bitten. Shaking out the material, she saw nothing.

Something was wrong. *Chance was gone.* Going up on her hands and knees, she searched the river area where the women had been. There was no one in sight.

Chance knew how she felt about being left alone. How could he disappear? Terror threatened to fill her chest but she pushed it down.

He would be back. He had to come back.

Off in the distance, downriver, clothes were hanging over a rope strung between two trees. There was a movement. One of the items disappeared from the line. *Chance.* She watched another piece of clothing being snatched away.

He would have to cross the field and come upriver again to get her. It would be safer if she met him. Quickly pulling on her pack and putting his bag across her chest, she carefully left her hiding place. With her body as low to the ground as possible she worked her way across the field. A dog barked. She crouched down. Her calf burned. She couldn't worry about that now.

Waiting for further noise and hearing none, she hurried to the jungle edge and along it to where she'd last seen Chance. There he was, pulling another item from the lie. She moved again to where she'd seen him duck out of the trees.

Chance's eyes went wide when he saw her. He handed her a couple of articles of clothing and nodded his head downriver. He didn't give her a chance to respond before he took his bag from her and quickly moved to the river and down the path. They walked at a rapid pace for a good while before he stepped off the trail.

Out of sight he turned to her. "You scared me to death, showing up like that."

"And you left me."

"I planned to be back before you woke."

She glared at him. "Don't do that to me again."

Chance studied her a second then said, "I won't. I promise."

She believed him. "I saw you and knew you'd have to double back for me so I decided to meet you."

"Smart girl."

"So what did you get us?" She rubbed her calf. It was still stinging. What had bitten her?

"Something for us to sleep on and a couple of clean shirts."

Ellen grinned. "I look forward to high-style living tonight. Shouldn't we get moving?"

"You're starting to sound like me." Chance smiled back and headed down the trail. Ellen had almost scared the life out of him when she'd shown up near the clothesline. He had really misjudged her when he'd first met her. Ellen had a backbone of iron.

When she'd announced that she was going to take the lead he couldn't help but be proud. If he had been in her place he would have been tired of following as well. The woman was full of surprises. His mother and ex-wife would have given up before they'd even got started. He wasn't used to having such a resilient woman in his life. *Life?* Could he really have her in his life? Would she stay with him?

He set a steady pace and Ellen kept up. A couple of times he checked behind him to see how she was doing. There was a determined look on her face, but occasionally her face was twisted as if she were in pain. Her feet must really be bothering her.

It was drawing close to evening and he had started to look for a place to stay for the night when the sounded of rushing water reached his ears.

"Is that a waterfall?" Ellen asked with enthusiasm.

"Sounds like one." If luck was with them they might have a good safe place to sleep and an opportunity for a fire. Even a bath.

They made a turn in the path and the water disappeared over the edge of a cliff.

He called back. "Are you up for a little climbing?"

Ellen shrugged. "Do I have a choice?"

"Not really. But if all goes well it'll be worth it."

"Lead on, then."

Over the next half an hour they made their way around and down to the pool of water at the bottom of the falls.

"It's amazing," Ellen said.

"It is. Honduras has incredible falls. I'd leave you here but I know you'd have none of that so come on and let's see if we can find a room for the night."

"Here?"

"Sure." Chance led the way around the pool toward the falls. He made a few maneuvers across rocks until they had worked their way behind it. There was the small cave he was looking for. It was large enough for them to remain dry and still have a small fire.

Pulling his bag off, he dropped the clothes on top. Speaking loudly, he worked at being heard over the roar of the water. "Your hotel room for the evening."

Ellen looked around. "It's wonderful."

"I need to look for something dry enough to burn before it gets too dark. Are you going to be okay here by yourself or do you want to come with me?"

"Aren't you worried about the smoke being seen?"

He smiled and pointed to the falls. "It'll blend in with the mist. We're safe. Hopefully we can have dry clothes."

She looked unsure a moment then straightened her shoulders. "No, I'll be fine here."

"I won't be long. Why don't you get that trash we have in our packs out to use as starter?"

It took Chance longer than he'd expected to find something in a tropical rain forest dry enough to burn. The entire time he was gone he worried about Ellen being frightened. He did manage to locate some dry leaves and small sticks. He and Ellen wouldn't have a bonfire but it would be something to dry clothes by.

With arms full, he made his way back to the river. He started to take his first step on the rocks when he saw her. Ellen stood naked beneath the falls. Her arms were raised as she held her hair out to let the water reach each strand. He'd never seen anything more breathtakingly beautiful or more uninhibited.

He should leave. Let her know he was there. But he couldn't.

Ellen turned, giving him a profile view of her delicious curves. His body hardened. Her breasts were high and her stomach flat. There was an arc to her behind that made his hands itch to hold her. He stood mesmerized by her splendor, unable to put a thought together beyond the acknowledgement of the desire building in him. Waiting and watching, he didn't want to disturb her or break the spell.

Ellen did it for him. She stepped out of the water. The gold of the evening sun caressed her skin as she walked to a nearby rock and gathered her clothes. She pulled on her shirt and pants and ducked behind the falls.

Chance remained where he was until he had control of his breathing. By the time he'd made it back to their hiding place some of his libido had eased but at the sight of Ellen it climbed again. He had to regain some perspective. It didn't help that Ellen's underwear lay in a small pile nearby.

The tension was thick between them. She wouldn't meet his gaze. Was she feeding off his emotion? Had she known that he'd been watching? It was as if the easiness between them over the last two days had disappeared and been replaced by the disquiet of heightened awareness of the weeks before. As alluring as Ellen had been as a water nymph minutes ago, he had to focus on them surviving. They needed to have a fire, eat and tend their feet. Those needs took precedence over his sexual cravings.

But those carnal needs pulled at him with each look he gave her.

He squatted and let the pile of brush fall from his arms. "Ellen, look in the side pocket of my bag and you'll find a round silver tube. Would you hand it to me?"

She did as he asked and included the trash as well.

He placed the paper under the brush and opened the watertight container, removing two matches.

"I should've known you'd have something up your sleeve to start a fire with."

"I keep them in case I have to go old school with sterilizing a needle. You just never know."

"Like this time."

He gave her a tight smile. "This was more than I planned for." Striking one match against the other, he quickly placed them on the paper. He slowly added some of the material he'd gathered until they had a small fire. "Bring your clothes over here and spread them out to dry. I wish this was going to be large enough for you to get your pants dry after a wash but I don't think they'll dry by morning. At least our underwear and shirts will be cleaner."

"Are you hungry?" she asked.

"Yes. I could eat."

"That was sort of a dumb question." Ellen picked up what little food they had and joined him beside the fire.

She gave him half of the food from the rag and ate the other. "That leaves us with one food bar."

"Hopefully we'll be in Saba by tomorrow night."

"As much as I've enjoyed this walk through the jungle, I have to admit I'm looking forward to seeing the resort again." She put the rag back in the backpack.

"Not New York? I would think after this you'd want to go home."

"No. Most of all I'd just like a good shower."

Chance looked at her. "I thought that's what you were having a few minutes ago." Even in the glow of the fire he could see her blush.

"You weren't supposed to see me."

He stood. "How was it?"

"Wonderful."

"If you'll keep the fire going I think I'll give the falls a try as well."

Ellen watched Chance leave. She wasn't sure why she had suddenly turned bashful around him. It was as if they had been fighting for their lives every hour of the last two days and she now felt safe enough to think of living. The intimate space they would share for the night only added to that awareness. She still tingled all over with the knowledge he had watched her bathe. For how long?

The waterfall had looked so inviting. She hadn't felt nastier in her entire life. Dirt mixed with sweat, her clothes sticking to her, pants less black than tan. Her hair had been a mass of tangles with bits of leaf and twigs. No one at home would have recognized her. The rush of the water had called to her. She had planned it to be a quick bath but she'd become caught up in the heavenly feeling of the water flowing over her and had stayed longer than she'd intended.

Ellen looked at the falls. She couldn't see Chance

through the rush of water but she could picture him beneath it as water washed over his shoulders and ran down his chest. What if they didn't make it home the next day? Were caught? Never had a chance to be together?

What would it be like to really spend a night in his arms? Life was too short not to have that pleasure.

She spread the blanket out near the fire and stored their packs. Her leg let her know it was there as she moved. Sitting down, she pulled her pants leg up and twisted so she could see the back of her calf. There was a red welt just above where the top of her boot came. She had been bitten. It was tender and warm. There wasn't much she could do about it now. She'd check it again in the morning.

Pulling Chance's pack to her, she found the ointment and gave her feet some much-needed attention. Her blisters now had blisters. She dreaded putting her boots on in the morning. At least her socks had been rinsed, which would help cut down on infection. She would lose one of her big toenails, if not both.

Chance joined her. His hair was wet. He'd pushed it away from his forehead. A lock of it hadn't stayed in place. Bare-chested and with his pants low on his hips, he strolled toward her. The fire reflected off his still-damp skin. Every nerve in her body was alert to him.

He laid his clothing beside hers. There was something oddly intimate about their undergarments drying next to each other.

"You need to get some sleep. We have another day of walking ahead of us." He put another piece of brush on the fire.

He continued to stand as if he wasn't going to join her on the blanket. "You aren't going to sleep?"

"I think I'll sit up for a while."

"Then I'll keep you company unless you've had enough of it."

"I don't think that's possible." A stricken look covered his features as if he'd said something he hadn't meant to.

"We haven't had that talk yet," she said just loud enough that she could be heard over the falls.

"Ellen, I don't think—"

"You're right. I don't want to talk." She stood. "I've spent the last two days worrying about dying."

"Ellen…"

She stepped around the fire. "There might not be another day, another time and I want to celebrate being alive. With you." Placing her hands on his shoulders, she went up on her toes and kissed him.

Chance grabbed her around the waist. Pulling her against his chest, he brought her feet off the ground. His mouth devoured hers as if he was hungry and a banquet was being served.

CHAPTER SEVEN

HOW LIKE ELLEN to take the initiative. Chance wasn't going to turn her away again. The gentleman in him he'd left in that hovel days before. He was going to accept what was offered. All of Ellen.

He would inhale her, touch her, have her. Totally take what he'd desired for weeks.

His body was tense with anticipation. With one hot kiss his manhood stood ready. He craved everything about her.

With her still in his arms he walked around the fire to the blanket. She wrapped her arms around his neck as they went. Cupping the back of his head, she held his mouth to hers. Her tongue caressed, twirled and mated with his, mimicking the very things he wanted to do to her.

Chance hadn't planned this. But he wanted it. Needed her.

She was right. They had spent the last few days fighting for their lives. He didn't want to battle himself or her about the attraction between them. Now it was time to feel her against him for the pleasure of her, not for the need to survive. Chance eased her down his body and brought his hands up under her shirt tracing the lines of her body. Stepping away, he pulled her shirt over her head and dropped it to the stone floor.

She was stunning, standing before him. The flickering firelight touched her in places he had every intention of savoring. He cupped one of her breasts. Slowly, he pulled his hand away, caressing the breast from beneath. Ellen shivered, adding to his delight. He reveled in her soft sound of pleasure.

The pads of her fingers drifted over his chest then downward to the edge of his pants and around to his side. She slipped a finger beneath his waistband and moved it across his skin.

His manhood tightened. Strained against the front of his pants.

She grabbed a handful of material and pulled him to her.

Chance took her mouth again. This time she brought a leg up his, circling it with hers. He broke the kiss and looked into her eyes. "I desperately want you but I can't make any promises."

"Tonight isn't about promises. It's about being alive. Enjoying life."

She hadn't said it but he knew her too well not to know she cared deeply for people and that meant she didn't take relationships lightly. Should he let this continue? For his sake? Hers?

A hint of a smile came to Ellen's lips. "Remember what I said that day when I was polishing the girl's nails? A moment of pleasure is better than none. If something happens to you, I'd always regret not having you like this."

That brick wall Chance had built around his heart had just taken a battering. He couldn't let her get hurt. "This isn't some storybook adventure that's going to end in a happily-ever-after."

"Have I ever said that's what I want?"

She hadn't, and for some reason it stung that she didn't expect it.

Her hands ran up his ribs and down his arms. "What I'm saying is that I want you. I know you want me. I feel it." She flexed forward. "There might not be another time. We may not get out of this. I don't want any regrets. Not being with you would be a great regret."

Chance knew about regrets and disappointment. He'd experienced both a number of times in his life. With his mother. His sister. His ex-wife. Ellen wouldn't be one of those. He would see to that right now.

Cupping her face with his hands, he gave her a gentle kiss. "You deserve a big comfortable bed and someplace clean."

"I don't care as long as you are there."

Bam. There went another chip in the wall.

Pulling her against him, Chance savored the feel of her bare breasts against his chest. His mouth found hers again then moved over her cheek to kiss the hollow behind her ear. She tilted her head as if asking for more.

He found her waistband and unfastened the button. Deliberately, he pulled the zipper down. Her pants fell to her feet and she pushed them away. His mouth left her ear to travel over the ridge of her shoulder and down to the tip of one breast.

His mouth took it, sucked. Running his tongue around the nipple, he teased.

A soft, sensual sigh filled the air as Ellen combed her fingers through his hair.

Chance pulled away and blew over the damp mound he was giving attention to. Ellen's moan turned to a groan.

His length twitched. How much longer could he stand not having her? What would she sound like when she found release?

Cupping the other breast, he took it into his mouth, giving it the same attention as he'd lavished on the first. She held his head, encouraging him. Chance's mouth left her breast to kiss his way up her neck and capture her lips. The meeting of mouths was wild and hot.

Her hands went to his pants and released them, pushing them over his hips to the ground. She didn't hesitate before she wrapped her hand around his staff and gently stroked. If she kept that up he would combust before they made it to the blanket.

Chance moved back and she released him. "I'll lose control if you touch me."

"I don't care." Her voice was husky, which did nothing to ease his need.

"But I do. You deserve more." He kissed her deeply. One of his hands followed the curve of her shoulder, skimmed her breast to brush the line of her hip. The palm of his hand skimmed over her stomach before his fingers teased the curls between her legs.

She tensed in his arms.

He slid a finger between her folds and pulled away.

Ellen shook, making a delicious sound of protest.

Chance cupped her center then slowly pulled a finger between her folds. Her stance widened as her tongue entered his mouth. She clung to his shoulders. Using one finger, he went deeper, finding the wet, hot opening of her desire. He dipped the tip of his finger inside. Ellen hissed close to his ear. Bringing her leg up around his, she offered him clear passage. He took it, pushing his finger completely into her. She bucked, going up on her toes.

He removed his finger and pushed into her again. Her hips flexed against him. She clawed at his back. Retreating, he thrust again. This time Ellen pushed down on his hand. Pulling his finger away, he entered her again. Her head fell back. Her hair was wild around her shoulders as she cried her pleasure and withered against him.

It took all Chance had within him not to throw Ellen to the ground and hammer into her.

Instead he held her, watching the soft look settle over her face as she eased to earth once more. The experience was something he'd never had with a woman before. It left a feeling of satisfaction he wasn't familiar with but desperately wanted again.

Was that another brick being knock away?

Ellen relaxed against him. He removed his finger and grasped her waist. Their gazes met. Hers was dewy. She gave him the tiny smile of a woman who'd found something special. He stood on top of the world because he was the one who'd given it to her.

That was an awesome responsibility. Did he want to carry that? Could he take that gamble?

Ellen placed a hand in one of his, went down on the blanket and pulled him to her.

Chance didn't resist. He couldn't.

"You deserve some attention." Her voice was deeper and even sexier than before.

"It's not necessary."

There was a look of concern in her eyes for a second then her lips turned upward. "Oh, but I think it is."

Ellen wanted to give Chance some of the pleasure he'd given her. She wasn't inexperienced but nothing she had felt before compared to what Chance's touch had done to her.

When he'd said it wasn't necessary she'd feared he was running away again. She wasn't going to let that happen.

Lying on her side, she faced him. His masculinity was almost more than she could comprehend. Holding his gaze, she reached out and placed her hand on the pectoral muscles of his chest then ran her index finger over his skin. Slowly she traced his ribs, dipping and rising as she moved downward.

She glanced up to see that Chance's pupils had dilated. They burned with desire. Her actions were having the effect she desired. Circling his belly button, she enjoyed the inhalation of his breath as she watched his skin react to her touch. It was exciting to see this strong, masterful man respond to her. Her hand followed a line of hair downward until she reached the head of his manhood. She ran the tip of her finger over him and watched the length twitch.

Chance growled and pulled her hand away.

Grinning, Ellen shifted so that she could push his shoulders to the blanket. That done, she straddled him. She kissed his jaw and moved down to the valley of his neck and onto his chest. As she went one of Chance's hands glided over her hip. When her tongue slid across his breastbone, he cupped a butt cheek and gently squeezed.

She rose above him. Looking into his eyes, Ellen slowly came down to kiss him. It was a kiss of not only passion but of heartfelt longing and caring.

Chance took control and rolled her to her back. One of his legs came to rest over hers. "I can't last much longer. I promise you slow next time."

Her heart swelled. He thought there would be a next time.

Ellen lifted her hips, pushing her center against his leg. She throbbed for him. Blood rushed in her ears. She needed him as well.

Chance settled between her legs, his manhood coming to rest at her entrance. He supported himself on his elbows as he looked down at her.

A stricken look crossed his face. "We have no protection."

Ellen's hands found his hips and pulled him to her as

she lifted upward. "Don't worry. I have it taken care of." She reached up and kissed him with everything in her. She refused to let him leave her again.

Chance slipped into her until she held all of him. Ellen gripped his forearms and wrapped her legs around his waist, bringing him closer. He pulled back and pushed forward then did it again. Each time tension coiled tighter in her. She wiggled, begging to have more. Chance gifted her with a hard thrust.

Ellen squeezed her legs tighter around him, bowed her back as he pressed into her. Squeezing her eyes shut, she reached, searched and grabbed for what she needed. Finding the pinnacle, she came apart. She remained rigid, taking all Chance had to offer, until she started the blissful float downward.

Her legs fell away from his hips. Before she could think straight again Chance drove into her. Slowly at first, then faster he stoked. Her hands tightened around his neck. He grasped her hips and held her firmly against him. His mouth took hers and whatever else he wanted. Heat flared in her. She grasped his shoulders. It couldn't be happening again. Chance gained speed. Her scream of pleasure mixed with his groan of release as he sent her to the stars once more.

Chance held Ellen close as they lay on the too-small blanket. Her head lay against his shoulder and her arm rested across his chest with her hand buried under his hair. One of her legs wrapped around his and her foot was cupped in the arch of his.

She fit like she belonged. Perfectly. What would it be like to have her like this all the time?

He'd never been more satisfied in his life. She was everything he'd never thought to have in a woman. Beauty, intelligence, strength, passion, perseverance and most of all an easy smile. He shouldn't think like that but having Ellen in his arms made him want to dream again. She'd brought that back to his life.

Her hand moved over his shoulder and teased his earlobe.

He looked at her. "Hey, there. I thought you were asleep."

"Mmm… Just resting." She stretched against him, running her fingers across his belly.

"You keep that up and I'll have to retaliate."

"I don't have a problem with that." She kissed his neck. "Didn't you promise me slow next time?"

Chance kissed the top of her head as his hand caressed the under-curve of one of her breasts. "I can go slow. But the question is can you stand it?"

Ellen's hand drifted to his hip. "As long as you can."

He took the challenge and they both won.

They were still basking in a cloud of satisfaction while in each other's arms when Ellen said, "Tell me about your childhood."

Chance couldn't help but flinch. Why did Ellen want to know about that? He'd rather talk about anything else but that and his ex-wife. She'd already heard that sordid story.

"I was a baby, then a child and now a man. Pretty typical stuff."

She gave him a playful swat on the chest. "I know well that you are a man. But what I want to know about is Chance the little boy."

Ellen wasn't going to back off from this. That wasn't who she was. He might as well tell her and then she'd quit asking. "I was raised in upstate New York. My father was a world-famous surgeon even when I was a young boy. He traveled and spoke a lot. We had everything money could buy but he was never around. My mother adored him." Chance had worshiped his mother. "But my father was so wrapped up in his life that he barely saw her. He liked the jet-setting, being the big shot, and he like the women that went with that recognition. I'm not sure why they ever married."

The same question had occurred to him when Alissa had left him. Had he, like his father, been so wrapped up in his work that he hadn't been taking care of what he'd needed to do at home? Had it been fair to ask a woman to live his lifestyle? The question still nagged at him.

He looked at Ellen. Her golden hair was spread out over his chest and shoulder. Her fingers ran along the center of his chest as if she couldn't get enough of him.

"How sad. Your mother must have been so lonely."

"She was."

"What happened?"

His chest tightened. "How did you know something happened?"

"By the tone of your voice."

Had he become that transparent? Or was she just that in tune with him? He wasn't sure which idea disturbed him more. "She left. Later I was told she joined a commune-type place. As far as I know, she's still there. I went to see her once when I was in college but she said she didn't want to see me. I never tried again."

Ellen's arm went to his waist and she gave him a tight hug. "Oh, Chance, I'm so sorry."

She'd lost her mother as well. If anyone could empathize it was her. "You understand too well, don't you?"

Her head nodded against him. "Mothers are important." She didn't say anything for a few minutes. Her voice wobbled as she said, "I watched my mother die."

Even during this ordeal she'd never sounded so close to tears. They shared a huge loss but hers had been far more traumatizing. He pulled her close. If only he could take her pain away. "Sweetheart, I'm so sorry."

Chance understood her agony. Knew the need of a child for comfort that only a mother could give. Or the smell of perfume that was hers alone. A whisper of a kiss on the cheek as she went by or that safe feeling when being tucked in at night.

Yet despite their similarities in background, Ellen saw the world as a sparkling place while he saw it as tarnished. She seemed to bubble even in the situation they were in now. He wanted that in his life.

Moisture touched his skin. Strong, resilient Ellen was crying for two children who had lost their mothers. Chance's chest tightened. His father not caring was painful but his mother's defection was devastating. At least Ellen hadn't felt unloved. He squeezed her close as she cried. "I'm sorry about your mother too."

Minutes later she composed herself again then said, "Who would have thought we'd share something so awful?"

He kissed the top of her head. "I, for one, would prefer to remember something else we've shared."

Ellen moved to look up at him with eyes that were still misty. "Why, Dr. Freeman, I believe there might be a romantic under all that gruff and bluster."

He smiled. "Don't get that rumor started."

At least they had moved past that emotional moment but they continued to hold each for some time.

Finally Ellen asked, "Will you tell me the rest of the story now? Did your father come home then?"

"Yeah, just long enough to put me and my sister into boarding schools."

"You have a sister?"

"I do."

Ellen grabbed a shirt and pulled it on. "But you've never said anything about her."

He shrugged. "I don't really know her."

"How can you not know your sister?"

"Pretty easy when I only saw her once a year at Christmas."

"What? That's horrible."

"Maybe so, but that's the way it was."

"Still is, I gather." Ellen sounded as if she was accusing him of doing something appalling in a court of law.

He sat up and faced her. "We're just in two different worlds. She has her life and I have mine."

"So you didn't even have each other to lean on when your mother left. No wonder you have issues with women. Pushed me away," she murmured.

Chance stiffened. "Don't start analyzing me."

"It was more of an observation."

He didn't like that much better. Had Ellen seen something about him that not even he was aware of?

"Where's your father?"

"He died a couple of years ago."

"I don't know what I would have done without my father. He's been there for me all the way."

"That must be nice."

"It is, most of the time."

Chance was relieved they had moved past the subject of him. "Most of the time?"

"I told you, he tends to watch over me too much."

"I can understand a father wanting to protect you."

She chuckled. "I guess you can. You act like him sometimes."

"Is that so bad?"

"What, that you act like him? Or that he is overprotective?"

"The overprotective part." He studied her. Her hands were clasped in her lap in a ball.

"It is when you want to do more than work on the upper

east side and in a hospital for women having their faces and breasts done."

He ran his palm lightly over one of her nipples. "Which you need neither of."

Ellen caught his hand and held it. "Thank you. But I wanted to work where people needed me. Where others weren't as willing to go."

"So what made you want to do that?"

"I don't know really. I guess it was because of what my doctors and nurses meant to me."

She waited as if she were in deep thought. He knew her well enough to know she would tell all if he just had the patience to wait.

"I still stay in touch with them."

"Who?"

"My doctor and nurses. I was in the car with my mother. I was in the hospital for weeks afterwards."

"That's why you balked the first day."

"Yeah. I've not done much emergency care and it takes me a second but I come around."

"And you did. And did great."

"Thanks. But that's not what you thought then. I saw it in your eyes."

"Guilty. But tell me about your father."

"He was devastated after my mother's death. He was at the hospital with me but he was so broken he wasn't much good around me. It was the doctors and nurses who looked after me. Brought me fast food. Talked and played with a scared little girl. I decided then that I wanted to be like them.

"It took a while but my father found his way out of his grief to see me again and then all he could think about was not losing me. I understand that but it can be stifling. When I went to work at an inner-city clinic he pitched a fit and hired a bodyguard to watch over me. Let's just say there was a large discussion over that. I didn't tell him until the night before I left to come down here that I was coming. Even then I didn't tell him where. I'm sure by now he knows about the resort."

Chance was sure her father didn't know the exact spot they were in now or they would have been rescued. If he ever met her father Chance was sure there would be hell to pay. A father who worried over his daughter that deeply wouldn't like her running for her life in the jungle or sleeping with the man who was responsible for the situation. It was just as well this thing between he and Ellen would end when she left Honduras. Why did the thought gnaw at him so much?

"At least your father cares. Mine hardly knew I was alive."

"That shouldn't have happened to you. I'm surprised you became a doctor like him."

"I was good at science and math. Medicine was—is— in my DNA. But I wanted to be a very different type of person from my father. From the beginning I wanted to help the less privileged."

"You are different. I can't see you not watching over the people you love and showing you care. Look what you're doing for the people of this country."

Her conviction had Chance wanting to believe her. He gave her a kiss that had nothing to do with wanting her sexually and everything to do with appreciating her large heart and loyalty. He needed both in his life.

Chance stood. "Enough talking or you'll have me telling stories of how I misbehaved in school."

"You were a troublemaker?"

"Only until the headmaster sat me down and said a few pointed words that made me think." He reached out his hand. "How about a moonlight trip to the falls?"

"Aren't you afraid we might be seen?"

"We won't stay long. I just keep thinking about you bathing and how much I wished I'd joined you."

"With an invitation like that, how can I refuse?" She took his hand.

Ellen couldn't remember ever being this uninhibited with a man before. She let Chance remove the shirt she'd pulled on and then held his hand as they carefully stepped over the rocks and into the falls under the full moon.

The ache in her leg had been forgotten as Chance had turned her mind toward what he'd been doing to her body. Then her entire attention had been focused on what he'd been saying. She was surprised by how open he'd been that she'd hung on each of his words.

Now there was an aching throb in her calf but as Chance pulled her under the falls it was eclipsed by the touch of his hands running over her waist and hips. She threw her head back and let the water wash through her hair as he kissed her shoulder and cupped her breasts.

There was something wanton, liberating, almost wicked about standing out in the middle of the world with no clothes on as a man loved her body. A tingle in her center grew to a pounding as blood flowed hot within her. She was a siren calling to her mate.

Her hands skimmed over Chance's wet arms and down his back as he kissed the outside of one breast. As he stood there she pushed his hair away from his face. His manhood, thick and tall, found the V of her legs as his mouth came to hers. His hands cupped her butt and lifted. She circled his hips with her legs. Chance shoved once and completely entered her. She held tightly to his shoulders. He eased away and pushed forward. She shuttered. He plunged deeper and joined her in the pleasure.

Chance released her, letting her slid down his wet body. He kissed her deeply then led her out of the falls and over the rocks. "As much as I'm enjoying your body, we need to get some sleep. We still have a day of walking tomorrow. We aren't out of danger yet."

"Boy, you have a way of putting a damper on the afterglow."

He gave her a quick kiss as they returned to their hiding place. "I'll do better next time but I want us to make it to the next time." Picking up a few sticks, he put them on the fire, which had turned to coals. "We need to dry off and get some sleep. As much as I hate to say this, we should sleep in our clothes in case we need to make a quick getaway."

Ellen picked up her underwear and began putting them on. "Is that your way of telling me you've seen all of my body you want to?"

Chance stepped to her and tipped her chin up with a finger. "I could never get enough of looking at your body."

Warmth went through her, settling in her heart. She wanted this moment, this feeling between them, always.

CHAPTER EIGHT

CHANCE WOKE. HE was hot. Too hot. On the side where Ellen rested. She was running a fever.

She groaned and sat up. Her eyes were red and face flushed. Little beads of sweat lined her upper lip.

Chance touched her cheek and confirmed what he already knew. This wasn't good. They already had a day's worth of travel ahead but with her sick it would slow them down.

"I don't feel well."

"I'm not surprised. You're running a pretty high fever. I'll check it in a minute. Do you hurt somewhere?" If they were lucky it was an intestinal problem from the food or lack of it.

"My leg."

He searched her face. "Your leg?"

"Something bit me yesterday when you were stealing clothes."

"Why didn't you say something?" She should have told him, especially after the number of bite cases they'd seen at the clinic. She knew better than to let something like that wait. Panic started to clench his gut.

"Show me."

"Can I have a drink of water first?" She lay back on the blanket.

Ellen was already too weak to sit up for any length of time. Chance picked up a bottle. Going down on one knee, he put an arm around her shoulders and supported her. Slowly she drank.

"Can I sleep a little longer?"

"Sure, sweetheart. Sleep while I look at your leg. Which one is it?"

Ellen stretched out her right leg. "Calf."

Chance pushed up the leg of her pants to reveal a large angry place that covered her calf from the back of her knee to her ankle. In the center there was a boil surrounded by deep purple. His heart constricted. Ellen should be in a hospital. Even if he lanced it the risk of infection was too great and she truly couldn't walk then.

"I wish you had said something." He wanted to shake her and hug her at the same time. They had little water, no food, and now Ellen was seriously sick. His concern for them getting out of this mess today had escalated a hundred percent.

"I was going to, but I was busy doing other things last night." There was humor in her voice.

"We were both thinking of other things last night."

Now he carried that burden of guilt. He should have stayed focused on their problem; instead he had been satisfying his need for her. That was another issue. He wasn't satisfied. Not by a long shot. But he wouldn't be misdirected by his desire again. It could mean Ellen's life and he couldn't abide anything more happening to her. He had to get them out of this new situation and Ellen safely home.

She started to rise.

"Stay put. I'm going to give you a quick exam. Then we'll need to get moving." Chance pulled his bag closer and removed his stethoscope then the thermometer. "Let's see how high your fever is while I'm giving you a good listen."

Her grin was weak as she said, "I like the good things you give me."

How like Ellen to speak frankly, even about a night of passion. He kissed her forehead. "I enjoyed it too. Now stop distracting me and let me see how you're doing."

"I'm distracting you?"

"Sweetheart, you've been distracting me for weeks." Chance placed the stethoscope on her chest. Her heartbeat was steady, which was encouraging. He checked her pulse and blood pressure. They were up a little bit. Removing the thermometer, he wasn't pleased. He searched his med bag and found a bottle of aspirin. It wouldn't do much for the fever but it was better than nothing.

"Do you think you're up for some walking?" He was sure she wasn't but they really had no choice but to get moving. She wouldn't last another day in the heat and rain with that leg.

"Sure."

He didn't expect her to say anything different.

"Could I have that half of a bar now instead of later?"

"That's a great idea. We'll share it for breakfast. I also want you to take a couple of aspirin for me." He handed her the bar, medicine and set a bottle of water down beside her.

They ate in silence.

Done with her bar, Ellen said, "I'm sorry, but I'm going to need your help with my boot."

Chance assisted her with getting the boot on her foot but could only lace it up loosely around her calf. He was afraid that before the day was over she would be in real pain.

When they were done, he packed the bags except for

the rag the boy had placed the food in. He pulled the strap of his bag over his chest and shrugged into the backpack.

"What're you doing?" Ellen stood beside him. "I'll carry the backpack. That's my job."

"Today you get a day off. Come on, let's get going."

They headed out from behind the falls. Chance stopped a few times to make sure no one else was around.

When they came to the pool, he dipped the rag into the water, wetting it thoroughly, then wrung it out. "Ellen, come here." She stepped closer to him. He wrapped the rag around her head. "This'll help keep you cooler."

Her gaze found his. "Thank you. You're a good person, Chance Freeman."

Coming from her, the simple compliment sounded like he was receiving a great honor in front of thousands. He brushed her lips with his. "You're quite a woman yourself, Ellen Cox."

Chance set a slower pace than he had the days before but even then Ellen was lagging behind. What had at first been a slow walk had now turned into one that included a limp. They stopped often to rest but that didn't seem to give her any more energy. With each stop he wet the rag and retied it across her forehead.

Her fever eased at one point but by midmorning it had returned with a vengeance. He was going to have to find another way to get them to Saba sooner rather than later. Ellen couldn't continue the way she was going. During one of their rests he'd looked at her leg. It was more inflamed than before. Walking hadn't helped.

It hurt him to see her in pain. Yet she still didn't complain.

"Chance, I'm sorry I got us into this and now I'm holding us up."

"For starters, you didn't get us into this. I agreed to see the boy's father. I knew the risks. That's all on me. As for your leg, yes, you should have told me sooner but there isn't much more we could have done. You didn't get bitten on purpose. So enough of that kind of talk."

"My, you are being all noble. But, then, that's who you are."

She made the statement sound as if she knew few people who were noble and admired him for it. He liked having Ellen think he was someone special.

By noon, he had to walk beside her while she leaned on him in order for her to move. Each time her injured leg touched the ground she winced. They had stopped again to rest when Chance said, "I'm going to have to carry you."

Thankfully the land had flattened out. The river was wider and slower, letting him know that were getting close to the coast.

Ellen shook her head. "How long would you last, doing that in this heat? Leave me and go for help."

"What?" She'd been terrified when he been gone for only minutes. He couldn't leave her with a dangerously high fever out in the jungle alone. "No way. We're in this together."

"I could never forgive myself if something happened to you because of me."

Chance cupped her face. "I think that's my line. Now, let's not talk about it any more. We're going to try you riding on my back for a while."

"Okay, but you let me have the packs."

He removed them and helped her on with them.

"Okay, you ready?" He squatted so she could reach around his neck.

She did so. Her heat seeped through his shirt. He wrapped his arms under her thighs and lifted her on his back as he stood. Chance started down the path. It wasn't an easy trek but it was far better than seeing Ellen's misery. They made it further than Chance had thought they would before he had to rest. Ellen could hardly keep her eyes open she was so consumed by fever. He had to find help soon or she would be in real danger of having lasting side effects.

"It's time to go again." She offered little help getting on his back. The fever was taking her energy.

Again Chance trudged down the path. There wasn't a dry stitch of clothes on either one of them. Sweat poured from where their bodies met. He leaned forward so that Ellen rested on his back more than held on. She'd long ago become heavier and her arms more relaxed. Had she passed out?

The river now stretched out more like a placid lake. High grass grew on each side of the path. The jungle was far off to the sides, affording them little protection. The only plan Chance had for them finding cover was to go into the grass and lie down, hoping they weren't seen. He'd reached the point that he needed someone to see them. It would be an opportunity to get help for Ellen.

With an amount of relief he hadn't known it was possible to feel, he heard the sounds of life carried over the water. There must be a village close by. He took Ellen to a spot far enough off the path that he believed she would be safe. He then eased her from his back and to the ground. There was no argument. She was unconscious. At least she wasn't feeling any pain.

He removed the packs and placed his under her head. Checking her pulse, he was glad to find that it was strong but she burned with fever. He pulled a bottle out and poured a few drops of water into her mouth. Watching her swallow, he gave her some more. He then drank a mouthful, leaving the bottle beside her in case she woke.

Kissing her on the forehead, he headed back to the path at almost a run. He hated leaving Ellen by herself but at least she was unaware he was doing so. That way she wouldn't fear being left alone.

When he reached the river he continued his pace along the path. After a couple of turns he came to a village of stilted homes built out over the water. These were much nicer dwellings constructed of finer material than those he had seen before. Still small, they appeared as if they might have more than one room.

Boats were tied below a number of them. Maybe he could find someone to take him and Ellen downriver. He continued running. A couple of children played in a bare spot at the bottom of a ladder to one of the huts. They chattered when they saw him and a woman stepped out onto the porch. Raising a hand to her forehead as if blocking the sun, she watched him approach.

Chance slowed his pace to a jog. He didn't want to scare away any aid he might find. "I need help," he called in Spanish. "A woman is sick."

A couple of other villagers exited their huts.

"I'm a doctor. I need to borrow a boat."

A young man joined the children as if in protective mode.

Chance stopped before he got too close to the first hut. "I have a sick woman with me. We need to get to Saba. I can pay for the boat. I'm Dr. Chance Freeman. I work with the Traveling Clinic out of La Ceiba."

Hopefully they had heard of the clinic. Maybe someone they knew had come to it.

The young man spoke up. "I know of it."

"Can you help me?" There was desperation in every word. Chance would get down on his knees and beg if he had to. All his fear was for Ellen. Her life. Had she woken? Found herself alone? He'd promised not to leave her again, yet he had. "Will you take me downriver to Saba?"

The young man looked around at the women then back at Chance. "I have no boat."

"What about these?" Chance waved his hand in the direction of the boats under the huts.

"Not mine."

The woman standing above them said, "Take my husband's. But you better return it."

"Come," the young man said, and headed toward the boat under the hut.

He didn't have to ask Chance twice. The man untied the boat and held it. The craft reminded Chance of a canoe with a flat bottom. There were no benches to sit on so he took a seat on the planks. The vessel seemed water-worthy enough but at this point it didn't matter. He needed to get back to Ellen. The man pushed away from shore, using a long-handled narrow paddle.

"We must go upstream, two bends in the path." Chance pointed in the direction he wanted them to go.

The man nodded and pushed against the bottom of the shallow riverbed, turning the boat so that Chance sat in the front. They headed upstream. Keeping the boat close to the shore, the man maneuvered them toward Ellen's hiding place. Even with the regular flap-flap of the water against the hull, they weren't moving fast enough for Chance. Worry circled like a wild animal in him.

"Here." Chance pointed to the shore. "Stop here."

The man directed the boat to land and it had hardly hit when Chance stepped out. He didn't wait on the man before he found the path along the river and backtracked to where Ellen waited. Running through the grass, he found her where he had left her. She looked as if she hadn't moved.

He went down beside her and lifted her head to his thigh. "Sweetheart. Wake up."

"You left me."

Great. If he didn't already feel horrible.

"I did but I'm back now. I found a boat and someone to take us to Saba."

"Good. I'm looking forward to sleeping in a bed with you."

"That sounds wonderful to me too but right now we need to get you to a hospital."

The young man arrived and looked down on them with curiosity.

Chance scooped Ellen into his arms. Her head rested against his chest. Even in the tropical weather he could tell her fever was still running high. "Please get the packs," he said to the man. Chance didn't wait to see if he did as he had asked. His concern was for getting Ellen to medical care as soon as possible, even if he had to steal the boat.

It wasn't an issue. The man passed him and Ellen on the path and was waiting at the boat when they arrived. Chance laid Ellen in the bottom then climbed in and sat behind her, situating her head against his thigh.

She sighed and closed her eyes. The man pushed the boat out into the river. Soon they were in the main channel.

"How long to Saba?" Chance asked over his shoulder.

"Dark. Maybe sooner."

Chance wasn't pleased with the answer. That was three or four hours away. He brushed Ellen's hair back from her forehead. She mumbled something unintelligible. Her soft skin was damaged from the sun, her lips parched and swollen. She was dehydrated. The list could go on and on.

Her hand found his and held it against her cheek. "I'll be fine."

Chance kissed the top of her head. "Sure you will." He wouldn't allow himself to think otherwise.

What in her made her so tough? It had to have been when she had been trapped in the wreck with her mother.

She'd known pain on a physical and emotional level that most people never experienced. How long had they waited for help? What had the pain been like as she'd healed? For her, this bug bite wasn't unendurable. She'd learned early in life what she could withstand.

He'd been playing her protector when Ellen was already a survivor.

Chance looked down into her beautiful face. She had the strength that it took to live and work here. Ellen didn't give up, she persevered. She wasn't a quitter. When she made a commitment it was forever. Could he open his heart enough to accept that?

If Ellen died Chance was afraid he would too. Despite what he had already lost in the world, his family, his wife, Ellen would be the greatest loss. When had she cracked through that wall and stepped into his heart? Had it been when she'd pulled out that hot pink nail polish, or stood up to him about his feelings for her, or her determination to care for a patient? Whenever it had been, she'd done it. He'd fallen for her.

The knowledge didn't make him feel better. He looked down at Ellen again. She just couldn't die now that he'd found someone who he knew with all his heart would stand by him the rest of his life.

Over the next few hours he bathed her head, neck and chest with the wet cloth, hoping he could keep the fever at bay. He did manage to get some water down her. But she needed so much care that he didn't have available. Even unconscious most of the time, she clutched his hand.

The sun was low in the sky when the man said, "Saba."

Relief washed through Chance. They were finally back in civilization.

"Help's not far away, sweetheart." He brushed a damp strand of hair away from Ellen's face. "We'll have you in a hospital soon."

Ahead Chance saw a high, modern bridge spanning the river. He'd heard of it but had never seen it. It was a major thoroughfare over the river and to the coast. And an answer to his prayers.

"I stop," the young man said as he pulled over to a pier. "Water too low past here."

Chance stepped out of the boat with Ellen in his arms and with the help of the man. "Thank you. I hope I'm able to repay you one day," Chance said, then hurried toward land.

He searched the area. Now he had to find a phone to call for help or someone to take them to the hospital. Determination and anxiety mixed, becoming a lump in his chest.

Chance hurried up a wide path with low green vegetation on each side toward houses. The path turned into a hard-packed dirt road wide enough for two cars. The houses lining the road were square and made of cinder block and plaster with only man-sized alleys between them. Chairs sat outside many of them.

Wasn't someone around?

The boy of about ten played in the street up ahead. "Help. Hospital."

Eyes going wide, the boy looked at him then ran into a nearby house.

He had to look like someone straight out of the child's bad dreams. With three days of growth on his face, his clothes dirty and smelly, and holding a woman burning with fever in his arms, he must look horrible.

A heavy woman appeared in the door of the house the child had run into.

Hope swelled. "Please help me. I have a sick woman. I need a phone or a way to the hospital."

"No phone. The boy will take you to someone who can help."

The boy was already headed up the street. Chance lifted Ellen more securely against his chest and followed. They walked a block and the boy ran up to a man talking to a group of other men. He pulled on the man's arm. The boy pointed to them. The man stepped away from the group and came toward Chance.

"I need a hospital. Do you have a phone? A car?"

"Car. Come this way." The man directed Chance toward a rusty and dented old sedan. Chance had never been so glad to see anything in his life. Opening the back door, the man then moved away so that Chance could place Ellen inside.

She opened her eyes for a second. "Where are we?"

"In Saba and on our way to the hospital, sweetheart."

"I like sweetheart."

Chance couldn't help but smile. "Good. I like calling you that."

As ill and in pain as Ellen must be, she still had a positive attitude. She'd told him she was tougher than she looked and she was right. Her life hadn't always been easy but she'd managed to find humor and wonder in it.

Convinced by his first impression and his past prejudice that she was weak and needy, he'd learned through this ordeal she was actually the stronger one of the two of them. He'd not been pushing her away for her good but his. What if he pursued a relationship and she rejected him? Would he survive the loss? Would he regret it more if he didn't try?

"No hospital close by," the man said.

Chance was afraid of that. "Where?"

"San Pedro Sula." The man glanced at Ellen. "I take there."

That hope started to build again. Chance had never been there before but that didn't matter. Ellen needed care.

They bounced over rocks and through ditches as the

car rattled up the unpaved street. The going was excruciatingly slow for Chance but they were moving toward help for Ellen. He was sitting in the back, with her head resting in his lap. Checking her vitals for the second time since they had left the boat, he was terrified by what he found. Her heart rate was becoming irregular. Her blood pressure was very high as well as her fever.

He looked up when the tires of the car hit pavement and his teeth quit knocking together. The car picked up speed and they were soon rolling over the high bridge that Chance had seen from the river.

"How far?"

"Thirty minutes," the man called back over his shoulder.

Did Ellen have that kind of time? Ellen started mumbling, throwing her head back and forth. She was delirious.

Guilt flooded him. Chance had never felt more helpless in his life. Here he was a doctor and he couldn't even help Ellen. He should have put her on a plane straight home the minute he'd seen her. This country and the type of work the clinic did was too dangerous. She should be someplace less demanding.

They left the city and drove along the highway into a less populated area. The hot wind coming through the open windows did nothing to make him feel more comfortable. They sped down the road but it wasn't fast enough for Chance. Houses started showing up again as they approached what he desperately hoped was San Pedro Sula.

The man pulled off the highway and made a few turns until he entered the drive of a pink sprawling building with a flat roof. Instead of stopping in front of it, he drove under the awning with the word *Emergencia* on the sign.

As the car came to a stop, Chance opened the door. He

lifted Ellen into his arms and headed for the glass doors. As he came to a desk he said, "I'm Dr. Freeman. This woman needs medical attention now."

A nurse in a white dress came toward him with concern on her face. "This way."

Chance followed her down a hallway to an exam room that looked like something out of the nineteen-fifties, but it appeared clean and adequate. Beggars couldn't be choosers and he was glad to have anything that would offer Ellen a chance to live.

He placed Ellen on the examination table. "I need a suture kit. An IV set up. Any penicillin-based medicine you have. *Stat*." He started unlacing Ellen's boot.

The nurse stood there stunned.

A man in a white lab coat came into the room. "Who are you and what are you doing in my ER?"

"Dr. Freeman, of the Traveling Clinic. My friend needs medical attention. She has been bitten by a spider. Her fever is high. Blood pressure up and her heart rate irregular. She is dehydrated, hasn't eaten in three days and sunburned."

The doctor said something to the nurse but Chance paid no attention to their conversation.

Chance was done explaining himself. He had Ellen to see about and no one was going to prevent him from doing so. After removing her boot and sock, he asked the nurse for scissors and she handed them to him. Without hesitating, Chance started cutting away Ellen's pants leg. His lips tightened when he saw her wound. There was no way she wasn't in extreme pain.

"Help me roll her to her stomach." He didn't speak to anyone in particular but the doctor came forward to assist him. Together they settled Ellen so that Chance could see the wound clearly.

What he needed to clean the wound showed up on the

table beside Ellen. It wasn't the sterilized plastic covered prepackaged set-up he normally used but he was glad to see the instruments. Over the next hour he opened and cleaned the wound. While he was busy the nurse took care of starting an IV. As he worked, he checked to make sure it was done to his satisfaction.

Chance began preparing to bandage the wound when the Honduran doctor said, "The nurse will take care of that. It's time you tell me what's been going on and for you to be examined."

The idea of arguing with the doctor crossed Chance's mind but by the determined look on the man's face it wouldn't make a difference. "Agreed. But I need to make a phone call first."

Ellen's eyes flickered open. For once her leg wasn't screaming with pain, taking her to the point of tears. The last thing she remembered was Chance carrying her piggyback.

She looked around the room. It was a simple one with white walls and very few furnishings. A hospital room? It reminded her of the black and white pictures on the history wall of the hospital where she'd done her fellowship. Her gaze came to rest on a sleeping Chance leaning back in a chair far too small for him. Clean-shaven and dressed in clothes that were probably borrowed, he looked wonderful.

When he woke would he gather her in his arms? She wanted that. Desperately.

They were out of the jungle. Safe. He hadn't been hurt. She was alive. They had shared something special. Did he feel the same way? By all his actions he must. He had cared for her tenderly. She remembered him brushing her hair back. Speaking to her encouragingly. Begging her to hang in there until he found help.

But wouldn't he have done that for anyone? Chance was a dedicated doctor.

He'd said no promises. Had never spoken of tomorrow other than when they were going to get out of the jungle.

Chance stirred. He blinked.

"Hey." Her voice was little more than a whisper.

He sat forward. Urgency filled his voice as he asked, "How're you feeling?"

No sweetheart. She wanted to hear him say sweetheart. "Better. Thanks for saving my life."

He shrugged. "I'm just sorry you had to go through that."

Fear built, swirling around her. Why didn't he touch her? Kiss her? Had something changed? She fiddled with the hem of the bedsheet. "I think we both went through it."

"You got the worse end of things." He stood.

Why didn't he come closer? Chance walked across the small space. He looked at her.

"It couldn't have been great fun carrying me around on your back." She paused. "Tell me what happened after I passed out."

He relayed what she was sure were the highlights and little of the drama that had gone into getting her to safety. "Where are we?"

"San Pedro Sula for now." He turned and paced the other direction.

They were interrupted by a nurse entering. She spoke to Chance. "We are ready."

"Ready for what?" Ellen asked.

Now he looked at her. "I called your father. He has sent a plane for you."

Ellen sat up in bed. "You what? You had no right to make that kind of decision for me." Her head swam and she leaned back.

"You need attention that can't be given here. It's my

responsibly to see about you. You should be in a hospital in the US and checked out completely. Your body has been through a major ordeal. You need to be seen by a cardiologist."

"I don't need you to see about me. I'm a grown woman who can make her own decisions."

"Yeah, and see where that got you." He moved across the room again.

"It could have been you instead of me who was bitten."

He gave her a pointed look. "But it wasn't."

"What about you? Are you coming? You went through the same ordeal."

"The doctor here checked me out."

"But I'm feeling better." She was weak but she wouldn't admit how much.

"You've been out of your head for most of two days. You need to go home and get healthy."

"When will I see you again?" Ellen reached out a hand. She saw the hesitation in his face before he walked over and took it. His hand was large, warm and safe. She never wanted to let it go.

"I don't know for sure."

"You're running now. Just like you did when you came down here."

"What're you talking about? I'm not running anywhere."

"You're running away from me. You can't hide here forever, you know. One day you're going to have to face the fact that you have to take a gamble on someone again. We aren't all like your mother and your ex-wife. Some of us can be loyal."

He pulled his hand away. "This is not the time or the place to be having this conversation. You don't need to get upset."

Ellen wanted to snatch his hand back but he'd crammed

both in his pockets. She didn't care about anything but him. This was her heart on the line. "Okay, if we don't talk about it now, then when?"

He looked toward the wall instead of at her. "I don't know."

"See, there it is. You're shutting me out."

Chance's look met hers. He growled, "I'm not! I'm thinking about your safety. You could have been killed out there."

"I'm a big girl. I make my own decisions. Can take what comes my way."

"And down here those decisions can get people killed. Get you hurt."

"What're you trying to say?"

"That in your fight for freedom you can be reckless. Can get people hurt. Get yourself hurt. Sometimes you need to think before you act. You go all in, heart leading. No wonder your father feels the need to shelter you."

If she didn't feel so awful she'd climb out of the bed and stomp her foot. "That's not fair."

Two men that looked like orderlies entered with a squeaking gurney. She and Chance said no more as the men settled her on it. They wheeled her from the room and down the hall. Chance walked at her feet.

As they lifted her into the ambulance Chance said, "It's for your own good."

Her gaze remained locked with his as the attendants pushed the doors together. "I don't need you to protect me, I need you to love me."

The doors clicked closed. Ellen held a sob threatening to escape.

The nurse that was riding with her patted her shoulder. "The doctor must care a great deal to sit by your bed for two days and nights."

If only he would admit it.

CHAPTER NINE

CHANCE HAD BEEN miserable before. But never on this level. He missed Ellen with a vengeance. Everything that happened at the clinic reminded him of her. Each child they saw he imagined Ellen teasing a smile out of him or her. Anytime an unusual case came in he wanted to discuss it with her.

The nights were the worst. He wanted Ellen in his arms. All he had to do was look at his hammock on his porch and think of those moments they had spent there. Taking a shower became something to dread instead of something to look forward to at the end of a long hot day. It reminded him too much of standing in the falls with Ellen.

How had she managed to fill all the cracks in his life to the point he almost needed her to breathe?

His staff had taken to not asking him anything unless it was medically related. He'd given the bare minimum of information about Ellen's and his time on the run. But beyond that he didn't want to talk about the fear, guilt and relief he'd suffered through over the three days they had been in the jungle and, worse, those when she had been so sick. He certainly didn't want to discuss those intense life-changing moments when he and Ellen had made love.

Love. That had been such an elusive emotion in his life

he would have sworn he had no idea what it was. Then in had waltzed Dr. Ellen Cox. Bright smile, infallible attitude, and fortitude that could withstand the worst situation. And it had. He needed someone in his life like that, but did she need someone in hers like him?

A guy who felt he had nothing to offer her. One who chose to work in a developing country. A dangerous one. With Ellen's background, would she really be content to live and work here with him? She had seemed to love it when she was here as much as he did. Would she feel the same way after she fully recovered?

Anticipation and insecurity hit him at the same time. He'd given up on having a wife, really caring for someone, long ago. But Ellen had him thinking *Can I?* again.

She deserved someone who could sustain an ongoing relationship. He'd not ever managed to do so. Was it possible for him? History said no. Could he learn? The real question was that if he wanted Ellen, was he willing to try?

She'd been disappointed in him when she'd found out he had a sister that he didn't stay in contact with. Maybe he should start there. Would Abigail be interested in seeing him? Could they be a family after all these years? Did they even have anything in common outside being from the same dysfunctional family? Every fiber in his being said Ellen would be pleased to know he'd tried. That alone was enough reason to make an effort. But something deep inside him was screaming for him to do it for himself as well. See if he could handle a relationship.

Ellen wiped her cheek and declared she'd shed her last tear over Chance Freeman. She'd not heard anything from him in the six weeks since she had been home. Not a word.

She was cycling though the steps of grief and she was firmly on anger. As far as she was concerned, she could stay on that emotion for a long time. If she saw him now it might be dangerous for him.

Michael had called and invited her out to lunch the Saturday after Thanksgiving. She had been tickled to see him. He'd filled her in on what had been going on with the clinic and had told her a few funny stories about the patients but that was about it. She was hungry for information about Chance but the only thing Michael had said was that he would be home during the Christmas holidays.

How could Chance act this way after what they had shared in the jungle? After she had exposed her heart? Had she misjudged the type of person Chance was? Keeping the resentment at bay was difficult. Even when her mother had died she hadn't felt this abandoned. She hadn't had a choice. Chance did. If anyone should know how she was feeling it should be him. So why didn't he care enough to do something about it?

When he did come to the States, would he call her? Ask to see her? How could a man be so smart yet so dense? She clenched her teeth, almost as angry with herself for caring as she was with Chance.

That went for her father as well. He'd been harping on at her for weeks to take a job at the big teaching hospital in the city. He'd even had one of his buddies call and put in a good word for her. Today was the day that they had the talk that was long overdue.

She had given her apartment up when she'd left for Honduras so her father had insisted that she stay with him until she figured out what she was going to do next. That wasn't a question. She already knew what she was going to do. Return to Honduras, and if not there then someplace that really needed her.

Her father had had a fit when she had announced the week before that she was on the schedule at the clinic where she had worked in the city. The conversation had gone something like, you could have been killed, you are lucky to be alive, you should be grateful, you need to think about what you are doing. She didn't expect today's discussion to go much better but what she had to say needed to be said.

Chance had accused her of being reckless. She'd never thought of herself that way. Her father had put her in a box of protection that she had wanted to get out of but which had made her take chances. When her mother had died she'd learned at a young age that life was short, but had she really become irresponsible with her decisions?

The last thing she wanted to do was put anyone in danger. She knew from her and her mother's accident that poor decisions could cause horrible outcomes. Did she get so caught up in what she wanted that she didn't think about others? Had she been reckless where Chance was concerned?

She'd made reservations at her and her father's favorite café and arrived early enough that she had gotten them a table in the back. Despite the hustle and bustle of Christmas shoppers stopping for a break, they would have a quiet place to talk.

"How're you feeling?" her father asked, after he'd kissed her and taken his seat.

He was a large, burly man who looked out of place in a suit despite having worn one most of his life. Ellen liked nothing better than being pulled into one of his bear hugs. They had never had a real disagreement until she had informed him she was going to Honduras. She had not left on good terms and had returned to him telling her he'd told her so. Today's conversation wouldn't be an easy one.

"Much better. I'm not having to sit down as often at work as I did the first few days."

"You went through some ordeal. Dr. Freeman didn't

tell me a lot but from the look of you when you got to the plane you had been close to death."

Her father had come for her himself. Had even brought their private doctor with him.

The waitress came to their table for their order.

"I'll have afternoon tea," Ellen told her.

"I'll have the same," her father said. As the waitress moved away he continued, "I don't know what I would've done if I had lost you. It isn't fair to put me through something like that. Sometimes you're so like your mother."

There it was. The guilt. Had her mother really been reckless or just enjoying life? Even if Ellen was like her mother, her feelings and desires had merit. She deserved to live her own life.

"I'm sorry. Maybe I do need to be more careful but that doesn't mean I need to give up my dreams just to make you happy."

She had to make it clear she wasn't going to live in a bubble just for him. That she needed his love and support but not at the cost of what she wanted. She'd learned life was too short for that. More recently, and in the past.

"Dad, it didn't happen to you. I was the one who had the reaction to the spider bite."

"Yes, but I was the one scared to death that I might lose you."

What little she could remember about Chance after she'd become sick, he had been scared too but he had still praised her for her strength, encouraged her to keep going. He'd been concerned about her but had never wanted to hold her back. Her father wanted to do just that.

"Yeah, it was pretty frightening in parts. But I'm here."

"And that's where I want you to stay."

"That's what I want to talk to you about."

His bushy brows rose.

"Daddy, I'm going back to Honduras if the clinic will

have me. If not, then I'll go to another Central American country to work."

Her father's palm slapped on the table, rattling the silverware. "Haven't you had enough? After what happened to you?"

"Daddy, I know you love me. I know I'm all you have. But this is something I'm compelled to do. I'm grown, heaven's sake I'm a doctor. I'm needed there. I wished you would understand but if you don't, that is fine. I have to go anyway."

Her father studied her. "Does this have something to do with Dr. Freeman?"

She looked away. "Some, but not all."

"That's what I thought. I had him checked out. He's known for having women falling for him."

Her chest tightened. She could understand why. She certainly had. "That may be so but that doesn't mean he doesn't do good work. That the Traveling Clinic doesn't have value."

"There's plenty of work you can do here. Of value. Did you even talk to the hospital about the job?"

"Daddy, I'm not going to. That's not where I belong."

The waitress returned with their tea. They sat quietly until she had finished placing the tea stand in front of them and left.

"I love you, Daddy. I do, but I have to be true to myself. I know you have lost. I have too. I miss Mother every day. I know you worry about me. You've worked to protect me. But you can't do that forever. I'll get hurt. Bad things will happen to me. That's life. What I need is your support. Encouragement."

Her father ate without saying anything. He finally looked at her. His eyes glistened. The last time she'd seen him close to tears had been when he'd sat beside her bed in the hospital and had had to tell her that her mother had died.

"I love you dearly. The only thing I've ever wanted to do was keep you safe. See that you were cared for."

"You have."

"I do support you. Want the best for you, but you can't stop me from worrying about you."

She placed her hand on his arm. "I know and I love you for it."

For the rest of their time together they talked about their plans for Christmas and what gifts they might like to receive. They were pulling on their coats to go out into the snowy weather when Ellen asked, "Dad, have you ever thought about dating? You're still a young man."

Those brows of his rose again. "What brought that on?"

She tugged at his lapel, lifting in around his neck. "I just think that everyone should share their life with some-one who cares about them. You've concentrated on me long enough. It's time for you to live."

"Have you found someone you want to share your life with?"

"I thought I had."

Her father kissed her forehead and tucked her arm though his. "One thing I've learned in this life is that anything can happen."

Did she dare hope?

She returned to her father's penthouse to prepare for her shift at the clinic that evening. An envelope lay wait-ing on the table in the hall with her name on it. Inside was an invitation to a gala event to benefit the Honduras Traveling Clinic.

Would Chance attend? Did she care if he did?

Chance had been in the States a week. There had been meetings at the foundation and a couple of speaking engagements. Ellen constantly called to him. If he went to her would she even speak to him after so much time had passed? She had to be mad. He couldn't blame her.

He'd kept tabs on how she was doing. Once he had called and spoken to her father. Not known for being easily intimidated, Chance's conversation with Mr. Cox had been an uneasy one. He was a man who loved his daughter deeply and Chance had put her in danger. It wasn't something her father was going to forgive quickly. Their discussion had been to the point but Chance had learned what his heart so desperately wanted to know. Ellen was doing well. Had recovered. For that Chance would be forever grateful.

He also checked up on her through Michael. He had seen her at Thanksgiving and Chance was jealous. What he wouldn't give to just see her for a second. Make sure for himself she was fine.

When Michael had returned he'd had enough compassion for Chance that he hadn't made him ask about Ellen. Michael had offered right off that he'd had lunch with Ellen.

"She's back at work at the same inner-city clinic she was at before she came down here." Michael had spoken to everyone at the dinner table but had given Chance a pointed look. "Says she coming back here or another Central American country as soon as the doctor gives her a complete release. Which should be soon."

Karen spoke up. "We sure could use her here."

In more ways than one. Chance ached with the need to touch her, hold her. See her smile.

"You should talk to her when we you go to the States next week, Chance. Get her to consider coming back here," Pete added.

"Yes, you should speak to her," Michael stated. "She asked how everyone is doing."

Michael looked at him again. There was a deeper meaning to his words, he was sure.

Would Ellen really want to see him? He'd done the one thing that could destroy her trust.

Called her father. She'd said she wanted his love. Could he give it? Take a chance on her leaving him? Maybe she had changed her mind. After all, their relationship had been during a fight for life. They'd been emotionally strung out. Had what she'd said about wanting love been in the heat of the moment?

What Ellen had done was make him determined to contact his sister. See if he could repair that bridge. He'd put off seeing her long enough. Gripping the phone with a knot in his throat, he remembered what they'd said to each other at their father's funeral. She'd invited him to their father's house for the will reading. Chance had had no interest in ever going there again. He'd told her she could have the house and everything else, that he only wanted the cabin. It was about two hours away and gave him a home base when he was in country.

"But you'll keep in touch, won't you? I would like to know how you are doing."

Chance had just nodded, making no commitment. She'd called him a few times but when he'd not returned them the calls had become fewer then died away. His sister had left him too. Or was it more like he'd pushed her way? Had he done the same with Ellen?

The phone rang almost long enough that Chance thought he had a reprieve. Just as he was preparing to hang up a woman answered.

"May I speak to Abigail? Tell her it's Chance."

"Chance?" The sound of disbelief had him regretting so many things he'd left undone and unsaid.

"Abigail?"

"Yes."

"I'm in town until after the Christmas holidays and I was wondering if you would like to have lunch?"

The pause was so long that he was afraid she might have hung up. Then there was a sniffle on the other end of the line. "Why don't you come here for dinner? Tomorrow night at six."

"Okay, I'll be there."

Chance drove up the drive to the large Tudor-style home built among the trees in an affluent neighborhood. This was his childhood home. There were few happy memories here for him.

He stood outside the front door for a minute before he knocked. As if she was standing behind it, waiting for him, the door opened and Abigail reached out and took him in her arms. "It's about time, Chance-man."

That had been her nickname for him growing up. He forgotten about it.

"It's about time." Now she was using that big-sister reprimand voice.

"I know. I should have come before."

She pulled him into the house and closed the door. Her husband and children waited in the hall. The excitement in her voice couldn't be denied. "Stan, Chance is here. Wendy and Jonathan."

Chance was caught up in a whirlwind of hugs and hellos. What had he missed all these years?

Dinner was served in the same room where dinner had been served when his father had come home but this time it wasn't a meeting of a family that was unsure of each other but of one glad to see each other. Chance hadn't enjoyed a meal more since Ellen had left.

To his great surprise, his sister knew about his work and the family had numerous questions about the Travelling Clinic and Honduras. The discussion was open and frank, with none of the tension he'd expected.

As the kitchen help began clearing the table, Abigail suggested they have coffee in the other room. The living room was the same place but the furniture had been replaced with a more modern version. What really held Chance's attention were the pictures. They were of the smiling and happy group of people who now lived in the house. There were even a couple of pictures of him and Abigail as children. Here he had been part of a family and hadn't even known it. Abigail had not abandoned him.

Her husband and children joined them for a while but slowly drifted away as if they were giving him and Abigail a chance to talk.

"Chance, I'm so glad you are here. I have missed you."

"I've missed you too." To his amazement he meant it.

"I'm sorry we've been so distant for so long. I wished it had been different."

He did too, but couldn't admit it out loud.

"I should have done better as the older sister in keeping in touch. I shouldn't have given up. You are my family."

She had cared. Abigail had carried a burden as well. "There wasn't anything you could have done. That was on me."

"When you came home from school at Christmas you were so different. I couldn't seem to reach you any more. After Daddy died you just never came around again. It was like you blamed me as well as Dad for sending you away."

He had. His mother had been gone. His father hadn't wanted him and his sister had said she couldn't take him. There had been nothing secure in his life and he'd wanted nothing to do with her betrayal.

"I wish I could have made it different for you. Fixed it so you could stay with me, but Daddy would have none of it. He said I was too young to see about you and that you were going to learn to behave. That sending you off to school was the way to do it. I fought for you but he wouldn't let you stay."

All this time Chance had believed she hadn't wanted him around. Had blamed her.

"Those weren't happy years for me either and I know they weren't for you. I hated that we were separated. I hated more that you wanted nothing to do with me. After a while I didn't know how to bridge the gap. Then you wouldn't let me and I stopped trying."

"Part of that is my fault."

"Then let's just start here and go forward. Promise me we'll see each other often. After all, we are family."

Family. That sounded good. "You have my word."

"We'll see you at Christmas." It wasn't a question but a statement.

"I'll be here."

"Chance, you may not want to talk about this but I just want to let you know that I saved your half of the inheritance for you. It's been in the bank, waiting on you."

He would never have thought he would be interested in the money but he knew where he could put it to good use. "Thank you."

"You're welcome. I would've never felt right about keeping it."

After his evening with Abigail and her family Chance saw his past and his sister in a different light. Had he been unjust in his view of Ellen too?

Could he humble himself and beg enough to convince her he loved her and would never let her go again? He could if that was what it took to rid himself of the unceasing ache for her.

CHAPTER TEN

CHANCE PULLED AT his tux jacket. He didn't make a habit of dressing up in one and he knew why. They were uncomfortable. Here it was a week before Christmas and he was going to some fancy party. He much preferred a T-shirt and cargo shorts.

He wasn't fond of a dog-and-pony show but he'd participate in the gala if that was what it took to raise money for the clinic. Tonight's event in the great hall of the Metropolitan Museum of Art, if successful, should raise enough money to supply the clinic for the next year and give him start-up funds for a permanent building.

What he really wanted to do was find Ellen and beg her to forgive him for being such an idiot. If his sister could welcome him back, maybe Ellen could too. He had a feeling he would have to work harder where Ellen was concerned.

From wealthy and socially known families on both sides, maiden and married, his sister was well connected. To Chance's shock she'd been on a committee that helped fundraise for the clinic for years. Abby's group had already had this event planned before he'd called her. She'd asked him to attend and say a few words about his work in Honduras.

The great hall of the Met was already crowded with

guests and more were arriving by the time Chance made it there.

"Doesn't the place look beautiful with all the twinkling lights and the Christmas tree?" his sister said beside him after they had left her wrap and the men's overcoats at the cloakroom.

Chance was sure he would have been overwhelmed by the event if it hadn't been for his social training during boarding school. He certainly didn't attend anything like this in Honduras.

Was Ellen here? If she wasn't, he would leave to find her.

Chance didn't see her in the crush of people. He'd had his sister send her and her father an invitation. It wouldn't be like Ellen not to show up. Despite how she might feel about him, she would be supportive of the clinic. In this environment, he hoped she might be more favorable to listening to him plead for her forgiveness.

A woman who Abigail whispered to him was the head of the fund-raising committee took the stage and asked for the crowd's attention. She thanked everyone for coming and introduced him, requesting he come forward.

As he spoke he scanned the room. *Was she there?* Once he thought he saw Ellen but if it was her she'd moved out of sight. He gave his prepared speech, which included sharing about how a visiting doctor had communicated with young girls over fingernail polish, pointing out that the smallest things could make a big difference. Ellen had taught him that. That the work wasn't just about the grand scale but the small everyday efforts and relationships the clinic was building.

When he had finished, the committee chair returned to the stage. "We have a little something different planned for this evening. We're going to have the men make a pledge of support in order to dance the first dance with a woman of their choice. Would anyone like to start the pledging?"

There was a soft murmur around the room then a man in the middle of the crowd raised his hand. "I bid a thousand dollars for a dance with my wife."

"Come on, is that all Margaret is worth?" the committee chair said with a smile. "You can do better than that, Henry."

"Make it five, then," the man called.

"That's better. Please come up and sign your pledge card and escort your partner to the dance floor. Anyone else? Come on, gentlemen, what's a dance worth to you?"

"I bid five thousand dollars for a dance with Miss Jena Marshall," called a young man.

"I bid six for the same lady," another man said.

"Make that seven," the first man came back.

The chairwoman looked at the other man but he shook his head. With a smile she said, "Miss Marshall, I believe you have your partner."

From Chance's vantage point beside the stage he could see the smile on the girl's face. While the committee chair was encouraging another bid, he caught a glimpse of Ellen. A joy so large filled him to the point he didn't know if his chest could contain it.

"I bid ten thousand dollars for a dance with Ellen Cox," said a man Chance couldn't see.

Without hesitation Chance lifted his hand. "I bid fifty thousand dollars for a dance with Dr. Cox."

Heat swept over Ellen. Her heart did a fast tap dance and she stood stock still. A hush had fallen over the crowd and everyone looked toward her.

She knew that voice. It called to her in her dreams. The voice she hadn't heard in weeks until tonight.

Her body had jerked and flushed when Chance's name

had been called to come to the stage just half an hour earlier. Her traitorous heart had flipped. *He's here!*

Why hadn't Chance gotten in touch with her? *Because he doesn't care.* After so many weeks of not hearing from him that could only be the answer. Despite that, his informative speech, which was filled with knowledge and passion for what he did, had her falling in love with Honduras and him all over again.

She stood glued to the floor until someone nudged her forward. The crowd separated as she moved to meet him on shaky legs. Chance's bid made her feel dizzy. Why did he want to dance with her? He could have given the money to the clinic without involving her. Where had he gotten that kind of money?

Ellen had smiled when the interesting pledge twist had been announced. It could either be a flop or a hit. Ellen had been interested to see which. She had watched as her father had made his way to the front of the room. His amazing bid had blown her away. He knew how important the clinic was to her, even if he didn't support her working there.

Now Chance stood in front of her. He was so handsome in his tux it almost hurt to look at him.

A flutter of excitement filled her midsection. She had to remind herself of how angry she was. So why was she so pleased to see him?

The band played the first notes of a waltz.

Chance offered his hand. "May I have this dance?"

She said in a low voice, "I don't want to."

There was a surprised gasp from a few people around them.

He met and held her gaze. "Sweetheart, I'm sorry."

"Don't call me that," she hissed. "It's been almost two months since I've spoken to you."

His smile never wavered. "Let's not fight about it here. We can find someplace private to talk after our dance."

Ellen heard the pleading in his voice and took his hand.
It was like coming home to touch him again. He led her
to the dance floor and there his arm came to rest at her
waist. She could hardly breathe. Her hands shook. She
worked to push the pure happiness down, to stop it from
overflowing and washing her anger away. They moved
across the floor. Chance was an excellent dancer. But
even if he hadn't been, she was in heaven by just being
in his arms again.

You are mad at him. Remember that.

"I've missed you."

Could she trust him? Was he playing at something?
She'd already spent two months in misery. Her feet quit
moving. "You think you can literally waltz in here after
not speaking to me for weeks and I'm going to fall at
your feet?"

"No, that's the last thing I thought. With you I was
fully anticipating I'd have to fight my way back into your
good graces." He pulled her closer.

Ellen pushed against his shoulder, putting some space
between them. "Just where did you get fifty thousand
dollars?"

"Let's just say I came into some money. By the way,
you look beautiful. That green is gorgeous on you."

She couldn't help but warm at his praise.

"How're you feeling? How's your leg doing?"

"Now you're showing interest?" She wasn't going to
give him the chance to hurt her further.

He didn't ease his hold as he whispered close to her
ear, "I've always been interested."

"You have a funny way of showing it. No phone calls.
No handwritten letter. Not even an email or text."

He twirled her away from him and then brought her
back to his chest. "I deserve that. And more. But I have
checked on you."

She glared at him. "When?"

"I spoke to your father after you'd been back in the States a couple of days. And Michael gave me a report."

"At least *he* cared enough to see me when he was here."

"I'm sorry. I should have called you. I have no excuse but that I was a coward. I screwed up."

"Well, you're right about that."

He lowered his voice and searched her face. "How are you?"

"Do you really want to know?"

"Yes, I want to know everything about you. I've missed you."

"I'm fine. I've been back to work for a number of weeks. The leg is healing nicely." She purposely filled her voice with sarcasm. "I had a good doctor."

"Yeah, but not much of a human being."

"You expect me to disagree with that?"

"I really am sorry. If you'll forgive me I'll spend the rest of my life trying to make it up to you."

Hope soared within her. What did he mean by the rest of his life?

The number ended and Chance released her from his arms but continued to hold her hand. "I'd like you to meet my sister and her husband."

"What?" So he had contacted his sister. She was so surprised she didn't stop him from leading her off the dance floor.

He grinned. "You sure are using that word a lot. I've never known you to be at a loss for words."

Leading her to a group of people standing near the refreshment table, he waited until a couple broke away.

"Abigail and Stan, I'd like you to meet Dr. Ellen Cox," Chance said. "She worked at the clinic for a while. I'm hoping to convince her to return."

Ellen's eyes widened. She stared at him. Chance wanted her to return?

"It's so nice to meet you, Ellen. We appreciate all the work you have done. I know Chance will be glad to have you join him again." His sister's smile was sincere.

Ellen's head was spinning with all that Chance had said. She hoped she made all the proper responses to Chance's sister's remarks. Had she walked into a third dimension where everyone understood what was happening but her?

Chance broke in on the conversation and said to his sister, "If it's okay with Ellen, I'm going to take her somewhere so we can talk privately. I'll see you at the hotel tomorrow."

Abigail nodded.

He kept a hand on Ellen's waist as they sidestepped their way toward the cloakroom.

"Why do you think I want to talk to you?" Ellen asked.

"Don't you?" He kept her moving, not giving her time to argue.

A number of times people stopped them to ask him a question or make a comment. Keeping a hand on Ellen, he smiled and gave a short answer then made an excuse to move on.

"I think what you haven't said in the last few weeks speaks loudly enough."

He handed their tickets to the attendant and collected their coats.

"Please, let me explain."

The clerk handed him Ellen's full-length hooded cape, with white fur inside and the same green as her dress on the outside, edged with fluffy fur. He placed it over her shoulders.

"You look like a Christmas fairy." Chance was mesmerized. "I thought you were beautiful before but you take my breath away."

"Not too over the top?" She made a half-twirl.

It was the first really civil thing she had said to him all night. She was coming around slowly. "You're amazing."

She smiled at him. His heart flipped. He was headed in the right direction. Pulling on his overcoat, he beamed back at her. "I have missed you."

Bundled up, they stepped through the outside doors into a snowy night.

"It's beautiful." Ellen looked up into the sky illuminated by the lights of the skyscrapers. "I love this city at Christmastime."

Chance offered his elbow as they made their way down the numerous steps to the street. "It's completely different from Honduras."

"Which is equally beautiful in its own way." She took his arm but he was sure it was more out of the need for help than her having forgiven him. Ellen wouldn't go easy on him. He had hurt her deeply. They continued downward. "Where're we going?" she asked.

"How about a carriage ride?"

"Now you're turning into Mr. Romance?"

"That's my Ellen. Give no quarter."

"I'm not yours."

He needed to slow down. Give her time to think. Stopping, he looked at her a second. "Maybe not, but I'm hoping you will be. Just hear me out, please."

She nodded and he led her to a horse-drawn carriage parked on the street. It was decked out in white lights and bells for the season. He spoke to the driver and then helped Ellen into the carriage. With her settled in the seat, Chance joined her and pulled the heavy blanket waiting there across their waists and legs, tucking it around them.

"Warm?" he asked.

"Mmm…"

The horse started off at a slow clop-clop and continued as they turned into Central Park. The jingle of the bells on the horse's rig only added to the perfect winter dream feel of the moment.

"It's been forever since I've taken a ride through the park. I've never done it in the dark while it's snowing." She raised her face to the sky. "I love the sound of the bells. It's magical."

"Sort of like standing under a waterfall," he said softly.

"Yeah. Just like that." Wonder filled her voice.

She was softening. He took her hand under the blanket.

Her eyes came around to pierce him with a look. This was the Ellen he knew so well. "Why haven't you called?"

There it was. The hurt. Raw and deep.

"Because I didn't want to face what I feel."

She continued to glare at him. "I like that answer."

He brushed a snowflake from her cheek. "I thought you might. I'm sorry, Ellen. I was an idiot. There hasn't been a moment I haven't thought of you."

"You had a fine way of showing it."

"I know. You made me think about caring for someone again. But that brought the fear of rejection. I had to face my past before I could ask you about a future."

"So you reached out to your sister?"

Chance nodded. Ellen squeezed his hand. It was as if that one action had shown her that he meant what he was saying.

"I'm so proud of you. That couldn't have been easy."

"You know that if you had died it would have killed me."

Ellen pulled her hand from his and cupped his cheek. Her hand was warm against his cold skin. "I'm made of tougher stuff than you give me credit for."

He covered her hand with his. "I know that now. You have more than proved it. I love you, sweetheart."

A smile spread across her face. "That's all I've ever wanted. I love you too."

He held her close and kissed her. Her lips were cold against his but they soon warmed.

"I told my father I was returning to Honduras or another developing country," Ellen said, with her head against his shoulder.

"How did he take that?"

"Better than I thought he would. He still wants to protect me but he is also starting to understand my need for independence. This time he knows I'm not rushing into a decision."

"No more being reckless?" Chance asked.

"I promise to think twice before I react."

"And I promise to let you be who you are without holding you back."

She gifted him with a bright smile. "I love you, Chance Freeman. I also promise to never leave you."

His hands cupped her cheeks and kissed her softly with all the love in his heart. "If you tried, I would come and find you. I love you."

Chance had found what had been missing in his life. It was all right here in his arms.

* * * * *

WHITE CHRISTMAS FOR THE SINGLE MUM

SUSANNE HAMPTON

Thank you to the wonderfully talented and incredibly witty Mills & Boon authors who shared this writing journey with me...Scarlet Wilson, Kate Hardy and Tina Beckett. You have made writing this book like a road trip with new friends. You all helped to make it a joyful experience and one I will never forget.

And to my amazing editor, Nicola... thank you again for your guidance and unending patience as we brought this book to life.

CHAPTER ONE

IT WAS FOUR in the morning and snow was gently falling in the darkness like tiny stars floating to the ground when Charlie Warren awoke from a nightmare that was all too familiar. Beads of perspiration trailed over his half-naked body. The nights it happened were less in number than the year before but they still came with a regularity he found strangely comforting. Feeling the pain was better than feeling nothing. Or facing the fear of letting go completely. That was something he could still not bring himself to contemplate.

For the few hours that sleep claimed him during those nights, Charlie would relive the moments of impact. Sounds echoed in his mind, each as haunting as the one before. The buckling metal and splintering glass as his car skidded out of his control and slammed into the old oak tree. It was the crash that had claimed his wife and had come close to claiming Charlie's sanity. He would wake and in the deafening silence lie motionless in his bed thinking over and over about the conversation they should have shared that fateful night. The one when he told his wife it was too dangerous to venture out. The one when he firmly and resolutely refused to take the risk on the treacherous road. The conversation he would regret for the rest of his life that they'd never had.

Some nights were worse than others and on the very worst the nightmares began the moment his head hit the pillow and ended as he sat bolt upright woken by either the ringing of the telephone or his alarm clock. Both signalling he should head in to the hospital, the only place that gave him purpose.

But this night he'd been woken from his tortured sleep by the sound of a falling branch outside his window. The weight of the snowfall had been too much for the narrow branch and it had snapped, crushing against the leadlight window. It had not broken the glass, merely scratched down the panes as it fell, making a noise not unlike a dying animal's scream.

Still damp with sweat, Charlie rushed to the window believing an injured deer might have roamed into his property, but he quickly saw the silhouette of the damaged tree lit by the moon. There were no streetlights as Charlie's home was on a large estate. The seven-bedroom, seventeenth-century, run-down and previously unloved manor home was undergoing much-needed renovations so he was sleeping downstairs on the leather chesterfield in the sitting room while work was being completed on the upstairs part of the house.

The stone slate roof had been in a state of disrepair for too long and the ceilings had been damaged in most of the upstairs rooms. The master bedroom was due to be finished within a few days. The rooms were all empty and waiting to be filled with new furniture although Charlie had no burning desire to see any of it, let alone choose it, so he had left those decisions up to the decorator. He wasn't rushing to move back into the master bedroom. He had not shared it with anyone for two years and he had no plans of sharing it again. His wife, Alice, had begun the renovations and he was seeing them through to completion in her honour. After that he did not know what he would do with the home.

Or himself, for that matter. Other than work, he had no plans for the future.

As always, once Charlie had been woken he found it hard to fall back into a sound sleep again. He read for a while and then tried once again to sleep. But slumber evaded him so he slipped on his heavy winter dressing gown, tied it loosely around his hips, headed into his kitchen and made himself a coffee. While memories of the accident monopolised his dreams, it was the impending arrival of the Australian *in-utero* surgeon that dominated his waking thoughts, leaving him both anxious and irritated about her potential interference.

The hospital's decision, or more precisely Assistant Head of Obstetrics, Oliver Darrington's decision, to fly the specialist over to consult infuriated him. In Charlie's opinion there was nothing to be gained and everything to lose. The quadruplets were only weeks away from being big enough to deliver and, as the attending OBGYN, Charlie thought any deviation from the treatment plan should be his decision. *In-utero* surgery carried risks that he did not consider warranted. And he wouldn't readily agree with the procedure without proof it was the best way forward.

As he looked out over what many would call a joy of the Cotswolds at Christmas, the majestic sight of dawn breaking over the snow-capped hillside, Charlie barely noticed any of the landscape. With his blood pressure beginning to rise, he sat down at the large oak kitchen table, sipping the coffee that was warming his fingers.

Dr Charlie Warren was unable to appreciate anything because he was preparing himself for a professional battle.

This time his words of caution would be heard. And heard loudly.

'What on earth do you mean, *there's no need for me to scrub in*?'

Juliet Turner spun around with confusion dressing her brow and a surgical gown covering her petite frame. 'My patient's on the operating table, prepped for an open foetal repair of a neural tube defect. I *have* to scrub in. This can't be postponed.'

'It hasn't been postponed, Dr Turner,' the theatre nurse told her. 'The surgery's going ahead today. It's just that you're not the surgeon operating.'

Juliet's nostrils flared behind the operating mask. 'That's even more ridiculous. There has to be a mistake.'

'No mistake, Dr Turner. Another *in-utero* specialist has been brought in to take over,' the nurse replied firmly. 'He's already arrived, and in gowning now. Orders came from further up the food chain than me, so don't go shooting the messenger.'

'*He's* in gowning! I'm sorry, Angie, but this is absolute nonsense,' Juliet said as she returned her focus to lathering her hands and forearms as a visible protest. She wasn't backing down and had no intention of relinquishing her role. Kelly Lester would have her surgery and her baby would have the best chance of a normal life. And she was operating as scheduled.

Being a female in a male-dominated profession had taught her to stand up for herself very early on. She had known entering the profession that women were at least twice as likely to drop out of surgical training programmes as men, making her well aware that it would not be an easy path and a shrinking violet would not succeed. During her studies her father, also a surgeon in the same field, often told her that, while half of the medical students in Australia and New Zealand were female, women made up less than ten per cent of fully qualified surgeons. It was a harsh reminder that she would have to be strong, focused and have a voice to survive. And she was going to use her voice whenever needed. Loud and clear.

It appeared that day was going to be one of those occasions.

'I will not allow another surgeon to just step in now without a damned good reason. I know this is not at the patient's request. I spoke to her only an hour ago.'

'No, it wasn't the patient who has requested the change, Dr Turner, and I understand you're taken aback but I'm just passing on the message, not making the decision. However, I'm telling you the decision's final. You really do need to stop scrubbing. Having sterile hands won't change the outcome.'

Not hiding her irritation, Juliet turned off the flow of water with the foot control. 'Well, we'll just see about that.'

'On the bright side, your replacement will no doubt meet with your approval. You've worked together more than a few times.'

Juliet was doubly confused with the smirk on Angie's face. None of it made any sense but if she was to believe the nurse, and she had no reason to doubt her, she was being replaced without notice or reason. 'I don't care who's been brought in to take over, it's still madness,' Juliet replied as she pulled her surgical cap free and the mass of brown curls dropped around her face. At that moment, the replacement doctor entered the scrub room.

'Really,' she announced, shaking her head in disbelief. 'This is becoming more and more ludicrous by the minute. They call you back here two days after you retire. What is this craziness? I've a patient about to be anaesthetised and I'm told I'm not operating. Will someone please explain the absurd rationale behind all of this? And who made the call to replace me as Kelly's surgeon?'

'The hospital director…but with good reason,' he replied.

'I can't think of one.'

'You have to prepare for your trip.'

Juliet paused for a moment with a perplexed stare. 'For goodness' sake has everyone gone completely mad? My trip's not until the middle of next week. I've got five days to prepare for the lectures and board the plane, but Kelly's baby needs this operation now if he's to ever walk.'

'That's where you're wrong…not about Kelly and her baby—you're right on that one, I just finished reading the notes and the surgery's urgent—but your trip's not next week. It's tomorrow. You're leaving on an eight o'clock flight in the morning.'

'Tomorrow? But why?' Juliet dropped her head into her hands still damp from the antibacterial wash. 'The lecture is not until next Thursday.'

'You're not delivering the lecture in Auckland… you're off to the UK—'

'The lecture's been cancelled?' she cut in.

'No, the lecture is going ahead…'

'But without me?' she asked as she pulled free her

surgical gown and dropped it unceremoniously in the bin alongside her discarded cap.

'Yes.'

'And the surgery's proceeding too, just without me?' They were framed as questions but Juliet's tone made it obvious they were statements that she was none too happy about.

'That's right.'

'And I'm off to the UK?' she continued with the volume of her voice escalating and increasing in speed with each word. 'Before I go completely loopy, just tell me why my schedule is changing before my eyes without my approval?'

'The call came through from Cheltenham just now.'

'Cheltenham? As in the Cotswolds?'

'One and the same.'

'And who over there's making decisions without consulting with me?'

'The decision was made by four babies.'

Juliet blinked and shook her head. 'Four? You're speaking in riddles and you know that frustrates me.'

'Apparently the Assistant Head of Obstetrics at Teddy's, which is the maternity wing of the Royal Cheltenham hospital, spoke with our Head of Obstetrics about the quads. Almost twenty-nine weeks' gestation, suffering twin-to-twin transfusion syndrome. Two sets of monozygotic twins. While the girls are fine at this stage, the boys have developed the TTTS. Oliver Darrington believes you're the best chance that the quads have of all surviving should the parents agree to the *in-utero* laser surgery. And Professor Le Messurier just approved your secondment.'

'That's all very flattering but why am I being called in at the eleventh hour? If there was a risk, I should've been consulted upon the initial diagnosis. Surely being quads they would have been having weekly scans and intense monitoring and they'd know at Teddy's that the earlier the intervention, the better the outcome.'

'Apparently the quads were being closely monitored throughout the pregnancy, but the TTTS diagnosis has only just been made,' her replacement continued as he began scrubbing in, and over the sound of the running water he continued his explanation. 'The girls have separate placentas while the boys have one shared placenta so they were being scrutinised for any signs of transfusion. Up until now there was no indication of anything being amiss. It was picked up when the patient presented in what she thought was premature labour.'

'Caused by the amniotic fluid imbalance affecting the recipient twin.'

'Again, apparently but you'll know more details when you get there.'

'But the lecture in Auckland?'

'Handled. I'm not sure who's your proxy but your focus needs to be on the quadruplets. Darrington's worried it could deteriorate quickly and there's an increased risk they could lose at least one of them if you don't get over to Teddy's immediately, and of course we know the risks if one dies to the remaining foetuses. The parents have been briefed and want to be fully informed so they can consider *all* options, in particular the *in-utero* surgery.'

'Anything else I need to know?'

'Just one thing…the attending OBGYN, Dr Charlie Warren, is averse to fetoscopic laser surgery. Believes the risks are too great so no doubt he'll be challenging you.'

Juliet took a deep breath. 'Looks like I'll be catching

a plane tomorrow morning to meet Dr Warren's challenge and convince him otherwise.'

'I hope he knows what he's up against.'

'He soon will.' With her head tilted just slightly, and the remnants of bewilderment still lingering, she looked at her replacement. 'Okay, Dad, looks like Kelly and her baby are in your hands now.'

'Don't worry, honey. I'll do you proud.'

CHAPTER TWO

'DR TURNER, WE'RE about five minutes away from the Royal Cheltenham hospital.'

The voice of the immaculately suited driver made Juliet lift her tired eyes to meet his in the rear-view mirror. They were warm and smiling back at her but with a curiosity that she had been so very accustomed to over the years. She was well aware that she didn't look her thirty-three years and many apparently found it difficult to believe she was a doctor let alone a surgeon. Her curly brown hair and spattering of freckles along with her petite frame, she realised, didn't help her quest to be taken seriously. She had no time for make-up except for a natural lip gloss to prevent her lips from cracking, and that too added to her young appearance. It also helped her go under the radar and not gain the attention of the opposite sex and, although it wasn't her primary motivation, it was a welcome side effect.

But despite the general consensus, she was both a surgeon and a mother and she took both roles incredibly seriously. Her work, she loved with a passion, and her daughter, she loved more than anyone and anything in the world. And more than she had ever dreamed possible.

'Thank you,' she responded as she gently turned to

stir the little girl fast asleep and leaning against her. Running her fingers down the child's ruddy cheeks, she softly kissed the top of her head. 'Wake up, Bea, my precious little sleepyhead.'

The little girl silently protested at being disturbed and nestled in tighter to the warmth of her mother's woollen overcoat. Her eyelashes flickered but her eyes were far too heavy to open.

'Well, I hope this part of your marathon travel's been pleasant,' the driver commented.

'Very pleasant, thank you.'

'So how many hours have you two been travelling to be here this morning?'

'I think it's about thirty five hours, but it feels like for ever,' she replied with a little sigh, thinking back over the logistical nightmare they had survived. 'We left Perth early yesterday, Australian time, had a layover in Singapore before we headed on to Heathrow, and then the sixty-mile trip to the Cotswolds with you,' Juliet added as she continued to try and wake her still-drowsy little girl as gently as possible. She wasn't sure just how coherent she was but didn't want to appear rude. She had a lot on her mind, including the impending *in-utero* surgery on the quadruplets within the week. The reason she had been seconded halfway around the world at a minute's notice.

Keeping all four babies viable was everyone's focus. And something everyone agreed could not be done with Juliet on the other side of the world. Well, almost everyone agreed. She knew she would have her work cut out convincing the quads' OBGYN, Dr Charlie Warren. She presumed he would be leaning towards bed rest, high-protein diet and medication for the quads' mother. It was conservative and Juliet was surprised that he was not encouraging the laser surgery. She'd had no time to research the man but assumed he might be perhaps closer to the driver's age and had managed previous TTTS cases in that manner. But once he heard her argument for the surgery, surely the traditional English physician would see that her method had clear benefit? Particularly once she stated her case and the supporting statistics. How could he not? With both hospitals agreeing that Juliet was best placed to undertake the procedure, all she needed was the parents' approval. She was not about to allow Teddy's overtly conservative OBGYN to question the validity of her surgical intervention. It was an argument she was more than prepared to have. And to win.

But that wasn't the issue that had weighed most heavily on her mind on the long flights over to the UK. It was her parenting. How responsible was it to drag her daughter with her? she had wondered incessantly. And with less than twenty-four hours' notice. The poor little girl barely knew what was happening. The only thing that she could really comprehend was a plane trip to see snow.

Up until that point Juliet and Bea's lives had been so settled and planned. Some might say overly so, and among those were Juliet's parents. They had openly encouraged her to take Bea with her and together enjoy the opportunity to travel. In her home town, Juliet's mother looked after Bea three days a week and the other two days Bea was in childcare only five minutes from Juliet's workplace at the Perth Women's and Children's Medical Centre. When the proposition of travelling to the UK had been forced upon her, Juliet's parents had quickly had to push her out of her comfort zone and into embracing the opportunity. Her mother had imme-

diately brought the suitcases down from the attic and
personally delivered them to Juliet's home and offered
to help her pack. Juliet didn't doubt it would be better
for the quads for her to be there but it was not just *her*
any more. She had her daughter to consider in every
decision she made.

'I just hope I'm doing the right thing in dragging Bea
to the other side of the world for such a short time,' Juliet had muttered in the car on the way to the airport at
five-thirty in the morning. Her father had been driving,
her mother next to Bea in the back seat.

'That's just it, honey, it might not be a short time,'
her father reminded her as he pulled up at traffic lights
and turned to his daughter. 'You don't know when the
quads will arrive and it's best you stay until they do.
There could be post-operative or postnatal complications, so it's better to remain there up to the birth.'

'I know you're right, but this whole trip is so rushed,
I've had no time to prepare mentally. I know it's too
late, but I can't hide the fact I'm having second thoughts
about everything.'

'It's an amazing opportunity to consult at Teddy's
and no one can come close to your level of expertise,' he
said with pride colouring his voice as the lights changed
and he took off down the highway. 'It's part of a teaching hospital, and along with assisting those four babies,
not to mention their mother, you can add value to the
students', interns' and residents' learning experience.
You're the best in your field, Juliet. And I should know
since I've operated alongside you more than once. It's
time you took your skills out to the world, not just in
research papers and journals and lecture tours, but in
person in an operating theatre.'

'Dad, you're completely biased.'

'Nonsense, your father's right. We're both proud of you and you need to take that knowledge and expertise where it's needed most. Those babies and their parents need you,' her mother argued from the back seat. Her voice was soft but her tone was firm. Gently she kissed the top of her granddaughter's head. 'While we'd love to have Bea stay with us if it was for your three-day trip to Auckland, this is not three days. Poor little thing, she would fret terribly without you for any longer than a few days and visiting the UK will be such a wonderful experience for her too. It will be her first white Christmas.'

'And mine,' Juliet said, but her tone lacked her mother's enthusiasm as she drummed her fingers nervously on the leather upholstered seat. There was an uneasiness stirring in the pit of her stomach.

'Exactly, so stop questioning your decision. It's made now, you're both going,' her father piped up as he took the turnoff to Perth International airport in the dawn light. 'You've been hiding away, Juliet. You're not the only professional woman who's going it alone as a single mother. It's not the eighteen hundreds, and you don't need a man to help you realise your dreams. You have your career and Bea.'

She was hardly *going it alone*, in her opinion, with all of the help her parents provided, she thought as she looked out of her window and up into the still-darkened sky. But her father was right, she mused. She didn't need a man to experience or enjoy life. She and Bea would be just fine on their own. The plane would be up in that same sky in less than two hours, the sun would be up and they would be heading off to the other side of the world. To see four babies…and snow.

Juliet tried to muster a smile for everyone's sake. Her

parents were always forthcoming with their very modern wisdom and they were generally right about everything. The quads needed surgical intervention and Bea needed to be with her mother. And Juliet could hardly stand being away from her daughter for a day, let alone the possibility of three or four weeks. So if Juliet went, then so would Bea.

Initially she wasn't sure how she would manage but when the information had arrived via email the night before, providing the details of the onsite hospital crèche, it had given Juliet no valid reason not to say yes to everything. Besides which, the tickets had been arranged. There was no turning back. And so it was that, with less than a day's notice, Juliet and Bea had left their sunburnt homeland behind and were on their way to Teddy's.

'It's a beautiful part of the world,' the driver announced, bringing Juliet back to the present. 'I've lived here for almost thirty years. Raised my children and now my grandchildren. You'll be sure to love it too.'

Juliet smiled at the way the man praised his home town. 'I won't be here quite that long, but long enough to enjoy the stunning scenery.' She looked out from the car window across fields blanketed in snow and dotted with trees and bushes in variant shades of green, all dusted by a fresh layer of white drift along the fences. It was so picturesque and a very long way from the long hot summer days of home. Since she could not turn back she had decided that she needed to accept her decision and be excited to share her first white Christmas with Bea. While she knew it had the potential to be a stressful time for her, with the impending surgery she would be performing, she was glad the two of them

were together. They were like two musketeers off on
an adventure.

Juliet had long accepted there would never be a third
musketeer in their lives and that suited her fine. She
didn't need a man in her life. Apart from her father, the
rest just brought grief. Even in a new country, a man
she had not laid eyes upon, Dr Charlie Warren's objec-
tion to her surgical option was another piece of proof
that men caused unnecessary anguish.

And she didn't need any more of that.

'So you're only here for a short visit, then?'

'I'm consulting at Teddy's for a few weeks. I agreed
because it was a short term. I couldn't keep my daughter away from her grandparents for too long. They'd
miss her terribly.'

'I can see why. She's a proper little sweetie,' the
man added, clearly wanting to keep the conversation
flowing.

Juliet guessed him to be in his mid-fifties. He looked
a little like her father, quite distinguished, greying
around his temples with a moustache and fine-rimmed
gold glasses. Her father was a chatty man too, even in
the operating theatre. Perhaps it was his age that made
it easy for her to talk to this man. There was no hidden
agenda. Just pleasant conversation.

'Thank you. She's my little angel and she's a real
sweetie.'

'She's got your curls and pretty eyes. I don't think her
father got much of a look-in there. My granddaughter's
just the same, spitting image of her mother.'

Juliet felt her stomach sink a little, the way it always
did at the mention of Bea's father. The man who had
caused more anguish than she had ever thought possible. A man who didn't want *a look-in*. He was the one

time she had let down her guard and the reason she would never do it again. After the one romantic night they had shared, he had walked away and never looked back. Married the fiancée he had forgotten to mention to Juliet while he was seducing her. And as quickly as he had swept into her life, he was gone. Well before she had discovered she was having his baby. Two months after the night they spent together, Juliet had caught sight of his wedding photo complete with huge bridal party in the society pages of the local newspaper.

She had instantly felt overwhelmingly sad for his new wife.

Heaved twice with morning sickness.

And sworn off men.

For ever.

Juliet paid the driver and asked him to take her bags to the boutique hotel where she was staying for a few nights. The hospital had contracted the car service and, after their conversation, she felt she could trust him to take her belongings, including Beatrice's pink fairy princess suitcase, and leave them with the hotel concierge. Being over fifty meant he fell in the trustworthy category. Men under forty had no hope in hell of being trusted with anything belonging to Juliet.

Not her suitcases…her medical decisions…or her heart.

With Juliet holding Bea's gloved hand tightly, the two of them stepped inside the warmth of the main entrance of the hospital to hear the heart-warming sound of piped Christmas carols. Juliet slipped off her coat and laid it over her arm and then unbuttoned Bea's as she watched her daughter's eyes widen at the sight of their surroundings. Teddy's, as the hospital was affectionately known, was certainly dressed in its Christmas best. Neither Juliet nor Bea had seen such a huge tree and certainly not one as magnificently decorated as the one that filled the glass atrium. It was overflowing with brightly coloured baubles, and tiny lights twinkled from behind the gold tinsel generously covering the branches. Their eyes both scanned around the foyer to see a Santa sleigh and carved wooden reindeers welcoming patrons to the hospital tea room and all the staff appeared as happy as both Juliet and Bea felt at that moment.

'Ith very beautiful, Mummy.'

'It is indeed.'

Taking hold again of her tiny daughter's hand, Juliet approached the information desk and introduced herself and mentioned her appointment with the OBGYN with whom she would be working.

'I'm sorry, Dr Turner, but Dr Warren hasn't arrived yet. He was due an hour ago but, to be honest, I haven't heard anything so I can't be sure what time we'll see him.'

Juliet's expression didn't mask her surprise. She had flown almost eight thousand miles and had arrived on time and Dr Charlie Warren, whom she assumed to be a resident of the Cotswolds and who therefore had a significantly shorter journey, was the one late for their meeting. She was not impressed and hoped he had a darned good explanation since she and Bea were each in need of a bath and some sleep and had gone without both to meet with him.

'Is Oliver Darrington available, then?'

'Mr Darrington's on surgical roster today so, I'm sorry, he won't be available until after four-thirty.'

Juliet was trying to think on her feet. And both her feet and her brain were tired. 'Then while we're waiting for Dr Warren perhaps I can take my daughter to the crèche.'

'Of course, that's on this floor but the other side of the building overlooking the visitor gardens,' the young woman told her. 'If you follow the corridor on your left to the end then turn right, you'll see it.' Then smiling, she added, 'And hear it. It's quite the noisy place with all the little ones.'

Juliet hesitated; she didn't want to walk away with Bea and have Dr Warren arrive. She checked her mobile phone for messages. Perhaps Dr Warren had been delayed and sent the hospital a message that hadn't reached Reception but had been relayed to her in a text. It seemed logical and it would give her an indication of how much time she had to settle Bea into the crèche, but after quickly finding her phone she discovered there was no such message.

'I suppose I shouldn't be surprised,' she muttered under her breath. 'Another unreliable man.'

'Pardon, Mummy?'

Juliet looked down at the angelic face staring back at her. 'Nothing, sweetie, Mummy was just mumbling. Everything's just perfect.'

'Okay,' Bea replied as her eyes darted from one festive decoration to the next before she began pulling her mother back in the direction of the main doors.

Juliet knew everything in their lives was not perfect but she would make it as perfect as she could for her daughter. She would devote her life to ensuring that Bea never felt as if she was missing out on anything. Particularly not about the lack of a father in her life. Juliet often felt sad that, while she enjoyed a wonderful relationship with her own father, Bea would never experience that bond. Although, she conceded gratefully, while the special father-daughter relationship would never be a part of her daughter's life, an unbreakable grandfather-granddaughter relationship had already formed. Juliet's father and Bea were like two peas in a pod and seeing that closeness brought Juliet joy.

She was drawn back to the current situation, caused again by a man. Bea's grip was tight and she was clearly on a mission as she tried to pull Juliet along. Juliet tugged back. 'It's so cold outside, darling. Let's stay in here where it's nice and warm.'

'But, Mummy, it lookth like the top of my cake.'

'What looks like the top of your cake, sweetie?'

'Out there,' the excited little girl replied as she pointed to the snow-covered ground. The branches of the trees and even the cars that had been parked for a few hours had been blanketed.

Juliet had to agree that it did look like Bea's fourth birthday cake. Her grandmother had baked a triple-layer strawberry sponge cake with a generous covering of brilliant white icing and decorated with four different fairy tale princesses for her beloved granddaughter. But this was not a cake, it was their reality for the next few weeks, and, despite her reservations and her annoyance with Charlie Warren, it was very pretty. Postcard pretty. And it was the first time either of them had seen snow up close and she couldn't blame her daughter for wanting to go outside and enjoy it.

'But I need to stay inside and wait for the doctor. He'll be here any minute, *I hope*, and I don't want to miss him when he arrives because after my meeting with him you and I can go to the hotel and have a nice nap.'

'*Pleeease* can I play in the snow?'

Juliet felt the sleeve of her blouse being tugged by

two tiny hands, still gloved, and Bea's eyes were wide with anticipation and excitement. Juliet looked out to the fenced area near the entrance doors. There was a park bench, see-saw and a small slide and the playground was secured with a child safety gate. It was clearly a designated area for children to play on a sunny day but it wasn't a sunny day. It was freezing cold, overcast and the ground was covered with snow, which she knew was the draw card for Bea but a cause for concern for Juliet. Although she didn't want to impose a fear of almost everything onto her daughter, she couldn't help but worry.

After a moment she took a deep breath; she had made her decision. 'All right, you can play outside but only if we button up your coat again, put on your hat and keep your gloves on…and only for five minutes. And I mean five minutes—you'll catch a terrible cold if you stay out any longer.'

'Yeth! Yippee! Thank you, Mummy.'

With trepidation, Juliet buttoned up her daughter's heavy overcoat, pulled a knitted cap from her bag and popped it over Bea's mass of honey-blonde curls, pulling it down over her ears, and then slipped on her own coat again before walking the little girl outside into the wintry weather. She was still worried about leaving Bea for even five minutes, but common sense told her it would be safe. It was ten o'clock in the morning not the middle of the night and it was no longer snowing.

Her father's words rushed back into her head, 'You can't keep Bea in bubble wrap. Let her have some fun sometimes or she'll grow up scared of taking chances. Who knows what she can do in life if she's allowed to really live it? She might even become a surgeon like her mother…and grandfather.'

Although Juliet loved her work, she wasn't convinced

medicine was the life she wanted for her daughter. Part
of her wondered if the lack of a social life due to the
years of heavy study load, and then the long shifts at
the hospital as an intern, then as a resident didn't assist
Bea's father to deceive her. She was far from streetwise
about men. She'd had friends but never a love interest
until she met him and he'd swept her off her feet and
into his bed. Making her believe their night together was
the beginning of something more. She wanted Bea to
be wiser and not naive about the opposite sex.

But that was many years away and this was a playground. But it was still making Juliet very nervous.

She paused at the playground gate and looked down
at her daughter, trying unsuccessfully to mask her concern.

'Mummy, I'll be good, I promith.'

Juliet realised she was being silly. It was only a children's playground and one she could see from inside
and so too could all of the staff in the hospital foyer
and the tea room. Juliet needed to meet with the now
quite late Dr Warren. There might be a message from
him any minute. She also wanted to meet the quadruplets' mother as soon as possible to discuss her treatment plan. Bending down and looking Bea in the eyes,
she said, 'Mummy has to talk with the nice lady at the
desk inside. I'll be back in five minutes. You know my
rule—don't talk to strangers.'

Bea nodded. 'Okay.'

With that Juliet closed the childproof gate with Bea
inside the playground wearing an ear-to-ear smile, already making small snowballs with her tiny gloved
hands. Juliet tugged again on the gate to check it was
closed properly before she headed back inside. She

doubted she would leave Bea for five minutes, estimating it would only take two to check again on Dr Warren's whereabouts and see if there had been an update on his ETA. And she would be watching her the entire time through the large glass windows.

Charlie Warren pulled into the Royal Cheltenham hospital astride his black motorcycle. Both he and the bike were geared for riding in the harsh winter conditions of the southern English countryside. The sound of the powerful engine reverberated across the grounds as he cruised into the sheltered area of the car park. Charlie climbed from the huge bike that would have dwarfed most men, but, at six feet one, his muscular frame dressed in his leather riding gear stood tall against the bike. He removed his snow-splattered black helmet and heavy riding gloves and ran his still-warm fingers through his short but shaggy blond hair. It was cold riding to work every day, even brutal his colleagues would tell him some days in the middle of winter, but Charlie wouldn't consider for a moment taking a car. He couldn't; he didn't own one. Not any more and not ever again. He hadn't driven a car of any description in the two years since the crash.

Two years and three days to be exact. The anniversary was only a few days earlier, and, he assumed, was the reason the nightmares had returned. He knew he would never forget the date. It was the day the life he loved had ended.

After that, little brought him joy outside his work.

He had nothing to look forward to each night he rode away from the hospital. So he didn't stay away from Teddy's for too long.

* * *

Juliet watched Bea giggling as she climbed carefully up each rung of the tiny ladder on the slide. Her gloved hands gripped on tightly, her tiny feet, snug inside her laced-up leather boots, struggled a little not to slide, but she still smiled a toothy grin at her mother. Juliet loved seeing her daughter so happy and she smiled back but her smile was strained. Worry was building by the minute as she watched her only daughter take each slippery step, but her father's words resonated in her head, forcing her to stay put. Reminding her not to run to her daughter or call out, *Climb back down…it's dangerous.*

No, on this trip she would heed his instructions and let her daughter have a bit of fun after all and the slide was only a few feet tall.

What could possibly go wrong?

Bea looked down at each rung then back to her mother. Juliet could see that Bea thought she was such a big girl and seeing that reinforced that her father did know best. Juliet had to let Bea try new things. She had to unwrap the cotton wool that she had lovingly placed around her daughter…but only just a little.

Juliet gave a little sigh and resigned herself to her four-year-old's growing independence and her desire to encourage it but her fear at the same time. She wondered how she would cope when she turned sixteen and asked to get her driver's permit. Mentally she shook herself. *That's twelve years away…you have time to prepare for it.*

With any luck Dr Warren would arrive before then, she sniggered to herself.

At that moment, a smiling Bea lifted her right hand and waved at her mother. But Juliet didn't have time to smile back as she watched in horror as Bea lost her concentration and then her footing. She gasped out loud as her daughter's tiny hands lost their grip too. Helplessly Juliet watched from inside the building as Bea fell backwards to the ground.

CHAPTER THREE

CHARLIE SAW THE small child fall from the playground equipment. He was only too aware that while there was a thick blanket of freshly fallen snow in some places, in other areas there was only a thin covering. The shade the trees gave in summer when they were covered in lush green leaves was lovely but the branches had acted as natural canopies preventing the snow from building up to a level that would have broken her fall. He felt a knot in the pit of his stomach at seeing the child lying motionless on the ground and he rushed across the car park.

While it wasn't an overly tall slide, the child, he could see, was very tiny. As he drew closer he could see there was no one with her. Why would anyone leave a child out in the freezing weather unattended? He looked around and there was no one in sight. No one running to help. Fuelled by concern for the child and anger at the parent or parents, he raced to the gate.

'How damned irresponsible,' he muttered under his breath and shook his head. But his words were driven by something deeper. His dreams of being a father had ended the day his wife died and that made it even harder to see that this child had been left alone. If he were the father he would protect his child at any cost and he would never have left one so tiny out in the cold. Alone.

He undid the safety latch with a sense of urgency as he heard soft moans coming from the child he could then see was a little girl, lying still on her side. She was conscious. He quickly crossed to her and knelt down. 'You'll be okay, honey. I'm a doctor at this hospital. I just want to see if you've been hurt.' He kept his words to a minimum as he could see just how young she was.

'Where'th Mummy? I want Mummy.' Bea's eyes suddenly widened and began to fill with tears.

'We'll try and find Mummy,' he said as he wondered the very same question.

Where the hell was the little girl's mother? And her father?

As he began to check her vital signs he guessed she was between three and four years of age. 'Where does it hurt?'

'My arm hurths,' she said, abruptly sitting upright with tears running down her ruddy cheeks.

Charlie was surprised but relieved to see her level of mobility and suspected her tears were fuelled by fear and pain in equal amounts. 'Anywhere else?'

'No. It'th jutht my arm. Where'th Mummy?' Her chin was quivering and the tears were flowing freely.

Charlie reassured her again they would find her mother as he continued his medical assessment. As she awkwardly tried to climb to her feet, it was obvious to Charlie that she had only injured her arm so he scooped her up ready to take her to the emergency department. Neither a stretcher nor a paramedic team was needed and he wanted to get her out of the bitter cold air immediately and into the warmth of the hospital where she could be thoroughly assessed.

'Put my daughter down now!' Juliet's loud voice carried from the gate to where Charlie was standing.

Charlie's eyes narrowed on her. 'I'm a doctor, so please open the gate for me and step aside. This child's been hurt,' he told her as he approached with Bea still firmly in the grip of his strong arms. 'I'm taking her to have an X-ray.'

Juliet hurriedly opened the gate. 'She's my daughter. I can take her,' she said, reaching out for Bea, but Charlie ignored her request and moved swiftly, and in silence, in the direction of the emergency entrance with Juliet running alongside him.

'I said, I can carry her.'

'I heard you but I have her, so let's keep unnecessary movement to a minimum.'

Juliet nodded. It was logical but she still wished her injured daughter were in her arms, not those of the tall, leather-clad stranger who was supposedly a doctor. 'I saw her fall but I couldn't get to her in time.'

Charlie's eyebrow rose slightly. 'That's of no consequence now. I saw her. I'll get her seen immediately in A&E and then you can perhaps explain why she was left unattended out in this weather at such a young age.'

'Excuse me?' Juliet began in a tone that didn't mask her surprise at his accusatory attitude. While she thought it was unfair and unjust it also hit a raw nerve. 'I wasn't far away—'

'Far enough, it would seem, for me to get to her first,' Charlie cut in with no emotion in his voice. As the three of them entered the warmth of the emergency department, the feeling between them was as icy as the snow outside. 'I need her name and age.'

'Beatrice, but we call her Bea, and she's four years and two months.' Juliet answered but her voice was brimming with emotion. Overwhelming concern about Bea and equally overwhelming anger towards the man who was carrying her child. How dared he be so quick to judge her?

'Four-year-old girl by the name of Bea, suspected green stick fracture of the forearm,' he announced brusquely to the nursing staff as he took long, powerful strides inside with Juliet following quickly on his heels. Charlie carried Bea into one of the emergency cubicles and laid her gently on the examination bed. With the curtains still open, he continued. 'We need an X-ray *stat* to confirm radius or ulna fracture but either way, if I'm correct, we'll be prepping for a cast. And bring me some oral analgesia.'

'Ibuprofen, acetaminophen or codeine?' the nurse asked.

'One hundred milligrams of suspension ibuprofen,' Charlie replied, then, as it was a teaching hospital and he was aware that three final-year medical students had moved closer to observe, he continued. 'Generally paediatric fracture patients have significantly greater reduction in pain with ibuprofen than those in either the acetaminophen group or the codeine group and they suffer less negative side effects.'

'What'th happening, Mummy?'

'The doctor,' she began before she shot an angry glare over her shoulder in Charlie's direction. She was impressed with his knowledge but not his attitude towards her. 'Sweetie, the doctor thinks you may have broken your arm when you fell from the playground slide so he'll take a picture of your arm with a special machine.'

'Will it hurt?'

'The machine won't hurt you at all but they will have

to very gently lift your arm to take off your coat and then take a picture. So the doctor will give you some medicine so it doesn't hurt.'

The nurse returned with the ibuprofen and Charlie asked Bea to swallow the liquid.

'Please do as the doctor asks because it will make the pain go away,' Juliet told her daughter with a smile that belied how worried she was. 'Don't worry, Bea, I'll be with you every minute. I'm not leaving your side.'

'That'd be a nice idea,' Charlie put in, with sarcasm evident in his voice just enough for Juliet alone to know the intent of his remark but no one else. Without looking up, he signed the radiograph request the A&E nurse had given him.

Juliet took a deep breath and counted silently to three. It was not the time to tell him just what she thought of his snide remarks, particularly not in the presence of her daughter and the medical students. But that time would come once everyone was out of earshot. And he would hear in no uncertain terms just what he could do with his unwarranted opinion.

'Can you please complete the paperwork?' the nurse asked of Juliet. 'We only need the signature of one parent.'

'Bea only has one parent,' Juliet said flatly before she accepted the clipboard from the nurse and hurriedly but accurately began to complete the details so she could expedite the process and allow Bea to have the X-ray. She wasn't sure if the doctor had heard and she didn't care as Bea's parental status wasn't his concern.

'Dr Warren,' another young nurse began as she neared the trio with a clipboard, 'would you like me to call for the paediatric resident so you can return to the OBGYN clinic?'

'No, I'm here now, I'll finish what I've started.'

'Of course,' the nurse replied. 'Then we can take the patient down as soon as the paperwork is completed.'

'Dr Warren? Dr Charlie Warren?' Juliet demanded as she fixed her eyes on Charlie for a moment. He was not the borderline elderly OBGYN she had pictured. Dr Charlie Warren, she surmised, was closer to his early thirties.

'Yes. Why do you ask?'

Juliet didn't answer immediately. Instead she ensured she had not missed any details on the admissions form before she signed and returned it to the nurse. It gave her a few moments to compose herself and reconcile that the man treating her daughter was the OBGYN who had stood her up for their meeting and the one who wanted to oppose her treatment plan for the quadruplets. He was already very much on the back foot but, with his obvious bad attitude, it did not augur well for them working together.

'Well, Dr Warren, it appears that you owe me an apology since you're the reason why my daughter is in here.' Juliet wore a self-satisfied look, one she felt she more than deserved to display.

'I hardly think so. I just pulled into the car park when your daughter fell. We both know that I had nothing to do with her accident so let's not waste time trying to shift blame. Leaving a child this young alone is something I am not sure I can fully understand…or want to.'

'That's where you're wrong. You have everything to do with the accident because if you'd been on time for our meeting my daughter would not have stepped outside to play.'

'Our meeting?'

'Yes, our ten o'clock meeting,' she began. 'I'm Dr

Juliet Turner. The *in-utero* surgeon who has flown half-way around the world and managed to be here on time for a meeting about your quad pregnancy patient, and, I might add, we travelled straight from the airport. My daughter needed to stretch her legs for a minute after such a long journey, so I allowed her to play in the fenced area that I assumed would not be open unless it was in fact child-safe while I enquired further about your arrival. If heavy snowfall changes the safety status of the area then it should be closed. You may like to speak to the hospital board about looking into that matter.' Juliet had not taken a breath during the delivery. Adrenalin was pumping out the words. She was scared for Bea. And extremely angry with Charlie Warren.

'Dr Turner? I had no idea…'

'Clearly…and apparently no time management either.'

Charlie was momentarily speechless. Juliet felt momentarily vindicated.

She noticed a curious frown dress his brow. Then she also noticed, against her will, that his brow was very attractive, as was his entire face. She had been focusing on Bea and not noticed anything much about the man who had whisked her daughter unceremoniously into A&E. But now she noticed his chiselled jaw, deep blue eyes and soft, full mouth. In fact, each moment her eyes lingered on his face she realised he was in fact extremely handsome, even when he frowned. His powerful presence towered over her with long, lean legs and his leather riding gear accentuated his broad shoulders. She shook herself mentally. His manner was both judgmental and conceited. Alarm bells rang in her head. Why were her thoughts even teetering on noticing him past being her daughter's emergency physician? He was just another arrogant man and one she was going to be forced to work with in some capacity.

In a perfect world she would have nothing to do with him once he had finished treating Bea. But she also knew that they didn't live in a perfect world. And not seeing Charlie Warren again wasn't possible. They would be consulting on the high-risk patient until the birth of the four babies.

And she was well aware that, after challenging her parenting, he would shortly be challenging her treatment plan. There was no way this working relationship was going to run smoothly. And she doubted with his attitude he intended to play nicely.

'I had additional house calls this morning as I needed to cover another OBGYN's patients. He's down with the winter virus that swept through Teddy's. With both patient loads it look longer than I anticipated, but point taken. I should have called in.'

Juliet couldn't help but notice him staring at her. It was a curious stare, no longer angry or accusing.

'I understand covering for ill colleagues happens but a text would have been prudent,' she continued, ignoring his reaction, suspecting like everyone else he was looking at her as if she weren't old enough to be a surgical specialist. She had grown tired of that look and in Dr Warren's case she wasn't about to give him any leeway. Nor was she about to give her unexpected reaction to him any acknowledgement. Her tone was brittle but with his masculinity hovering around eleven out of ten he was making it difficult not to be a little self-conscious despite her ire.

'We can speak further about my delay later, Dr Turner, but let's get Bea into Radiography and ascertain the extent of the fracture,' Charlie announced, breaking her train of thought.

Juliet did not respond to Charlie as she wasn't sure what exactly she would say. Her equilibrium was beyond ruffled and she was struggling to keep her thoughts on track. She returned her attention to Bea, and stroked her daughter's brow. 'Mummy and the doctor will be taking you on this special bed to have that picture now. And then if the doctor is right and you have broken the bone in your arm then you will have a cast put on until it's all healed.'

'What'th that?'

'You know when Billy, the little boy from playgroup, fell over last year and he had a bright blue plaster on his arm? And everyone drew pictures on it with crayons? That's a cast.'

Bea nodded. 'I drew a star and a moon.'

'That's right, and it was a very beautiful star and moon.'

'Can I take it off? Billy couldn't take it off.'

'No, you won't be able to take it off but it won't be too uncomfortable,' Charlie chimed in with a voice that Juliet noticed had suddenly warmed. She wasn't sure if that warmth was directed at Bea alone or if he was attempting to be nice to Juliet as well. 'There's a soft bit inside and a hard layer outside that stops your arm from moving so that it can heal.'

Juliet turned back to face Charlie to ask another question and immediately wished she hadn't. He had moved closer and his face was only inches from her. His cologne was subtle and very masculine. She tried to keep the same professional demeanour but dropped her eyes, refusing to keep the courtesy of eye contact for two reasons. One, she was still fuming and wait-

ing for an apology that she doubted she would ever
receive, and, two, she didn't want to risk falling into
the dark blue pools that were more blue than any she
had ever seen before. She didn't want to forgive him
for his appalling behaviour. Without all of the facts he
had jumped to a conclusion that was unjust. But her
hormones were overriding her good sense. It was completely out of character for her. She was angry and she
never paid attention to men, good-looking or not. And
she would be damned if she would allow it to happen
that day. Or any day in the future.

She quickly decided she didn't want to hear an apology from Charlie. If one was not offered it would mean
that she could then remain furious with good reason,
keep the man at arm's length and her mettle would not
be tested. If he made amends, he might prove to be a
distraction on some level that she didn't want. Although
she knew her sensible side would win, she didn't want
to waste any time on some ridiculous internal battle of
hormones versus logic. Particularly when she had a very
real battle to fight with the very same man.

Coughing, she cleared her throat in an attempt to
gain some composure. Dr Warren's nearness was, for
some inexplicable reason, threatening to awaken something in Juliet she had buried a long time ago. And it
didn't need digging up now. That part of her life was
over. Perhaps it was just sleep deprivation, she wondered. She had not travelled for so many hours straight
before either. Nor had her daughter ever suffered an
injury of that nature. It had to be the series of events
stacked against her that was messing with her logic.
Making her emotions a little unstable. It wasn't her. It
definitely had to be the combination of factors, she decided, not Charlie Warren himself. Suddenly she had

everything back in perspective, the way she liked it. Charlie Warren was her daughter's doctor and her potential nemesis.

'Will you be using fibreglass?' she asked, quieting any sign of emotion. Her heart was no longer beating madly and the butterflies were one by one exiting her stomach. She was proud of herself for so quickly once again gaining control of the situation. Although she was still disturbed the *situation* had presented in the first place.

Jet lag, she quickly told herself. Definitely jet lag.

'If Bea needs a cast we'll use fibreglass and, since it will be difficult to expect Bea to keep it dry, I'll use a waterproof lining too,' Charlie told her.

'Billy had blue but I don't like blue,' Bea said softly, looking down at her arm.

'We have pink and yellow and I think red too,' Charlie responded with his mouth curving to a half-smile and that did not go unnoticed by Juliet.

'I like red for Chrithmath…but pink ith pretty… I want pink,' Bea announced.

Juliet smiled at her daughter. As she lifted her head her eyes met Charlie's eyes staring back at her and her heart once again began to pick up speed. It was madness for certain. The intensity of his gaze wouldn't allow her to look away. It was as if there was something deeper, something hidden behind the outer arrogance. Warmth and kindness seemed almost trapped inside him.

And she couldn't ignore, no matter how much she didn't want it to be true, and how much she'd fought it over the years, that there was a tiny part of her craving warmth and kindness from a man like Charlie.

CHAPTER FOUR

'UNFORTUNATELY BEA HAS a distal radial fracture…but at least it's non-displaced so we should be grateful for that news.'

Charlie turned back from the radiographs on the illuminated viewer in the room to see Juliet holding her daughter closely. He could not help but notice the tenderness in her embrace and the obvious love Juliet had for her daughter. He had been wrong about her, he admitted to himself as he watched her gently kiss the mop of blonde curls on the top of her daughter's head. He had not accompanied them to the radiography department. Instead he had excused himself to change into street clothes he kept in his office and then met them back in the emergency department.

Their eyes met and he paused in silence for a moment. He hoped she had not noticed him staring longer than was necessary but he could not help himself. Despite their professional differences, there was something about Juliet that was making him curious. Making him want to know more about the single mother with the Australian accent; the very pretty face; the spitfire personality; and the adorable daughter. He had noted her mention Bea only had one parent. Whether she was widowed, divorced or had never married, he didn't know. And it was none of his business.

It was out of character for him to be distracted by anything or anyone. Least of all someone he had only just met. But he could not pretend even to himself that he had not been distracted by Juliet, and it was not just her appearance. She was a conundrum. A surgeon who looked closer in age to a first-year medical student while he knew she would have to be in her thirties, with an academic record that would come close to that of a professor and an attitude when provoked of a bull. Not to mention a love for her child that was palpable. He had not met anyone quite like Dr Juliet Turner before.

Charlie was never thrown by anyone or anything. Charlie Warren's life was organised and predictable. It was the only way he could function. He had few friends, save his colleagues during his work hours. Socialising was a thing of the past although he had been forced to attend the recent hospital fundraiser, escaping as soon as decently possible.

He spent any time away from the hospital alone and preferred it that way. In more than two years, Charlie had never experienced any interest in anything other than his work. Returning home only to sleep and prepare for the next day's surgery or consultations. His patients were his sole passion in life. And now the Australian *in-utero* expert, with whom he completely disagreed on a professional level, was rousing his curiosity in knowing more about her.

And it was unsettling.

The second anniversary of the accident had just passed and it was a day he wanted to do differently every night as he lay alone in his bed reliving the hell that had become his waking reality. One he couldn't

change. One he had accepted a long time ago that he
would live with for the rest of his life. And to be spending any time thinking about a woman other than his late
wife was ridiculous.

But as much as he fought the distraction, he couldn't
control his wandering thoughts.

He wondered for a moment what life had dealt Juliet. Just being a surgeon would have provided struggles
along the way. He had found the study and workload
gruelling and he was not raising a child alone. Whether
or not her status as a single mother was recent he was
unsure. She looked to him like a waif but she had the
fire and fight of someone a foot taller and he assumed
she would have faced life head-on. His wife had been
similar in stature but very different in demeanour and
profession. She was quietly spoken, and a local Cotswolds girl who managed a craft shop in town. She spent
hours quilting and running the little store that doubled
as a social hub for the local community.

Charlie doubted that Juliet would have any interest
in quilting. But it bothered him greatly that questions
about the woman holding her daughter had suddenly
and unexplainably captured his thoughts.

He was grateful that Juliet had been distracted by the
nurse coming back and looked away. For some unfath-
omable reason he was struggling to do just that. The
woman before him was nothing close to the stoic surgical specialist he'd been expecting and he was shocked
at just how much he had noticed about her in such a
short space of time.

And he was angry and disappointed with himself
for doing so.

Juliet forced herself to blink away her wandering
thoughts. Charlie Warren was nothing close to what

she'd been expecting. His white consulting coat covered black dress jeans and blue striped shirt. He was still wearing his black motorcycle boots. The combination of the leather and gunmetal hardware of his boots was both edgy and masculine. It had to stop. She had not flown to another hemisphere to find herself distracted by the first handsome man she met. First handsome, *arrogant* man who would be her work colleague for the next few weeks.

She felt butterflies slowly returning just knowing he was so close to her. Close enough to reach out and touch her. Not that he would…nor would she want that, she told herself sternly. But it was as if she could see there was something more to the man who had rudely stood her up and then berated her for inattention to her daughter. Was his brash exterior a shield? She wasn't sure as she tried in vain to analyse the ogre. Perhaps it was the way he had rushed to Bea. As a man and as a doctor, he had not hesitated to help Juliet's daughter. He had lifted her into the safety and strength of his arms the way a father would. The way Bea's own father never would and the way no man other than her grandfather up until that day had done.

But it was romantic nonsense. He was just the tall and not so dark—more dusty blond—handsome stranger of happily ever after stories that she knew didn't really exist.

There wasn't anything more to this man, her practical self was saying firmly and resolutely despite how her body was arguing. He wasn't even nice let alone the type to sweep her off her feet. He was far too brusque and cold. What was going on in her tired mind? she wondered. It had to be international time difference setting in. Most definitely. It couldn't be anything else stirring her thoughts into chaos. She needed a good night's sleep and all would be as it should be. And she would be looking at her colleague as just that, a colleague. And if his strong, borderline obstinate opinion about her plans on surgical intervention with the quadruplets' mother remained, they would in fact shift from colleagues to adversaries.

She took solace in the idea that their differing opinions would add another protective layer to the armour she wore very comfortably.

'Hmm-hmm...' Juliet coughed. 'I said I'm happy there's no need for a closed reduction.'

'That makes two of us,' he replied, turning back to the radiographic films.

'So there'll be no intervention to realign the bones, just a cast as we already discussed, then?' Juliet continued as she fought to keep her thoughts professional.

'It's standard practice to give the arm a few days in a sling to allow swelling to subside,' Charlie explained to everyone in the room. 'But I'm concerned at Bea's age she may cause further damage if we don't protect the fracture with a cast. There's a marginal amount of swelling around the fracture site but not enough to warrant risking further damage by allowing it to be without protection.' He then asked the nurse to prepare for the cast while three medical students, who had quickly become part of the furniture, continued listening intently. The nurse moved swiftly, while the medication still kept Bea's pain at bay. 'And we need pink. That is the colour you want, isn't it, Bea?'

Bea looked up and nodded.

'Then pink it is,' he told her. The nurse helped Juliet to carefully roll up Bea's long-sleeved top that she had worn underneath the woollen jacket that was still under Juliet's arm.

'You were all layered up, weren't you, young lady?' the nurse commented with a smile. 'Rugged up for our chilly winter?'

Bea nodded and watched as her mother and the nurse worked gently to lift the clothing free so the cast could be applied.

'It's a nice loose top so it should roll down again afterwards, but the jacket will never fit so we'll have to just rest that over her shoulders and go shopping for a cape,' Juliet mentioned as she dropped the little coat on the nearest chair.

Charlie began the process of applying the cast, explaining to Bea in simple language every step, while also including a short tutorial for the students' benefit as they stood observing the process from the sidelines. Juliet listened to the way he spoke so tenderly to her daughter and she felt the flutter of the annoying butterflies emerging once again. She hated the feeling but she was unable to control it. His manner and tone to Bea made him appear almost fatherly. She sternly told herself it had to be his standard bedside manner…but she wasn't completely convinced.

'Applying a cast is quite a simple procedure,' he began as he turned his attention to the students. 'I'll begin by wrapping several layers of soft cotton around the injured area. Today I'll be applying a short cast that extends from the wrist to just below the elbow as the break is a distal radial fracture so extending further than that would cause unnecessary discomfort to the patient.' Charlie worked at wrapping Bea's tiny injured arm, and as he spoke the fibreglass outer layer was being soaked in water. Gently he wrapped the fibreglass around the soft first layer. 'While the outer layer is wet at the moment, it will dry to a hard, protective covering. I'll make some tiny incisions in the cast to allow for any potential swelling.'

In less than thirty minutes, Beatrice Turner was the proud owner of a pretty pink cast. And her mother could not help but be impressed with the way in which Dr Charlie Warren had attended to her daughter, executed the delicate procedure and managed to deliver a tutorial to the students. All the while continuing to look devastatingly handsome. She shook herself mentally and tried to remind herself of his initial overbearing attitude. But it was difficult when he was displaying such empathy to the little person she loved most in the world.

'Now you need to rest this arm quite still for about an hour, Bea,' Charlie said. 'The nurse will keep an eye on it and we'll leave your top rolled up for the time being.'

Bea just looked at the cast. Her eyes told the story. They were filled with confusion. It had been an overwhelming experience for her and she wasn't taking in much of what was being said at that moment.

'And we can give you a sling to hold it up because it might get heavy over the next few weeks.'

Still Bea just sat in silence. Juliet suspected it was a combination of jet lag and the pain beginning to resurface.

'Mummy will be here,' she told her softly as she stroked her hair.

Juliet waited for another snide remark, in fact she hoped for one, but Charlie made none. She didn't like not having a reason to dislike the man.

'It may get itchy, Bea, and if it does you can tap on the outside and that might help, but don't put anything inside like a pencil because it might scratch your skin and we don't want germs in there.'

Juliet watched as Bea tilted her head slightly with a curious expression on her beautiful face. She knew her daughter was still a little confused by everything that had happened so quickly. It was a lot for a four-year-old to take in such a short amount of time.

'Is there anything else we can do?' Juliet asked, holding Bea's free hand and quickly trying to recall her training in paediatric fractures during medical school. It had been so long since she had graduated from her general medical studies before specialising and she was stretching her memory.

'It would be best to sponge-bathe Bea so that the cast doesn't fill with water in the bath or shower. While the outside of the cast is waterproof, as you know, the inside isn't, even with the special lining. It needs to be kept dry, so no lotions or oils either.' He paused to recall the other instructions that once rolled off his tongue as an A&E resident. 'And if the itching starts to bother Bea, you can use a cool hairdryer to blow air in around the edge of the cast and check now and then that she hasn't hidden small toys or sweets inside the cast. Believe it or not, during my A&E rotation I had more than one child think of it as their secret *hideyhole*.'

'No doubt,' Juliet said with a smile that she hadn't thought previously she would ever display in Charlie's presence. Her defences were slowly melting as his bedside manner warmed the room. She began a mental inventory of Bea's belongings, wondering if she'd brought anything that small with her on the trip. She felt certain as she looked at the tiny gap that Bea's possessions would not fit inside.

'I'm sure you'll have it under control,' Charlie said

to her before he turned his attention once again to the medical students. 'Along with asking the parents or caregivers to check the cast regularly for cracks, breaks, tears and soft spots, what else would you ask them to look out for and what would warrant medical attention?'

'Pain that doesn't get better with the prescribed pain relief,' one of the students offered.

'Yes, anything else?'

'If the child complains of feeling numb or tingly in the vicinity of the fracture,' another chimed in with a self-satisfied smile.

'Good.'

'Blisters inside the cast,' the third student said confidently, then continued, 'and fever, or any significant increase in temperature.'

While being a tutor was nothing new to Charlie, doing so back in A&E was a change of pace and very different subject content but he didn't want to exclude the students. 'Well done. You seem to have a good understanding of the basics of paediatric fractures.'

The A&E resident poked her head in at that moment and directed her conversation to the medical students. 'If you're finished here, there's suspected tetanus in bay three and gallstones in bay seven. Take your pick.'

Charlie grinned. 'It's been a while since I've heard a call for one of those conditions. It's usually onset of labour or unexplained abdominal cramps over in Teddy's.'

The three looked at Charlie for approval to leave, which he gave in a nod, and they left, as did the attending nurse, leaving Charlie and Juliet alone with Bea.

'Well, it looks as if we're all finished, then,' Juliet offered in a voice that did not give anything away about the effect Charlie was still having on her, being so near.

His natural affinity with her daughter was thawing parts of her she wanted to remain frozen.

'I think we are.' His eyes once again locked on hers for just a minute but long enough to make her heart race just a little faster.

She swallowed nervously, growing more irritated with herself by the minute. Behaving like a schoolgirl experiencing her first infatuation was not her usual demeanour, nor one she intended to entertain. Not for another second. Reinstating herself as the quads' surgeon, not Bea's mother who had a borderline crush on her daughter's doctor and her own soon-to-be colleague, was a priority.

Biting her lower lip, she tried to channel someone very different from herself. A detached, bumptious persona she had created over the years when people looked at her like a child and they needed reminding of her medical credentials. And it would work perfectly at that moment. 'It's best, then, that we reschedule the *in-utero* surgical consultation that you missed earlier. If you can provide me with overnight obs about both the mother and babies, we'll be off to the hotel so Bea can rest and I can brief myself on their progression and return this afternoon.'

Her voice had suddenly morphed from warm to officious. And as she stood her relaxed posture had become stiff. Her body language screamed confrontation. But Charlie didn't appear to take the bait as he helped Bea down from the examination table. Although his tone returned once again to something more formal and detached.

'I'll email you the updates, Dr Turner.'

She felt she had been successful. The atmosphere in

the room had cooled and for that she was grateful. It was just the way she wanted it.

'I appreciate that, Dr Warren.'

'Great, I'll leave you both in the A&E's care and head up to visit with Georgina and Leo. They're waiting for my update on their babies' treatment plan, because since the diagnosis it appears the recipient twin is now struggling.'

Juliet froze on the spot. 'Georgina and Leo Abbiati? The quads' parents?'

'Yes.'

'But that's why I'm here. Why would you not include me in that consultation? And why would you not update me immediately?'

'Because you just excused yourself.'

'No, I didn't,' Juliet argued with her nostrils beginning to flare. 'I excused myself from *our* meeting. Not the meeting with the quads' parents. I thought that was scheduled for this afternoon.'

'It was, but yesterday I decided to bring it forward since the condition had deteriorated slightly. Which is what I just mentioned.'

'What exactly do you mean by "deteriorated slightly"?'

'There's more amniotic fluid so the uterus is almost at capacity. It might be a good idea to do an amniotic reduction.'

'I'll need to assess her immediately,' Juliet told him. 'And I wouldn't be considering the reduction if we are undertaking the laser surgery in a few days.'

'Whether the laser surgery will go ahead is still to be decided by the Abbiatis.'

'And without me, it would appear. Didn't you think that it would be nice to consult with me about treatment plans? I thought we would meet at *ten this morning*, you would brief me on the current viability of all four babies, the affected babies' condition and the mother's status and I would take that into consideration and then, with a consolidated treatment plan, meet with the parents late today.'

'I scheduled it for now as I thought you'd want to meet with the parents immediately.'

Juliet drew a deep breath. She needn't have worried she was warming to him because Charlie Warren had very quickly given her a cold shower when he'd returned to being a dictator with a medical degree. She wasn't sure if he had taken her cue or it was his intention all along but either way any attraction she had felt instantly disappeared.

Juliet had to think on her feet. She would not be made to appear less than professional by not attending the consultation. This was about the option of surgical intervention. Not Charlie Warren's conservative treatment plan. Waiting for the birth was not in her expert opinion the best way forward. The best chance was surgery to remove the offending artery and save all four babies and she wanted the Abbiatis to have all the facts before they made their decision.

'I want to meet with them as soon as possible.'

'Then let's go. I'm meeting with them in fifteen minutes.'

'What about Bea?'

Charlie looked down at Bea's little face and his heart began to melt. If life had been different he would have been looking at the face of his own child every night. He or she would have been younger than Bea but he and his wife had planned on children. Four of them if possible. Leaving the hospital every night to return to his wife and those much-loved children, to read them bedtime stories and tuck them in to sleep, was his dream but instead he returned to an empty house in the middle of renovations that he didn't care about. His life was as empty as his house.

And suddenly the daughter of the overbearing woman who shouldn't have any effect on him was doing just that. He wasn't able to define what made her special—perhaps it was because she was like a tiny angel with a broken wing. Although he did not feel her mother had fallen from heaven.

'I said, what do you propose I do with my daughter?' Her voice was firm but not much more than a whisper. She didn't want Bea to feel she was in the way or not wanted.

'Bring her along to my office and I'll ask one of the nurses to keep an eye on her,' he told Juliet as he patted Bea's hand.

'I don't feel comfortable with that.'

'Then go home…'

'Go home?'

'I meant go back to the hotel and we'll arrange a second consultation tomorrow.' Charlie walked over and opened the door. 'We're all finished in here,' he told the nurse as he left A&E.

'So you won't postpone the consultation until this afternoon, then?' she asked, exasperated with his attitude and following slowly on his heels with Bea in tow.

'No, definitely not. Postponing has the potential to make both parents extremely anxious, not to mention Leo's taken time away from the family business to be here.' Charlie pressed the elevator button for OBGYN on the second floor and turned back to face her.

Juliet's gaze swept the hospital corridor as she rubbed her forehead. In her mind, the Abbiatis needed to be provided with both treatment plan options to consider. Charlie would no doubt suggest a 'wait and see' treatment plan or next propose medication as an option. After sleeping on it, the second option of surgical intervention, she conceded, would be the scarier of the two to Georgina and Leo. The delivery gap between both might sway them to what was not in their best interests. Nor the interests of the babies.

She felt trapped.

'Fine, we'll do it your way. I'll attend,' she said as the three of them stepped inside the empty elevator. 'But I'll need a few minutes to find the crèche and settle Bea in.'

'Fine, you have ten minutes.'

'Can't you delay the consultation for half an hour?'

'No.'

'No?' she repeated incredulously. 'Not, perhaps…or I'll see what I can do? Who made you the final decision maker? Oliver Darrington actually seconded me here, not you.'

'But I'm Georgina's OBGYN, so I make the final decision on this case. It's how we run it at Teddy's. Check with Oliver if you like, but he will without doubt defer to me.'

'I don't have time to chase down Mr Darrington.'

'Good because I'm already running behind.'

The doors of the lift opened into OBGYN. The waiting room was full and all eyes turned to them. Charlie considered compromise was in everyone's best interest. 'I'll give you twenty minutes to settle Bea into the crèche, Dr Turner. Then I'll begin the Abbiatis' consultation in Room Two-Thirteen.'

With that, Charlie disappeared down the corridor leaving Juliet and Bea standing opposite the nurses' station. Juliet realised immediately that the middle ground he had offered had more to do with circumstance than generosity of spirit. The patients were all looking in their direction and had clearly been the impetus for the change in tone. She was well aware that he had the potential to be a medical ogre when out of earshot of others.

'Dr Turner?'

Juliet looked up to see a very pretty willowy blonde nurse smiling back at her. 'Yes.'

'Hi, I'm Annabelle Ainsley. I'm the head neonatal nurse,' the blue-eyed woman told her. 'We've been expecting you.'

Juliet guessed the nurse to be in her mid-thirties as she stepped out from behind the station with her hand extended.

'Juliet Turner,' she responded as she met her handshake.

'And who is this gorgeous young lady with the very pretty coloured cast?'

'My daughter, Bea.'

'Hello, Bea,' Annabelle said.

Bea gripped her mother's hand a little tighter as she looked up at the very tall nurse. Her long blonde hair was tied in quite a severe style atop her head that made her appear even taller.

'Pink's my favourite colour in the world,' Annabelle continued and bent down a little to come nearer to the little girl's height. 'I love it so much I even have pink towels and pink soap.'

Bea loosened her grip a little. 'Me too,' she replied with her toothy grin and then smiled up at her mother before she continued. 'I have a pink bed.'

'Yes, you do, and a pink quilt. In fact your room is a pink palace,' Juliet agreed.

'Wow, that's awfully special. I wish I had pink sheets and a pink quilt.'

Juliet was happy that Annabelle and Bea were engaging but she was becoming increasingly concerned about the timeframe she had to get to the consultation and she knew she was hiding the fact well.

'Is there something I can help you with?' Annabelle asked.

'Yes, actually there is. I need to find the crèche as soon as possible. Dr Warren and I'll be meeting with the Abbiatis shortly and I need to settle Bea in, and I haven't had a chance to look over the last two days' obs for Georgina as I've been travelling—'

'I can help with all of that,' Annabelle cut in.

'You can? That would be wonderful. Thank you so much.'

'Not at all,' Annabelle replied with a smile. 'I've just finished my shift and I have no plans so what if I take Bea to the crèche? It's on the ground floor, and I'll wait with her while you meet with Georgina and Leo. Bea and I can chat about all things pink.'

'That's so kind of you,' Juliet said as she turned back to the lift. 'We'll have to hurry though as I have less than fifteen minutes to get to the crèche and back here for the consultation.'

Annabelle took a few long steps and pressed the down button. 'If I may make a suggestion…what if you wait here and I take Bea to the crèche so you can read over Georgina's notes? I've just refreshed everything after the ward rounds, so you can sit at the nurses' station and read up for a few minutes. I'll ask one of the nurses to take you to Room Two-Thirteen when you're ready. It would be less rushed and you'll be up to speed on the babies and mother's condition in plenty of time for the appointment.'

Juliet was so grateful the world had given her a twenty-first-century Florence Nightingale but she also felt torn letting Bea go with a nurse she had known for less than five minutes. A brief internal battle prevailed, fuelled a little by Charlie's initial judging of her parenting, but common sense and her need to attend the consultation won out. 'I think Bea should be okay to go with you. She attends childcare two days a week.

'Is it all right with you, Bea, if the nurse takes you to the crèche? It's like Pennybrook back home when you go and play with the other children when Grandma and Grandpa don't have you. It's not far from here and I'll be there in about an hour once I've seen the very special patient we came all this way to help.'

'Are you going to help the lady with four babies in her tummy?'

'Yes, I am.'

'Okay, Mummy. I think you should go. Grandpa told me that you need to help the lady have the babies.'

Juliet smiled. Sometimes Bea was so wise and practical for a four-year-old. Spending quality time with her grandparents had brought an older perspective to her life and for that Juliet was grateful. She kissed the top of her daughter's head and watched her and Annabelle step closer to the opening doors of the elevator. Bea's fear, that was palpable in A&E, had all but disappeared. Annabelle did look a little similar to one of the pretty child-carers back at Pennybrook and that, Juliet surmised, went a long way to making Bea feel comfortable.

'And you can meet the other children at the crèche. They're all very nice,' Annabelle added as she reached for Bea's little hand and stepped inside the now fully open doors. 'And you can tell me about everything you have back in Australia that's pink. Do you have a pink kangaroo too?'

'No, that would be silly,' Bea said, giggling. 'But I have a pink bear and a pink...' The doors closed on Bea's chatter and Juliet felt herself smiling as she waved goodbye. Annabelle was a lovely addition to an otherwise dreadful day and she was so grateful for her assistance.

As Juliet took a moment to gather her thoughts she knew, with Bea under control, she could concentrate on the task at hand. Making sure that Charlie Warren was put in his place. She had not travelled halfway around the world, not to mention spent years qualifying in her field, to be contradicted by him without having an opportunity to deliver all of the facts. *In-utero* surgery was the quads' best hope and she would be damned if she would stand by and have Charlie convince the Abbiatis otherwise.

Juliet returned to the computer at the nurses' station and caught up with the Abbiatti quads' and their mother's observations before heading off in the direction of Georgina's room. She stood at the T-junction reading the room signs to ensure she had the right wing.

'So let's get you around to meet the parents of the infamous four,' Charlie said, startling Juliet and making her spin around. It was a voice that she would now recognise anywhere. 'I didn't want you to get lost on the way to the consult. I want the Abbiatis to hear your plan and make up their own minds. Despite what you may think, I do play fair.'

'Um...thank you,' she said with a little frown causing a furrow on her forehead. He wasn't playing fair in her books. He was on a mission and the way he looked, the way he spoke, his seemingly impeccable manners, none of it was playing fair.

He ushered her in the direction of the patient's room and she walked alongside him refusing to acknowledge to herself how he was unnerving and confusing her. Since Bea was born, Juliet felt confident in her appraisal of men and their intentions very quickly. No matter how cleverly they spun a story or expertly delivered a well-versed pick-up line. They were all the same and she knew not to trust them.

But Charlie, she had to silently admit, was the most difficult case to sum up that she had stumbled upon to date.

They walked in silence for a few steps, but as they neared the ward Charlie stopped and turned to face Juliet. 'There's something I've been wanting to say to you.'

Juliet's eyes widened and quizzically looked everywhere but at Charlie. She really didn't want to look into his eyes, not in such close proximity. Finally her gaze came back to him. His look was intense and she swallowed nervously.

'What is it?' she asked, not sure she wanted to know but equally puzzled. Even now, in his white consulting coat, he looked as dashing and irresistible as he did in his head-to-toe black leather motorcycle gear. His broad shoulders were not hidden underneath the shapeless clothing. A body like his could not be masked by anything. His boots very loudly announced bad boy even if the rest of him was temporarily dressed to indicate tame. There were definitely two sides to Charlie Warren.

'I've had time to reflect on my earlier behaviour and

I wanted to apologise for jumping to a conclusion about you,' he told her.

Damn! Juliet swallowed again. How she wished with every fibre of her being she had refused the secondment and remained in Perth. Safely tucked away from what Charlie Warren could risk making her feel. It was scaring her. She had known him for less than two hours and he was confusing her more than she'd thought possible. All of her reservations and irritation about Charlie seemed to vanish, with the sound of his voice. It was a bedroom voice. Husky and innately masculine but with undertones of compassion….and tenderness.

Why did he have to apologise? Being angry was her best line of defence. Now what would protect her from herself…and whatever she might begin to feel about Dr Charlie Warren?

CHAPTER FIVE

'GEORGIE, LEO…' CHARLIE BEGAN as Juliet entered the room carrying some handwritten notes on a clipboard along with the printed obs. 'This is Dr Juliet Turner. She is the *in-utero* surgeon who has travelled from Australia to consult on your pregnancy. She will be providing another option with regards to the condition the boys have developed. I must say upfront that I'm not supportive of this option for reasons I have already explained. However, Dr Turner has flown a long way to explain the procedure and answer your questions so I will hand over to her.' He paused and turned his attention to a very stunned Juliet. 'Dr Turner, let me introduce Leo and Georgina Abbiati.'

Juliet couldn't believe that he had just put doubt in the Abbiatis' minds before she opened her mouth. Despite his apology and consideration in ensuring she made it to the consult, he was not giving her any other professional courtesies. She stepped forward with her hand outstretched. 'Very pleased to meet you.'

Juliet knew she was up against his bias. He was stubbornly conservative and not open to accepting proven progressive procedures just as her father had suggested. It was not what she would expect at face value from the motorcycle-riding doctor. The two seemed miles apart.

She drew a deep breath hoping Charlie would leave any further opinions until they were alone in his office and show a mutual professional respect and, as he said, *hand over to her.* She was not about to back away from her belief that the *in-utero* surgery was the best and most logical option for the patient. In the limited time Charlie had given her, Juliet had read the last few days' patient notes and it was exactly as she had first thought: an open and shut case in favour of laser surgery. The twin-to-twin transfusion needed to be halted immediately.

'It's a long way to come just for our babies,' Leo said as he tenderly stroked his wife's arm. 'And we appreciate it. This is a huge decision for us to make. It's our babies' lives we're talking about.'

'Of course it is and I was more than happy to travel here so that you and your children have options to ensure for the best possible outcome,' she replied empathetically. 'The hospital board and the Assistant Head of Obstetrics believed it necessary for me to come and discuss the next management strategy that can be employed. Can you please tell me what you know about your babies' condition, so that I don't repeat anything that either Dr Warren or Mr Darrington have already covered?'

'We know that the two girls are okay and the two boys are sharing an artery or something so one of our boys is getting lots of blood and the other one not enough. Georgie's been having a special diet hoping to get all of them big enough in case they came early anyway. She's twenty-nine weeks tomorrow.'

'You certainly have an overall picture of what's happening. Twin-to-twin transfusion syndrome, or TTTS for short, is a condition of the placenta that affects identical twin pregnancies. The placenta itself is shared unequally by the twins so that one of your sons is receiving too little blood to provide the necessary nutrients to grow normally and the other too much and so his heart is being overworked. Your TTTS was diagnosed at stage three, which is already advanced, and unfortunately has progressed to stage four.' Juliet paused. She knew that she needed to be honest but what she had to say would be hard for the parents-to-be. 'I am not telling you this to add to your concerns but I need to tell it how it truly is and, while the recipient baby is coping at the moment, if we do not surgically intervene that can change quickly and he can suffer heart failure. If that happened, it would immediately cross to stage five and we cannot save him and you will only have three babies. And even then their survival will be compromised.'

The expressions on Leo's and Georgie's faces fell further. 'What do you think, Charlie?'

'I agree with Dr Turner that the boys' condition is serious but I feel the high-protein diet has assisted with the babies' gaining weight and if we continue on that path we may be able to deliver within the next two weeks if necessary.'

Juliet felt as if she were playing a polite game of medical ping-pong but she had to keep serving. 'I would like to commend Dr Warren for the exceptional care he has provided to you and your babies up to now, but unfortunately your boys' condition has worsened. I'm not convinced that without surgical intervention you'll be able to carry four healthy babies for long enough for a good outcome,' Juliet countered.

'But I don't understand why it happened,' Leo said, oblivious to the battle of medical opinion that was being waged very politely in his wife's room. 'We've asked everyone and everyone has told us we did nothing wrong, but you're the specialist. Be honest, was it something we did?'

'Not at all,' Juliet answered. 'It's something that the medical experts can't predict. The events in pregnancy that lead to TTTS are quite random events. The condition is not hereditary or genetic, nor is it caused by anything either of you did or didn't do. TTTS can literally happen to anyone having multiple births at any stage up until about thirty weeks.'

'So it's definitely not our fault?'

'Absolutely not,' Juliet responded again honestly and without hesitation.

'Charlie and Mr Darrington told us that but it's nice to hear it from you.'

Georgina's expression, on hearing confirmation about the cause of her babies' condition, was subdued but Juliet was happy that at least unwarranted guilt would not be another struggle for the quads' mother.

'We know the boys are in trouble but are there any risks to Georgie from the TTTS?' her husband asked as he looked at his wife with loving concern.

'That is something we have to consider, and another reason your wife is in Teddy's on bed rest,' Juliet continued. 'Carrying quads is in itself quite taxing on a woman's body and that stress has been increased by the TTTS. Her uterus is being stretched past what is normal for pregnancy—'

'Should you just wait then and take the babies in two weeks as Charlie says and not put Georgie at any risk?' Leo cut in.

Without giving Charlie time to interrupt, Juliet answered quickly. 'Actually no. That could've been a consideration if, since the diagnosis two days ago, the condition had not progressed, but it has and, for want of a better word, aggressively. I'm not convinced that the recipient baby would survive until thirty-one weeks. If the pregnancy was just twins, we could deliver at twenty-nine weeks. However, with quads the babies are still very small so if we can prolong the pregnancy another few weeks by having the laser surgery, the babies will be bigger when they're born and that will make their lives easier. At the moment they are all less than three pounds and we no longer have time on our side to observe their growth.'

'Like you said, Dr Turner,' Georgina responded, 'we agree that Charlie has taken such good care of me up until now we're really struggling to think about ignoring his advice. Perhaps we should have the needle and stay with bed rest.'

Charlie drew in a deep breath, plumped out his chest, and in Juliet's opinion looked like a pigeon about to mate. His polite interruptions made her believe their professional battle would lean towards a gentleman's sword fight, but a fight nonetheless, and she was right. But for the good of the mother and her babies, she would not hold back. There would be a level of professional courtesy, but she would not cower to him. Juliet was prepared to argue on the evidence-based merit of surgery and then leave the decision where it should lie. With the well-informed parents.

'While the needle you spoke of, an amniotic reduction, can work well in stage one patients, you have moved past this option very quickly. Teddy's brought me here to discuss laser surgery and the benefits and they would not have flown me halfway around the world if there was any doubt that surgery was a viable and preferable choice for you.' Juliet paused for a moment, then continued with a serious timbre in her voice. 'But

I won't lie to you, there are risks in the surgical route as there are with any surgery, but the benefit far outweighs the risks. I also must let you know that if you choose to proceed with the laser surgery, then it would need to be this week. On Thursday or Friday at the latest as time is not on our side if we decide to help your sons surgically. If we leave it too long, your body will make the decision for us.'

Juliet watched Georgina's and Leo's expressions darken. It was a lot to process and, while she had not wanted to put additional pressure on either of them, she felt all the facts had to be stated. Time was unfortunately not on their side and that was the harsh realisation they all needed to accept. To deliver four living babies, something had to be done. She just prayed they chose surgery.

'Can you give us more details, like what the surgery involves and how long it will take?' Leo asked as he ceased stroking his wife's arm and reached down to hold her hand tightly.

Juliet stepped away from the bed to give the couple a little more space. Hearing news and making potential life-and-death decisions, she knew, was overwhelming and they needed to feel safe together in their own space. 'Of course,' she began and then noticed that Charlie had brought her a chair. She wasn't sure if he was being gallant and considerate or if he was trying to make her appear weary. She didn't waste time deciding which it was, instead choosing to graciously accept the chair and continue.

'The operation involves endoscopic surgery using a laser beam to cauterise the offending arteries and halt the exchange of blood between your boys. Each baby will remain connected to his primary source of blood and nutrition, the placenta, through the umbilical cord. The use of endoscopic instruments allows for short recovery time and no effect on the other babies and would be done only once during the pregnancy.'

'Dear God, we pray if we go ahead it's just one time,' Leo interrupted as he looked into his wife's tear-filled eyes. 'Georgie's been through so much over the last eighteen months with the three rounds of IVF, and that was unsuccessful, and then finding out we're having four babies conceived naturally. And now this heart-breaking news about the transfusion while I was away.'

'Leo, you're suffering as much as me, and you had to make the trip to New York,' she told him as she mopped the tears that threatened to escape. Her eyes were reddened from too many nights of crying. 'We've *both* been through so much and we're doing our best to stay strong together.'

'And we will. No matter what, we'll get through all of this. And we'll take our babies home to where they belong. Their *nonni*, all four of them, are waiting to meet their grandchildren.'

Juliet nodded. 'That's my plan and I'm so pleased to hear your positive outlook. That's exactly what your babies need.'

'Ah, you know Italians, we're a strong race and our children will be fighters too.'

'Goodness, Leo,' Georgina said. 'You sound like my father!'

'Well, it's the truth,' Charlie added. 'You and Georgie have been strong and focused since the diagnosis and that's why you should not completely rule out continuing on the current conservative path.'

Juliet swung around on her chair with a look of indignation. She could not believe what she was hearing. Charlie clearly had not *handed over to her* as he'd promised. Fuming but unable to tell Charlie how she felt, Juliet regained her composure, turned back to the couple and continued. She would let Charlie know in no uncertain terms how she felt about his interference, after the consultation. But for the moment she intended to calmly give Georgina and Leo all the information so they understood it was their choice, and theirs alone.

'Minimally invasive fetoscopic surgery is the name of the procedure and it is aptly named because it's *minimally* invasive. It involves small incisions and I will be guided by both an endoscope and sonography. Essentially it's keyhole surgery so far lower risks than open foetal surgery, which is completely opening the uterus to operate on the foetus.'

'But there's still a chance it could go wrong?' Leo asked anxiously, looking from Juliet to Charlie.

'Yes, but not undertaking the surgery has equal if not greater risk,' Juliet said honestly and, armed with further facts, she elaborated. 'I do not want you to be under the misapprehension that the safer choice is doing nothing as that is quite incorrect. In the past the twin survival rate with severe TTTS was very low, around ten per cent before ultrasound made it possible for us to make an early diagnosis and the introduction of laser surgery. I think you should consider taking advantage of this medical advance. In years gone by women had no choice but to wait and pray they did not give birth to a stillborn baby. As I have mentioned excess amniotic fluid caused by the TTTS is causing your uterus to grow to an unsustainable size. It's a condition called polyhydramnios, and it can cause premature labour.'

'I have a fifty-four-inch waist now.'

'Yes, that's a combination of four babies and the fluid

and it will continue to increase,' Charlie added. 'We're monitoring that and can continue to do so, and perform the amniotic reduction procedure.'

Juliet bit her lip again. Charlie was not allowing her much space to move.

'Georgina, you will be monitored in hospital until all four babies are born, no matter your decision. However, I'm suggesting surgery because there are four very tiny babies still growing inside you and they need optimum time to grow. The final decision rests with you.'

Georgina shifted on the bed and raised her feet again. Her rounded stomach was still covered by the sheet and lightweight blanket, but only just. Her pretty face was almost hidden by the mound that held her precious babies. Juliet knew the young woman's ribs would be excruciatingly tender from the pressure of four babies.

'So you can definitely separate the blood supply?' Georgina finally asked.

'The tiny telescope in your uterus will allow me to find and destroy all the connecting vessels. This is the only treatment that can *disconnect* the twins.'

'How common is it for parents to choose laser surgery?'

'Laser surgery is now performed all over the world as more and increasing numbers of progressively attuned doctors are convinced that this will lead to the best outcomes.' Juliet's words were directed at Charlie but she did not pause over the words or look in his direction. Two could play at the same game. 'Most physicians worldwide agree that placental laser surgery results in the highest numbers of healthy survivors.'

'Including those in the UK?' Leo enquired.

'Yes, particularly in a hospital like Teddy's.'

Georgina and Leo gave each other a knowing look. 'Would I be awake?'

'Yes, Georgie, you'd be awake. You would be under conscious sedation and local anaesthetic for this procedure. We need you and the babies to be relaxed and pain free during the procedure but there's no need for a general anaesthetic.'

Leo straightened his back, took a deep resonating breath and looked at Charlie. 'Charlie, by what we're hearing, and the urgency of everything, are we right in thinking we have to make the decision tonight? It's a lot to take in and not a decision we want to make in a hurry.'

Charlie cleared his throat and stepped a little closer. 'Not quite tonight but, yes, if you choose Dr Turner's surgical option you would only have a day or two to make that decision. However, my plan would not see you making any changes other than looking at prescribing heart medication as pills given to Georgie, or injected directly into the twin if he is showing signs of heart failure. We can also look at another therapy using medication to decrease the urine output in the recipient and lessen the amount of amniotic fluid that is causing Georgie's uterus to expand.'

Juliet bit her lip. She could counter but chose not to do so. She had said enough and if they chose the non-surgical option she would remain on staff at Teddy's to help in any way she could, including the delivery. But she hoped they would choose her way forward and she would be able to use her surgical skills to increase the babies' chances of survival and happy and healthy lives.

Georgina and Leo looked at each other with what Juliet knew would feel like the weight of the world on their shoulders but their love for each other still shone brightly in their eyes. Finally Leo spoke. 'Is it all right if we sleep on it?'

'Of course,' Charlie and Juliet said in unison then they too looked at each other. But it was not lovingly; their look was more of an aloof stare.

Juliet had felt as if she were on a roller coaster since she'd touched down at Heathrow, and even before that with the last-minute packing. But now it was a different type of roller coaster. The emotional type. And for which she had not willingly purchased a ticket, nor even had any idea she would be experiencing. But in the few hours since Charlie had stepped into her life and lifted her tiny daughter into his arms, she had ridden highs and lows that she'd never imagined. He was opinionated and brash; considerate and caring; her old school colleague and stubborn opponent; and still, to her annoyance, attractive.

He was quite the package and she definitely didn't want to peel back too many layers or get too close. Charlie was confusing her and, working together for the next few weeks, she wondered how successfully she could avoid getting to know more about him. A conservative, bad-boy biker with attitude who seemed to adore children, or at least her child. Could he be any more complex? She doubted it.

And she wasn't convinced she wanted to understand Charlie Warren.

CHAPTER SIX

WITH LEO AND GEORGINA left alone to think everything over, Juliet had a chance to meet the rest of Teddy's nursing staff. Although Juliet had seen the Royal Cheltenham hospital emergency department up close and personal with Bea, Charlie knew that she had not seen Teddy's properly, so he took it upon himself to offer to show her around the centre dedicated to babies and birth. But not before setting the parameters of the working relationship in his mind.

'I think you would have to agree that we both behaved quite poorly in there,' he began, thinking that they should get everything out in the open and start afresh. 'Fortunately not that Georgina or Leo noticed.'

'I'm sorry, are you questioning *my* behaviour?'

'I'm just saying that we could have handled things a little more diplomatically.'

'So you're saying that we *both* behaved poorly and *we* could have handled things better?'

Charlie frowned. 'Yes, as I also said, it was done in a very polite manner so that the Abbiatis did not sense any professional tension, but you have to admit we were walking a fine line.'

Juliet's hands suddenly took pride of place on her hips as she began pacing, then drew to a halt in front of him. 'I can't believe what you're saying and I refuse to accept culpability for your, as you Englishmen say, *poor form*. I was seconded over here and you were clearly the one stirring doubt, if not confusion.'

Charlie studied Juliet's face. Even angry, she was very beautiful. And Juliet was clearly angry. She was riled up and ready to pounce on him for even suggesting that she had participated in the battle of wills. It was apparent when challenged Juliet was like a cat with an arched back. He wondered what made her so defensive. Had she been on the receiving end of too many challenges over her career? Or was it more than that? Was her attitude of fight or flight born from something outside work?

He suddenly stopped his line of thought mid-journey. What she did or did not do outside work was not his business. Whatever had caused, or was still causing, Juliet to fight back was not his concern. She was a grown woman, who had no doubt endured some heartache and some of life's lessons, but that did not excuse her from professional scrutiny.

Charlie eyed Juliet again. In fact he had barely taken his eyes away from her. All five feet four inches. But despite her petite appearance, he had quickly learnt that she was no shrinking violet. And he doubted she would tolerate fools either. He quickly realised that he wasn't about to win the argument. And suddenly, to his surprise, he was willing to accept the decision was where it needed to be, with the parents of the babies at risk. They had been given the facts. He couldn't do any more.

'Fair call, Dr Turner,' he offered. 'I'm sorry for the start we've had. Shall we begin again? Let's put the consultation behind us. One way or the other it looks as if we'll be spending time together so we should try and make this work.'

Charlie wasn't sure what had motivated him to call a professional truce but it seemed the right thing to do. He hoped she knew his words were genuine. He was calling a ceasefire. It was a masculine apology but sincere nonetheless. And one he hoped that she would accept.

She extended her hand. 'Truce accepted, Dr Warren. Let's agree to disagree and allow the Abbiatis to decide without further interference.'

As he met her handshake the warmth of her skin against his almost made him recant the apology so they could return to adversaries. He pulled his hand free as soon as he was able.

'We're both clearly passionate about what we do and that's a great thing so we will just have to respect our differing opinions and work alongside each other as best we can,' he said.

'Yes, and one of us will clearly be pleased with their decision and the other disappointed but we will simply wear it,' she added.

Charlie said nothing for a moment as he looked at the tiny powerhouse standing near him. She was without doubt one of the best in her field, and, despite not agreeing with that particular obstetric intervention, he had immeasurable respect for her skills. Her reputation had preceded her. But there was something other than respect simmering below the surface for him and it was making him uncomfortable. Very uncomfortable.

He walked in the direction of the large digital directory board in Reception. 'It might be a good idea if you took a look around and familiarised yourself with Teddy's. It would be best if you met everyone and knew where everything was in case you're needed.'

'You mean for *when* I'm needed?' she responded.

'Let's wait and see.'

The introductions soon became an induction. As she met each of the medical staff she learnt about the layout and workings of Teddy's. The nursing staff gave Juliet a message from Annabelle, letting her know that Bea had settled in well and that she was enjoying a light lunch with the other children while listening to a story. Knowing that, Juliet decided to keep on the tour and learn as much as she could about the hospital.

The reputation of Teddy's had been a driving force in Juliet's accepting the secondment. The opportunity to consult and operate in a hospital with facilities second to none in all of Europe was too good to refuse.

Juliet thanked Charlie for showing her the ropes.

'Not at all. It's been an eventful start for you and I hope Bea will be all right tonight. I know I don't have to mention it, but just give her a little oral analgesia if she has trouble sleeping and she should be fine by tomorrow.'

'I will.'

As Charlie watched Juliet walk away he realised that he hadn't wanted the tour to end. He had enjoyed his time with Juliet. She was challenging him and he felt the closest to alive that he had in a long time. They came from polar opposites. Both geographically and professionally. She was forging new ground surgically and he was of the belief that monitoring with minimal surgical intervention was the better method. But despite their differences, he admired her courage.

He had been an OBGYN for many years, and his conservative approach had always provided great outcomes for the mothers and the babies. Although as he walked back to his office he admitted to himself that he had not dealt with the complication of TTTS in quadruplets. As he sat down behind his desk, to stretch his legs out and read his emails before another ward round, he conceded they were on an even playing field with regard to experience. Neither had a track record that could negate the other. So neither one of them could say with any evidence that their treatment plan was better. It was purely subjective and tainted by preference.

Juliet for taking risks.

Charlie for avoiding them every day since he had taken a chance on the icy road and lost.

Juliet and a very tired Bea arrived back at their hotel late in the afternoon. Bea had enjoyed her time at the crèche and was not in a hurry to leave. Juliet suspected it was due to the fuss that Annabelle and the children had made of her. After lunch and the story, her mind had been distracted from the traumatic start to the day by the children all wanting to draw pictures on her cast and ask questions about koalas and kangaroos. She'd been the centre of attention and she'd managed that role well. When Juliet had popped up to collect her, she'd looked through the large glass window that was decorated with paper cut-outs of snowflakes to see Bea happily playing with the other children. Juliet had been convinced earlier in the day that bringing her daughter on the trip was a terrible idea, but as she'd witnessed her smiling and happily playing despite the cast the idea had left terrible territory.

A classic Georgian property, not too far from the hospital, had been restored and refurbished as an exclusive, eleven-room boutique hotel and it would be their accommodation for a day or so until Juliet could source something more practical for the two of them. Their room was toasty warm with a large bed covered in far too many oversized pillows and the softest mattress. The warmth was created by an antique radiator and the all-white decor, complete with heavy damask drapes and matching bedspread, was elegance in abundance. She felt very spoilt as the hospital board had insisted on covering the cost of the expensive room until she secured something else, in addition to her business-class flight and that of her daughter.

Back in Perth, she lived in a small home not too far from her parents and equally close to the hospital and Pennybrook childcare centre. When she'd purchased the three-bedroom house, it had been a very practical decision. It was a nice house but not ostentatious. Understated in its exterior appearance and equally in the interior. Juliet wasn't in love with her home but the location meant she could drop off Bea and collect her easily from childcare or her grandparents' home. Most decisions after Bea was born were practical. And never rushed. Up until this trip, Juliet had considered and reconsidered every move she made. Although Charlie clearly thought she was a risk-taker in suggesting the surgical intervention, she thought just the opposite. She carefully weighed up the risks, and never blindly jumped into anything. She had learnt the hard way by rushing into a relationship with Bea's father and she never planned on doing that again.

In fact, she swore on it.

The ambience of their hotel room was something Juliet loved almost immediately, along with the breathtaking scenery of the Cotswolds. It surprised Juliet that, while she had worried she would feel out of place, she quickly felt comfortable in the South Midlands of England. She was a long way from home but she didn't feel entirely lost.

As they sat at the small mahogany card table that doubled as a dining table for two, eating their room-service dinner of a hearty beef stew and finished off with a homemade apple pie, Juliet felt as if she had been transported back to another time. Bea managed to eat her children's size serving even with her sling in place and Juliet felt sure she would sleep well with a full tummy.

But no matter how stunning the room, Juliet had to admit the gorgeous antique bath positioned by the large bay window was completely impractical for a four-year-old with a cast. She felt so sorry for her tiny daughter as she stood her next to the porcelain wash basin and used the fluffy white washcloths to give her a freshen up. It would have been too awkward to place Bea into the free-standing and very deep bath. She needed to check the bathroom of the longer-term accommodation before she signed anything, she thought as she dried Bea and slipped her into snuggly warm pyjamas. Fortunately the pyjama top was made of a stretch knit and quite loose fitting so she could slip it over the cast. But working around her daughter's broken arm was not how she'd seen the first day ending.

With Bea snuggled in bed after some pain relief and drifting off to sleep, Juliet ran a bath for herself.

'Mummy,' Bea called out sleepily across the warm room.

'Yes, sweetie, what is it?' Juliet asked as she took a nightdress out of her suitcase, which was open and lying alongside Bea's. Juliet decided there was no point unpacking and using the ample white built-in wardrobe, which blended into the wall colour, or the ornately carved chest of drawers. They wouldn't be staying long enough.

'Why duth Grandpa call you honey and not Juliet?'

'He's just always called me honey since I was a little girl.'

'Ith that becauth he'th your daddy?'

'I guess so. It's his special name for me because I'm his daughter and everyone else calls me Juliet.'

'Charlie called me honey…'

Juliet stopped what she was doing. 'When?' she asked with a puzzled look.

'When I fell in the playground and he picked me up. Duth that mean Charlie could be my daddy?'

Juliet felt her stomach fall and her heart race as she dropped closed her suitcase. Her fallen stomach was the reaction to the unexpected daddy question and just thinking of Charlie in the role of Bea's father made her heart race. She swallowed a lump that had risen in her throat. Charlie's handsome face appeared in her mind. She no longer pictured Bea's father or even thought of him when she looked at Bea.

But now she suddenly pictured Charlie.

With legs shaking, Juliet walked back to her daughter and sat beside her, stroking her face and watching her tired eyes struggle to stay open. They were slowly closing as she kissed her gently. Juliet was trying to find the words to answer Bea. She was still too young to understand what had really happened and why she didn't have a daddy.

'No, my sweet, Charlie is not your daddy. But one day when you're much bigger we can talk about your daddy.' With that she pulled up the covers over her daughter.

'Okay.'

'Sweet dreams.'

As Juliet tiptoed back to the bath she heard her daughter mumble, 'Mummy?'

'Yes, sweetie.'

'I think Charlie would make a nice daddy.'

Juliet felt momentarily overwhelmed. It was obvious now that her daughter missed having a father. With a heavy heart, Juliet removed the last of her clothing in the soft light of the bedside lamp and climbed into the steaming bubbles, where she remained for a good half an hour thinking about her life and about Bea's. Her daughter's question was spinning along with all the others she had for herself. Her mind was on overload and Bea's innocent curiosity added another weight. While the travel was beginning to take its toll, the question of Bea's paternity was now an issue and one that she had no idea how exactly she would answer. Soon she would want more answers. And Juliet would have to answer each and every question as honestly as she could without letting her know that her father was a cad.

Juliet's eyes felt heavier and heavier as she reached for an oversized towel and stepped carefully from the bath. She was exhausted. Mentally and physically. It had been a whirlwind since she'd stepped off the final plane at Heathrow. Then she admitted silently the whirlwind had begun before she and Bea had even boarded the first aircraft. The push to hand over her patients at the Perth Women's and Children's Medical Centre in a matter of hours and packing their suitcases in temperatures hovering around one hundred degrees for freezing cold weather and all the while questioning the practicalities of travelling with a four-year-old. As she dried herself and slipped the nightdress over her head she heard the soft breathing of her sleeping daughter and knew that no matter what happened or what they faced they would do it together. And they would be just fine.

Barefoot, she tiptoed over to her side of the bed, slipped in between the brushed cotton sheets, turned down her mobile phone and turned off the bedside light. Sleep overtook her the moment her head rested on the softness of the duck-down pillows.

'Mummy, wake up! Someone'th here,' the lispy voice announced.

Juliet opened her eyes to see Bea standing beside the bed and looking in the direction of the hotel-room door. There was firm and unrelenting knocking. Not brash but loud enough to seem urgent. Juliet climbed from her bed, kissed the top of her daughter's head and grabbed her robe from the end of the bed where she had dropped it the night before.

'Who is it?'

'Charlie Warren,' came the response, but even without his self-identification his voice told her immediately that it was him.

Juliet's brow knitted. What on earth was he doing at her door? The heavy drapes stopped her seeing how dark or light it was outside but she imagined it was early; she felt as if she had barely been asleep.

'Is there something wrong? Has Georgina progressed to stage five?'

'No. Georgina's stable but they've made their decision and I thought I'd let you know first-hand.'

Juliet crossed to the door, running her fingers through the messy curls. She didn't care at that moment about her appearance. She just hoped the news was good and they had chosen surgery. She opened the door ready to ask that question when she came face to face with a vision head to toe in black leather. Suddenly she felt senses that had lain dormant for many years awaken without warning. Charlie stood before her, once again dressed in his leather riding gear, and holding his helmet in his leather-gloved hand. The same hand that had so tenderly applied Bea's cast the day before. This was the man that called Bea *honey* and made her think he might be her father. The look was intoxicating and took her breath and words away but allowing him into her life scared her too.

'Are you okay?'

'Yes,' she finally managed. 'You startled me. I was still asleep. I'm as keen as you to know the answer but it's still so early. Did the Abbiatis call you in the middle of the night?'

'No,' he replied. 'They spoke to me on my nine o'clock rounds.'

'Nine o'clock rounds?' she asked incredulously.

'I called your phone but it went straight to message bank and you didn't call back so here I am.'

'I never heard your call,' she told him with a slight frown. 'What time is it now?'

Charlie looked at his watch. 'Nearly ten-thirty.'

'Really? That means we slept for twelve hours.'

'I've been watching TV, Mummy.'

Juliet looked down at her daughter, who had cleverly managed to slip on her sling, and then turn on the cartoon channel on the television.

'I can't believe I slept in that long. You must be hungry, darling.'

'A little.'

Charlie smiled. Bea was adorable and he was beginning to feel that there might be a slim chance Juliet might be just as lovely if he got to know her better. He admired the fact she told him exactly how she felt. She didn't tiptoe around him like everyone else who *felt sorry for the widower*. He could see it in their faces and hear it in their voices. He had attended the hospital fundraiser in the hope the staff would see him as something other than a recluse. Charlie liked that Juliet was unaware of his wife's death and he assumed that was why she was able to stand up to him. She was the first person to do that in two years. Being around her made him realise he missed being challenged and being held accountable.

And her conviction in her treatment plan for Georgina Abbiati made him feel slightly less concerned about the surgical intervention although he still did not agree.

'What if I take you two ladies out for brunch?' He wanted to spend more time with the beautiful woman with the messy hair and the gorgeous smile who was still dressed in her robe. He couldn't explain it to himself—it was as if he had known Juliet and Bea for more than one day. His attraction was more than skin deep and it defied logic and his promise to himself that he would never get involved with anyone. But standing so close to Juliet, he felt that promise fading and the desire to know her increasing.

'Is this a brunch to break good news or bad?' she asked without a smile. 'Are you here to brag of your victory and tell me that the Abbiatis have chosen your conservative treatment option? Is that the reason you've come in person?'

Charlie was taken aback. He had not seen that reaction coming. His agenda had been very different. He just felt a pull to be with Juliet, to learn more about her away from the hospital, and against his better judgement he had decided to act upon it. Now he knew that was a stupid idea. Reckless in fact. He barely knew Juliet and, for some ridiculous reason, he wanted to spend his free time with her. And with Bea. Suddenly he was grateful she had given him the perspective he needed. He had no business being at her hotel. He should have left a message and waited until she had arrived at the hospital. He was better off alone.

It was the way he liked it.

And the way it should be.

'You're right, it was a bad idea,' he said as he stepped back and opened the hotel-room door. 'I'll leave you ladies to enjoy your late breakfast alone. And by the way, Juliet, the Abbiatis decided on the fetoscopic placental laser surgery. I guess I was just the gracious loser in a professional differing of opinion…offering to share a meal.'

With that he closed the door on Juliet.

And to stirrings he knew he had no right to act upon.

CHAPTER SEVEN

'CHARLIE, PLEASE WAIT,' Juliet called down the passageway. She couldn't follow him dressed in only her robe. 'I'm sorry, I was rude and ungracious.'

Charlie stopped long enough to turn and see her in the doorway. Her messy hair, the spattering of freckles across the bridge of her nose, and her pretty amber eyes that looked genuinely remorseful. He was grateful that she had sent him walking. It was for the best. She was too close to exactly what he didn't have room for in his life. And definitely didn't deserve. A pretty, intelligent woman with a fighting spirit. And a daughter who was cute as a button.

'Apology accepted. I'll see you at the hospital later, then. I've an opening at one-thirty if you would like to meet. We need to schedule in the surgery, brief the theatre team and then book another pre-op consultation as soon as possible.'

His tone was brusque and he didn't wait for a reply as Juliet watched him disappear out of sight. She closed her bedroom door and raced to the window with Bea in tow. Pulling back the heavy damask curtains to see him emerge from the building and climb onto the shiny black bike that he had parked in the small guest car park. He pulled down his helmet, and turned his head.

Nervously she dropped the curtains before he saw her watching him. It appeared Dr Charlie Warren, intentionally or unintentionally, was going to make her second day in the Cotswolds as confusing as the first.

Charlie rode away but not before he noticed Juliet looking from her window. He saw in his rear-view mirror that she had closed the curtains as quickly as she had opened them. While he had accepted her apology he couldn't help but wonder as he headed along the leafy streets on his way to Teddy's what had made the Australian specialist so quickly think the worst of him.

Admittedly, the previous day he had been the one to jump to conclusions, and perhaps had not been his professional best at the consultation, but he had apologised for both. And to make amends and let her know that he would not challenge the Abbiatis' decision he had driven over to tell her in person. But once he'd known that neither Bea nor Juliet had eaten, it had felt natural to offer a shared brunch.

As he rounded the next corner, he told himself that it was his olive branch. But there was more to it and, as he righted himself on the large motorbike before the next curve, he silently accepted that Juliet had broken through his tough exterior shell. She had made him think of more than work. More than the mothers and the babies and the families he was helping to create. In twenty-four hours she and Bea had reminded him of all those things he'd wanted and dreamed of before the accident. Before the loss of his wife made him lose hope in the future.

But her reaction to his reaching out was unexpected. Shooting him down by questioning his motives.

Was it jet lag or was Juliet Turner always on the defensive? He wasn't sure but, with his hand on the throttle, he rode a little faster than usual. Although Charlie had grown up in the stunning Cotswolds countryside, he appreciated the architecture and landscape that defined the part of England he called home, but not that day. Instead of noticing the Regency town houses and their intricate ironwork balconies and painted stucco façades or the rolling green hills that were blanketed in pristine snow, he could only picture Juliet's face as he travelled back to work. Equally confused about what made Juliet so quick to judge…and what had really driven him to deliver the news in person.

Juliet knocked on the door. The brass plate read Dr Charlie Warren, OBGYN. She was in the right place.

'Come in.'

Juliet opened the door and entered with mixed emotions. She was thrilled that the surgery would take place and the quads would in her opinion have the best chance of survival, but her behaviour at the hotel a few hours earlier still bothered her. And underneath she knew that was because Charlie Warren was affecting her and she was confused and scared.

But despite those feelings unnerving her, the fact the obstinate but handsome OBGYN had reached out to her made her feel a little special. Perhaps that was why she took extra time to choose her outfit. A long black knitted dress that hugged her slim hips. It had a roll collar and she had added a silver necklace and a black patent boot with a medium height heel. It was her smart apology outfit, she told herself. The previous day's travelling clothes were for comfort and that morning he had seen her in her pyjamas so she wanted to show a level of professionalism in her dressing. There was no other reason for her to wear the figure-hugging dress.

The tight knit also kept her warm. Cheltenham was a cold place. That was all.

How could there be any other reason? It certainly wasn't to impress Charlie Warren the man.

'Hello, Juliet. Please take a seat. I won't be a moment. I'm just emailing through a medical report to a GP in London.'

'Thank you,' she said as she sat in the chair opposite him.

Juliet took the time to let her gaze wander around the office. But there was nothing telling about any of it. No personal belongings that jumped out and showed her a little about Charlie. No photos, just a couple of certificates that provided evidence of his qualifications. Without appearing nosey, she searched from her vantage point for something that would let her know more about him. There was nothing. No hint. It appeared that Dr Warren had no life outside his work...or if he did he was hiding it.

"I have taken the liberty of booking the operating theatre,' he began as he turned his attention to Juliet. 'And also confirming with the Abbiatis that the surgery will be on Friday.'

'Thank you.'

'Don't thank me, I'm just extending a professional courtesy on behalf of the board.'

Juliet frowned. His change in demeanour was extraordinary. But she knew she had been the cause. Her earlier reaction was cold and dismissive and just plain rude.

'Juliet, don't misread my actions for a change of mind. It isn't. I still don't think that surgery is the best option and, while I will not raise the issue again with the parents as they have made their decision, I still have grave concerns.'

'Well, I'm grateful that we can agree at least to provide a united front even if behind the scenes there is still a great divide.'

Juliet noticed a flick in his jaw. Finely covered with dark blond shadow, it was defined but tense.

'A very great divide.'

'May I ask why?'

'Because I know you have experience in TTTS and this procedure, your papers prove it, but you have never, according to my research, undertaken this with quads.'

'I have with triplets,' she argued.

'Once,' he returned. 'I read your notes.'

'Yes, once, but successfully and I am not operating on all four. Only two of the four are involved.'

'That's where you're wrong. You're exposing all four to a risk.'

'I agree but the benefits outweigh the risk—'

'I don't agree with that rationale. You're risking all four babies to save one and even success with that foetus is not guaranteed. It could take up to a month after the baby is born to know if there are any residual effects from the surgery. And even a year later in some cases long-term side effects have been diagnosed.'

'But the child may not live at all if we don't proceed.' Juliet slumped a little in her chair. Her apology meeting was turning sour quickly. Charlie's defensive stance was back again. She hoped she would have been more gracious if she had been the one assisting him with his treatment plan instead of the other way around. But she accepted that was easier said as the victor and her reaction a few hours earlier, suspecting he was delivering bad news, didn't show any sign of gracious defeat. Perhaps they were alike after all. But she would never know because she was the one who had won this battle.

'I've been performing this procedure for many years and before proceeding the Abbiatis will be fully informed of the risk.'

'One additional baby complicates things ten-fold and I'm not sure that you'll be experienced enough to deal with those complications should they arise.'

Juliet decided to stand and signal the end of the meeting. It was going nowhere and it was pointless in her opinion. 'I don't see any value in going around in circles. The parents have agreed, Teddy's board flew me over and the theatre is booked thanks to you. It would appear the surgery is a fait accompli.'

'If it's not successful, I'll be noting my objections in a report to the board.'

'I would expect no less,' she replied as she crossed to the door. 'Will I have an office during my secondment? I think it would be a good idea so that I can have some time to look over the reports privately.' Her eyebrow was raised as she looked directly at Charlie. She hoped it was a look that didn't leave room for questions or second-guessing. It was a demand not a polite request that he could choose whether to approve. He had taken it back to adversarial colleagues. They were right back to where they started.

'I'll see what we can do.'

'Now that's settled, I'll be back tomorrow with my laptop ready to log on and begin the pre-op preparations.'

Juliet chatted with the nurses and asked to meet the midwife who was looking after Georgina.

'That's Ella O'Brien,' Annabelle offered. 'She's not on today but will be back tomorrow.'

Juliet thanked her and then left to visit Georgina.

'Leo's just gone home to get me some fresh clothes. I guess you heard we're going ahead with the surgery.'

'I did, and I must say I'm very pleased. I truly believe it's the best option.'

'So do we,' Georgina said with nerves and a little doubt still evident in her voice. 'We really like Charlie but we got to thinking if the board has flown you all the way here then they must believe in the surgery too. We didn't think they would go to that much trouble and expense if it wasn't something they believe worthwhile. We just don't know why Charlie doesn't feel the same way as them.'

'Dr Warren is a great doctor, and he has every right to have a different opinion. Medicine can be quite subjective at times and sometimes doctors differ but they both want the best for the patient. Dr Warren's taken the very best care of you up to now but the board do agree that the laser surgery will give you the best chance of taking four babies home with you.'

'We pray every day for them all. We've named them, you know.'

'That's wonderful. Are the names a secret?'

'We have told our family and Charlie, Ella and Mr Darrington. We like Graham and Rupert for the boys and Lily and Rose for the girls.'

'I feel very honoured to know, and they are the loveliest names,' Juliet said sincerely. She thought they were such sweet, old-fashioned names but they didn't sound very southern European at all.

'I guess you're wondering why they sound so English and not Italian.'

'You're a mind reader.'

'Not really, I think we're going to be asked that a lot but our families moved here from Italy many years ago. Leo and I met at Italian school so traditions are important but since we both come from huge families, I have five siblings and Leo has eight brothers and sisters, so the grandparents all have grandchildren named after them, and more than a few cousins share names too. We wanted our babies to be different. It's not that we don't love our culture, it's just we want them to have their own identity, which will be difficult enough with two sets of identical twins, let alone if they share names with their cousins. So we have our parents' blessings to give them very special names.'

'Were you born here, or in Italy?'

'Leo and I were both born in London. Leo's grandparents did very well producing rice and maize in the region of Abbiategrasso, in Lombardy in Italy, and that's where his surname originated. They sent his father to London for an education with the hopes he would return to his home, but instead he graduated from law, met a beautiful young Italian woman, married and settled in London raising Leo and his brothers and sisters. My grandparents' background was in grapes and olives in Umbria. My father was also sent to London for higher education and along with his international commerce degree came an English bride, my mother, who loved all things Italian including my father. And soon,' she said, looking down at her oversized belly, 'there will be another instant generation of Abbiatis a long way from Italy.'

'Well, I think the names are just gorgeous and I'm sure the children will make you very proud as they grow up.'

'So you're privy to the babies' names too?' came a deep and now familiar voice from the doorway. 'Well, I must say you've become a member of the Abbiati family more quickly than I did. It took me the best part of a month before that information was entrusted to me.'

Juliet turned to see Charlie in the doorway to the private hospital room.

'I feel quite special at this moment.'

'And so you should, for you know the names of the children you have been given the opportunity to save.'

Juliet suddenly felt the weight of the Abbiatis' decision fall squarely on her shoulders. She swallowed hard, unsure if unsettling her was Charlie's intention. If so he had succeeded.

'I will have a great surgical team, experienced—'

'And ready for the unexpected,' Charlie cut in.

Juliet was not impressed. She had hoped his doubts would not be voiced any more but apparently that was not the case. At least she was pleased his delivery was subtle enough not to cause any concern to Georgina. She was still unaware of the professional rivalry. For that Juliet was grateful.

'I would expect no less from any team, primed for success and prepared for the unexpected, but in this case I doubt there will be any surprises. We know there are four babies, and we know there's one problem to solve and then bed rest for you for another few weeks until they are all healthy and a good size for delivery. And on that note, Dr Warren and I need to discuss the procedure and have a scheduled meeting now.'

'We do?'

'We do.'

'Then, Georgie, I will see you later,' Charlie said as

he followed Juliet from the room. Once they were out of earshot, Juliet did not hold back.

'You promised you would not try to unsettle my patient. She has made her decision and there is no point in you questioning them now.'

'Your patient? Georgina is my patient and has been for nineteen weeks since the quads were identified.'

'Well, she'll be your former patient unless you promise to cease this interference.'

'Since when does advice to my patient constitute interference?' he asked as he headed in the direction of his office.

'From where I'm standing that's exactly what it is and I won't stand for it. So please back off or I'll be forced to go to Oliver Darrington and ask to have you removed if he wants me to stay.' Juliet kept up with his fast pace.

'Is that a threat?'

'I'm not sure… I guess if you don't accept your behaviour to be tantamount to undue interference then I really don't have to acknowledge whether mine is a threat.'

'I said in front of Georgina that you have the opportunity to save her babies. They chose your procedure. It's now in your hands. A fact. And as for the team expecting the unexpected, that is my way of saying they are experienced and the Abbiatis have nothing to worry about. My words were designed to bring comfort to the quads' mother and by the look on her face they did just that. Did she look panicked?'

Juliet considered his words and began to think she might have overreacted again. 'Well, no.'

'That's because I know my patient, I've been treating her for almost three months now and I have built a good rapport with her.' He stopped outside his office.

At that moment, an orderly appeared wheeling a trolley laden with boxes. 'This is the last of the archived records, Dr Warren. A desk is being brought up from storage along with a chair and a sofa. Oh, and I've asked the cleaning crew to freshen up the office next door for the Aussie doctor as you requested and the flowers you ordered will be here first thing tomorrow. I'm sorry the office wasn't cleaned up this morning when you asked but we've been flat out. I wasn't sure if she'd arrived yet but it will be all done by lunchtime.'

'I guess your office will be ready for you to move in tomorrow, then, Juliet,' Charlie said as he left Juliet alone with another onslaught of thoughts.

Each one of them making her feel smaller by the minute. She had once again misjudged Charlie and in the process demanded something he had already planned on providing. Before he graciously asked her out to brunch to give her the good news. Suddenly she thought the ogre's shoes were more befitting her feet.

Juliet collected Bea without trying to find Charlie and offering to thank him. He had already organised an office for her before she'd made the demand earlier in the day. She felt foolish and thought better than trying to make amends yet again. She had made a habit of offending him that day just as he had of offending her the day before. He had made an effort to be courteous but the orderlies hadn't been able to deliver. The fact she did not have an office was not his fault.

And the flowers he ordered? What on earth did that mean? After the disastrous start to the day, and the terrible ending, he still wanted to make her feel at home with flowers. This man was more of a riddle by the minute. Just when she thought she had worked him out, he surprised her. Only this time it was a nice surprise and an extremely humbling one for Juliet.

Somehow she would make amends. But exactly how would take some time to figure out.

'Mummy!' came the little voice. 'I have a friend. Her name's Emma.' A little girl with flaming red hair and a toothy grin was holding Bea's hand. 'We played yesterday. And we played today. She'th such a good drawer. Her mummy'th a doctor too.'

'Hello, Emma.'

'Hello,' the little girl replied in the softest voice.

'Can Emma come home and play?'

'That would be lovely one day if her mummy says yes, but just not today, Bea, because we have to find another place to live. Somewhere with a nice bath and your own room.'

Bea studied her mother's face for a minute. 'Okay, Mummy,' she finally said with a smile. 'Bye Emma. See you tomorrow.'

'Bye, Bea,' the little girl replied before she ran back to the toys on the play mat in the centre of the room.

Juliet popped her daughter's woollen cape over her shoulders and led her to the car they had hired that morning. She was happy that Bea had made a new friend so quickly. She definitely had much better social skills than her mother, Juliet thought.

'I've found two houses that might be nice so we might just pop in and see them. A man with the keys is meeting us at the first one in half an hour. We can't stay in the hotel because it doesn't give us much room and the bath just won't do. It might be nice to have your own room—perhaps one day this week Emma might come over and play.'

'I hope so,' Bea said as she looked out of the window at the buildings as they drove down the main street of the town.

Juliet suddenly spotted a quaint tea room. 'Would you like something to eat?'

'Yeth, please.'

'Let's see if this little restaurant has Devonshire cream tea,' she said as she checked her rear-vision mirror, then pulled the car over and parked.

'What'th that, Mummy?'

'Scones and jam and cream.'

'Yummy!'

Almost an hour later and quite full on the fluffy scones, homemade raspberry jam and freshly whipped cream, Juliet and Bea arrived at the first house. It was a fully furnished cottage only ten minutes from Teddy's. She pulled her small sedan into the lane beside the house, unsure of where else to park, and walked briskly around to the front gate. The lettings agent was already there. He looked about sixty years of age with a happy face with a ruddy complexion, strawberry-blond hair and wearing a tweed coat and a scarf.

'Good afternoon, Dr Turner. I'm Eugene Parry.'

'Hello, Eugene,' Juliet said as she approached him with her hand extended. 'Please call me Juliet.'

'Certainly, Juliet,' the man said as he unlocked the front door of the thatched-roof cottage. 'It's a lovely little place, this one. Just came back on the market for renting a week ago after the temporary bank manager left. They found a local to fill the role so the other one headed back to London leaving this vacant and you can have it on a monthly basis. No need for a long-term contract.'

Juliet stepped inside and was immediately taken by

how cosy the home felt. It was small but very pretty inside.

'Two bedrooms, as I said, and an eat-in kitchen along with this sitting room,' Eugene said as they stood in the middle of the carpeted room. It was a little cold but Juliet knew with the flick of a switch the heating would change that quickly. 'There's a lovely garden room out the back, which is delightful in summer but not so nice in the chilly weather. Oh, and there's a bath and shower in the newly renovated bathroom.'

Juliet was happy to hear those words and took Bea by the hand to look around. The pretty tastefully wallpapered sitting room more than met her requirements with a large floral sofa and a big leather armchair, a coffee table and a large television. The master bedroom was very simply decorated in tones of blue, with a queen-sized bed and attractive blue-and-cream-striped curtains and a cream damask quilt cover. A free-standing dark wood wardrobe took up one corner of the room and the other corner held a matching large dresser with an oval mirror.

'Where'th my room?'

'Let's go and find out.'

And they did. And it was just perfect. It was painted in tones of peach and there were two twin single beds and a white dresser and robe. The curtains were peach floral with yellow window ties. And there was a four-foot fluffy yellow rabbit sitting under the window beside a toy box.

'The owners have two granddaughters and they used to come and stay but now they're all grown up so they've left it here for others to enjoy.'

'I like it, Mummy.'

'I like it too. We'll take it.'

* * *

Aware that the next few days would be hectic leading up to the surgery, Juliet decided, once she had signed the rental agreement, to leave the hotel and move into the cottage immediately. The estate agent was happy as the hospital provided a reference and a guarantee. So Juliet was approved instantly. He had given her the keys and explained how the heater and the stove worked and left.

'Well, Bea, it looks like we have our own little home for the next few weeks. I've rented it for a month so we can stay here for Christmas and New Year's Eve.'

'Do we have milk and biscuits?'

Juliet smiled at Bea's funny random question and the look of worry on her daughter's face. 'We will get some milk and biscuits and a few other things. In fact, we should go now and stock the pantry before the shops close.'

Together they locked up, hopped back into the car and headed off to fill the cupboards and refrigerator with all they would need.

And as she drove into town Juliet realised she was no longer anxious about being so far from home. Despite her topsy-turvy relationship with Charlie Warren she was suddenly feeling quite at home in the Cotswolds.

Without warning she began to question if in fact it was because of him that she was feeling so at home.

CHAPTER EIGHT

IT WAS FIVE o'clock in the afternoon when they returned. Bea was napping on the sofa, with the heater warming the house, and dinner for two was cooking in the oven. Juliet had bought half a dozen small pork chops and decided to roast them with root vegetables. She thought they could have leftovers the next night. The house was quiet and the delicious aroma of the cooking made her think of home. She looked at her watch and did the mental arithmetic and quickly realised it was one in the morning back home. While she knew her parents loved her, one a.m. was not the time to test the depth of those feelings. She would wait until morning. She had called from the airport to tell them she was safe and since then they had each sent texts. There was nothing else to report. Nothing had happened. They hadn't really met anyone. As she put her feet up on the ottoman and leant back into the softness of the cushions, she realised that technically wasn't correct. Bea had met her new best friend, Emma.

And Juliet had met Charlie. Complicated, handsome, argumentative Charlie. She closed her eyes for a moment.

Who was he really?

And why was he making her think about him when

he wasn't around? For almost five years, she had not given a man another romantic thought, until now.

Dinner was lovely and they both ate well, then Juliet washed the dishes before she gave Bea a nice warm bath, paying particular care to keep her cast dry. As she wrapped her daughter in a fluffy bath sheet before slipping her into her pyjamas, Juliet smiled at the little girl and thought how strong she had been. She couldn't have been more proud of her daughter. She didn't fuss or complain about it at all. Bea just worked around the cast and made the best of it. She was indeed a very special little girl. Despite having her own room, and thinking it was very pretty, that night she decided to sleep with her mother in the big bed. And after her favourite story, they both fell asleep around eight o'clock.

Bea dreamt about a princess who fought dragons and won…and Juliet's sleep began with a dream of Charlie.

It was close to ten when Charlie stood staring into the darkness from his kitchen window. The tap was running and steaming water was filling the sink where he had placed his dinner dishes but it was as if he were somewhere else. Somewhere other than in his home alone, the way it was every night that he didn't work late at the hospital. The silence made him feel even more solitary but that night he chose not to have the noise of the television. He didn't want white noise providing pretend company. He suddenly felt as if he wanted something more. The lightness of heart that he felt when he was near Juliet and Bea was something he had not expected. And something he could not fully understand nor thought he deserved. He lifted his gaze to see the haze of the full moon trying to break through the heavy clouds just as he was trying to step out from behind the guilt that was burying him. But he knew he had as much chance as the moon had.

The next morning was an early start. Along with meeting with Georgina and Leo, Juliet wanted to brief the surgical team to ensure there were no questions around the procedure. Bea needed help to dress in a stretch knit track suit and then after a hearty breakfast of porridge and honey the two set off for Teddy's.

'Ith the hothpital really called Teddy'th, Mummy?'

Juliet smiled as she drove. 'Yes, it is.'

'Like a teddy bear?'

'Yes, just like a teddy bear.'

'That'th silly. It'th a hospital for babies, not for teddy bears.'

Juliet laughed along with her daughter as she turned into the hospital car park. She loved that Bea could see the funny side of life at an early age. She had taken after her grandfather with that trait and clearly the ability to make friends quickly. After the uncomfortable situation with Charlie the day before, Juliet knew she was most definitely missing that skill.

But worrying about being friends with Dr Charlie Warren was not about to take precedence over what mattered and the reason she had travelled to the *teddy bear hospital*.

The day would be busy and she had a lot to accomplish. From a risk-management viewpoint, she needed to have contingency plans in place should the babies react poorly to the procedure. While she saw no reason for it not to proceed smoothly, guaranteed success was never a given and Juliet was always prepared for both the best and worst scenarios and everything in between. Should the laser surgery initiate early labour, she wanted Charlie on the team. She just had to ask him and then wait for the lecture about unnecessary risk she knew would follow. Despite this, she would not exclude him from the theatre as she valued his skills as an OBGYN. She just hoped and prayed she didn't need to call on it.

Her mind's focus was on ensuring that it went like clockwork. There were four babies, two parents and four grandparents who were stakeholders with a heartfelt interest in the surgery being successful. Not to mention Oliver Darrington and the board who had covered the cost of her temporary relocation. The surgery would not be lengthy but it would be intricate. She intended on spending time letting the theatre staff know exactly how she operated and what she needed. She knew this would not be the first laser surgery procedure at Teddy's, but she would not take any chances with miscommunication around the operation on these babies. The staff needed to be fully aware of her expectations. She wanted Lily and Rose to grow up with their brothers, Graham and Rupert. And she would do everything in her power to make sure that happened.

It was not until she saw the black motorbike parked outside the hospital that her thoughts returned to Charlie. At least that was what she told herself, when the butterflies returned to her stomach at the sight of the shiny black road machine. She knew it wasn't the truth because she had fallen asleep thinking of him, dreamt of him and then woken with his handsome face firmly etched in her mind. She hoped he had cancelled the flowers for her office after the words they had shared the previous day. She wanted him to be spiteful and give her reason to dislike him. She didn't want to believe that underneath the gruff exterior lay a good heart.

She had told herself for too many years that a man like that didn't exist and she didn't want to doubt herself.

After dropping Bea at the crèche and watching her daughter and her new best friend, Emma, hug each other excitedly, Juliet made her way to her office. She knew it was adjacent to Charlie's office. She walked past with her laptop computer under her arm ready to settle into her new workplace. As his door was ajar, against her better instincts she felt compelled to look inside. She crossed her fingers that he was not there and she did not have to address her poor behaviour first thing in the morning. This time her wish came true. Charlie was nowhere in sight. But she knew that she would have to face him. Soon. Avoiding him would only last for an hour or so as they needed to consult further on Georgina and the quads, but it would give her time to find the right words to say. An apology on her behalf was deserved. She just wasn't sure how to deliver it.

Her second wish was that the flowers were not in her office. Bracing herself, she opened the door. There was no floral arrangement in sight. Unexpectedly her heart fell. She had no idea why. It was her wish that he'd cancelled the order so she could hold that against him. But part of her had apparently, and unconsciously, hoped he wouldn't. She'd hoped he would be gallant and still have a beautiful bouquet waiting for her as a welcoming gesture. She hadn't expected it, until she'd heard about it. And at that moment she'd realised that deep inside Dr Charlie Warren was a gentleman. Despite her knowing they came from opposite sides of opinion, the fact that he had arranged an office for her and even thought of flowers made her believe in chivalry.

If only for a second.

But the lack of flowers, she knew, was fed by her

own actions. She tried to remind herself it was only flowers, but the fact there were none still stung. For a few wonderful moments when she'd realised he had gone to the effort and trouble for her, she had felt special.

And she could not remember the last time a man had made her feel that way.

But it wasn't to be, Juliet decided as she dropped her oversized shoulder bag on the chair and her computer bag on the desk. Charlie had chosen to cancel the flowers, or perhaps give them to someone else. There would no doubt be a number of young women in the hospital who would be flattered to receive them. Perhaps he was even dating one of them. With his looks and position he would be quite the catch, she thought. But she wasn't fishing. She was very happy to live her life without a man who might disappoint her. She and Bea would be happy together.

And she didn't need any flowers.

She was glad she hadn't dressed in something as figure hugging as the previous day. There was no point. She was at the hospital to concentrate on the quads and nothing else. Juliet hung up her heavy overcoat on the coat stand near her desk, then smoothed down her black woollen skirt and checked her black-and-white-checked blouse was still properly tucked in. She did have very pretty black patent pumps with a kitten heel, so she hadn't entirely tried to hide her femininity. And she was also wearing her signature French fragrance. It was light and floral.

She remembered reading in one of her self-help books that she'd purchased when her trust in men had been broken four long years before that, *'When there isn't a man in your life to make you feel special, expensive perfume can.'*

She wasn't sure it would fill the void for ever, but it had worked up to that point.

Checking her emails, she noticed that Oliver had scheduled a meeting with the surgical team. She had sent a list of required staff for the procedure the day before. She'd wondered if she should consult with Charlie as the OBGYN about it, then decided it might become another debacle so decided to consult with Oliver. She was looking forward to getting to know the team and going over the procedure so that the babies had the optimum chance at leading normal, healthy lives. She couldn't see Charlie's name on the list and wondered if he had chosen to withdraw or if Oliver had made that decision for him.

Suddenly, there was a knock on her open door. She lifted her eyes to see the freshly shaven, impeccably groomed subject of her thoughts. His crisp white shirt highlighted his slightly olive complexion, and once again his blue eyes caught her attention. They appeared even more vivid from across the room.

'May I come in?'

'Of course,' she said, trying to keep the rhythm of her heart from racing and bringing a blush to her cheeks. She doubted she would be successful so she launched into the much-needed apology. 'I'm very sorry about yesterday. I behaved so poorly and I'm not sure how to make it up to you. It was professionally reprehensible, not to mention just plain awful, on my part to speak to you that way after you had made the effort to deliver the Abbiatis' decision in person.'

Charlie stood in silence for a moment and she was unsure how he would react.

'Apology accepted, Juliet,' he said, taking long purposeful steps across the room and very quickly closing the gap between them. His cologne filled those senses that his very being hadn't already claimed. 'You travelled a long way, it can't have been easy without much notice and I'm sure you have a lot on your mind. Let's just agree to disagree. I will not change my mind about the surgery and you, I can very clearly see, do not agree with the benefits of waiting.'

'You're right,' she returned. 'And it's very generous of you to accept my apology. I'm honestly not normally so rude—in fact I don't think I'm ever really rude at all. *Normally.*' Normally covered many different things for Juliet that day. Quite apart from not *normally* hopping on a plane with less than a day's notice, *normally* she didn't find herself fighting her attraction to a colleague.

'Let's call a truce,' he replied.

'Done,' she agreed, hoping that the heat she was feeling hadn't made her cheeks glow.

'I have something for you in my office. I'll be back, then we can discuss the Abbiatis.'

'Sure,' Juliet responded, not entirely sure at all what Charlie had for her but suspecting it was the update on the quads' condition. Juliet prayed it had not worsened during the night. She had intended on heading to Georgina's room as soon as she had read her emails. She wanted to speak in more depth with both Georgina and Leo about the surgery that was scheduled in two days. The risks needed to be explained again and the permission signed for surgery. Both parents had to accept that, while this was the best way forward, there would still be risks.

Juliet was deep in thought when she heard Charlie

return. With a large arrangement of the most beautiful flowers.

'Oh, my goodness,' she said, getting to her feet as she watched Charlie place them on a small table by the window. 'They're gorgeous. You shouldn't have.' It was a lovely round arrangement, as if it had been picked from an English garden. Although she knew it wouldn't be from a garden in the snow-covered Cotswolds. She could see foxglove, hollyhock, snapdragon, sweet peas, roses and a few sprigs of lavender. It was the prettiest arrangement she had ever seen. And as she moved closer she could smell the delicate scent of the flowers' perfume.

'Glad you like them,' he returned. 'But I can't take the credit, since they're not from me. The board asked me to order them as a thank you for coming all this way on short notice.'

'Oh,' she mumbled, feeling silly and trying to mask the disappointment she was feeling.

'I thought I'd test the water before I brought them in case you were still upset and planned on throwing them at me. I know I didn't make it easy on you and we really did not get off to a good start.'

Juliet knew she had been crazy to think a man like Charlie Warren would buy flowers for her. She felt very foolish for thinking that he would.

'I agree we got off on the wrong foot,' she managed to reply. 'But…it's all sorted now.'

Little was truly sorted in Juliet's head. She had been entertaining romantic thoughts and even having dreams about a man who had just followed the instructions of a board and ordered flowers. At least she knew exactly where Charlie was coming from.

'Actually I haven't bought flowers since…' He

paused, then stopped the conversation completely and walked to the door in silence.

Juliet thought Charlie was about to let her into something about him. The man who had an office devoid of photos or personal belongings. There was no visible history or connection to another person or persons. And no hint of a life outside the hospital. She didn't want the opportunity to know more about him to pass. 'Since?' she prompted before Charlie could leave.

Charlie drew a deep breath and turned to face her. 'Not since my wife died. There were so many flowers at the funeral that I couldn't face another flower again. Besides, there was no one to buy them for after that.'

Juliet's disappointment was quickly pushed aside by the shock of what he had said and the instinctive reaction to comfort him. She was momentarily speechless.

Her emotions were once again swinging like a pendulum.

And he was gone.

CHAPTER NINE

CHARLIE LEFT JULIET'S office before she had a chance to offer him any words of comfort or condolence. Juliet watched as he rushed out of the door, confirming matter-of-factly on the way out that they would meet with Georgina and Leo an hour later. There was no further reference to his wife or being a widower. He did not put a timeline of context to his statement. He apparently had another important appointment and one that oddly seemed to lift his spirits when he spoke about being needed elsewhere. He had quite literally dropped an emotional bombshell and run before she could say anything. The swing of the pendulum grew wider by the minute. Charlie mentioned he couldn't be late for his tough taskmaster. She couldn't think who would be harsher than himself but clearly there was someone in the hospital giving him orders. And he jumped. But jumped willingly. While the news was sad, Charlie seemed strangely upbeat as he left.

Juliet thought better than to try to learn more. He had said enough. He was a widower, and she was a single mother. Facts about each other that she had to remind herself had no relevance to their working relationship. But it was not news she had imagined hearing from him.

But it suddenly did make sense. And she could understand better why he appeared to not have a life outside Teddy's. He would have lost the life he knew when he lost his wife.

Trying to push thoughts about Charlie from her mind, she read the medical updates that had been emailed to her and sent an email to her parents, informing them that she would call in the next day or so once she had everything under control. Although she wasn't sure exactly when that would happen. She doubted while Charlie was around, or, more accurately, while she was anywhere near Charlie, that everything would be under control. He was complex and perhaps even still grieving and she was confused.

She wasn't sure she would ever really know Charlie Warren.

But she did still need to ask him to be in Theatre. She had assumed he might have attended, but after seeing the theatre staff listing and noticing his name was not there she wanted to raise it with him. It had slipped her mind in her office, but a lot did when he was around.

She had to put him back in context. He was Georgina's OBGYN and having him there would make Juliet feel more secure. She tried to tell herself it was purely from a risk-management viewpoint, but it was more than that.

With half an hour until she had to be with Georgina, Juliet decided to pop in and check on Bea. After stepping out of the elevator, she rounded the corner and saw Bea and Emma happily helping the childcare assistant to put Christmas decorations along the hallway window ledges of the crèche. It was difficult with her arm in the cast but she was managing to pass the sparkly tinsel to the young woman and Bea beamed with delight as she watched it being secured in place with tape. Juliet grew prouder of her daughter by the minute. She had adjusted to the move, albeit only for a few weeks, so well. She had made friends, not dwelled on her broken arm and was loving the opportunity to do new things.

Juliet wished she were as resilient. She was still carrying around scars that should have long healed. It was as if she had her broken heart in a cast, and she had spent almost five years dwelling on it. She certainly needed to take a leaf out of her four-year-old daughter's book on how to cope with adversity and still enjoy life. She was still allowing Bea's father to affect her life's choices. To affect the way she saw other men. She was punishing all men for the mistakes of one and feeling sorry for herself in the unnecessary process. Her daughter was a better example to her than she was being in return.

And, she quite harshly reminded herself, she hadn't lost the person she had committed to spending her life with the way Charlie had. She had been seduced and dumped by a man she barely knew and it hurt. But she had the most wonderful daughter to love while Charlie had no one. He had lost the woman he loved. His scars would with good reason run deeper. She needed to put on her 'big girl' panties and stop letting the past rule her future.

Juliet decided to get in the Christmas spirit and offer to help with the decorations. But as she drew closer she discovered the three of them had a fourth helper.

'Charlie,' Bea called out sweetly. 'We need more tinthel.'

Juliet moved back out of sight and watched as Charlie stepped from inside the crèche and ruffled Bea's hair. 'Of course, boss. I'll get it for you now.' With that, he walked back inside the doorway and emerged carrying a large box with tinsel overflowing from the top. He placed it within Bea's little reach and then stepped back. 'Do you need any more help?'

'No, thank you, Charlie. You can go and meet my mummy about the babies but maybe you can come back and help.'

'I certainly will.'

Juliet realised the identity of the taskmaster that Charlie was meeting. She controlled the urge to laugh at the way Bea was throwing around orders and at the same time blink back tears as she watched a man who had lost his wife act almost like a father to her daughter.

Bea's banter with Charlie was so relaxed. Her orders were delivered in a cute voice, and with the best intention of getting the job done, but they were orders nonetheless. And she was only four. What made it more poignant was the fact that Charlie was taking them. She sincerely doubted anyone older than Bea could get away with being so forthright with a man like Charlie.

She suddenly worried that Bea might be auditioning him for the role of her daddy. Juliet felt torn as she walked away in silence. She and Bea would not be in the Cotswolds for ever and she didn't want her daughter to get too attached, but at the same time it was wonderful to see Bea so happy in Charlie's company. She bit her lip as she suspected with little effort it might be easy for her to become attached to Dr Warren herself. Particularly with what she now knew about him.

With her mind spinning, Juliet headed back to Georgina Abbiati's room. She needed to focus on the real reason for her travelling to Teddy's. And it was not to become involved with a complicated man. No matter how wonderfully he treated her daughter. And no matter how she felt herself warming to the handsome widower.

* * *

'So do you feel comfortable and understand fully everything I've told you about Friday's procedure?'

'I think so, Dr Turner. I mean, we've made our decision and we're not backing down now. Sorry, Charlie, but I think we've made the right decision,' Georgina said with a slight waver obvious in her voice.

Charlie nodded and, true to his word, said nothing.

'But I do have two more questions if you have time,' Georgina continued.

'Of course. I have all the time it takes to make you feel at ease and comfortable. Fire away,' Juliet said as she took one final glance at the morning's observations of her patient, including the results from the daily ultrasound she had requested. The boys' condition had remained stable and the girls were unaffected.

'I know I will have a local anaesthetic and sedation, but will I feel anything at all?'

Juliet had been asked the same question many times. 'There will be no pain, perhaps a small amount of dull tugging, but also there is a slight risk your uterus can react to any interference with contractions. Not sufficient in most cases to bring on labour but it may feel that way to you. There will be no pain, just tightness if a contraction occurs.'

'Will Charlie be in the theatre too?' Leo asked as he looked over towards Charlie. 'Just in case Georgina goes into labour.'

Juliet turned to Charlie and with equally baited breath awaited his response. She wasn't sure if Oliver Darrington was still to make the final decision on the attending OBGYN or attend himself.

'Of course,' he announced with conviction and keeping his focus on Georgina and Leo.

His words allowed Juliet to take the next breath and a smile spread over her face.

'I'm your OBGYN, and, while I have the utmost faith in the skills of Dr Turner and the team, I'm your back-up plan. If the need arises, and I'm not pre-empting it, but should the laser surgery hasten labour, I will be bringing Rupert and his siblings into the world.'

Juliet was happy with his explanation. It had not been delivered in a manner that would elevate the Abbiatis' fears, in fact just the opposite, and for that she was grateful. Charlie was playing fair.

'And I'll be very happy to have Dr Warren in Theatre. No one knows you better than your OBGYN so his presence and skills are invaluable.'

Juliet could see from the corner of her eye that Charlie had turned his head in her direction. But she didn't reciprocate. It had the potential to be a moment that she was not ready to face. Mutual admiration and respect, coupled with what she had witnessed downstairs with Charlie helping Bea. It would have been an emotional overload that she could not afford at that time.

She was feeling more than a little vulnerable. To her feelings and to Charlie Warren.

Charlie was many things and increasingly she was seeing he might even have the potential to be wonderful, but she was not looking for a man. Wonderful or not. She doubted her heart would survive. Besides, she was not staying and she did not want to start something she could not finish.

'If that's all for the moment, and you know you can page me any time, I will head off to brief the theatre staff.'

'Georgie, Leo,' Charlie began as he edged closer to Juliet's direction, 'I'm in that meeting too, so we will see you later. Rest lots, try not to stress and write down any questions so you can ask either Dr Turner or myself when we call in.'

'That went well,' Juliet began as they walked down the corridor towards the elevators. She still did not make eye contact. 'I'm glad you'll be in Theatre. It wasn't articulated on the list.'

'I was waiting to be invited. You're the lead surgeon, so it was a professional consideration on my behalf to wait until I was asked.'

'I was going to do that today.'

Charlie eyed her suspiciously. 'Well, I guess I invited myself so, like the idea or not, I'll be scrubbing in with you on Friday.'

'I like the idea. Very much. Thank you,' she said as she pushed the button for the elevator with her pulse racing a little but a sense of contentment washing over her knowing Charlie would be there with her during the operation.

Twenty minutes later, Juliet was winding up her briefing to the theatre staff, a number of whom were pressed for time as they were due to scrub in for another procedure that afternoon. She had already gone over her theatre equipment requirements, spoken to the anaesthesia team and nursing staff. All of the medical team involved in Georgina's procedure, bar the one medical student and two interns on maternity rotation, were experienced with TTTS laser surgery, although none on more than two babies. Four was outside everyone's experience. Including Juliet's. And she did not hide that fact from the team.

'While I have performed fetoscopic laser surgery on

triplets, I will not deny that on quadruplets it will be a slightly more challenging procedure. However, the direct visualisation through the fetoscope will allow us to successfully perform a targeted and focused laser termination of the vascular communications directly responsible for the TTTS and effectively separate the placenta into two components, one for each foetus. With each baby having its own placental mass, and the removal of this communication, there will be an interruption to the transfusion process and we should stabilise the situation so we can advance to a gestational age where the four babies in this situation all have a greater chance of survival. Does anyone have any further questions?'

'If the parents of the quads did not agree to the surgery, what would the risk be to the other three babies if the recipient baby went into stage five heart failure and died?'

Juliet could see the question came from one of the interns. 'That's a very good question. If one foetus was to become non-viable through cardiovascular complication arising from the TTTS, then it would put all three remaining babies at high risk of death, injury or disability. Essentially the fetoscopic laser procedure has taken what was until relatively recently a lethal placental disease and turned it into a manageable condition if detected early.'

The specialist team were all silent. Each nodded their understanding.

'Just one more question. If the outcome of moving forward with this intervention is pre-term delivery, are you certain that you're sufficiently prepared for the arrival of four twenty-nine-week gestational babies with a current average weight of less than three pounds?'

Even without hearing the voice or seeing the man,

Juliet knew the question had to come from Charlie, who was standing with folded arms at the back of the room. She took a deep breath. But instead of feeling resentment or interference, she appreciated the question. It was fair and one he had every right to ask in that arena and one that others might have been wondering about.

'Yes, Dr Warren, that's why we have assembled a multidisciplinary team who can deal with all potential outcomes including pre-term delivery. In addition to Ella, who is Georgina's midwife, and two anaesthetists, Mr Darrington has already approved the four neonatal intensive care nurses and two neonatologists who are here with us today, and a senior paediatrician, paediatric resident and a paediatric cardiologist, all of whom I assume you will recognise on the day but can't be at this briefing. In all we will have sixteen in the medical team, three observing and four incubators in Theatre. All of which, God willing, will be under-utilised on the day.'

Surrounded by Theatre staff, many in scrubs, Juliet suspected the imminent laser surgery for his patient became more real in Charlie's mind, giving rise to his ongoing concerns.

'Good, I'm not surprised you have it under control, Dr Turner. Let's hope we don't need any of it,' he said, then turned and walked away leaving a tiny grain of doubt in Juliet's mind.

Juliet never operated with doubt over anything. She needed to manage it immediately.

CHAPTER TEN

'CHARLIE, MAY I see you for a minute?' Juliet asked at the same time as she knocked on his open door. She had excused herself from the pre-operative meeting with the medical team and followed him back to his office. 'I need to ask your advice with regard to a question hanging over Friday's procedure.'

'What would that be at the eleventh hour?'

'It's hardly the eleventh hour.'

Charlie rolled his eyes as Juliet stepped inside his office and closed the door behind her. Normally she would have shown professional courtesy by involving him in her plans earlier but his initial reservations had ensured that did not happen. She stepped closer to his desk and looked him directly in the eyes. 'I should have asked for your input around the team. I realise it may have come across as if I've gone behind your back and made arrangements with your Assistant Head of Obstetrics with no input from you as the quads' consulting OBGYN.'

'What's done is done,' he said as he continued rifling through the paperwork on his desk.

Juliet pulled out the chair opposite and sat down. 'I am sorry about the way I've handled this. I've been a bit like a bulldozer.'

His gaze lifted from the paperwork and met hers. 'Perhaps a mini dozer.'

She smiled. 'I really do appreciate you agreeing to be there in the surgery with me. Not for protocol…just because I need you there.' As the words slipped over her lips she surprised herself. Juliet never admitted needing anyone. And it wasn't just to make up for what she had done. She meant it. She actually needed Charlie.

He said nothing for the longest moment, leaving Juliet wondering what he was thinking.

'Let's just hope the procedure doesn't induce an early delivery because all four are too small for my liking.'

'I agree, that's why I need your advice around my contingency plan for that occurrence. Do I have everything in place? You've delivered more babies at this hospital than I've seen in my life and I'm not afraid to say that I feel a little like a fish out of water and I want your advice on how we can best prepare for the worst.'

Over the days since she had arrived, despite their disagreements, she knew Charlie was a great OBGYN. It was his passion for what he believed to be best for his patient that fuelled his stubbornness. Juliet knew he cared over and above and, while she conceded he was not one to take risks, perhaps that would make their collaboration perfect. He could temper her risks, mitigate the strategies and together they could find the best way forward.

'What is it you want to know?'

'I want to know if we have sufficient staff on board for starters. And if we don't, I need you to tell me who's missing. Oliver has left it up to me, and I would like your input.'

Finally he looked up and spoke earnestly. 'I think you're fine with the surgical team. Each and every one is the best that Teddy's has to offer and I don't think you want to further crowd the operating room. My concerns would be around the anaesthesia.'

'Why would that be?' she asked with her curiosity piqued as she shifted to the edge of her chair.

'If the laser procedure was to be the catalyst for preterm delivery of the quads you would be looking at a Caesarean if the babies were to have any chance of surviving. They would be barely twenty-nine weeks' gestation, and babies that premature would not survive the birth canal. There would not be sufficient time for an epidural to be administered so you'd be forced to use a general.'

'So we'll have that option on hand?'

Charlie stood and walked around to the front of the desk, crossed his legs and looked directly at Juliet. 'I think you should try to avoid general anaesthesia.'

With a frown, Juliet continued the questions. 'How can we though? You just said yourself that our only option if labour was to commence as a result of the laser surgery was a GA.'

'No, I said that it would be the only option if we weren't fully prepared.'

'So you think we should have an epidural in place for the procedure rather than the local anaesthetic and conscious sedation?'

'Yes, that way we'll have both bases covered. It would meet your needs during the fetoscopic procedure, but allow a Caesarean to be performed immediately any signs of distress were detected from any of the babies.'

'It makes perfect sense.'

'Glad you agree.'

'Am I missing anything else?'

'No, I think we've covered it all now.'

They both felt the other trying to meet halfway. It was almost as if the slate had been wiped clean in a very short time by them trying to understand the other. It was starting to resemble a collaboration of minds and skills. And each of them was pleasantly surprised.

Juliet wondered fleetingly if there was a chance it could possibly become a collaboration in another sense. Then just as quickly she pushed that from her mind. She didn't need any complications in her life. And she knew Charlie Warren would be a very big complication. And if she fell for him, a very big heartache that she couldn't risk.

'I know we won't agree on the procedure,' she began with her mind back in appreciative colleague mode, 'but I value your advice. I'll meet with the anaesthetist tomorrow and brief him on the changes and then let the Abbiatis know. I'm glad we agree on this.'

'I'm glad too,' Charlie offered as he suddenly saw Juliet in a very different light. He had seen glimpses over the previous days but only in short bursts, before her need to bring home her opinion took over masking the woman he was seeing clearly again now. Suddenly he felt the defensive armour he had worn close to his chest for two years loosening a little. He had not meant to tell her about losing his wife but the words had just spilled out and he was not sorry. Letting Juliet know about his past seemed natural. In fact everything about being around Juliet suddenly seemed very natural.

'It's been a long morning,' he suddenly announced. 'And I'm quite hungry as I skipped breakfast. Would you like to join me for lunch?' He felt as if he was getting to know the real Juliet and it had been a long time since he had wanted to get to know anyone. Her interest in seeking his opinion, despite their opposing stands on the procedure, made him feel as if his advice meant something to her. And she had not pried into his personal life. He had told her about losing his wife and she had left it alone. He appreciated that respect of his unspoken boundaries.

'That would be lovely, Charlie, but I'm due to collect Bea. Would you mind if she joined us?'

'Not at all.'

Charlie was already smitten by Bea. She was a tiny version of her mother. Just as bossy, just as beautiful… and just as endearing. Her innocent joy of everything festive was making him see Christmas through her eyes instead of a man who had lost his wife at that same time of the year. The distaste he had held for anything close to celebrating was losing ground under the spell of the tiny decorator with a love of tinsel.

'Did you know that Charlie helped me with the tinthel on the windowth?'

'Did he indeed?' Juliet asked as she sipped her Earl Grey tea in the downstairs hospital tea room. Juliet did not want to let on she had witnessed Bea ordering Charlie around. It still brought a smile to her face as they sat together having a light lunch. Charlie had suggested they could head into town to have something to eat, but Juliet was well aware that he had a patient in labour and already beginning to dilate and thought better of taking him away. The roads were icy and she knew he would be taking his motorbike and the thought of him racing back in bad weather if the labour turned into a delivery without much notice did not sit well with her.

'Yeth. He was a very good helper. And he carried the boxthes.'

'Because you were a very good boss,' he said, with his eyes laughing. 'And you can't carry boxes of tinsel with a broken arm.'

Juliet laughed and looked over at Charlie. He was the most complex man she had ever met. He had so many layers and she wasn't sure why but when he lowered his guard around Bea in particular she could see how very special he was. Juliet watched him smiling down at her daughter. His affection for her was palpable. And it made Juliet happier than she could have imagined. Not that she was looking for a father for her child, but if she had been Charlie would definitely have been a good choice.

Even Bea knew it.

'And how exactly did carting tinsel for a four-year-old became your role?' Juliet asked as she watched Bea happily sipping on her oversized chocolate milkshake. She felt certain the ladies in the tea room had found the largest cup and filled it to the brim. Bea's little legs were swinging back and forth as she gleefully watched the toy train, driven by a tiny Santa, circling a smaller Christmas tree in the corner of the tea room. Cotton wool covered the base of the tree like freshly fallen snow and it had been sprinkled with silver glitter. Juliet could see her daughter was in complete awe of it all. Juliet finally felt she could relax and exhale over her decision to bring Bea with her to the UK.

'I wanted to check on Bea's cast,' Charlie continued. 'I know you would have been keeping an eye on it, but I wanted see how my workmanship had stood up to the rigours of a four-year-old. Before I knew it I was recruited to decoration duty.'

'Be careful, knowing my daughter, she'll soon have

grand plans of taking the tinsel to any part of the hospital that is not looking festive.'

'Oh, she's already scoped the entire floor and has plans of hospital-wide decorations!'

As they chatted over roast beef and mustard sandwiches all signs of animosity had abated, and for that Juliet was grateful. She could see that Charlie was a good man, a guarded, opinionated and stubborn one, with an overly cautious nature, but nevertheless a good man with a sad past. They spent a little while comparing the Australian landscape to the Cotswolds and then Charlie unexpectedly excused himself and made his way over to a very pregnant woman.

Juliet watched as he chatted with her for a moment and the two of them returned to the table.

The tall, ash-blonde woman was wearing a very tired smile and said, still chatting to Charlie, 'I can't join you but thank you for asking, Charlie. After they make my sandwich, I'll be heading home. I just finished up a long surgical repair of anomalous pulmonary veins on a newborn. It went well but I need a good sleep. I'm exhausted.'

'I'm not surprised. You're pregnant and insist on keeping up a fairly heavy surgical roster. You'll have to slow down soon,' he told her. 'But while you're waiting for your food, let me introduce you to Dr Juliet Turner and her daughter, Bea. Juliet's the *in-utero* specialist brought here from Australia to assist with the quadruplets.'

Sienna approached with her hand extended. 'Welcome aboard, Juliet. I hope you enjoy your time here.'

'Thank you,' Juliet said as she met Sienna's handshake, immediately liking the other woman.

'Sienna is Teddy's neonatal cardiothoracic surgeon,'

Charlie explained. 'And one of the very best so we're fortunate to have her.'

'Said by Teddy's best OBGYN,' Charlie's very tired, very pregnant colleague told Juliet. 'But I should go... It's nice to meet you, Juliet. Perhaps we could meet up for coffee soon.'

'I'd like that, thanks, Sienna.'

'Mummy, ith that a printh?' Bea interrupted.

Juliet turned her attention to her daughter. 'Is what a prince, sweetie?'

'The man up there,' Bea said, pointing at the large television screen in the corner of the tea room. 'Ith he a printh?'

Juliet watched the news coverage and read the footnotes on the screen. 'Yes, he is a prince. It's Crown Prince Sebastian Falco of Montanari.'

'Does he have a printheth?'

'Not yet, sweetie, but he is engaged to be married and they're making quite the fuss of him. I suppose if you're a prince they will make a fuss of everything you do.'

'Will I ever be a printheth?'

'You're already *my* princess,' Juliet said as she kissed her cheek.

Sienna suddenly grabbed the seat that Charlie had offered. Juliet noticed she had also suddenly drained of colour.

'Is everything all right?' Juliet asked. 'Would you like some water? You look terribly pale.'

Charlie rushed to the cooler and, taking a bottle of water, undid the cap and passed it to Sienna. 'Get this into you.'

Juliet didn't understand what had happened as she watched the woman stare at the screen as if she had seen a ghost. She said nothing as she sipped her drink and then looked away from the screen and into the distance.

Charlie's pager abruptly beeped. 'I've been summoned. Looks like there's another baby about to enter the world. Will you be all right, Sienna? Should I get Oliver to take a look at you?'

Sienna shook her head. 'No, I'll be fine. I've suddenly lost my appetite. I really need to go home.'

Juliet walked Sienna to her car, and made sure the other woman was safely on her way. She thought that Charlie was right, that Sienna needed to look at slowing down as her pregnancy progressed. It was obviously taking its toll on her.

The next day, Juliet managed to meet with the anaesthetist to discuss the change of plans. He agreed that the dual purpose epidural would be the better option and that information would be passed on to the rest of the team. She then headed to Georgina's room to let her know the change to the preferred anaesthetic and explain the benefits of Charlie's suggestion of an epidural. The results of the daily scans were emailed through to both Juliet and Charlie and thankfully there had been no change to the TTTS status and Juliet wanted to pass this information on as well.

She checked in at the nurses' station and was told that Leo had headed home to let the family know the latest update and have a good night's sleep at Georgina's insistence. He had spent a few nights at the hospital since his return from New York and she knew he would fuss over her if he stayed that night and not get any rest himself. Juliet knocked on the door and asked if Georgina would like company.

'If you have time that would be lovely,' the mother-to-be answered as she invited her to sit for a while. 'I've been here less than a week and I'm going a little stir crazy. I can't imagine how women confined to bed for months cope.'

'You do what you have to do, and, believe me, if you were told bed rest for nine months to have healthy babies, you would do it. It's just a mother's natural instinct.'

'I suppose I would,' Georgina agreed. 'But I would still be a little loopy by the end.'

Both women laughed before turning the subject to something a little more serious. Juliet wanted to know about the supports in place for when the babies finally went home. While it wasn't her role, she was interested to know how much assistance would be available as she reinforced the fact that four babies would be an enormous workload for the next few years.

'The babies' grandparents live very close to us, and I have a housekeeper, so I won't be struggling in terms of running the house,' Georgina answered. 'I'm very fortunate, and I know that Leo will be very hands-on too.'

'Leo's also running the family business, so he may not always be able to help, so please don't try to be brave if you feel overwhelmed at times. Let those around you know if you are struggling,' Juliet told her. 'Get extra help and take some time for yourself, even if it's just a ten-minute soak in a bubble bath. It will help you to re-energise, regroup and get right back to being a mother.'

'That sounds like you've been through it.'

'I have, believe me, but not with four babies. I only had one, she's four years old now, but it was a full-time job for me for the first few months.'

'Didn't your husband help at all?'

Juliet paused before she answered, thinking back

for a moment to when Bea was a baby and then to even before that, to how scared she was as the delivery date drew closer. The fear that engulfed her some days knowing that she would be bringing up Bea alone. And how some nights she lay awake worried that she would not be enough for her daughter. That she wouldn't cope. But she did.

'I wasn't married. I'm a single mother.'

'And a surgeon,' Georgina responded. 'That's amazing. You're bringing up your daughter alone and holding down a career.'

'It's not been that difficult. Bea's almost at school now.'

'But you've done it by yourself and flew all the way over here from Australia to help my babies. I think you're the one who should take time out and have a bubble bath!'

Ella stepped into the room as the women were still happily chatting. She was there to take Georgina's blood pressure.

'I think I will head off and leave you in Ella's care,' Juliet said as she stood up to go. She wanted to go back to her office and confirm that everything was on track. 'I will see you and Leo in the morning.'

With that Juliet walked back down to her office and as usual she looked into Charlie's office as she passed by. It was a habit that had formed quickly but she was grateful he wasn't always there or it might have seemed awkward. This time he was there, sitting on the sofa with his feet up reading. It looked like a report of sorts but she didn't stop.

Not until she heard him call her name and she turned back to see him standing in the doorway.

'How are Georgina and Leo holding up?'

'Georgina's doing very well and Leo's gone home. She wanted him to rest for tomorrow,' Juliet told him, still feeling warmed by the affection the parents-to-be shared. 'They would have to be the sweetest couple, so in love and looking out for each other. Truly beautiful.'

Charlie didn't comment and Juliet suddenly felt terrible for bringing up their marital happiness. She felt so insensitive and decided to change the subject rather than add to her verbal blunder.

'What about you?' she asked to break the uncomfortable silence. 'Did the baby have an uneventful entry into the world? It must've been a quick labour for you to be back here already.'

'It was her fourth,' Charlie said, clearly keen to move away from discussing Georgina and Leo's love story. 'She was a pro. Her baby boy was delivered in forty-five minutes and she has three more at home to match. There will be no shortage of men to mow the lawns in that household.'

Juliet assumed the conversation would end there and made a mental promise to herself to be more sensitive but Charlie continued the conversation. 'Is Georgina fine with the change to the anaesthesia, then?'

She paused mid step and turned back to him, elated that there was no damage from her inappropriate comment. 'Yes, she understood why you thought it would be best. And I'm sure, because the suggestion has come from you, she feels very comfortable. I think she's happy we're working closely together—it makes her feel better about everything.'

Charlie had heard the overall details the day before but wanted some clarification around a few of the finer details. He invited her back into his office and they talked through everything from the preoperative medication to the post-operative care. He was impressed that Juliet was thorough, focused and left little to chance. It was how he liked to operate. He wasn't one to ever take unnecessary risks.

They were winding up the conversation and Juliet mentioned heading down to collect Bea. 'You apparently said you could look at staying here longer if needed to one of the midwives.'

'That's right. I'll stay until the babies are born.'

'And after that?'

'I'm not sure. If there's a position here, and the need for my skills, I may look at my options. But my family and friends all live in Perth, quite close by, which is a great support for both of us and of course my mother and father still keep watchful eyes on both of us. I'm fortunate but some may find it odd that they still fuss over me at my age.'

'Helicopter parents?'

'You could say that, but with all good intentions.'

Charlie nodded. 'Well, they let you out of their sight to make this trip at least.'

Juliet laughed. 'They actually pushed me onto the plane. I wasn't convinced that I should come here but they insisted.'

'Then they can't be too overprotective. You and Bea have travelled a long way and you're definitely not under their watchful eyes now.'

Juliet smiled. 'What about you?' she enquired. 'Are your parents here in the Cotswolds?'

Charlie's smile seemed to drop instantly. The cheery disposition Juliet had been enjoying seemed to slip away and she wished she hadn't asked. She prayed they too hadn't died. That would be a heavy burden for someone to bear. She watched as he stood up slowly and walked to the window, looking out into the distance. He didn't appear to be focusing on anything in particular.

'It's none of my business, really you don't have to answer.'

Charlie stared ahead, still saying nothing for a few moments. 'No. My parents both passed while I was in medical school. They left me a sizable inheritance to ensure I could complete my studies but they left me alone. No brothers or sisters.'

'I'm so sorry.'

'It was a long time ago and it only hits home occasionally. Usually around holidays like Christmas when it's all about family time.' Charlie rested back into his chair. 'On the subject of family, I overheard you tell the nurse in A&E that Bea only has one parent. And tell me if I'm overstepping the line but are you widowed like me…or divorced?'

Juliet reached into her bag for her bottle of water and took a large sip. She had known the subject could arise but she wished it had not been that day. She had no intention of blurting out to him details around her irresponsible one-night stand. She was a doctor and she slept with a man she didn't know and fell pregnant. Juliet accepted that it wasn't the eighteen-hundreds, as her father had often said, but the circumstance of Bea's conception, in her eyes, still made her look fairly naive and irresponsible.

Charlie was so conservative in almost every way and to announce that, *By the way I was reckless, slept with a man I barely knew, trusted him when he said he'd handled the contraception and as a result became a single mother, but the rest of the time I'm incredibly responsible…except of course for the day we met and Bea was alone in the playground and fell…and last week when*

I decided on a minute's notice to drag a four-year-old halfway around the world.

Any way she looked at the situation, she felt that Charlie might judge her.

But then why did she care? His opinion shouldn't matter. But it did. She had been silly enough to trust a man who didn't deserve that trust the night Bea was conceived and naive enough to think there would be more than one night. Perhaps even forever.

She doubted that Charlie ever threw caution to the wind and for that reason she felt anxious about confessing her stupidity. But just as Charlie had told her about his wife and his parents she felt she should give him the same level of honesty.

'Bea's never met her father but he is alive and living somewhere in Western Australia.' There it was said. Out in the open. And she knew the floodgates were also open to the barrage of questions that would follow. And she would answer all of them truthfully. Or not answer them at all.

'May I ask why?'

'It's for the best,' she mumbled. 'It's just that he's not a good person. To be frank, he's the worst type of bad.'

'Really?'

'Truly.'

'Do you want to talk about it?'

She momentarily closed her eyes and took a shallow breath. It was a risk to tell such a man about her stupid night, very stupid night with a serial womaniser. It made her appear as young and naive as she knew she looked.

'Then you don't have to...'

'No, I want to...' She swallowed pensively. 'The reason Bea's father has never met her...is because we haven't seen each other since I became pregnant.'

'So he left you when he discovered you were having his baby?'

'Not exactly. He left long before I knew.'

'How long before?' he asked.

'He left the morning after I became pregnant and he's married so there's no point going there.'

'Married?'

'He wasn't at the time…but he married a few weeks later. He was apparently engaged when we met but I had no idea. I discovered later, much later, he was a serial womaniser. He married before I had even known I was pregnant.'

'But he should have been held accountable. A man can't just walk away from the responsibility of his own child.'

That was what Juliet's father had said despite not knowing the identity of the man. No one knew the identity of the father, not even her parents. It was Juliet's secret. Perth was not a huge city and she did not want her father to confront Bea's father and tell him what he thought. It would have opened a Pandora's box and she thought that Bea might be the one to suffer the most.

'It wasn't long after the wedding I discovered he and his new bride were expecting triplets.'

'How did you discover that?'

'A cruel twist of fate had his wife's OBGYN reach out to me when a complication arose during the pregnancy. I couldn't bring myself to consult on the case so I deferred to another neonatal surgeon. How could I operate on the children of a man I despised so completely? If anything had gone wrong I feared that I'd have questioned myself for eternity and far more than anyone else ever would for sure, but it wasn't worth the risk.'

Charlie sat shaking his head. 'Still he should provide support for his daughter. It must be hard as a single mother, financially and emotionally.'

Juliet rested back into the generous padding on her high-backed chair. 'It is but I wouldn't change a thing. I adore Bea. She's my world.'

'She's adorable…despite her father. That must be because she's got more of you in her.'

Juliet smiled up at the man who was close to capturing her heart but she wasn't ready to let him. She still couldn't risk being hurt again.

'Thank you.'

'It's definitely his loss,' Charlie began before shifting the direction of the conversation slightly. 'Will you ever let Bea reach out to him?'

Juliet felt a warm feeling rush over her with his words. She would never have expected Charlie to say something like that. He wasn't judging her at all. He hadn't reacted the way she had feared.

'With three children under his belt and, from the gossip around Perth, more than a few post-honeymoon flings and another one or two since the birth of his children, I don't want him in her life. He's a real-estate developer with no conscience and both the means and opportunity to entertain other women and he's been doing that for a very long time. I will be thinking long and hard about allowing Bea to be the fourth, and unwanted, child of the man who enjoyed a pre-wedding fling with me despite having a fiancée at home waiting for him.'

'And if she asks about her father growing up?'

Juliet had not decided how she would respond when

Bea asked about her daddy. And invariably she would one day.

'I'm not sure how I'll handle it. Despite my feelings about the man who fathered Bea, he's after all half of Bea and I want my daughter to grow up proud of who she is, not doubting herself because of her father's despicable behaviour. It's a dilemma I'll face later. Although I must admit recently I'm beginning to believe it will perhaps be sooner rather than later. Almost all of Bea's little friends at playgroup have fathers and Bea's beginning to talk about their *daddies*. She has a grandpa who had just retired but then… But that's another story. Anyway, he is more than thrilled to be the male role model but I know it's not the same as having a daddy.'

Charlie didn't reply. Bea was a wonderful little girl and didn't appear to be suffering from paternal neglect so obviously Juliet's father was a great surrogate. She was a sweetheart and many men would be proud to call her their daughter and watch her grow up under their watchful eye. Be there to unwrap Christmas presents together, buy her first bike and then her first car and of course scrutinise boyfriends who would never be good enough for his daughter.

Suddenly Charlie began to suspect if he wasn't careful he might just be one of those men. 'Look at the time—it's getting on and I have some paperwork to catch up on tonight at home,' he said abruptly, collected his leather briefcase, said goodnight and left his office.

Bea was happily playing in her room with cartoons on television and Juliet had just folded the last of the towels from the dryer, all the while thinking about Charlie. She could think of little else as she stacked the towels in the airing cupboard. With the empty basket in her arms,

Juliet made her way into the sitting room. She could see the front porch through the lace-covered bay window.

Her jaw dropped and she almost dropped the basket when she saw who was standing on her doorstep.

CHAPTER ELEVEN

'OH, MY GOODNESS, what are you doing here?' Juliet squealed as she opened the door. She couldn't have been more surprised...or happier. 'Quickly come in from the cold!'

'It was your father's idea. He thought that we could help with Bea while you concentrate on the quads' surgery.' Her mother embraced Juliet, then stepped aside for her husband to do the same.

'It's a challenging surgery and we don't want you worrying about picking up Bea from the crèche,' her father chipped in as he carried one of the suitcases inside and then hugged his daughter warmly. He turned back for the other one still on the porch, then closed the door on the bitterly cold night air.

'Or worrying if she gets a sniffle with the sudden change in climate,' her mother added as she looked around the cosy sitting room of the cottage.

'Oh, my God, why didn't you tell me you were coming?'

'Because you would have said we were fussing—'

'Which you are...but I'm very glad you like to fuss.'

'And we missed you both terribly.'

'It's been less than a week.'

'See what an only child has to suffer. Two parents

who miss you after less than a week and follow you to the other side of the world,' her father continued as he placed the second suitcase down. 'So learn from us and give Bea some brothers or sisters in the future or she'll be doomed to having a helicopter parent hovering around like us!'

Juliet smiled. 'If I'm half as good a parent as you two, then Bea will be a lucky girl.'

'We are the lucky ones, Juliet. You make us both very proud.' Her father hugged Juliet again and then stepped away a little as his eyes filled with tears of happiness.

Juliet could see the emotion choking him and knew all three of them would be a mess if she didn't change the subject. 'So when did you decide to fly out? And how did you arrange it so quickly?'

'We had passports so we just rang the travel agent. We've booked into a hotel nearby for tomorrow but they didn't have a spare room tonight.'

'You'll do no such thing. There's plenty of room here.'

'We don't want to put you out. We'll just stay tonight if that's okay. We can sleep on the sofa.'

'Don't be ridiculous. You'll stay here...now how long are you able to stay?'

'Till you get sick of us,' her mother replied.

'Then you'll be here for a long time,' Juliet said. 'What about a nice cup of tea?'

'That would be lovely,' her father said.

'Well, actually, we've booked one of those river cruises through France and Spain,' her mother added. 'That's the week after Christmas.'

'I thought you had planned that for next July? You were going to enjoy summer in Europe. Leave the Australian winter behind and thaw out over here.'

'That was our plan but we brought it forward. No point flying out twice. It's a long way for two old people.'

Juliet laughed. 'Hardly old but you'll be missing the sunshine on your cruise.'

The three of them looked up as Bea came running down the hallway. 'Grandma! Grandpa!'

'Here comes all the sunshine we need,' her father said.

Juliet's parents both dropped to the ground, her father a little more slowly due to the arthritis that plagued his knees. A group hug ensued with lots of kisses.

'I knew Father Chrithmath was real,' the little girl said with a toothy grin.

'Of course Father Christmas is real, but why do you say that?' Juliet asked as she looked at the three of them nestled together on the rug on the floor.

''Coth I asked him to bring Grandma and Grandpa here to play in the snow with me and have Christmath food and everything.'

'How did the surgery go for Kelly Lester?' Juliet asked as they sat by the fire after settling into Bea's room. Bea was happy to move in to Juliet's room and sleep in the big bed and give her room to her grandparents. 'I got your email that the procedure was successful but how is Kelly progressing post-operatively?'

'Good, very good,' her father answered as he reached for a homemade cookie. 'She's a strong woman, lots of family support and, although there will still be hurdles as to be expected with spina bifida, the chances have been greatly improved of the child walking by about the thirty-month mark, which I know was your prognosis. And we both know without surgical intervention the little boy would never have walked or really enjoyed a quality of life.'

'Look at you two. Like peas in a pod,' her mother said as she finished her second cup of tea.

'You liked the tea, Grandma?'

'Yes, I did, Bea.'

'Would you like some more?'

'No, thank you, sweetie. But what I would like is to hear about how you got that cast. Mummy rang and told us how it happened but it did sound very scary.'

Momentarily distracted from her cup of hot chocolate, Bea looked at the cast intently. 'I fell from the slide and broke my arm.'

'Are you feeling better now?' her grandfather asked as he lovingly watched his granddaughter.

'Yeth, Charlie made my pink cast.'

'It's very pretty and has lots of beautiful drawings,' her grandmother replied.

'Yeth, my friendth drew them,' Bea told them, then, pointing at the image of a sunflower, she continued. 'Thith one is by Emma, my betht friend.'

'Well, she's very clever and I'm sure very nice.'

'Charlie ith very nice too, and very tall. Like a building,' Bea said as she jumped to her feet and stretched her hand up as high as possible. 'He'th Mummy'th friend and he'th going to get us a Chrithmath tree. A really, really big one.'

'Did Charlie offer to get a Christmas tree for the house?' Juliet asked with a curious frown. He had not mentioned it to her.

'Yeth, Mummy, he told me he would get a beautiful tree for uth.'

Juliet's parents looked at each other with a knowing smile.

'Don't go there,' Juliet said, shaking her head. Since the strange way he'd left off with Juliet, she wasn't sure about him. She felt that he was hiding something from her and she wasn't sure she wanted anyone that complex in her life. 'He's the OBGYN, and to be honest, most of the time, quite difficult to work with. It's taken almost all week to finally come close to understanding him. He's conservative and stubborn and fought me every inch of the way about the *in-utero* surgery.'

'Why did he attend to Bea? Since when do OBGYNs attend to paediatric fractures?'

Juliet drew a deep breath and put down her spoon. 'He's the doctor that rushed to Bea in the playground. The doctor I was waiting for inside and he was running late. He arrived at the hospital at the same time Bea fell.'

'Serendipity…'

'Mum, please, I said don't go there.'

'Is he handsome?'

'Mum…'

'It's a simple question, Juliet. Is the nice doctor who saved Bea, and is now, according to our granddaughter, *your friend*, who is going to buy you a Christmas tree, handsome?'

Juliet swallowed. 'Yes, he's handsome…and incredibly difficult at times—'

'And also with a very kind streak by the sound of it too,' her mother cut in.

Juliet's eyebrow was raised as she returned her attention to the last few crumbs of cookie on her own plate. She wasn't going to get into an argument. Her mother had said the truth. Charlie did have a chivalrous and kind side to him and she didn't want to think about that.

'He'th nice,' Bea added, completely oblivious to her

mother's opinion of Charlie. 'We put up tinthel, and pretty thingth around the hothpital.'

'Really? Not what I would have thought was part of an OBGYN's job description?' her mother said without making eye contact with Juliet.

'Particularly not one who's difficult...' her father mused, looking at his wife.

'Let's not forget stubborn,' her mother commented with a wistful smile.

Juliet stood up. 'Have you finished?'

'With this conversation or the cookies?' her mother asked with a cheeky grin.

'Both!'

'Remember, if there are any issues or just for peace of mind, if you need or want to stay at the hospital and monitor the quads' mother, you know your mother and I are here to look after Bea.'

'I still can't believe you flew all that way just so I could focus on the babies,' Juliet said as she gathered the last of her things, wrapped her scarf around her neck over her heavy coat, pulled on her knitted cap, kissed Bea and headed for the door. They had all enjoyed a restful night's sleep and Juliet felt good about the impending surgery.

'If Bea needed you in the future, you would do exactly the same.'

Juliet knew that was the truth. She would indeed do anything for her daughter, at that time or any time in the future.

'Despite what you say, Juliet,' her mother added as she sipped her early morning cup of tea and prepared for the cold gust of air as her daughter opened the door, 'it's not easy being single and raising a daughter and having a career that makes you responsible for other people's lives. You have a lot on your very slender shoulders.'

'But I love it. It gives me purpose and I can't imagine doing anything else,' Juliet told them both as she stepped onto the porch and closed the door behind her.

'I know,' her mother replied as she looked over at her husband, reading the local paper. 'The apple indeed did not fall too far from the tree.'

Georgina and Leo were waiting outside Theatre when Juliet arrived. With her hair tucked inside a disposable cap, and dressed in a hospital gown, Georgina had been prepped for the surgery. She was lying on the trolley with the sides up ready to be wheeled inside by the theatre staff. Leo was holding his wife's hand tightly and trying to put on a brave face but Juliet could sense the fear that was mounting by the minute.

'I will be scrubbing in for your procedure now,' she told them as she patted Georgina's arm. 'And, Leo, you can scrub in with me. I know that Georgie will want you right beside her during the procedure.'

'Sure.'

'Any questions?'

'Yes,' Leo said with a cheeky smirk. 'How hot does it get in Australia in summer?'

Juliet was surprised by the question. It was definitely left of centre. 'Quite hot in Perth, well over one hundred degrees on our hottest days. I left only a few days ago and we'd been through a heatwave—we had three days in a row that reached over one hundred and five degrees.'

'That's hot. Maybe spring would be nicer.'

Aware that time was ticking, and the medical team would be waiting, she quickly asked, 'For what, exactly?'

'Georgie and I have decided, should all of our babies come through this happy and healthy…' he paused for a moment and smiled lovingly at his wife '…that in honour of you we're going to take them all on a trip to Australia before they start school. We were planning on showing them Italy, but I think an adventure down under would be more fun for the six of us. Besides, Georgie and I have been back to Italy a few times but we've never seen a kangaroo up close and we can tell the girls how an Aussie doctor saved their brothers and, if you're home, perhaps we could call in and say hello.'

Juliet thought it was such a sweet sentiment and optimistic. It was what would pull them through whatever lay ahead. 'And I will put the barbie on for all of you.'

'I'll cook the pasta,' Georgina added from the trolley.

'And I'll bring the vino,' Leo chipped in as the theatre staff began to wheel his wife into surgery. Juliet couldn't help but see through his jovial façade that a tear trickled down his cheek. She patted his arm. 'Georgina is in good hands and so are your babies.'

Juliet then took Leo to scrub in.

'Heads up to the medical student and interns with us today, if you have questions about any of this procedure, ask. We will be using a laser to coagulate the shared blood supply between two of the four babies. This will be more complex with the four foetuses and will take considerable time to map the shared arteries and veins but it will be done. So we are all in here for the long haul.'

Charlie was pleased to hear the conviction in Juliet's voice.

'After this procedure I am hoping the two babies

currently affected by the TTTS will be able to grow to their maximum size without complications.'

The epidural had taken effect and Leo was behind the blue surgical sheet holding his wife's hand. Everyone present in Theatre was wearing the protective goggles in preparation for the laser, including Georgina and Leo. Juliet carefully inserted the fetoscope and, guided by the screen, began the arduous task of locating Rupert, otherwise known as Baby A. Once this was done she traced his umbilical cord back to the placenta and began the process of identifying the offending arteries. Secure in the knowledge she had the first communication located, Juliet utilised the laser to cauterise the artery.

Charlie held his breath. That was only the first; he was well aware there were more to locate and sever. Juliet continued mapping the vascular placental linkages and painstakingly cauterising each one. The procedure was progressing slowly but successfully. Charlie was still cautious. Any disruption to the uterus he knew was risky. With only two veins to cauterise, Juliet announced they were on the home stretch and everyone in Theatre felt instant relief sweep over them.

'Well done, Juliet,' the anaesthetist announced. 'Great outcome.'

'I said home stretch, not completed,' she countered cautiously as she pushed down on the foot pedal for the laser and severed the second to last. 'We still have one to go.'

Charlie was impressed with her reply. She had every reason to gloat that close to seeing the end in sight but still she was hesitant to accept praise. He also realised that he had been wrong to judge the procedure. Perhaps, in fact, Juliet had made the right call with the quads.

And if the babies all continued to grow, they would be able to prolong the pregnancy for at least a few more weeks until the uterus became too large, but by that time the babies would be all viable and have a good chance at a healthy life.

The final artery was the most difficult to locate due to Baby B's position. All eyes were on the monitor as Juliet carefully manoeuvred around the tiniest twin.

'We have a problem,' the neonatal cardiologist announced. 'Baby B's struggling, he's clearly in stress.'

Charlie stepped forward again to observe the screen. The invasive procedure had been delayed by the fact it was four babies, not two, and it had adversely affected the smallest quad.

'I'm ceasing laser now,' Juliet told the room, then quickly but delicately removed the fetoscope but it was too late. Without warning Georgina's water broke. The operating table was saturated with the amniotic fluid of the boys. The girls, in a separate sac, were unaffected but that would not mean they were safe. If the boys were to be born, so would the girls.

'I'll take over from here. We're in labour and delivering,' Charlie announced as he removed his protective laser glasses, switched them for clear glasses and stepped up to the operation table. He looked over the blue curtain to the Abbiatis. 'Georgie, Leo, your children are on their way,' he said, before turning his attention back to the immediate task. 'Nurses, please prepare for a Caesarean section—we have four twenty-nine-week foetuses that are neither large nor strong enough to pass through the birth canal.'

Immediately Juliet stepped back as she watched the surgical tray swing around in reach of Charlie. She approached Georgina and Leo, leaving the operation table free for Ella and the other midwife to approach and assist.

'The epidural was our safety net,' Juliet said softly. 'It won't be too long before your babies are born.'

'But…they're…too…tiny,' Georgina stated with fear paramount in each staggered word.

'They're small but, thanks to Dr Warren's suggestion of the epidural, we're more than adequately prepared. There'll be no delay in delivering all four babies and that is an important factor. They will be assessed by the neonatal team and then moved quicker to neonatal ICU.'

Carefully but with haste appropriate to the situation, Charlie made the first incision at the base of Georgina's engorged stomach, cutting through the outer layer of muscle. Then carefully he prised open the first incision to reveal the almost translucent uterus that had been stretched to capacity with the four babies. Once through to that layer, Charlie cut the unbroken amniotic sac of the girls, and, reaching in, he carefully pulled free the first of the tiny infants. Carefully he placed the baby in the first neonatal nurse's hands while he clamped the umbilical cord. One clamp for the first baby, who was named by the team, Baby C. The second girl followed a few minutes later; it was Baby D and she had two clamps. Baby D was slightly larger and began to cry immediately. Quickly she was taken by the second midwife. Then came Baby A and finally the smallest of them all, Baby B, who had been against his mother's spine. Removing him from the womb proved tricky as he was the smallest and the most fragile. She could see the concern in Charlie's eyes but along with it was sheer determination. Finally he was pulled free, blue and almost translucent, but alive.

Juliet watched in awe as Charlie tenderly held the

tiny infant while the final cord was clamped. The paediatric team worked alongside the neonatal nurses to assess all of the babies. But it was Baby A that caused the greatest concern. He had been the recipient baby and, while not the smallest, his heart had been pumping furiously for the previous twelve hours as Georgina had teetered on the periphery of stage five.

Charlie's focus remained with Georgina. There were still two placentas that needed to be delivered and then the painstaking work of closing the Caesarean section. Juliet remained with Georgina and Leo. It was where she was most needed at that time. With a heartfelt admiration for Charlie, she watched as he expertly began to repair the opening that had allowed Lily, Rose, Rupert and Graham to enter the world.

'You're an incredibly skilled obstetrician and you have no idea how very grateful I am that you were in Theatre today,' Juliet commented as she removed the disposable gown over her scrubs. 'I'm just sorry you had to use your skills.' She was waiting for what she knew would follow. And what she knew would be a fair call. *I told you so.*

But it didn't. Instead, she received the most unexpected praise.

'I did okay, but your skills are second to none, Juliet. I observed you mapping the placenta's vascular pathways. Not an easy task with two babies, but with four it was a miracle and you managed to cauterise all but one artery. And if you'd been provided the time then the quads would still be happily tucked inside Georgina for another few weeks. But fate had another idea.'

Juliet pulled her surgical cap free. 'So you're not

upset that I tried. I thought you would be...and justi-fiably so.'

Charlie turned to face her. 'The opposite, actually.'

'Now I'm confused.'

'If you hadn't pushed for the fetoscopic laser sur-gery, Juliet, then Rupert's heart would've remained overworked for another twelve hours and it might have been too late. We wouldn't have done another scan until tomorrow and there's every chance he would have gone into heart failure during the night. We would not have had the opportunity to save him.

'I'm very glad you came all the way from Australia to fight me on this. You saved at least one baby's life. If not all four.'

CHAPTER TWELVE

'THANK YOU, CHARLIE. That was an unexpected compliment.'

'Perhaps unexpected but not undeserved. I think you know me well enough after the last few days together to know that I don't hold back my opinion, whether others want to hear it or not. In this case I hope you want to hear it. And while I didn't initially agree, you proved me wrong and that rarely happens.'

'As I said, your compliment was unexpected but very much appreciated,' Juliet said as she removed her surgical gloves and dropped them in the designated bin along with her surgical cap and gown. 'There were a few scary moments in there and I must admit I felt a little out of my depth more than once.'

Charlie slipped his surgical cap free and ran his fingers through his hair. 'You seemed pretty poised and in control even when it all went south.'

'I may have looked composed but my mind was the duck's feet paddling underneath at a million miles an hour. You were the star today.'

Charlie smiled at her analogy and Juliet thought it was the most incredible smile.

'Seriously, you need to take credit where it's due. Teddy's are so fortunate to have you on staff. You could move permanently to anywhere in the world. There would be so many hospitals that would love to steal you, of that I'm sure.'

'What about you?' he answered quickly, still looking into her eyes with an intensity she had not experienced.

The deep blue pools were threatening to pierce the last barriers of resistance to him. Watching him so expertly and confidently lead the team and deliver the four babies safely had brought a new level of admiration for him that she knew few, if any, other doctors could surpass. But Juliet still wasn't sure what he meant. Was he asking if she wanted to steal him? The answer of course would be yes, if she could dull the alarm bells ringing in her head and bury her doubts.

'I'm not sure what you mean?' she asked nervously.

He crossed his arms across his impressive chest and stepped out his legs. It was a powerful stance not lost on Juliet.

'I mean, would you seriously consider living and working here? Would you let Teddy's perhaps steal you permanently from your base in Perth?'

'I'm not sure.'

Juliet felt the intensity of his gaze upon her. She wasn't sure if he was waiting for her to say anything as he stood looking at her without saying a word. She felt her pulse quicken and she became almost breathless with him standing so close to her. Her skin tingled and he had not touched her. She wondered for a moment if she would or could say no to him touching her if they were somewhere else alone…and he tried to pull her to him.

'Are you hungry?'

Juliet was taken aback by his question. *Hungry for*

what? Her eyes widened and she felt excitement surge through her veins as she nodded.

'What if I cook us dinner at my place?'

'Your place?'

'Yes, my home's twenty minutes from here. You could follow my bike and I could whip us up something half edible and definitely better than the vending machine, which is your other choice if you stay here at this time of the night.'

'But what about Bea…?' she began to ask as her chest rose with a nervous intake of air.

'I don't think your parents will let her starve and they've more than likely eaten already. Bea may even be in bed asleep. It's almost eight o'clock.'

Juliet hadn't realised the time. It was true, it was late, and they all might have been asleep, not just Bea. She was trying to keep her emotions in check and remember it would be merely a dinner shared by two colleagues. She just had to keep remembering that fact and everything would be fine.

'Give me fifteen minutes to have a quick shower and change.'

'Of course. I could do with a hot shower to loosen my muscles as well. I'll meet you in your office in twenty minutes.'

Juliet walked away knowing she hadn't wanted anyone's company in a very long time. Not until that moment.

Juliet followed behind Charlie's bike along the winding road. The moon's halo lit his broad masculine silhouette as they travelled slowly through the darkened countryside. There was no other traffic, just the two of them on the road. Juliet felt herself mesmerised as he leaned into the turns and curves of the road. His was agile and strong and completely in control of the huge machine. He made it impossible for her not to stare in awe and a little bit of anticipation as he led her to his home.

Finally they pulled into the large estate and Juliet wondered if he had one of the cottages, but soon learned it was the stately mansion that was indeed his home. Even with just the moon lighting the grounds, she could see how magnificent the landscape and how grand his home.

'This is beautiful,' she said as she climbed from the car wearing jeans, a pullover and boots. Her hair was tied up in a makeshift ponytail and a thick scarf and coat rested on her shoulders. 'I've never seen anything quite like it.'

'It's a work in progress.'

'It looks wonderfully finished to me,' she replied as she followed him up the steps to the two-hundred-year-old home. 'It's simply glorious. Nothing quite like it in Perth.'

Charlie unlocked the door and held it open for Juliet to enter, before he stepped inside and closed the door. 'I'll put on a fire and start dinner then show you around, if you'd like.'

With her gaze scanning the furnishings and architecture of the beautiful interior, she nodded. 'I'd love that.'

The fire was roaring and the meat was ready whenever they were; it would take only a few minutes on the grill. Charlie reappeared in the doorway, aware that he was not in a hurry to cook or rush anything about the evening. The surgery, and everything that had happened over the last few days since meeting Juliet, had made him feel alive and made him hunger for more time alone with her, despite his better judgement. 'Would you like a glass of wine?'

'I do have to drive home.'

'Not for a while. Besides, you'll be eating and I'll give you only half a glass.'

'That sounds lovely. I won't head in until around one tomorrow so it might be nice to let my hair down.'

Charlie smiled. Seeing *Juliet* on the sofa, with her beautiful face lit by the fire, was a sight he had never imagined over the years of his self-imposed solitude. But it was a sight he was relishing. 'I'll be back.'

Juliet looked into the crackling fire and as another log was consumed by flames she thought how very different Charlie was from the man she'd first met. In five short days he had opened up and shown a compassionate, loving side completely at odds with the brusque exterior he had first displayed. Bea was smitten by him, and she felt sure if her parents met him they too would think he was very charming. An English gentleman with an English country manor. It was all very proper and lovely. A little like a fairy tale but she wasn't yet sure of the ending. Or indeed if fairy tales happened.

Charlie appeared with two glasses of red wine, Juliet's only a quarter filled.

'As I promised,' he said as he handed her the long-stemmed Waterford Crystal glass. Their hands touched as he gave her possession of the cold crystal and it instantly stirred an overwhelming desire to feel more than just her hand against his. His mouth immediately craved Juliet's full, inviting lips hovering only inches from his own. He let his gaze linger for a moment on her mouth, all the while wondering if it would taste as sweet as it looked. He pushed the cold rim of the glass against his mouth in a bid to control the mounting desire surging through his veins.

'Thank you,' she said as she climbed to her feet. 'Can I have the grand tour now? Do we have time?'

'All the time in the world,' he replied.

Charlie led Juliet around the ground floor. Leaving the generous sitting room, he showed her the kitchen with the butler's pantry, the dining room, which she noticed had been set for two, the utility room, a wonderfully inspiring floor-to-ceiling library, a study with a large oak desk and bookcase and a billiard room that housed an antique snooker table. As they entered each room he thought about kissing Juliet but then reasoning stepped in and made him keep a little distance. But each room was harder than the last.

'You said you were renovating but it all looks perfect to me.'

'I finished downstairs first then moved upstairs with the repairs and redecorating.'

'What's upstairs?' she asked, her curiosity driving her towards the staircase. She was fascinated by the house and couldn't wait to see more.

'The seven bedrooms,' he answered as he followed her lead and moved towards the grand staircase. 'Apparently all of them including the master bedroom are finished but I haven't seen them yet.'

Juliet thought the statement was odd and turned to him. She said nothing as she assumed he had been too busy to check it out, but she couldn't imagine not rushing home to see the progress every night, no matter what the time of day. He was very low-key.

'So where do you sleep?'

'Over there,' he said, pointing at the chesterfield.

'I'm accustomed to it now. I've been sleeping there for a few months while the work's been happening upstairs.' Charlie didn't tell her that he didn't feel any motivation to sleep in the new master bedroom alone.

'It's a very comfortable sofa, but if the master bedroom's finished then it's time you moved in. Let's take a peek.'

Charlie noticed everything about Juliet as she climbed the stairs ahead of him. Her slim hips swaying in her tight jeans with each enthusiastic step, the way her curls bounced when her head flicked from side to side as she looked at the antique framed paintings hanging on the wall, and the slender fingers of one hand gliding up the balustrade, the other hand encircling her glass. She was gorgeous, intelligent and sexy. And watching her, he suspected he was smitten. He wasn't sure if it could be more than that but it was still more than he had imagined ever feeling again.

By the time they had reached the large oak door of the master bedroom, Charlie knew he couldn't resist her any longer. He wanted to spend the night in the refurbished room. But not alone. He wanted to spend the night with Juliet. She had made him feel more alive than he had in years. She, and her little girl, had made him believe there could be life outside the hospital. He had been alone for so long, but now this sexy, desirable woman had stirred feelings that he'd never thought he would feel in his body and soul the way he did at that moment. And if all they had was that moment, he couldn't let it slip away without taking a chance.

Juliet tentatively opened the heavy door to the darkened room and Charlie brushed her shoulder gently as he reached around for the light. Her heart unexpectedly began to race with his touch. Nervously she swallowed and bit the inside of her cheek. She was at the entrance to Charlie's bedroom and she couldn't see anything. But she realised that she wasn't scared.

She couldn't see the future but suddenly that didn't matter either. She didn't need to have everything laid out. She felt safe. Safer than she could remember feeling before. The fleeting warmth of his body against hers caused butterflies to stir. As each second passed with him so close to her, she loosened her tether to fear. Pushing away the promises she had made to never trust again. With his warm breath on her neck, she felt herself feeling free to fall into whatever this could be. She didn't want to run away from her feelings.

As his fingers flicked on the light switch, Juliet found herself looking around at the elegant decor, in the soft lighting. But her focus was the imposing four-poster bed that dominated the room…and dominated her thoughts. It could be their bed for the night.

Suddenly everything felt right. The man standing so close to her was everything she could hope for and he was within her reach.

That bed would be theirs.

Her breathing became laboured with anticipation as she felt Charlie's strong hands on her hips. Gently but purposefully he swivelled her around to face him. Her mouth was only inches from his and it made the ache inside her almost overwhelming. With only the sound of their hearts beating, he searched her face for permission to kiss her and she smiled her consent as she reached up on her tiptoes to meet his lips. Taking her glass and placing it with his on the large oak dresser, Charlie scooped her up in his arms and carried her to the bed, where he laid her down and gently began to peel away her clothing. He slipped off her boots, tugged down her jeans and then slid her arms and body free of her jumper, revealing her white lace underwear.

Juliet watched and admired as he pulled free all of his own clothing, discarding each piece roughly to the floor. Finally, gloriously naked, he loosened her hair from its ponytail and then began to slowly remove the last remnants of clothing keeping them apart. With every part of his mouth and body he began to pleasure Juliet in ways she had not thought possible and ways she did not want to end. Willingly and wantonly, she gave into all of her desires for the man who had awakened the woman in her. And over the hours he loved her that night she gave a little part of her heart to him as they crossed the divide from colleagues to lovers.

Charlie looked over at Juliet still asleep. She was beautiful and loving and everything a man could desire. She had given herself to him willingly and, while it had been the most amazing night, in the soft light streaming from the hallway his actions hit home hard. He had taken the chance. For the first time in a very long time he hadn't denied his feelings but as he lay there looking out into the still of the darkness outside he knew he should have fought this harder. He should never have invited her to dinner, let alone to his bedroom. He regretted everything about the night. The sight of her peacefully sleeping tugged at his heart. A heart so damaged that it hadn't felt anything but pain for so long.

And now the pain returned two-fold. He had betrayed his resolve to live his life without love out of respect for Alice and now there was a second burden. He would be forced to hurt Juliet. A very special woman he did not want to hurt. A woman who did not deserve to be hurt. She was loving and trusting and she had given herself to him openly and honestly. He knew everything there was to know about her.

But she did not know everything about him. She had no idea that he could not let her into his life. Last night was all they would share. He could not accept happiness. He didn't deserve it. As he felt the warmth of her body against his he suddenly felt overwhelmed by the guilt that had been his constant companion for two years. Thoughts of Juliet and what might have been had their lives been different filled his mind. Her scent was on every part of his body and buried the guilt for those few hours but he knew it was only temporary. It wouldn't last and then he would bring her down too. She deserved better than to be with a man who would never be free to love her. He had to set her free.

'Good morning,' she softly said as she lifted herself up to meet his lips.

His mouth felt the warmth of hers but he ended the kiss before it deepened. The need for her was as strong in the morning as the night before but now he knew he had to fight it. It should never have gone that far.

'I'm sorry I fell asleep. I should have left a while ago. You invited me for dinner, not a sleepover.'

He sat bolt upright. If he held her close to him he would give in to his desire. He would take her again and feel her warm soft skin against his and that would make what he had to do more difficult. And more painful for both of them.

'That was my fault as much as yours. I guess we just got carried away by the heat of the moment. Yesterday was quite an intense day. But I'll get you some breakfast before you leave,' he told her as he lifted the covers, swung his legs down and found his boxer shorts and then a heavy winter robe lying on the chair beside the bed. 'I'm sure I can rustle up some toast for us. I'm going to head into the hospital and check on the quads and my other patients.'

'Is there something wrong?'

'No,' he lied. 'I just think we should get going. Last night was…well…special but I'm sure you agree not something we should repeat. It'd make working together difficult for the short time you still have here and neither of us would want that.'

Each word was carefully chosen to hide any level of emotion. What he wanted to do was to pull her into his arms and make love to her again, but he couldn't. He couldn't surrender to the emotions surging through him after they'd spent the night together. He feared his heart and soul were still in pieces and he needed to accept that in the harsh light of the morning. He was damaged and she needed a man who was still whole. Her tenderness and honesty made him feel worse. But he couldn't prolong what he knew he had to do. End it before it began. Not because he didn't care about her but because he feared caring too much.

'I'm really confused, Charlie. I won't lie,' she said as she pulled the covers up around her. 'After last night and…after what happened between us, why are you so distant to me this morning? You sound so cold and… just nothing like you were last night. Why are you in such a hurry for me to leave?'

'I'm not being cold. I'm being honest. Last night was great but we both need to see it for what it really is.'

'And what is that?'

'A great night together—'

'A one-night stand?' she cut in.

'Juliet, it was fantastic,' he said. 'But we're colleagues and I'm not looking for a relationship. I think the intensity of what we went through yesterday with the delivery of the quads heightened our emotions and we acted upon it.'

'So last night was just a fling after the surgery, a re-action to a successful outcome? Is that how you see it?'

Charlie used every ounce of his strength not to reach for her. Not to say how he really felt. Not to let her know that she was breaking through his defences and making him want more. That there was no one he wanted to be with more than her. But he couldn't.

'You can and will do far better than me. I was just for last night.'

'So in your mind it really was just a one-night stand?'

'That doesn't sum up what we shared...'

'But it's how you see it,' she spat back angrily.

'Well...'

'I can't believe this,' she said with anger and disappointment colouring her tone. 'You're no different from all the other men who want a quick roll in the sack with no strings attached—'

'That's not true.'

'Tell me how it isn't true. If this was only for one night then you should have let me in on that fact yesterday, before we fell into bed together. I thought we shared something more than that, or at least we could, given time.'

Charlie hated what he had to do and say. His heart wrenched. This woman was wonderful and loving but he could never be what Juliet needed.

'I didn't mislead you, Juliet. I don't think either of us thought too much about anything other than being with each other but now, in the light of day, we have to be practical. I need to be alone and you're not staying in the UK long term so let's not delay the inevitable.'

What he wanted, with all of his still unhealed heart, was to say that spending any more time with her and knowing he had to let her go would be unbearable. He was torn between the happiness that he felt around her and the guilt that he knew he deserved to carry.

The guilt that would ruin any chance for them having any sort of a future.

'Charlie, does this have something to do with your wife? Lots of people lose their partners but they go on to love again.'

'That has nothing to do with this,' he lied again. 'It doesn't matter why, it's just the way it is.' His voice was shaky as he tried to hold back what Juliet did not need to know.

'I'm not buying it. I think I know you almost better than you know yourself, even though that sounds ridiculous after a week but it's how I feel. So I need to know something. I need you to tell me what happened, Charlie,' she said. Her tone had softened. 'What happened to your wife? Because that has everything to do with your need to be alone. I know it has.'

Charlie's back stiffened and his jaw tensed. 'It won't change anything.'

'Perhaps not, but I want to know.'

He climbed from the bed and began to gather his clothes in silence. He did not want to open up old wounds.

'Charlie,' Juliet began as she leant against the bed head, the bedclothes wrapped around her still-naked body. 'I'll go. I know you want me to leave but you owe me an explanation for what is happening now. I need to know why you're rejecting us…and why you won't even try.'

'Fine,' he said as he inhaled and filled his tight chest

with air and stood in the middle of the softly lit room staring back at Juliet. 'You know I'm a widower and you know my wife, Alice, died two years ago. It was a car accident that claimed her life on the road that leads out of town. She died in the Cotswolds only two miles from this house and I wish every day that I could change places with her but I can't. She died and I am forced to live on.'

Juliet sat for a moment in silence. 'Charlie, I'm sorry that you lost your wife so tragically, but you can't change what's happened or trade places with her. Do you think she would want you to be living with that much sadness? Don't you think you're being hard on yourself? You're still here and you can live your life...'

'After I took hers? I don't think so.'

'What do you mean, after you took hers? It was an accident.'

'I was driving.'

'Were you drunk?'

'No,' he spat angrily. 'I would never get behind the wheel if I'd been drinking.'

'Then it wasn't your fault.'

He stood rigidly. 'She was excited about going to the dinner. I couldn't have been further from excited. The weather had been the worst we'd seen in years, I'd been in surgery all day and wanted to stay home but I didn't want to refuse her. I didn't want to appear selfish so I gave in. When I should have said no, I said yes. Despite my reservations, we headed out on the snow-covered roads, I lost control and I killed her.'

'No, Charlie, you didn't kill her. The weather, the road, fate, that is what killed Alice. You can't take responsibility for that. Factors came together to take her life.'

He paced the room. His hands were clenched tightly. 'We shouldn't have been on the road, in the weather. I should have been more cautious. I should've protected her. I was her husband; that was my role.'

'I bet you had driven in that weather many times without incident and you thought that night would be no different...'

'But it was different. I should've argued the point, and insisted we stayed in, out of the weather.'

'Even if you had done that, you know Alice could have been in an accident the next morning travelling to work. It could have happened any time. Or worse, she could have gone on her own and you wouldn't have been there for her. You tried to protect her. You were tired and yet you agreed and did your best to protect her by being with her.'

'But I failed and nothing you say can change this. I've felt this way since the day she died and I will feel this way until the day I die. And it's the reason I haven't driven in more than two years. I won't get behind the wheel of a car again. Ever. Please, Juliet, I think it's best that you leave.'

'Charlie, we can talk about this—'

'No.' He knew his coldness wasn't lost on Juliet and he wanted it that way. He had to push her away before he fell too hard and couldn't let her go. 'There's nothing else to say. I'm sorry if you were looking for more. But I'm not and never will be. You're a special woman, Juliet, but I can't... I suppose occasional lapses like last night will happen.'

Juliet stared back at him. He could see tears welling in her eyes. 'Lapses?'

'I'm sorry, you know what I mean.'

'If all of this is true, then you had no right to ask me back here last night.'

'I asked you here for dinner.'

'Then why didn't you leave it downstairs?' she demanded. 'Why did you show me the master bedroom?'

'I need to get dressed. There's no point discussing this further. We made a mistake last night. We shouldn't have overstepped the line. We work together and we should not have slept together. It won't happen again. I'll make sure of that.'

'You'll make sure of that?' she repeated solemnly. 'I'll make sure of it.'

'Juliet, I didn't mean to hurt you; you have to believe me.'

'I don't have to believe anything.' She climbed from the bed and began to gather her clothes. Angrily she pushed past him to the bathroom. She slammed the door shut and reappeared a few minutes later, dressed.

'There's just one more thing,' he said, determined to distance himself from Juliet and her tiny daughter. He knew it would sound heartless but it would ensure she stopped trying to help him.

'What?' she demanded.

'Would you mind telling Bea that the delivery she's expecting won't be arriving? The Christmas tree farm can't deliver. I'm truly sorry.'

CHAPTER THIRTEEN

JULIET ARRIVED HOME to see there were no missed calls
from Charlie. He hadn't so much as sent her a text, let
alone called to apologise or try to make it up to her.
Her face was damp with tears she had shed but most
of them had rolled down her cheeks on the short and
painful drive home just before dawn. The road was dark
and she felt more alone than she had ever done before.

It was her worst nightmare. A one-night stand with
a man with whom she had thought she might possibly
fall in love. If she wasn't already a little. With a heart
heavier than she had dreamed possible, Juliet had run
out of his home when he'd told her about the tree. She'd
known she had to leave. Without saying another word.

She'd had to turn her back on Charlie Warren just
the way he had turned his back on her.

But before he'd seen the tears she had promised herself all those years ago that she would never shed for
a man.

She had pulled into her driveway and crept into the
house before the sun came up and slipped into bed
beside Bea, feeling stupid and filled with regret. She
hoped her daughter would never make the same mistakes she had, twice. She wanted so much more for Bea.
She wanted her to feel real love, the kind that lasted for

ever with the bells and whistles and everything a man could give and that neither had given to Juliet.

She could hear her father snoring in the other room and knew her mother would be wearing the earplugs that had saved their marriage. Her father's snoring at times was like a long freight train rattling down the tracks, and, without the earplugs, she knew her mother would have gone mad from the sleep deprivation or divorced him. But she had found the solution in a pharmacy, popped them in her ears and had her happily ever after. For Juliet there was nothing in a pharmacy, no prescription or over-the-counter solution to her woes. She simply chose the wrong man and that was a problem that couldn't be cured.

In her lifetime Juliet had only chosen two men and both were wrong for her. And both were nothing more than one-night stands.

There would be no happily ever after.

She was, in her mind, the poster girl for stupid decisions with her one hundred per cent failure rate.

Bea had left the bed while Juliet lay with her eyes closed. Now she could hear her daughter giggling over the sound of the television in the other room. She could also smell fruit toast that she knew her mother or father had prepared for their granddaughter.

While her irresponsible mother slept in after a drive of shame home.

They had been careful, so at least she had no fear of another pregnancy. No, this time she had only gained a broken heart and damaged pride. Not to mention shattered dreams that what she had shared with Charlie in his four-poster bed would amount to more than a night. Climbing from the bed, she headed for the bathroom.

She needed to soak in the tub and try to wash the man out of her heart.

Only this time, she thought it would take longer and hurt more. Because this time she had believed in her heart it was real.

It was the weekend, and Juliet was not required at the hospital but she wanted to be there to see Georgina and Leo and also their babies. In general her role ended after the delivery, but the outcome of the Abbiatis' procedure was not what she had clearly hoped for and she wanted to check in with them. Despite what Charlie had said post-operatively, and what she knew to be true, she still felt responsible for the babies' pre-term arrival. It wasn't logical, it was heartfelt, and that was linked very closely to the outcome of becoming involved with Charlie.

Spending the night in his bed was illogical and... heartbreaking.

She left Bea playing cards on the floor with her grandfather. Snap was their game of choice. The house was lovely and warm and Juliet's mother was going to roast a chicken for lunch, then they thought they would all rug up in their winter best and head out for a walk through the town. Juliet wished she were in the mood to join them but decided to hide behind her work rather than pull them all down with her melancholy mood.

After parking in the hospital car park she made her way into the hospital. The chilly breeze seemed even colder that morning.

Juliet caught sight of Ella as she walked into Maternity. Worried that the midwife would sense immediately that she was upset, Juliet quickly realised that she had to avoid her. Ella had mentioned a few times how she was growing accustomed to Juliet's sunny personality and that day Juliet knew she was anything but sunny. With her head down, she waved and rushed past Ella, hoping she would assume she was in a hurry and not think anything of it. But she wasn't that lucky.

'Juliet,' Ella called to her. 'Do you know where I might find Charlie?'

Juliet shrugged her shoulders. She didn't want to be drawn into talking. She feared she might tell Ella that she hoped Charlie was rotting somewhere in hell. Or worse, burst into tears and confess how much she still felt for the man who had behaved so poorly. So she kept walking, offering Ella nothing. In Juliet's mind, it was best if she was the only person who knew about her foolish behaviour. No one else needed to know that she had actually believed, when he'd pressed his hard body against hers, that a man like Charlie wanted more than a fling.

With a deep breath to steady her emotions, she knocked on Georgina's door. There was another hurdle to face that day. Georgina and Leo and their questions about what went wrong.

'Come in,' came Leo's voice.

Juliet stepped into the room that was filled with flowers and family members. She suddenly realised she also had to face their family.

'Mum, Dad,' Leo began, then turned to the other set of parents and repeated himself. 'Mum, Dad, this is Dr Juliet Turner, the *in-utero* surgeon from Australia.'

Juliet attempted a smile. She was genuinely happy to finally meet Georgina and Leo's parents but it would have been a nicer meeting if it had occurred the previous day. Before the surgery had brought about the preterm delivery of the four babies...and before she had stupidly slept with Charlie and hated herself.

Moving closer to Georgina, she did not attempt to shake four sets of hands. The closest were folded, the next clasped, one set leaning on the window ledge and the final hands were arranging flowers. It was a little overwhelming and she suspected they were all making judgement calls on the laser surgery that had brought about the early arrival of the quads. And they had every right. While she'd known it was risky, she had forged ahead and in their eyes that was probably not the right decision.

'So you're the Australian doctor who performed Georgina's surgery?' one of the two older men said.

Juliet nodded and lifted her chin. The outcome was not perfect but Juliet still believed she had made the correct decision. The only correct decision she had made that day.

'Yes, I am. And I stand by my advice to operate. Despite the outcome, I believed then, and still believe now, that it was the best option, however—'

'Then we all owe you a huge debt of gratitude for saving our grandchildren.'

Juliet was taken aback. She'd thought both sets of parents, along with Georgina and Leo, would have been upset with her. Not grateful.

'Please take a seat. You must be exhausted after the day you had yesterday,' the taller of the two women said. 'We heard you stayed back to check on the babies. Have you seen them today? They're so tiny but the neonatologist is very hopeful they'll all pull through. They're tiny little Italian fighters.'

'You should have called Rupert Rocky instead!' Georgina's father suggested with a grin. 'It's not too late to change his name.'

'Rocky as in Rocky Balboa?' Leo asked, looking more than a little embarrassed.

'The greatest Italian fighter ever!' his father-in-law replied happily.

'Dad,' Georgina cut in, 'Rocky is a fictional character in a movie.'

'I know,' the older man replied. 'But Rupert's a fighter and the other three are just as strong. I know in my heart our grandchildren will pull through. And that's thanks to you, Dr Turner.'

'I'm not sure where this is all coming from,' Juliet admitted.

'Charlie was in early this morning to see me and check my stitches,' Georgina continued. 'He told me that, even though he was against the laser surgery, and despite it not going to plan yesterday, it saved Rupert's life because it brought on my labour early and he was born just before his heart stopped. A day longer and he would not have survived. You saved our baby's life, Dr Turner.'

'Charlie, is everything all right with Juliet?' Ella asked as she caught up with Charlie scrubbing in before visiting with the quads.

'Why? What makes you ask that?' His tone was defensive. He didn't want to be questioned by the midwife. They had been friends for a long time but he didn't want to feel forced to justify his behaviour to anyone. There was no other choice but to push Juliet away. He had to be cruel to be kind. While he regretted hurting Juliet, he knew if he led her on he would hurt her more. It would just take her longer to feel the hurt. She was looking for a happily ever after and he was not that man. He had a debt to pay. And it wouldn't allow him to love someone.

Particularly the way he knew he wanted to love Juliet. With every fibre of his being.

But he wouldn't.

'She rushed past me this morning, and snubbed me. Well, almost, I mean she waved at me but it wasn't like her. And I asked about you and she just shrugged her shoulders. She and Bea are always so lovely and she seemed upset today.'

'Perhaps she's drained after yesterday,' he suggested to deflect from the real reason.

'No, she's a pro,' Ella responded. 'She wouldn't react that way.'

'Just leave it alone.'

'You know, Juliet would be perfect for you, Charlie. I know you may not have thought about her that way, but she's beautiful, sweet and intelligent. You're both single. I think she could be *the one*, Charlie.'

'I like it on my own. It's been that way for a long time. I had *the one*, and I lost her. I don't need to hurt another woman.' It was true that it had been a long time but it was a lie that he liked being alone. It was a penance he made himself pay for the accident.

'It's been over two years since the accident—that's long enough for someone as young as you to mourn. Your wife wouldn't want you to go on punishing yourself.'

'I guess we'll never know what she wanted, because I killed her.'

'It was an accident—a stupid accident that no one could have averted. It's lucky you lived through it.'

'I'm not so sure I'd call myself lucky. I lost Alice.'

Ella shook her head. 'It was a tragic accident that you survived. You are not the first person to lose their partner. It's awful, but it happens and people have to go on and rebuild their lives.'

'It was stupid and reckless. I've no right to a happy life when my wife died with my hands on the steering wheel. I'll never forgive myself for that.'

'Charlie, I hope you know from the way Juliet and little Bea look at you, you might just be punishing more than yourself by pushing them away.'

Juliet saw Charlie around the hospital when she popped in to check on the quads over the next couple of days but he said nothing to her. He had every opportunity to try to make amends. To apologise. But he didn't try. She felt as if the world were crashing in. A world she'd dreamed she might possibly begin to build with Charlie. She knew it was too soon to have been thinking for ever, but she had. For the first time in a very long time. They had shared his bed for one night and after she'd left, they did not even acknowledge each other.

She had no idea how he could be so cold but she made a promise to herself as she heard his office door close.

She would never trust her instincts where men were concerned.

And she would never speak to Charlie Warren again. Although she doubted she would ever stop thinking about him.

CHAPTER FOURTEEN

IT WAS EARLY Monday morning when Juliet awoke. The sky was overcast and threatening to rain down on the still-damp earth. While she knew she had so much to be grateful for, it still didn't lessen the pain in her heart. But just like the dismal weather, it too would subside in time, she reminded herself. But how much time that would take she didn't know. Sitting in bed with Bea still sound asleep beside her, she thought back over the week since they'd arrived. So much had happened. The rushed journey over was probably the least eventful.

Bea's pink cast took her attention and she remembered the sinking feeling when she saw her fall to the snow. Instinctively, sitting in the warmth of her bed, with her little girl safely beside her, she still dropped her head into her hands. That fleeting but very real fear that something had happened to her daughter had been the worst feeling in the world.

And how she felt as she thought about Charlie, she accepted, was the second to worst feeling.

Losing him, after only having him for one night, brought sadness to her every thought. She had been stupid to believe there could be more. She had fallen into bed with a man once again without thinking.

Then she shifted her shoulders and lifted her chin.

It wasn't quite like that, she had to admit to herself. Charlie was not just any man. He was different. Charlie never lied to her, like Brad. He didn't scheme, like Bea's father. He had never hidden the fact he liked his life the way it was. Alone. But Juliet had thought she could change that. And his clear affection for her daughter had convinced her that he was ready to open his heart to love.

But he wasn't.

Both of them were wrong.

She wasn't sure what she would do. Extending her contract with Teddy's was yet to be negotiated so she still had the option of returning home. Or perhaps going on a river cruise with her parents, she thought wryly.

In the jumble of thoughts, she decided to get up and make some tea and let Bea sleep in a little longer. She tiptoed down the passageway into the kitchen and put on the kettle. She couldn't let herself fall to pieces. Bea deserved better. She was too young to witness her mother's heartbreak. Juliet's tears would have to wait until the middle of the night, when she could cry alone and wish for what might have been.

Looking at the clock, she realised it was later than she had thought. It was almost nine. Jet lag, she assumed, had finally taken its toll on her parents. That was for the best, she thought as she sat in her pyjamas and robe, holding the steaming cup of tea at the kitchen table. Her socked feet were inside her slippers.

She thought she heard a car, but presumed it was the neighbours or local traffic passing by. It wasn't the motorbike she wanted to hear. Biting her lip, and trying to hold back the tears threatening to spill onto her cheeks, she accepted that she would never hear Charlie's motorbike in her driveway.

A rustling and thumping suddenly began. And it seemed to get louder. Pulling back her kitchen curtains, to look out of her window into the neighbour's driveway, Juliet couldn't see anything. It was the oddest sound. Nothing she could really discern so she sat back down and sipped her tea. While some said tea solved everything, she doubted it would come close to resolving her problems.

The noise changed to heavy footsteps. And they were outside her house. She crossed the wooden floorboards to the front door expecting a deliveryman. She tugged her dressing gown up around her neck and braced herself for the inevitable gust of cold air as she opened the door.

But it wasn't a delivery man.

It was Charlie.

'What are you doing here?' Her voice was not welcoming. She was hurt and angry and disappointed and more confused than ever. And the reason for her tumultuous emotions was standing on her doorstep.

'I brought the Christmas tree I promised Bea.'

Juliet eyed him suspiciously as she looked to the side of the house where the six-foot tree was leaning against the wall. Snow was covering the deep green branches that had been tied up with rope.

'Why?'

'Because, as I said, I promised to do it. I won't let Bea down.'

But you would let me down, she thought. 'That's not what you told me,' she spat back. 'I'm heading off today with my father to collect one so you can take that one back. I don't want a tree or anything from you.'

Charlie didn't flinch. 'I know you're upset with me—'

'And does that surprise you?' she cut in angrily.

Charlie looked down at his snow-covered boots for a moment before he raised his gaze back to her. 'Not at all. I deserve your anger. I behaved terribly. And I want to make it up to you. Bringing you the tree is just the start…'

'But how did it get here?' she interrupted. She hadn't heard his motorbike and there was no delivery van visible outside.

'I brought it here.'

Juliet stepped onto the freezing cold tiles of the front porch.

'How?'

Charlie paused for a moment before he turned and looked over his shoulder. 'On the roof of the car. I tied it to the roof rack.'

'But you don't drive. You haven't driven since the accident. I don't understand.'

Charlie, momentarily and in deep thought, closed his eyes. When he opened them seconds later he spoke. 'I had to drive. They couldn't deliver the tree.'

Juliet said nothing.

'I borrowed the car from the Christmas tree farm owner.'

'How long since you've driven?'

Charlie looked into Juliet's eyes in silence for a moment. 'I haven't climbed into a car…since the accident. Not to drive or be a passenger. This is the first time in two years I've been behind the wheel. I had no choice but to drive because I couldn't let Bea down.'

'Thank you for the tree. I'll get my father to help me in with it later,' she said as she stepped back inside and began to close the door.

Without warning, Charlie's boot stopped it closing. 'There's more. We need to talk.'

Juliet shook her head. 'No, Charlie, we've said everything there is to say. I know how you feel. I know you like living alone. I get it. I don't agree but I accept that it's your choice and not mine. So let's leave it at that. But thank you very much for the tree. Bea will love it.'

'Please, Juliet. Give me five minutes. This is not just about Bea. I won't ever let you down again, if you'll let me make it up to you.'

She looked at his handsome face, his stunning eyes that were pleading with her, but she couldn't let him stay. She needed space to heal and listening to his reasons, his justification for being so cold, would not help her to shut him out for ever. He needed to leave before she could not control her need to stroke the stubble on his chin with her fingers, before she reached up to kiss his tender lips with hers the way she had that night.

'I'm busy, Charlie.' Her voice was cold but her heart was still warm and she wished it were otherwise.

'It's nine in the morning and I know you don't start until one today.' He moved his foot free. She could shut the door but he hoped with all of his heart she wouldn't. 'Please don't close the door on us. Not without hearing me out.'

'Why, Charlie? We've said everything there is to say. You want to spend your life living in regret. Living something you can't change. You can't bring your wife back and I don't want to talk about it any more. I can't compete with the woman you lost. I'm alive and I wanted to be there for you but you threw me away. I have my pride and I have my daughter. And you can have your lonely existence.'

'I never threw you away. I wanted you to walk away before I hurt you.'

'Perhaps you should have thought about that before

you invited me to stay the night,' she argued. 'You like being alone and I was just for one night. But that's not who I am. I want something more, something you can't offer. So just stay in your glorious house by yourself. It's how you like it.'

'It's not. But it took you coming into my life to make me realise that.'

Juliet frowned and began to shiver. The cold morning air had finally cut through her thick dressing gown and pyjamas and she felt chilled to the bone.

'Can we go inside?' he asked, aware that she was not coping in the cold.

'No,' she replied flatly. 'Everyone's sleeping and I don't want them to know about what happened between us. It's over and done and they do not need to be any the wiser that their daughter made another mistake.'

'It wasn't a mistake.'

'I disagree. I think me sleeping with you was a mammoth mistake. You were almost morose when we woke. I could see you didn't want me there with you.'

'I asked you to stay. I wanted you next to me.'

'Yes, maybe you did that night, but in your heart you knew it would be over when the sun came up.' Juliet began to shake from the bitter cold…and her breaking heart. 'I just wish you'd never invited me over in the first place. I wish I'd never stayed.'

'So you regret making love to me? Do you think falling into my bed and into my arms was the biggest mistake you could have made? Because I don't. It's just taken me time to work it out in my head. And my heart.'

Juliet was angry but she couldn't lie. She didn't regret making love to Charlie. All she regretted was allowing herself to fall in love with him. 'I don't understand your question. Why are you wanting to torture me? I haven't wanted to sleep with anyone in more than four years and then I make this huge error in judgement and believe that you're different, that perhaps you're looking for something more, but I was wrong.'

'You weren't wrong.' He pulled off his heavy jacket and gently placed it on her shoulders.

'You'll freeze,' she said, attempting to give it back as he stood in a jumper and shirt. The air was misty and damp, the ground outside covered with a fresh layer of snow.

His strong hands remained resting lightly on her shoulders as he refused to take back the jacket. 'I'm warm-blooded enough to survive while you hear me out.'

Juliet hated the fact that she couldn't argue that fact. Charlie had been warm-blooded enough the night they'd spent together to keep her fire burning into the early hours. She also hated that while his coat was heavy it felt good to have it wrapped around her. His scent, the warmth of the lambswool lining that he had heated only moments before. It felt as if it were all she would ever need but she knew it wasn't hers to keep. Because he wasn't hers to keep.

'Just let me say a few things and then if you want me to go, I will.'

'Just go now—'

'I can't and I won't. Not without telling you how I feel. How I've felt since I first laid eyes on you.'

'When you told me off for being a bad mother.'

'I didn't say those words—'

'But you thought it,' she interrupted, trying to remind herself, as much as him, why they shouldn't be together.

'I admit, I've been judging everyone but mostly myself for as long as I can remember...'

'Since the accident?'

'Yes. I've been confused and carrying guilt with me for so long that I felt lost without it. I was driven to punish myself since that day.' His voice was low and sombre.

'But it wasn't your fault.'

'You and everyone in this town have said that so many times,' he stated. 'But it was how I saw it.'

Juliet thought she heard something more in his words but she wasn't sure. 'How you *saw* it? So it's not how you *see* it now?'

Charlie looked at her and shook his head. 'It's not how I want to see it any more and being with you I know that's possible.'

'What's changed?' she asked, not daring to hope that he wanted her. And was ready to build a life with her. And with her daughter. The three of them as a family.

'I know that hurting you won't bring my wife back. Nothing can. I realised that as I've slept alone in my bed for the last two nights wanting you beside me. Wanting to feel your tenderness and love again. Being near you brought my spirit back and being with you and making love to you made me feel more alive than I thought possible. I won't let you go without a fight. I know that spending the rest of my life regretting the moment my wife and I climbed in that car two years ago won't change anything. I will still have a place in my heart for the woman I loved back then, but I don't want to lose the two special women who have come into my life now. I want to live in the present and build a future and I want to do it with you. I want you, Juliet, now and for ever if you'll have me, and I want to be the father that Bea needs. If you'll let me.'

'I never wanted to fight you on that. I just wanted to love you,' she told him with tears welling in her eyes.

'I know that, Juliet, and I'm sorry. The fight was never *with* you, the fight was *with* myself and my stupidity, my need to carry the guilt like a cross and my need to punish myself to make amends. I don't want to do that any more. In the week since we met, I have been questioning everything that's been my life, my reality for the last two years. You and Bea have made me want more. You've made me want a life that's free of remorse and sad memories. You've brought a light back that I never thought I would see again and warmth that I never thought I would feel. I don't want to live in the cold or the dark any more. I want to really live again. To have you by my side for the rest of my life.'

'What are you saying?'

'Juliet,' he said, dropping to one knee and wrapping her hand into the strength and warmth of his, 'I'm asking you to be my wife. To love me the way you did the other night. To share your life and to bring life back into my home and make me want to sleep in our four-poster bed and make love to you every night. Will you? Will you make me the man I want to be and the man I can be if you'll allow me?'

'Yes,' she answered with tears freely flowing down her face as she fell into his arms and kissed him as if there would be no tomorrow. 'Yes, of course I'll marry you. I love you, Charlie Warren.'

'And I will love you for ever, Juliet…and spend the rest of my life decorating Christmas trees with Bea… and the rest of our children.'

* * * * *

LET'S TALK
Romance

For exclusive extracts, competitions
and special offers, find us online:

 facebook.com/millsandboon

 @MillsandBoon

 @MillsandBoonUK

Get in touch on 01413 063232

For all the latest titles coming soon, visit
millsandboon.co.uk/nextmonth

MILLS & BOON

THE HEART OF ROMANCE

A ROMANCE FOR EVERY KIND OF READER

ODERN

Prepare to be swept off your feet by sophisticated, sexy and seductive heroes, in some of the world's most glamourous and romantic locations, where power and passion collide.
8 stories per month.

STORICAL

Escape with historical heroes from time gone by. Whether your passion is for wicked Regency Rakes, muscled Vikings or rugged Highlanders, awaken the romance of the past.
6 stories per month.

EDICAL

Set your pulse racing with dedicated, delectable doctors in the high-pressure world of medicine, where emotions run high and passion, comfort and love are the best medicine.
6 stories per month.

ue Love

Celebrate true love with tender stories of heartfelt romance, from the rush of falling in love to the joy a new baby can bring, and a focus on the emotional heart of a relationship.
8 stories per month.

Desire

Indulge in secrets and scandal, intense drama and plenty of sizzling hot action with powerful and passionate heroes who have it all: wealth, status, good looks…everything but the right woman.
6 stories per month.

EROES

Experience all the excitement of a gripping thriller, with an intense romance at its heart. Resourceful, true-to-life women and strong, fearless men face danger and desire - a killer combination!
8 stories per month.

ARE

Sensual love stories featuring smart, sassy heroines you'd want as a best friend, and compelling intense heroes who are worthy of them.
4 stories per month.

To see which titles are coming soon, please visit

millsandboon.co.uk/nextmonth

MILLS & BOON
MEDICAL
Pulse-Racing Passion

Set your pulse racing with dedicated, delectable doctors in the high-pressure world of medicine, where emotions run high and passion, comfort and love are the best medicine.